THE CLOCKMAKER'S WIFE

Daisy Wood worked as an editor in children's publishing before she started writing her own books. She has a degree in English Literature and an MA in Creative Writing from City University, London, and is the author of several works of historical fiction for children. This is her first published novel for adults. She divides her time between London and Dorset, and when not lurking in the London Library, can often be found chasing a rescue Pointer through various parks with a Basset Hound in tow.

The Clockmaker's Wife

DAISY WOOD

avon.

HarperCollins*Publishers*
1 London Bridge Street
London SE1 9GF

www.harpercollins.co.uk

HarperCollins*Publishers*
1st Floor, Watermarque Building, Ringsend Road
Dublin 4, Ireland

This paperback edition 2021

21 22 23 24 25 LSC 10 9 8 7 6 5 4 3 2 1

First published in Great Britain by HarperCollins*Publishers* 2021

A catalogue copy of this book is available from the British Library.

ISBN: 978-0-00-844463-1

Typeset in Bembo by Palimpsest Book Production Limited, Falkirk, Stirlingshire
Printed and bound in the United States of America by LSC Communications.

To Philip, with love and gratitude

Author's note

Big Ben – as the Great Clock at the Palace of Westminster has come to be known – is recognised around the world, a landmark that draws tourists like a magnet and tells Londoners they're home. During the Second World War, however, the clock held an even greater significance. In prison camps, cellars, attics and back rooms all over Nazi-occupied Europe, people secretly tuned into wireless broadcasts from the BBC – and for most of the war, the chimes of Big Ben were used to announce the nine o'clock evening news. People everywhere were encouraged to pray for peace as they listened, and this sacred moment was known as the Silent Minute. The great bell represented freedom and better times to come; as long as it tolled, at least one country resisted oppression.

The Clockmaker's Wife is a work of fiction. As far as we know, there was no conspiracy to destroy Big Ben on New Year's Eve in 1940; certainly, no evidence has ever been found. The Houses of Parliament had been bombed in September of that year and were to be more seriously damaged in May 1941, when the Commons Chamber was destroyed by incendiaries, but these episodes were incidental rather than targeted. Yet such a plan isn't inconceivable. St Paul's Cathedral had only been saved by a miracle a couple of nights before, when over a hundred thousand bombs were dropped on the ancient City of London. The Palace of Westminster was similarly vulnerable, and the loss of such a beacon of hope as the clock tower would have been a terrible blow to morale.

Despite this imaginative leap, I have tried to ground the plot and setting of my novel in historical reality. When I began dreaming up the story, renovation work to the clock tower was already under way and a visit in person was impossible. Yet I was lucky enough to experience the next best thing: a talk at the Houses of Parliament by one of the guides, Catherine Moss. She and her colleague, Lindsay Schusman, know all there is to know about Big Ben and I'm extremely grateful to them both for their help, so generously given. At the time of writing, these renovations are still some way from completion, but the results will surely be spectacular. I've come to think of Big Ben as an old friend, and a trip up the clock tower is top of my wish list when the world returns to some kind of normality.

I wrote much of this novel during months of lock-down due to the coronavirus pandemic. It's been a strange time, and one can't help noting the similarities and contrasts with wartime Britain as we currently battle a more insidious, invisible enemy. Researching London during the Blitz has left me overwhelmed by the extraordinary courage of so many 'ordinary' people, men and women just like Nell and Arthur, and in awe of the sacrifices they made to ensure the freedom of generations to come. I couldn't help thinking of my own grandmother, the original Daisy Wood, who lost her brother during the First World War and brought up her daughter, my mother, during the Second. How I wish I could talk to her now!

Prologue

London, April 1939

'Not much further,' Arthur calls down to Nell, who is labouring up the stone spiral staircase behind him. She's wearing new shoes that have rubbed a blister on the back of her heel, and it's been a long day, but she knows how much this visit means to Arthur so she perseveres. He's rightly proud of his work, maintaining the clocks at the Palace of Westminster, and she knows it's taken some negotiation with the Keeper of the Clock for permission to show her the greatest one of all: the huge turret clock that Nell in her ignorance used to call Big Ben. Arthur had quickly put her right. Big Ben, she knows now, refers to the vast bell that strikes the hours, rather than the clock itself.

She's learned a lot about this clock since meeting Arthur – or rather, she would have learned a lot, if she weren't so distracted by his steady brown eyes, gazing intently into hers, by the hollows under his cheekbones and the bluish stubble around his jaw, by that mysterious male presence that takes the words out of her mouth and the breath from her lungs. Sometimes they can talk for hours and it seems as though they've known each other for years; more often, she simply stares at the way his curly hair springs up from his forehead or the curve of his beautiful mouth and wonders how long she'll have to wait until he's kissing her. She thinks about him all the time. He's on her mind from first thing in the morning until last thing at night, and people have begun to notice. The headmistress has had to have sharp words with Nell about leaving her personal life at home.

So now she smiles back at Arthur and tells him she's fine, slips off her shoes and limps after him in her stockinged feet. First, he takes her to the clockmakers' room, where their tools and equipment are stored. Technically, Arthur is employed by Saunders, an external company of clock and watchmakers, rather than the Palace of Westminster. Yet the Palace is where he and his colleagues spend most of their time, winding, adjusting and maintaining the hundreds of clocks that mark the hours as Parliament goes about its business. And also when it's in recess, of course. There are two other clockmakers apart from Arthur: Ralph Watkinson (whom he likes) and Bill Talbot (whom he doesn't).

Their room is low-ceilinged, with short windows beneath the overhanging dials above. Arthur shows her the workbench where his tools are neatly arranged, ready for the morning.

'Sure I'm not boring you?' he asks, and she hastens to reassure him. 'You are a dear girl to be so interested,' he says, blushing a little, and his flush deepens when she catches sight of her photograph in pride of place on the shelf, self-conscious in pearls and an evening gown. Dropping his eyes, he exclaims over her lack of shoes and binds her bleeding heel with his handkerchief, taking such care that she melts under his touch. She's longing for him to kiss her when he straightens up, but instead he unlocks the door to an inspection hatch and shows her the weights running up and down the central shaft of the tower. She can just make them out, far below in the gloom. There are three weights, he explains, controlling the three gear trains by which the Great Clock operates: the striking train driving the hammer which drops against Big Ben, the chiming train that controls the quarter bells, and the going train that powers the clock hands. The striking and chiming trains are wound back up by electric motor when they reach the bottom of the shaft, Arthur says, but the going train has to be wound by hand, three times a week.

'Goodness.' Nell could listen to him talk all evening – although, to be perfectly honest, she pays more attention to his dimples than she does to the gear trains. He wants to share his great passion with her, and she knows this is a significant moment. Who would have thought the workings of a turret clock could be so romantic?

Arthur takes Nell's hand and leads her through the gallery behind the four huge dials. Dusk is falling and the light bulbs behind each clock face are blazing; people on the ground over three hundred feet below will be looking up to check the time as they hurry to meet friends or lovers, or head home after work. Nell peers up at the milky glass. She can't see through to the Roman numerals on the other side, but Arthur tells her they are over two feet high, and the minute hand is fourteen feet long. The scale is awe-inspiring.

After this excitement, they go up another flight of stairs to see the clock mechanism itself, an intricate arrangement of wheels, cogs, levers and ratchets laid out on a flatbed frame. The machinery was made in Victorian times; a work of art, combining beauty and precision. Nell's face is beginning to ache from all the smiling when a tremendous racket starts above their heads, the smaller bells ringing out the quarter hour. She and Arthur put their hands over their ears, beaming at each other. I do love you, she thinks, and wonders when she'll find the courage to tell him. Probably not tonight. He seems in a strange mood: preoccupied, distracted, distant. He's probably tired after a day's work, and of course he's worried about the current state of affairs on the Continent, along with everyone else. They had a long conversation about that alarming little man Hitler the other night. Arthur's parents are German but they moved to England before he was born – which, as things have turned out, was just as well.

At last the Westminster Chimes die away and the

fly fans high up in the room come to a noisy, clattering halt.

Falling well and truly under the spell of this extraordinary place, Nell hurries after Arthur, up another flight of stairs to the belfry where Big Ben hangs in state; a caged beast behind an iron fence, with the quarter bells arranged around him like planets orbiting the sun. She leans over the wire-mesh barrier to lay her hand against his great scarred side and stand for a moment, drinking in the quiet atmosphere. Arthur, however, is in a hurry. He wants to show her the Ayrton light, which is lit when either House of Parliament is sitting after dark. Frowning, he looks at his watch and hustles her towards the open metal staircase as though they're late for an appointment.

'Hope you don't mind heights,' he says, bounding up the first few steps without looking back. Nell follows, trying to ignore the open iron latticework beneath her feet and the wind that steals under her crimson coat, freezing her stockinged legs. When they climb out onto the balcony running around the lantern, she's glad of Arthur's hand to hold, and gladder still when he puts his arm around her shoulders and draws her close, inhaling the scent of her hair, which she rinsed in lavender water, just in case this situation might arise. They gaze out over London, quiet in the deep blue haze of evening. The dolphin streetlamps along the Embankment are shining like strings of pearls as the sinking sun outlines fleecy clouds in pink and gold; the lights of barges heading towards the docks gleam like fireflies on the water. Nell can see as far as Tower Bridge in one direction and Lambeth Bridge in another, spot the golden angel glinting on the memorial outside Buckingham Palace, and glimpse Nelson standing proud on his column at Trafalgar Square. The cars crossing Westminster Bridge look like Matchbox toys from this height, and the roar of the traffic is muted. She and Arthur are completely alone, with this extraordinary scene laid out before them.

The sight of his serious face casts a shadow over her happiness. Now, at last, she understands why he's brought her here. 'War's coming, isn't it?' she asks, so quietly that she might be talking to herself. 'You want me to see the city before everything changes.'

'I think it's inevitable, sadly,' he replies. 'And sooner rather than later.'

Now a terrible fear clutches her heart. 'Please don't tell me you're leaving. Are you about to say goodbye?' Ridiculous tears spring to her eyes; she'll blame them on the wind. He looks away, biting his lip. 'Don't go,' she begs, abandoning all trace of dignity. 'You needn't, Arthur, not till they send for you. Let other men play the hero.'

He takes her hand. 'I have brought you here for a reason, but it's not that,' he says, gazing into her eyes. 'We haven't known each other long, dearest Nell, but it's been long enough for me to have fallen head over heels in love with you. Let's make a home and grow old together. We might never be rich but I swear, I'll move heaven and earth to make you happy. Oh, damn,

I meant to do this properly.' He starts patting his pockets. 'Where is it? I'm sure . . . Ah, yes, here we are.'

He produces a small black box and, sinking to one knee, opens and offers it up to her. 'Nell Roberts, I'm only a humble clockmaker, but would you do me the honour of becoming my wife?' When she doesn't reply instantly he repeats, with the merest hint of desperation, 'Will you marry me, darling girl?'

Laughing and crying at the same time, lost for even the simplest of words, Nell helps Arthur to his feet. Her expression is all the answer he needs. He takes the ring from its velvet bed and slips it on her finger and then, at last, he kisses her; the most magical kiss there has ever been or will be again. At that very moment the world explodes as the bells beneath their feet begin to chime, followed by a few seconds of silence before the mighty hammer drops and Big Ben rings out in celebration. Arthur's timing is impeccable – naturally.

Chapter One

London, November 1940

Nell looked at the clock for what felt like the hundredth time. Arthur had never been home as late as this before. It was almost eight o'clock. What on earth could have happened? The bombers had been coming earlier and earlier – almost as soon as it was dark, sometimes – but so far the night had been quiet and the alert hadn't sounded, so he couldn't have been caught up in a raid. She went to the front room and pulled aside the blackout blind to look out. It was dark and quiet, the moon only a fingernail paring and a solitary searchlight roaming the clouds. She could make out the bulk of a couple of barrage balloons, bobbing and swaying from their moorings like vast tethered animals. The street was empty, apart from a couple of ARP wardens standing on the corner, playing their torches over the house that had been bombed a couple of months before. Rumour had it that a tramp had moved in, though no one had actually seen him. Nell dropped the blind; those men could spot a chink of light at fifty paces.

Sighing, she walked back down the hall, edging past the pram. The liver she had queued an hour to buy had been drying out in the oven since half past six; Arthur would probably break a tooth if he tried to eat it now. Upstairs, Alice gave a drowsy, half-hearted wail. Nell stood for a moment to listen, holding her breath, but the baby seemed to have settled down so she carried on to the kitchen, to find the largest mouse she had ever seen – could it even have been a rat? – running across the floor. She couldn't help screaming, and then of course Alice woke up and screamed too, and the house was in uproar when Arthur's key turned in the lock.

'Arthur! Where have you been?' she cried, clutching her sobbing baby, on the verge of tears herself. 'I was so worried! Supper's ruined and we've nothing else to eat except a tin of corned beef that I was saving for the weekend. I was trying so hard to make everything lovely but the house is infested with vermin and it's all too ghastly for words.'

'You poor thing. Here, give Alice to me.' Gently, Arthur scooped up the baby and walked her up and down, humming under his breath. Alice buried her damp face in his shoulder, hiccupped a couple of times and fell asleep.

'But you haven't even had time to hang up your

things.' Full of remorse, Nell took off his hat while he shrugged his arms out of his coat so she could relieve him of that, too. His clothes were cold and damp, and smelt of soot. 'Oh, I'm the worst wife in the world!' she burst out. 'I'm meant to change and put on fresh lipstick before you come home and here I am, nagging like some awful harpy. Can you forgive me?'

He smiled. 'As long as you can forgive me for being so late. And, darling, I wouldn't mind if you came to the door in sackcloth and ashes.' He kissed the top of her head. 'Why don't you make a pot of tea while I put Alice back in her cot and then we can decide what to do about supper and vermin.'

She shouldn't have mentioned the mouse, Nell realised, putting the kettle on to boil. Arthur might use that against her in their ongoing debate – it wasn't an argument, not yet – that was becoming increasingly heated as the bombing continued.

'So how was your day?' she asked him brightly when he came back downstairs. 'Is Mr Watkinson back at work yet?'

'Sadly not.' He took a sip of tea and gave a small involuntary shudder.

'Sorry. We're out of fresh milk so I had to use powdered.' What a terrible housewife she was.

'At least it's hot,' he said gamely. 'Well, warm.'

'Warmish,' Nell said, and they laughed.

'Talbot's been up to his usual tricks,' Arthur went on. 'I couldn't leave without checking the work he can't be bothered to finish. He's getting more slapdash than ever and he's not training the lad properly, either. Sam's picking up all sorts of bad habits. And when I point out where Talbot's gone wrong, he goes off at the deep end. He can't bear any sort of criticism. We need Watkinson to keep the peace. Still, enough of my woes. What's this about the house being infested?'

'I thought I saw a mouse,' Nell replied, 'but it was probably just my imagination.' She retrieved Arthur's plate from the oven and placed it in front of him. 'Now, do your best. I've eaten already.' Only potatoes and a slice of bread and marge, but she wasn't particularly hungry.

'I'm absolutely ravenous.' And he must have been, because he managed to polish off the liver and most of the potatoes that had collapsed into a heap of grey mush. They had learned to eat supper quickly, before the air-raid siren inevitably sent them hurrying to the shelter.

'I've got a surprise for you,' Arthur said, when he had forced down the last mouthful. 'Close your eyes and hold out your hands.'

He put something round and smooth in her cupped palms. She gasped when she saw it. 'An orange! Where on earth did you find that?'

'It fell off the back of a lorry.' He grinned, delighted by her reaction.

Nell dug her fingernail into the fruit's waxy peel and inhaled the sharp citrus scent. It had been months since she'd seen an orange in the shops, let alone held one. The skin was already wrinkled and the fruit probably wouldn't last till Christmas, more than a month away. She would keep it till the weekend, she decided, and share it with Alice and Arthur after tea. Maybe Alice could eat her segments in the bath, so as not to make a mess of her clothes. They were running low on soap powder and even a bib took ages to dry at this time of year.

'I want you to eat it all yourself,' Arthur said, as if reading her thoughts. He put his plate in the sink, scooped up her hair and kissed his favourite spot at the nape of her neck. 'You're looking rather run down these days, my darling. You know how I worry.'

She did indeed. He went on, 'Thought any more about what we discussed the other day?'

'I'm not going to change my mind,' she replied. 'We belong together, Arthur – that's what we've always said. Whatever this war throws at us, we'll face it side by side.'

He sat down again, his face serious. 'There's Alice to think about now. It's not fair to put her through all this, not when you could both be safe in the country.'

Nell stuck out her jaw. 'If the Queen won't leave London, I don't see why I should.'

'But the Queen lives in Buckingham Palace, not a terraced house in Vauxhall.'

Nell sighed. 'Let's not go over this again, not when we're both so tired. We're just going around in circles. We'll talk about it at the weekend, I promise.' She glanced at the clock. 'Nearly time for the news.'

They went through to the front room and Nell switched on the wireless. Now there was an added incentive to tune in: since the previous Sunday, Armistice Day, the pips introducing the nine o'clock news had been replaced by the chimes of Big Ben. Arthur had been so proud. People all over the country would be listening to that solemn sound, united in love for their country. She smiled at him across the hearth as the notes died away, but he was deep in thought and didn't notice. Sighing again, she turned her attention to the world beyond their small terraced house. There was encouraging news from North Africa, apparently: thousands of Italian soldiers were surrendering in Egypt and British troops had captured some fort or other in Libya.

She yawned, her eyes drooping. The siren hadn't sounded yet and it was getting late; perhaps tonight they would be lucky. 'Please, God,' she prayed to herself, 'let us not have to go to the shelter.' It was a selfish request, given the suffering some people had to endure, but she'd come to loathe the Anderson with a passion. The shelter stood in the garden of their neighbours, Mr and Mrs Blackwell, who had generously offered to share it when the raids had started, what seemed like a lifetime ago.

'We wouldn't hear of you going to a public shelter, Mrs Spelman,' Mrs Blackwell had said. 'Neighbours have to stick together these days.'

None of them had had any idea they would be spending so much time together, but London had been bombed relentlessly since that first week of September. Night after night, Nell had stumbled along the icy garden path, Alice clutched to her chest in a cocoon of blankets. Four slippery moss-covered steps led down into the shelter's chilly interior, where spiders and possibly rats lurked in every corner, and a frog had once hopped onto her foot; it had squatted there for a moment, staring at her in the light of a candle with its wet black eyes. Nell had always hated to be shut up in any confined space, let alone one that smelt of damp, mouse droppings and worse. She knew Alice felt the same. Most of the time, her daughter was an undemanding baby, but her small body would start to tense as soon as she caught sight of the shelter's forbidding entrance.

The Anderson was furnished with an easy chair near the entrance and two bunk beds standing opposite each other. Nell slept on the bunk above Mrs Blackwell with Alice in a Moses basket beside her, while Arthur took the berth on top of Stanley Blackwell. This ménage was completed by the Blackwells' elderly terrier, Jack, who lost control of his bodily functions at the first explosion and would whine throughout the night in a pitch that set Nell's teeth on edge. Outside, the sirens wailed, bells clanged, bombs detonated and buildings collapsed in an avalanche of brick and stone. Under the Anderson's turf roof, Mr Blackwell whistled or snored, Mrs Blackwell knitted and sucked peppermints and Jack keened. Arthur was restless, tossing and turning and sometimes talking in his sleep. Once he had even sat bolt upright and shouted something in German, which had sent Mrs Blackwell into hysterics.

It was kind of the Blackwells to let them use the shelter, Arthur reminded Nell; they didn't have to. Mr Blackwell had built it himself in his back garden and made a gate in the fence so the Spelmans could slip through from next door. Their garden was half the size of the Blackwells' and concreted over, otherwise Arthur would have put in an Anderson himself. They were lucky to have such good neighbours, Nell told herself as she lay sleepless through the wild nights. There was a surface shelter barricaded with sandbags a few streets away, but Arthur wouldn't hear of her using it. Those brick-built shelters were a death trap, he said; you were more likely to be killed by one collapsing on top of you than by being caught out in the street. And surely it was better to spend the night with people they knew, rather than strangers who might have all sorts of unsavoury habits?

Nell wondered about this. Mrs Blackwell's habitual expression was one of disapproval. Her lips were usually pursed and she frowned ferociously even when asleep. She felt sorry for Alice, and said so on numerous occasions. 'Poor little mite!' she'd remark, shaking her head as she tweaked back the blanket, exposing Alice to draughts. 'She's looking very peaky. London's no place for a baby, not at a time like this.'

Mr Blackwell, on the other hand, had a genial air and a variety of cheery maxims at his disposal. He'd retired from his job as a mechanic on the buses but had gone back to work once the war started; thankful to get away from Mrs Blackwell, Nell suspected. His bulk took up a lot of space in the shelter but he was a comforting presence, by and large – especially on the nights Arthur was fire-watching at the Palace of Westminster.

Now, the familiar, stomach-churning blare of a siren startled Nell awake. She opened her eyes to find Arthur smiling at her so tenderly that she couldn't help smiling back. 'There I was, hoping we might have a night off at last,' she said, stretching her arms above her head.

He helped her to her feet, hugging her fiercely for a moment. 'Chin up, old girl. This can't last forever.' She laid her head against his shoulder, breathing in the beloved smell of his soap and aftershave. 'Better not linger,' he said, detaching himself. 'You fetch the baby and I'll bring the valuables.'

Upstairs, Alice lay on her back, fast sleep with her thumb in her mouth and her dark hair sticking up in tufts. Nell couldn't bear to wake such a precious creature and take her to that awful place, to be pitied by Mrs Blackwell. Perhaps she would just pick her up so gently that she wouldn't stir, and they would sit together under the kitchen table, just the two of them. It would be cosy there, sheltered by the chimney breast. If Alice did wake up, she would sing her gently back to sleep. Arthur would understand.

Except, of course, that he wouldn't. There was nothing for it. Nell slipped her hand under Alice's damp, warm head that smelt of sugared almonds and lifted her out of the cot. Immediately, the baby's back arched and she let out a howl of protest.

'I know, I know,' Nell murmured, bundling her up in the quilt. 'I'm sorry, my darling. Time for the horrid old Anderson.'

By the time they were hurrying out into the garden, the night was lit up by parachute flares and somewhere close by, sticks of incendiary bombs were already screaming towards the earth. The crash of nearby explosions sounded in her ears and the ground over which she was running seemed to shake and tilt. She stumbled and nearly fell, holding on to the baby for dear life. Behind her, Arthur shouted something she couldn't hear. Alice might have been crying but it was impossible to tell, given the commotion.

Mr Blackwell was standing at the bottom of the steps in his siren suit and tweed cap, peering out into the night. 'There you are,' he said, as Nell threw herself down the steps with Arthur close on her heels. 'Thank goodness! Now we're all present and correct. Come in and make yourself comfy.'

A candle stuck in a saucer cast flickering shadows over the brick walls of the shelter. Its light revealed Mrs Blackwell sitting on the lower bunk, wearing an overcoat over her nightie and a pair of wellingtons. Her curlers were covered with a paisley headscarf. 'Comfy, in here!' She gave a bitter laugh and unwound another length of wool. 'Mind where you're treading, dears. Jack ate some tripe yesterday and it seems to have disagreed with him.' She began knitting with some ferocity. 'And how's the poor little mite?'

'Cutting another tooth, I'm afraid,' Nell replied, catching her breath. 'I've pinned a bickiepeg to her vest but she's not happy.'

'Of course she isn't,' Mrs Blackwell said. 'She wants to be safe in the country, where it's lovely and quiet, not stuck down here.'

'Cheer up for Chatham, wooden legs are cheap,' said Mr Blackwell obscurely, poking Alice with a beefy finger and making her howl.

Outside, the world split apart in a cacophony of thuds and crashes. How strange it was, Nell thought, to be shut up in this godawful spot with the Blackwells, of all people, while some unknown people up in the sky tried to kill them. Arthur took Alice from her arms while she hung up her coat and swept their mattresses for debris and snails.

'At least we've all made it down here safe and sound.' Mr Blackwell rubbed his hands together. 'I told you what Maurice said to his missus, didn't I? When she wouldn't leave the house without her dentures?'

'Yes, you did,' Nell said, smiling dutifully. Several times, she added in her head. Mr Blackwell worked on the principle that if a joke was worth telling once, it was worth repeating *ad infinitum*.

'He said, "Come on, Betty! Hitler's dropping bombs, not sandwiches!"' Mr Blackwell shook his head, chuckling. 'He's a caution, that Maurice. "Bombs, not sandwiches!" He just came out with it, quick as a flash.'

'Jam puffs would be more up Betty's street,' Mrs Blackwell remarked. 'She wouldn't bother bending down to pick up a sandwich. The woman's always had a sweet tooth, that's why she's so fat – even now, on eight ounces of sugar a week for the whole family. She must be taking Maurice's share, and the kiddies' too. Either that or she's getting a supply on the black market.'

What would Arthur and the Blackwells do if I screamed out loud? Nell wondered. They'd put it down to nervous exhaustion, probably, and they might well be right. Arthur had tried to help by advising her to meditate. Her body might be trapped in the shelter but her mind was free to wander at will. He, for example, imagined the chalet high in the Swiss Alps where he'd once spent a holiday with his German cousins: ten of them, crammed into a small hut that smelt of cedar wood and smoke, its shingles creaking under the weight of snow and icicles that hung like transparent daggers. They had been marooned, cut off from the everyday world by a soft white blanket that muffled the sound of their footsteps but sharpened their senses. He had never known such a profound sense of peace, never felt so intensely alive as in that pure, cold air.

Nell did her best to follow his advice. Her sanctuary was with him. He would be waiting for her up in the clock tower, making some minute adjustment to the machinery. He was single-minded; that was one of the things she loved most about him. Every task received his full attention, from heaving coal from the cellar to nudging the tiniest saw-toothed wheels and cogs into place with tweezers. When he looked at her with that steady, intent gaze, she felt as though she were being seen for the first time. In her mind's eye, the Great Clock would be running smoothly and the room would be quiet, apart from the steady chink of the pendulum rod every two seconds. Arthur would lay down whatever cloth or gauge he happened to be holding and take her by the hand. She could feel his warm palm against hers, smell the oil on his overalls. Together they would climb up to the lantern at the top of the tower and look out over pre-war London, intact and beautiful in the drowsy evening light – just as it had been on that unforgettable evening he'd asked her to marry him. The parks would be green and leafy, the small Wren churches still standing peacefully in ancient, unblemished streets. Even the shabby terraces of South London across the river would look picturesque from that height; she felt a nostalgic fondness for them now so many had been blown apart. Arthur's arm would be around her shoulder and – how could she have forgotten? – Alice, of course, would be on her hip, chubby and beaming.

To date, however, Nell had never made it as far as the belfry in her mind's eye. Her reverie would inevitably be interrupted by Alice grizzling, or Jack yapping, or Arthur mumbling, or Mr Blackwell snoring, or Mrs Blackwell harrumphing about on the bunk below – and sometimes all of these distractions at once.

'Goodnight, darling,' Arthur whispered now, giving her a peck on the cheek. 'Sweet dreams.'

She laid Alice in her basket on the top bunk and climbed up to lie beside her. The corrugated iron roof was only a couple of feet above their heads but she tried not to think about that. The baby began to cry and wouldn't be distracted by the soggy rusk, so Nell turned discreetly on her side and fumbled under her jumper. Alice had been weaned for over a month and her breast milk was drying up, but a feed usually comforted them both. Not tonight, though. She yelped as her daughter's new tooth sank into her nipple. 'Bottles from now on for you, young lady,' she whispered, readjusting her clothes. Alice was growing up fast; she was crawling already and soon she'd be into everything. Where could a child play safely in London? The parks were full of barbed wire and gun emplacements, the ground littered with lumps of shrapnel and broken glass.

She stroked the baby's head, humming softly, until Alice's breathing quietened and she grew still. A lull had descended on the fire storm outside and they were both drifting into sleep when the most tremendous crash seemed to pick up the shelter and shake it until its teeth rattled, like a dog killing a rat. Debris rained down from the roof onto Nell's face, Alice shrieked, Jack yapped and Mrs Blackwell screamed. Nell sat up, grabbing the baby to her chest. The bunk swayed beneath her, threatening to collapse. 'God save us!' Mrs Blackwell cried, rolling sideways out of the rickety structure, while Mr Blackwell bellowed for everyone not to panic.

'It's all right, sweetheart.' Arthur's steady voice cut through the chaos. 'I'm here.' She reached for his hand and clung to it, speechless, the baby sandwiched between them. 'We're safe,' he murmured, over and over again, and somehow she believed him.

The racket seemed to last forever. Eventually, after what might have been long minutes or only a few seconds, the pounding died down and an uneasy calm descended.

'That was a close one.' Mr Blackwell switched on the emergency torch, revealing a scene of disarray. Mrs Blackwell was scrambling to her knees amid a tangle of wool, her dressing gown and nightie riding up to reveal a sagging thigh. There was no sign of Jack, although a low moan under the other bunk and the stench of rotten eggs gave his presence away. A carpet of stones, dirt and shards of brick littered the upper bunks and the wooden pallets that served as the Anderson's floor.

Arthur smoothed Nell's hair away from her forehead, scanning her face. 'Hitler certainly put us through the wringer that time,' she said, smiling shakily. Alice took a shuddering breath before screwing up her face and letting out a piercing cry.

'All right, Enid?' Mr Blackwell helped his wife up. 'Mrs Spelman? How's the baby?'

'Fine, I think.'

'Nothing wrong with her lungs, at any rate,' said

Mrs Blackwell, dusting herself off. 'I wonder who's copped it this time.'

'I'll take a look in a minute,' her husband said.

'You will not,' she retorted. 'You'll stay in here till it's light. I'm not having you blundering about, falling into craters and God knows what.'

'All's well that ends well,' Mr Blackwell replied philosophically. 'At least we're still in one piece.'

'Nip of brandy?' Mrs Blackwell took a swig from her hip flask and held it up to Nell, who accepted it gratefully.

Arthur scooped Alice from her arms, cradling the baby's head with his hand. 'I'll sit with this little one in the chair for a while. Try to get some sleep, darling. With a bit of luck, the fun's over for tonight.'

Nell's heart was still thumping, her hands shaking and clammy. 'I couldn't possibly sleep.'

'Well, then, just lie still for a while.'

Despite her protestations, Nell managed to drift into a restless doze. Every now and then, she would open her eyes to see Arthur sitting with Alice in his arms, keeping vigil as he waited for the dawn.

Chapter Two

London, November 1940

It was fully light when Nell woke up properly. Alice was back in the basket beside her, fast asleep, Mrs Blackwell was sitting in the chair, smoking a cigarette, while Arthur and Mr Blackwell were talking somewhere outside the shelter.

'Morning,' she called, swinging down her legs.

'She's awake,' Mrs Blackwell called to the men, which was odd. Then she turned to Nell and said, 'Good morning, dear,' which was odd, too. She had never addressed Nell as 'dear' before.

Arthur's silhouette blocked the shelter's entrance for a moment; he ducked his head as he came in. Nell jumped to the ground to meet him. 'Has something happened?' she asked. 'Everyone looks frightfully serious.'

He took her by the arm. 'You'd better come outside and see for yourself.'

Mr Blackwell was standing at the top of the steps, surveying his garden. He turned to them, smiling uneasily, and offered, 'No use crying over spilt milk.'

The daylight dazzled Nell's eyes, dull though it was, after the long dark hours in the shelter. She could hear the usual morning sounds: the rhythmic sweep of a brush and its accompanying chink of broken glass, gushing water, the clanging of shovels and distant shouts. It was a weary, pointless sort of housekeeping but one couldn't let things slide or chaos would ensue. The acrid stench of smoke and explosives wafted towards her. A section of the fence had come down, she noticed, and a torn sandbag disgorged its damp, beige innards across the path. There were bricks and roof tiles littering the vegetable patch, shattered roof spars lying about and a large chunk of plaster which, oddly enough, was covered in their bedroom wallpaper.

Through a gap next to the Blackwells' house, where theirs should have been standing, she could see Mr and Mrs Jenkins' red front door on the opposite side of the street, and a telegraph pole leaning at a crazy angle amid a tangle of cables. There was no sign of their roof, or Alice's bedroom window underneath with the blackout blinds drawn across, or their kitchen door with the barrel beside it in which she'd tried to grow potatoes. Instead, water from a broken pipe ran in channels through a vast rubbish heap. The empty house on the right which shared the chimney with theirs had been demolished, too. She had seen houses with walls torn away to reveal the rooms inside, crockery still on the table and washing-up waiting in the sink, but there was nothing recognisable to be seen here. Her home had been reduced to a pile of dirty stone and splintered wood, and no amount of housekeeping could ever put it back together again.

'Oh, Arthur.' She turned to him, blank with shock.

'I know.' He squeezed her elbow. 'We never liked that house, though, did we? Far too dark and poky, you always said.'

'But what about our things? Our clothes, and books, and—'

Nell couldn't bear to continue. Nearly everything she and Arthur owned lay buried underneath the wreckage: her best frock, the one she'd been married in, Arthur's bicycle, his suit, his walking boots, the carriage clock he was so patiently rebuilding, his spare tools, their photograph album, all the jumpers and leggings her mother had knitted for Alice and even – oh, Lord! – the Silver Cross pram Arthur's parents had given them when Alice was born. It even had a name: the Ambassador, top of the range. Arthur was always scraping his shins on the coach-built chassis in the hall and threatening to leave it out for the rag-and-bone man, but of course he was only joking. The Ambassador was the most magnificent thing they owned. Or rather, had owned. How would she manage without it?

Arthur put his arm around her. 'We're safe, and so is Alice. Nothing else matters.'

That was easy for him to say. The house and its

contents represented Nell's whole world; without them, she had nothing to do and nowhere to be. Shaking off Arthur's grip, she picked her way through the debris to see if she could salvage some small reminder of the life they had led.

'Be careful not to touch any wires,' Mr Blackwell called behind her. 'Better safe than sorry! Fools rush in, etcetera.'

Nell's eye was suddenly caught by a burst of colour amid the dirty browns and greys of destruction. An orange – her orange – was balanced perfectly on a conical pile of stones, like the cherry on a cupcake. She picked it up and wiped away the dust. The fruit was intact, unblemished apart from a tiny mark in the peel her fingernail had made the night before.

'Look, Arthur!' she said, turning to show him the miraculous thing.

She tore off the peel and stuck her thumb into the centre of the fruit to divide it. The flesh was plump and sweet, tasting of how things used to be. Arthur had wanted her to eat the whole orange herself so she did, cramming the segments greedily into her mouth, the juice running in rivulets down her chin. Soon it was gone, along with everything else. Nothing could be saved.

'Here we are.' Arthur passed Nell a mug. 'Liberally sweetened, I'm afraid, before I could refuse. Apparently, people in our situation need sugar. Oh, and some custard creams.' He took them out of his pocket.

'That's all right. Beggars can't be choosers.' They exchanged weary smiles. 'Actually,' she said, after a few sips, 'this is the best cup of tea I've ever tasted. And biscuits, too. What a treat!'

'Well done, darling.' He patted her knee, his face grey with worry and fatigue.

A couple of hours earlier, they had climbed over the rubble that had once been their home to find the street busy with wardens and policemen. Hathaway Road had escaped relatively lightly; their house and the one next door were the only two seriously damaged and there'd been no casualties, but the power cables were down and a water main had been hit, so there would be no power or water for a few days. They had walked with their neighbours in a dreary procession to an emergency relief centre in a nearby church hall, Arthur carrying Alice in his arms. A few streets away, they had passed a team of rescue workers with sniffer dogs, digging through the ruins of a three-storey tenement building that had collapsed on itself like a house of cards. The heavier beams were being delicately removed one at a time by the swinging arm of a crane and an ambulance stood by with its doors open, stretchers at the ready. An elderly couple with coats over their night clothes sat on a pile of bricks to watch the scene; not even the promise of tea could lure them away.

The relief centre was already crowded with people in oddly mismatched outfits: curlers under headscarves, pyjamas tucked into wellington boots, evening dress and carpet slippers. Faces were dazed, dirty, uncomprehending. The atmosphere was one of weary resignation as people queued at various desks to report damage, arrange replacement papers and ask for help with urgent necessities. The woman in front of Arthur had been given five shillings and a new ration book, there and then, no questions asked. Vast urns supplied endless amounts of tea which would make everyone feel right as rain, said the ladies from the Women's Voluntary Service, who came into their own at times like these.

Nell and Arthur sat without talking, watching Alice try to pull herself up on one of the folding wooden chairs. She bounced up and down experimentally on her chubby legs, making hooting noises.

'Look at her! She hasn't a care in the world.' Arthur took their empty mugs back to the trestle table and returned to stand by Nell, his hand on her shoulder. 'Well, we've done all we can for the time being. The War Damages Commission should give us some sort of compensation and the landlord's been notified. Things could be a lot worse. We have our papers and our gas masks, and enough money to tide us over. And I know this pram isn't a patch on the Ambassador, but it's better than nothing.'

Nell glanced at the rickety contraption, which had probably been used to store logs in a previous existence. She would look like a tramp, pushing her baby in that. Yet Arthur had wheeled it back to her with such a look of triumph on his face that she knew she would have to put on a brave face. 'Thank you, darling,' she'd said. 'It'll certainly be a lot easier to manoeuvre.'

'So now, then,' he began, 'perhaps we'd better—'

'Actually, would you mind keeping an eye on Alice for a moment?' Nell interrupted. 'I need to step outside for a breath of air.'

He took a surreptitious look at his watch. 'All right. But I must be getting back to work fairly soon. Talbot will be getting away with murder.'

'I won't be long, I promise.' Nell turned quickly away. There was no sense in delaying the inevitable, but she needed to prepare herself for what lay ahead. She could guess what he was about to say and it was simply unbearable.

Outside, she leant against the wall and closed her eyes. She'd been lucky to have Arthur at home for so long, she knew that. He'd been declared unfit for military service because of a heart condition, although his was a reserved occupation so he wouldn't have been called up anyway. So many other families had been torn apart – in some cases forever. Her brother Harry was still missing somewhere in France. And now she and Arthur would be separated. The thought was so awful that for weeks she'd been refusing to entertain it. As long as they were together, she could survive this nightmare: the constant bombardment, the nightly terror and grim daytime reckoning. Arthur was a wonderful husband, always ready to help with the baby and bring back little treats for her, or think up ways to make her life easier. She would find her shoes polished in the morning, or the first snowdrops in a glass on the table, or a library book by her chair that he knew she'd enjoy.

They'd been married for a year and a half by now and, until the war, Nell had been happier than she thought humanly possible. The terraced house they rented had been cramped and dark, it was true, but that didn't matter as long as they were there together. They would tell each other tales from their respective days over supper every evening, and although the meals she produced while learning to cook were often rather odd, sometimes inedible, Arthur never complained. Afterwards, he would wash the dishes and she would dry them, and then they would listen to the wireless, or read books or the newspaper, finishing the crossword together before going up to bed. Nell's mother had warned her that although the wedding night might come as a shock, she had to let her husband do what he wanted or he'd find someone more obliging. The whole messy business would get easier with time. Yet Nell soon discovered there were things she wanted, too, and that her pleasure was as important to Arthur as his own. Bedtimes became earlier and earlier, and occasionally they didn't even make it up the stairs. Nell blushed to imagine what the Blackwells would have said if they could have seen the goings-on next door.

Arthur hadn't wanted to wait till the war was over before starting a family, which had surprised her as he was usually so cautious. 'Who knows when the fighting will end?' he'd said. 'Or what might have happened to either of us in the meantime?' When Nell found out she was pregnant, he'd said it was the happiest day of his life.

Nell hadn't felt ready for motherhood – and she still didn't, not entirely – but perhaps he was right. At least now she had his child to hold on to. Alice had Arthur's quizzical expression, his habit of looking seriously at an object from all angles, his gorgeous dimples. She had been born in March, around the time meat became rationed. So much had happened since then: Winston Churchill becoming Prime Minister, for a start, and then the war taking a turn for the worse. Holland surrendered to the Nazis, followed by Belgium, and Norway the month after that, and soon German troops were sweeping through Europe. Thousands of Allied soldiers were rescued from the beaches and ports of Western France but plenty were left behind – including her brother, Harry. No one could give them any information as to his whereabouts, and communication became impossible when France surrendered to Germany shortly afterwards.

Britain now stood alone in the fight against Hitler and the Nazis. 'We shall go on to the end,' Winston Churchill said in Parliament. 'We shall never surrender.' That was all very well yet sometimes, in her darker moments, Nell wondered whether going on till the end was the wisest course of action. Surely any sort of life was better than none, even under German occupation? Of course, she'd never have voiced her doubts to anyone, including Arthur. They all had to be relentlessly optimistic.

'Fancy a cig?' She opened her eyes to see a middle-aged woman in a headscarf standing beside her, offering a crumpled pack of cigarettes. Nell didn't like to smoke anywhere near Arthur, who disapproved of the habit, but suddenly she wanted to – very much.

'Thanks awfully,' she said, and then, 'Oh! You only have two left.'

'One each.' The woman grinned. Her spectacles were held together by sticking plaster and her front teeth were missing. Bombs not sandwiches, Nell thought, and smiled too.

'That's the spirit,' said the woman, passing her a cigarette. 'I've plenty more at home.'

I bet you don't, Nell thought, but she took the cigarette anyway and bent her head to the match. They stood for a while, smoking in companionable silence.

'I hate that bloody blasted Hitler,' the woman said suddenly. 'Hate him to buggery and back. If he were standing here right now, I'd give him a piece of my mind.'

'I'd give him worse than that,' Nell said. They spent an enjoyable few minutes discussing precisely what they would do to Hitler, by which time she felt able to go back to her husband.

She stood for a moment in the doorway of the hall, watching Arthur bouncing Alice on his lap and clapping her hands together between his while she chortled with delight.

'You win.' She sat beside them. 'I'll telephone my parents and ask whether they'll have us to stay. Me and the baby, I mean. I know you can't leave London.'

His shoulders sagged in relief. 'Oh, that's wonderful. Well done, darling. Your mother will be so pleased. It might take her mind off worrying about Harry. Just think, you'll be able to spend the whole night in a proper bed instead of that ghastly bunk. There'll be plenty to eat, and peace and quiet, and help with—'

'I know, I know.' He'd been telling her all this for weeks now. 'It makes perfect sense, except for the fact that we swore we'd stick together, no matter what.' She dug her fingernails into her palm.

'We can't carry on like this,' he said quietly. 'You must know that, deep down.'

'It's just that I hate to think of you here alone,' she burst out, although she'd resolved to make things easy. She was only human, after all. 'What about your meals?'

'That's not a problem. I shall take them in the staff canteen.' He patted her knee. 'I know how hard it's been for you, having to stand for hours in those wretched queues and worry about eking out our rations.'

'And where will you sleep?'

'Oh, there are plenty of shelters around Parliament – I can take my pick.' He sounded positively jaunty. 'Might even bag a spot in the crypt at Westminster Abbey. I'll be safe as houses there.'

But houses weren't safe anymore, were they? Nell thought miserably. Alice had begun to squirm restlessly on Arthur's lap, so she reached over to take her. He wouldn't give the baby up. 'I think she's tired. Let's see if I can get her off to sleep.' He held Alice against his shoulder, rocking her gently to and fro.

There were a few disapproving looks from the people nearby but Arthur was oblivious. Nell loved the fact that he didn't care about being thought soppy. So much for hurrying back to work, though. As if he could read her mind, he added, 'A few more minutes won't hurt. Why don't you ring your parents while I hold the fort here?'

There was no point in delaying the inevitable. Nell had to queue for a quarter of an hour to use the public telephone, and her mother was infuriatingly slow to understand what had happened. 'We're perfectly safe,' Nell repeated, 'but the house has been demolished. Could Alice and I possibly come to stay with you for a while?'

'Of course, it would be lovely to see you,' Rose began, 'but we're full to bursting with all these evacuees. They sent us another one last week so now we're up to five. Or is it six?' She sounded even more vague than usual. 'Hold on a minute. I shall have to see what your father says.'

'Can you be quick?' Nell asked. 'I'm running out of change, and there are a lot of folk wanting to make calls.'

She smiled apologetically at the people waiting in line while a muffled conversation took place between her parents. Eventually she heard a rustle and her father's voice echoed down the line. 'So you've been bombed out,' he began. 'Well, I always said it was only a matter of time, although I take no joy in having been proved right.' Nell gritted her teeth. 'Of course you and the baby must stay with us,' he went on. 'You'll always be welcome here and besides, your mother could do with the help. These children are running her ragged. When do you plan to arrive?'

'Would tomorrow be all right? The first available train? I'll try not to be too late.'

'Do your best. Goodbye, then.' Before her father could replace the receiver, there was a scuffle and her mother broke in. 'Nell? Are you still there? We've had some news about Harry. He's in a prisoner-of-war camp, in Germany, and we can—'

But then the pips sounded, and Nell had no more change. Dazed, she walked back to Arthur. 'Harry's alive. He's been taken prisoner.' It was too much to take in, on top of everything else.

His face lit up. 'That's marvellous. You see, darling, sometimes things work out, despite our worst imaginings. And look, Alice has dropped off.' She was lying on her back in the pram, her thumb in her mouth and the muslin cloth she liked to hold nestled against her cheek.

'Don't despair,' Arthur said. 'The Germans can't go on bombing us like this forever. As soon as it's safe, you can come back and we'll find somewhere else to live.'

'And Christmas is coming, so you'll have some time

off then,' Nell said. A flicker of doubt crossed his face; quickly supressed, but not quite quickly enough. 'Arthur? You will, won't you?'

He shifted uncomfortably on the chair. 'I hope so. I shall have to be back in London by New Year's Eve, though.'

'I'm aware of that.' Nell spoke more sharply than she intended. Of course there had to be a clockmaker on duty that night; the whole country would be waiting for Big Ben to ring in 1941 and nothing could be allowed to go wrong. She and Arthur would never be celebrating New Year's Eve together, but surely seeing him at Christmas wasn't too much to expect. And yet, plenty of other families would be spending the day apart. Why should theirs be any different? 'Sorry to be scratchy,' she added. 'It's been rather a night, that's all.'

'I really must go.' Arthur frowned as he put on his coat, already preparing himself for the day ahead. He gave her a brief, distracted kiss. 'We'll have a meal somewhere special this evening. I'll meet you at the Abbey at six.'

'That'll be lovely. I might go back to the house and see if there's anything to be salvaged.'

'Try not to worry,' he said, listening with only half an ear. 'Everything will be fine, I promise.'

Chapter Three

London, November 1940

Hathaway Road was swarming with people by the time Nell returned to it, pushing Alice in the awful pram. Four or five men were standing around in a crater in the middle of the street, inspecting the exposed pipes for damage. Nell glanced in herself as she went past. It was fascinating to see the complex arrangement of channels and cables that lay under one's feet, hidden in the normal run of things by hard core and asphalt. There was no privacy anymore, not even for Hathaway Road. London was being torn apart and people no longer averted their eyes: they peered into their neighbours' houses, stared at passers-by in pyjamas and dressing gowns, took buses to view the more spectacular bomb sites. Was it just nosiness? Nell wondered, manoeuvring around a lump of fallen masonry. Perhaps it was more a need to convince themselves this destruction was real, because it seemed so unbelievable – even when the evidence lay in front of one's eyes.

The elderly couple at number 19 were standing in their front garden, watching a workman fix a flapping tarpaulin over the roof. 'Oh, thank goodness you and the baby are safe,' said the woman, putting her hand on Nell's arm. 'We were so worried.'

They'd never spoken to each other before; Nell had no idea her neighbour even knew Alice existed. She smiled and walked on as though in a dream. There were a couple of wardens knocking on people's front doors, and as she approached her house, she could see the bossy one she'd never liked stooping over a heap of rubble on what used to be the front path. Mr Blackwell was there, too, taking off his cap to wipe his forehead before bending back to the job in hand. They were flinging bricks about and calling to each other in a brusque, manly way.

'There you are, dear,' Mr Blackwell said, catching sight of her. 'If we can salvage anything, we'll be sure to let you know.'

'Thanks awfully. I'm rather worried about the pram, and Arthur's bicycle. They were both in the hall.' Although looking at the heap of pulverised stone, Nell didn't hold out much hope. So she was officially 'dear' now; not that she minded. She wished suddenly that she could have had a jolly, uncomplicated father like Mr Blackwell, despite his maxims.

'Why don't you take the baby round to ours?'

he said. 'Sit down and catch your breath for a while.'

The Blackwells' house looked exactly as it had on the few occasions Nell had visited in the past, which seemed odd, given the devastation next door. She had always sat in the kitchen before but now she was shown into the parlour, a small room crowded with uncomfortable furniture.

'If only I could offer you a cup of tea.' Mrs Blackwell hovered in the doorway. 'Looks like we won't have gas before tomorrow.'

'Thank you, but I'm awash with tea,' Nell said, perching on one of the high-backed leather chairs that stood either side of the fire. 'Well, this is cosy.'

A fire roared in the grate behind a fender and the temperature was almost tropical; somehow the Blackwells always seemed to have plenty of coal. She took off the grubby cardigan Alice had been given at the rest centre and set her down on the floor, where she made a beeline for the coal bucket.

'Oh no, dear.' To Nell's surprise, Mrs Blackwell scooped the baby up and swung her into the air, pretending to drop her without actually letting go. Alice looked astonished, too, and then she laughed, grasping one of Mrs Blackwell's iron-grey curls in her chubby hand and tugging it. Nell was horrified but Mrs Blackwell didn't seem at all put out.

'I've found you something that's better to play with than dirty old coal,' she said, reaching into her cardigan pocket and producing an ivory teething ring with a silver bell attached. She put it in Alice's hand and set her down on the hearth rug.

'What a beautiful thing!' Nell exclaimed. 'It looks like a family heirloom.'

'Our Susan used to love that ring when she was teething.' Mrs Blackwell smiled, watching Alice gnaw on it for all she was worth.

'I didn't know you had a daughter.' The Blackwells had never mentioned children; Nell had always assumed they hadn't any.

'She died when she was six,' Mrs Blackwell said briefly. 'Pneumonia. These old houses aren't fit for kiddies.'

'I'm so sorry.' Nell's eyes filled with tears. She'd managed not to cry so far that day, despite everything, but this revelation was too much. 'I didn't know.'

'How could you? It's not something I care to talk about.' Mrs Blackwell clamped her lips in a thin line, indicating that her feelings hadn't changed.

Eventually, Nell managed to compose herself. 'Thank you for all your kindness,' she was able to say. 'We couldn't have asked for better neighbours. We shall miss you both, very much. I'm taking Alice to my parents' house in the country, you see, while Arthur stays in London. He can't leave his job. I hate the idea of us being separated, but—' She spread her hands and shrugged.

'But what choice do you have?' Mrs Blackwell said. 'You're doing the right thing, Mrs Spelman. The baby has to come first.'

The conversation was interrupted at that point by someone knocking on the window. Mrs Blackwell pulled aside the net curtain to reveal her husband, standing on the pavement with a broad grin as he displayed the Ambassador – dented, filthy, but more or less in one piece.

'Now there's a first,' she said. 'Don't think my Stan's ever touched a pram before.'

Nell pressed her face against the glass, unable to believe her eyes. It was a miracle. 'How on earth . . .?'

'The front door blew against it and kept off the worst of the damage,' Mr Blackwell called. 'The hood's been torn and one of the wheels is bent, but I can probably knock it back into shape.'

'Oh, that's wonderful! Thank you so much.' It felt as though an old friend had been brought back from the dead. She couldn't wait to tell Arthur. 'Any sign of the bicycle?' she added, but Mr Blackwell only shook his head.

'Once the pram is ready, I shall take this little one for a walk to the park.' Mrs Blackwell had picked up Alice again. 'You go upstairs and have a rest, Mrs Spelman, while you've the chance.'

The temperature plunged as Nell climbed up the stairs. She kicked off her shoes and crawled under the eiderdown in the Blackwells' spare room. In contrast to the parlour, it was sparsely furnished with a bed, a chair and a wash stand. The walls were papered in a pretty rose print and the curtains were pink. This must have been Susan's room, Nell thought as she closed her eyes. Oh, the sadness of the world! She could hardly bear it.

'Good heavens!' Arthur exclaimed as Nell approached, wheeling the pram with Alice sitting up in state like a queen restored to her throne. 'That thing really is indestructible.'

'Mr Blackwell dug it out,' Nell said. 'Oh, Arthur – I have so much to tell you. Where are we going for supper?'

'It's a surprise,' he replied. 'Follow me. Alice is well wrapped up, isn't she?' He narrowed his eyes. 'Is that a new cardigan she's wearing?'

'And a new bonnet, and new mittens, and a blanket for the pram. I'll explain once we're settled.'

They walked out of the Abbey into a cloudy night, past the barbed wire enclosing Parliament Square, across Westminster Bridge, and down the ramp to the Embankment. The Thames flowed silently past, the ripples on its surface occasionally revealed by a roaming searchlight. Nell had come to think of this stretch of the river as theirs. She and Arthur had done their courting here the previous year, as winter turned to spring and the avenue of plane trees burst into bright green leaf. And now a year and a half later, here they were: a family. Arthur turned to smile at her; there was no need for words. He led the way to their favourite bench with a view across the water to the golden clock face, its hands ticking their precious hours away. The time they had spent together back then seemed to fly past; there had been so much to learn about each other. Arthur had been a stranger whom she'd happened to notice on Westminster Bridge as she walked home one afternoon from the school where she taught in the back streets of Westminster. A dark-haired young man walking towards her had paused, staring for a moment with his hand on the balustrade as though he recognised her. Something in his expression made her smile at him, then blush furiously. A couple of days later, she was crossing the bridge again when he overtook her, walking in the same direction, then turned back to look. This time, he was the one to smile. She dropped her gaze immediately, her cheeks burning; when she looked again, all she saw was his back, disappearing into the crowd. It was surprising how disappointed she'd felt.

She found herself looking out for the dark-haired young man every afternoon after that – she never saw him in the morning – until, one day, a gust of wind sent her hat flying through the air. He happened to be walking behind her and had only to reach out a hand to catch it; she couldn't have timed the mishap any better had she been trying on purpose. They fell into conversation quite naturally, walking together across the bridge, and from then on, they saw each other every weekday. 'I can spot your crimson coat from the clock tower,' he confessed. 'Don't ever forget to wear it.' As the evenings grew lighter, they would stroll together beside the river, and soon they were meeting at weekends: going to the pictures, or for bicycle rides along the river to picnic in Richmond Park. Arthur told her about his work at Westminster; she told him about the battles she had with her unruly class and the occasional triumphs that made these battles worthwhile. Soon they were talking about everything: their childhoods, their families, Arthur's heritage – his German parents had moved to London at the turn of the century, where he'd been born – which naturally led to the worrying situation abroad. Hitler and Mussolini were becoming increasingly belligerent; the Prime Minister's policy of appeasement clearly hadn't worked. Across the water in the House of Commons, the call for action was intensifying. At the end of March, Chamberlain promised that Britain would come to the aid of Poland if that country were invaded, and the French government backed his pledge. War seemed inevitable.

Nell and Arthur were walking arm in arm by then, and that evening he kissed her on their favourite bench, the one with the best view of the clock tower. It felt wrong to be so happy at such a frightening time, but Nell couldn't help herself. She had fallen deeply in love. It seemed a miracle that this extraordinary man should feel the same way about her, that he should have recognised her from a crowd of strangers. Yet somehow they had found each other, and now she would never let him go.

'Here we are.' Arthur led her to that very same bench. They parked the pram beside it and sat in their accustomed places, Nell with her head resting against his shoulder. 'Warm enough?' he asked, stroking her hair.

She nodded, her heart full. The tower was shrouded in darkness on the other side of the river but still, she knew it was there. She liked to imagine the clock face watching over them: a reassuring presence that anchored her, keeping her steady.

'You're probably wondering about supper,' Arthur said, 'but fear not. I've brought a picnic.' He disengaged himself and took a parcel wrapped in newspaper out of his rucksack.

Nell inhaled the tantalising smell, suddenly ravenous. 'Fish and chips? Perfect!'

'Not quite as hot as they should be, but they'll have to do.' He laid the parcel on the bench between them, then produced a bottle of beer and a china mug from which to drink it, two linen napkins and a bar of chocolate for pudding.

'You've thought of everything.' Nell speared a chip with the little wooden fork and held it out to Alice. 'This really is a treat.'

'I didn't want to sit in a crowded restaurant,' he said. 'It should be just the three of us tonight: me and my two best girls.'

Nell felt the tears pricking at her eyes and was grateful for the cover of darkness. There was no point in making their parting more agonising than it had to be; she would be strong, too, and show him he had no need to worry. She managed to tell him how marvellous the Blackwells had been without crying, and about the loss they had suffered, and even about the bag of baby clothes that Mrs Blackwell had given her.

'Such lovely cardigans and leggings, and some dresses with the most gorgeous hand-smocking. There's even a christening gown.'

'I can't take this!' she'd told Mrs Blackwell. 'It belongs in your family.'

'There's only Stan and me left now,' Mrs Blackwell had replied. 'What's the point in us keeping a christening gown locked away in a suitcase? It's not as though we'll be having any more babies. You're a young couple, just starting out. And I should like to think of you having something nice, given what you've lost.'

'But—' Nell had begun, then stopped, unable to put into words what she was thinking.

Mrs Blackwell had seemed to understand. 'I've held on to the past for long enough, dear. It's time to let go.'

Nell didn't trust herself to repeat those words to Arthur.

Soon they had eaten every last greasy, delicious scrap. Arthur parcelled up the newspaper and empty bottle to throw away, then took a small package wrapped in tissue paper from his pocket and pressed it into her hands. 'This is for you.'

'What is it?' she asked, unwrapping the paper but unable to see its contents clearly in the dark.

'Just a watch. I thought it might come in handy.'

Not 'just a watch', Nell discovered by the light of her torch, but the most exquisite piece of jewellery. It hung from a ring on a long chain so she could tuck it under her jumper and feel its ticking close to her heart. 'Oh, Arthur!' she said wonderingly, 'I've never seen anything so beautiful.'

'I've been waiting for the right time to give it to you. It's been in the family for a while but I've cleaned it up and engraved your initials on the back.' He hung the chain around her neck and kissed her upturned face. 'Just think: every second that passes will be a second nearer the moment we see each other again.'

She couldn't speak.

He jumped to his feet. 'Right, on to the next adventure! I've found somewhere special for us to sleep tonight: the crypt at Westminster Abbey, no less.'

'The crypt?' Nell repeated, overcome by a sudden wave of dread.

Arthur laughed. 'Don't worry, nobody's buried there. It's actually rather cosy. You'll love it.'

Nell felt so faint that she had to sit down again on the bench and take a deep breath. Her stomach lurched. It was ridiculous to be superstitious, she told herself; Arthur was delighted with his plan and would be desperately hurt if she objected. Yet the fears that had been plaguing her all day now coalesced into a terrible certainty: this would be the last night they'd spend together. After they had said their goodbyes in the morning, he would turn and walk away, and she would have lost him.

Chapter Four

Westchester County, November 2021

'You mustn't worry about me,' Alice said, knotting her fingers. 'I'm perfectly happy here. Why wouldn't I be? Waited on hand and foot with more food than I could possibly eat, and the staff all such nice girls. So pleasant to talk to.'

Ellie felt ashamed that her mother should regard staying in a nursing home as such a treat; it was a sad reflection on her as a daughter. She should have visited Alice more often, should have taken her out shopping, for lunch or dinner – should at least have called more regularly. Yet her mother had always seemed so self-sufficient. She wasn't one for chatting on the phone, and she was so horrified by the cost of eating out that she always chose the cheapest thing on the menu, even if she didn't like it, which drove Ellie insane. They would end up fighting before the meal had even started.

'Have you made friends with any of the other residents yet?' she asked.

'Oh, I don't have much to do with them,' Alice replied. 'They're far too old and decrepit.'

'Says the woman who's in her eighties.'

Alice flapped a dismissive hand, then wrapped the paisley shawl more tightly over her sunken chest. She looked like a gypsy queen, sitting in the high-backed chair with a red silk scarf wound in a turban around her head, her dark eyes snapping and the skin taut over her cheekbones. She might not care to acknowledge her age, yet it was becoming harder to ignore: she'd fallen and broken her hip a few weeks before, and was taking a while to get back on her feet. The bones were healing but her confidence seemed to have been shaken. She certainly didn't seem in any hurry to go back to her second-floor apartment. Ellie had been visiting the nursing home every Sunday, and sometimes after work if she could face it, taking the commuter train out to the suburbs where she had grown up. It was strange, spending this time with her mother in the impersonal, sparsely furnished room. There was a television on the wall but Alice preferred to read or listen to audiobooks, or simply sit and stare out of the large picture window. They'd had longer conversations than ever before – sometimes more than once. Ellie had been shocked when Alice occasionally launched into the same story again, word for word, only an hour or so after first telling it. Most of the time, she was recognisably herself, but sometimes Ellie would catch a blankness in her mother's eyes that terrified her.

Now, they shared a companionable silence, looking out of the window. A man sat in a wheelchair smoking a cigarette with his lower leg, encased in plaster, stuck out before him like a battering ram. A station wagon drew up and four people climbed out: a man in a sheepskin jacket, a harassed-looking woman carrying a large Tupperware container, and two girls aged about six or seven, wearing identical green dresses embroidered with Celtic designs, white socks and old-fashioned black lace-up shoes. Their small heads were bent under the weight of curly nylon wigs, cascading from thick white hairbands that might have been bandages – as though they had recently undergone some strange form of surgery.

'Ah, the Infant Phenomena,' Alice remarked. 'Granddaughters of Mrs Curran, along the corridor. They'll be giving a display of Irish dancing after we've had lunch. I'm holding myself in readiness.'

Ellie couldn't help smiling, if a little sadly. There would be no grandchildren visiting her mother: Ellie was her only living relative in the States. Alice had a half-sister in England, Gillian, but she never mentioned her and they hadn't been in touch for years; the round robin letters Gillian used to send them at Christmas, describing her children's many and varied achievements, had dried up since her divorce.

'Tell me about your childhood, Mom,' Ellie said. 'Were you happy?'

'Not particularly.' Alice shifted in her chair. 'I don't understand this current obsession with happiness. When I was growing up, nobody expected to be happy – you just had to get on with things and make the best of them. We'd come through the war, you see. We were grateful to be alive. Or at least, everyone told us we should have been. One could never complain, no matter how hard life was.' She took a sip of water, her hand trembling a little. 'People are always whining about something or other these days.'

Alice had always been different. Ellie had adored her mom when she was tiny – Alice would spend hours reading to her and made up such wonderful bedtime stories – but as she grew older, her mother's singularity became embarrassing. Her classmates' moms had elaborate perms and wore velour tracksuits with sparkly white trainers. Alice favoured the flowing skirts and kaftans that had been popular when she was in her twenties. Bracelets jangled on her arms, she outlined her eyes with kohl and smelt of patchouli; her hair – dark then – was long and resolutely straight, unlike Ellie's unruly curls. Teenage Ellie wanted a mother who blended in with the pack, but Alice stood out in all sorts of ways. She had kept her English accent, for one thing, which sometimes made her sound condescending and snobbish. Even worse, she was a good ten or fifteen years older than the other women dropping off their kids at school. Ellie's teacher had once mistaken Alice for her grandmother; Ellie had been mortified, though her mother had only laughed.

'All the doctors said I'd never fall pregnant,' she used to recall, even in front of strangers. 'When my periods stopped, I thought the menopause had come early.'

Ellie wished the earth would swallow her up at times like these, like Rumpelstiltskin in the fairy story Alice used to tell, who stamped his foot so hard that he made a hole in the ground and fell into it. And then she would catch sight of her mother sitting by herself in the stands at a basketball game, or struggling uncomfortably to make small talk, and feel the fiercest rush of protective love. Her mom always made the effort, no matter what. She turned up to every match Ellie played and every concert she ever sang in, made tray bakes and pot-luck dishes whenever required, bought too much candy for trick-or-treating and sat up half the night sewing Hallowe'en costumes. Alice tried too hard, that was the trouble, and the results were usually wrong in some indefinable way: the dishes too elaborate, the outfits too fancy, the jokes somehow off. Ellie couldn't help wishing her mom would stay at home, give her a break from this constant burden of guilt. And then, overcome with remorse, she would hate herself even more.

She never worried the same way about her dad. Jeff was older, too, but so were a couple of her friends' fathers who'd divorced and married again. He was the kind of guy who could fit in anywhere, with an easy-going charm that made everyone want to be his friend. So many people came to his funeral that the service was relayed through loudspeakers set up outside the church. It must be coming up for twenty years since he died, Ellie realised. She was thirty-eight and had lived more than half her life without him. She went over to her mother's bedside table to gaze at the photograph Alice always kept close, taken on one of their family hikes in the Poconos. Ellie must have been about ten. She and her dad were walking ahead along the trail, his arm resting on her shoulder, the sun behind them so they were silhouetted against the dazzling light. Alice must have called out to make them turn around for the shot. What had they been talking about? Ellie wondered, looking at her absorbed, intent face. She should have paid more attention. Her overriding memory when she thought of her father was one of general, uncomplicated happiness.

A selection of Alice's other treasures had been arranged within easy reach: a triangular crystal for healing and tranquillity, a lavender bag that smelt only of dust, an embroidered handkerchief. Lying among them was one thing Ellie hadn't seen before: a round gold watch with a ring at the top, designed to wear on a chain. Its glass face was crazed with a spider's web of cracks; beneath them, tiny diamond chips glinted at the Roman numerals marking the hours XII, III, VI and IX.

'Where did this come from?' Ellie picked it up for closer inspection. 'It's beautiful.'

'I didn't steal it, if that's what you're implying,' Alice said haughtily. 'It was my mother's. My father gave it to her. She was wearing it when she died.'

The watch said five past nine, although the time was actually midday. Ellie turned it over. The initials ES had been engraved on the back: Eleanor Spelman, her maternal grandmother, and the woman after whom she had been named. She had been killed in the Blitz when Alice was a baby.

'I thought your father was German?' Ellie asked idly, replacing the watch. 'Spelman sounds like an English name.'

'His parents were German but they moved to England before he was born. The family was originally called Spielmann, I think. They anglicised the name to fit in, like so many people did at the time. My father was Arthur Spelman, and as English as they come.' She lifted her head towards the door, scenting the air. 'Something smells good. Will you be staying for lunch, darling?'

'I'm going to the Scardinos for Thanksgiving. I told you, Mom.' Ellie tried not to sound impatient. 'Are you sure you won't come too? They'd be so happy to have you.'

Beth Scardino was Ellie's best friend, and her mother Kathleen had been almost as close to Alice; the two women had met when their daughters were babies and stayed in touch ever since. Kathleen was the only close friend Alice had. The pair of them still lived not far from each other in the town where they'd raised their families, although Alice had moved into a smaller house and then an even smaller apartment after Jeff had died.

‘No, thank you, darling,’ Alice replied. ‘I’m not up to being sociable yet. And I’ve never been much of a one for Thanksgiving. Send Kathleen my love, though. I haven’t seen her for months.’

‘I thought she dropped by last week?’

‘Whatever gave you that idea?’ Alice asked. ‘Honestly, it’s hard enough to keep track of the days without you trying to confuse me.’

‘Sorry,’ Ellie said quickly. ‘I must have got it wrong.’

It had started to rain. Alice watched an elderly man struggling to open an umbrella for the short walk to his car, then repeat the battle to close it when he got there. She snorted. ‘Well, that wasn’t worth the bother.’

They sat quietly for a while, Alice stroking the fringes of her shawl. ‘I had the strangest dream last night,’ she said eventually. ‘I was waiting for my mother at a railway station – a proper one, like we used to have, with flowers in tubs and a uniformed guard, and a fire in the waiting room. She was arriving on one train and taking me away with her on another, and she’d promised to bring a picnic. Cucumber sandwiches with the crusts cut off, those little cheese triangles wrapped in silver foil and packets of crisps with the salt in a screw of blue paper. The train came in and a woman got off. She stood at the far end of the platform so I ran to meet her, but as I got closer, I realised it wasn’t my mother after all. This person was far too old and plain. My mother was beautiful, everyone said so.’

‘Do you have any photographs?’ Ellie wondered why she’d never thought to ask before.

'I seem to remember seeing some once, but who knows where they are now.' That anxious look crossed Alice's face. 'They were in a hatbox, I think, on top of the mahogany wardrobe. My stepmother threw a lot of things away. She was jealous, you see, because Nell was my father's great love. Mavis was second-best all along and she knew it. She was a butcher's daughter and rather coarse, despite her airs and graces. And no great shakes in the looks department, either.'

This was a familiar theme; Alice and her stepmother had never got on. Ellie surreptitiously checked the time on her phone.

'Am I boring you?' her mother asked.

'Of course not,' Ellie replied guiltily. 'I don't want to be late for lunch, that's all.'

'I'm glad you're going to the Scardinos. Kathleen will look after you.' Alice smiled. 'And Beth is such a lovely girl. She's getting married soon, isn't she?'

'That was a while ago, Mom. She has a baby now, remember? A little girl, Morgan.'

'What strange names children have these days,' Alice said crossly. 'They might as well have called the poor thing Bentley, or Morris Minor.' That frightened, lost look had come back into her eyes.

Ellie took her mother's hands between hers, smoothing her papery skin. 'Tell me about your father, Mom. What was he like?'

'Why do you want to know?'

'Because he's a part of our family.' And when you've gone, she added to herself, those memories will be lost forever. For months, if not years, she had been refusing to look ahead, unable to contemplate the world without her mother's prickly, loving presence. Now, perhaps, it was time to face reality.

'He was very sad,' Alice said after a while, 'and that could make him difficult. Losing his wife in the war must have affected him deeply, although I didn't understand that at the time. All I wanted was to leave home and start leading my own life.'

'And you never went back? Not even after I was born?'

Alice shook her head. 'We were so happy, Jeff and I. We'd even managed to accept not having children – and then when you came along, it seemed like a miracle. My life was perfect and you were so precious; I couldn't see any good in taking you back to England. Mavis was a bitter, discontented woman – the bad fairy leaning over the baby's cradle.' Alice gave Ellie a searching look. 'I might have made a mistake. I should have told you about your heritage, but I know so little myself. My father was a talented man. The Spielmanns had been clock- and watchmakers for generations in Germany, and he carried on the tradition. I think he looked after Big Ben during the war. You know, the famous clock at the Houses of Parliament?'

'Really? That's amazing!'

Alice frowned. 'I might have got that wrong.'

'And what about your mother?'

'A mystery.' Alice shook her head. 'Her name was Eleanor but people called her Nell, apparently she was beautiful, for what that's worth, and she was killed in the Blitz when I was a baby. My father couldn't bear to talk about her and now it's too late to find out. There's no one left to ask.'

'What about Gillian?'

Alice snorted. 'Gillian's a dead loss. She was born years after my mother died and anyway, I wouldn't trust a word she said. Remember those ridiculous letters she used to send?'

'She's family, too, though.'

'And?' said Alice, raising her eyebrows.

'And I might try to get in touch.' The words fell out of Ellie's mouth before she'd thought about them. 'She's gone back to her maiden name, hasn't she? There can't be too many Gillian Spelmans living in London. She might have some photographs she could send us – of your dad, if not your mom. That would be better than nothing. And I'll have a look in your apartment for that hatbox you mentioned.'

'Hatbox? I don't need a hat, I'm not going out.' Alice rubbed her thumb and forefinger together: a habit Ellie had recently noticed. Thankfully, they were interrupted just then by the dinner lady – as Alice insisted on calling her – bringing a tray bearing a plate of soup, a roll with a pat of butter and a bowl covered by a saucer. She put it down on the table and said, 'Here you are, Your Ladyship. Lunch is served.' In a friendly voice, though.

Alice lifted up the saucer to peek underneath. 'Apple pie!' she announced. 'Marvellous.' She turned to Ellie.

'But what will you have to eat? Shall I ask the girl to bring you a sandwich?'

'Thanks, but I have to go.' Ellie kissed the top of her mother's head. 'I'm having lunch with the Scardinos.'

'Oh, yes, you told me,' Alice said vaguely. 'I'm sorry, my memory's not what it was.'

'Don't worry about it.' Ellie adjusted the scarf which had slipped at a rakish angle over Alice's eye, to reveal strands of silvery hair.

'Stop fussing.' Her mother batted away her hand. 'I'm not a baby.'

Ellie put her arms around Alice and hugged her tight, resting her head for a moment in the hollow of her mother's bony shoulder. 'Love you, Mom. Everything will be all right, I promise.'

Chapter Five

Westchester County, November 2021

'Here she is! The guest of honour.' John Scardino swept Ellie up into a whisky-scented hug, pressing his stubbly cheek against her cold one. 'Hey, you're freezing! Come through to the kitchen and thaw out. Kathleen's having hysterics but that's nothing new. Down, Bailey!'

The crazy spaniel was leaping against Ellie's legs, whining with excitement. A familiar smell wafted down the hall: drifts of cinnamon and cloves, turkey roasting under a blanket of bacon, caramelizing sweet potatoes, cranberries simmering in orange juice.

Ellie let out her breath in a rush, the tension leaving her shoulders. She didn't need to feel guilty; Alice had been invited to the feast but she was happier in her own company at the moment, and there was nothing wrong with that.

'Ellie, darling!' Kathleen grabbed a saucepan from

the stove and jammed it down on the worktop, sending a bowl of potato chips skittering over the floor. 'Oh, hell,' she said, stooping to retrieve the bowl. 'Never mind, Bailey will clean up the mess.'

Wiping her hands down the front of her checked apron, she advanced, holding out her arms. Her cheeks were flushed from the heat of the stove and her short dark hair, threaded with grey, stood in spikes; Ellie could picture her dashing it away from her forehead with the back of her hand as she stirred too many saucepans and sliced too many vegetables they would struggle to eat. 'Honey, you look tired,' she said, hugging Ellie tight. 'How's Alice? I visited last week and we had a long talk about the good old days.'

'Give the poor girl a break.' John was already easing the cork from a bottle of wine. 'She hasn't even had time to take off her coat.'

'Mom's OK,' Ellie said, wriggling out of her jacket and dumping it on a chair. 'She sends all of you her love.' She fished around in her backpack for the present she'd brought. 'Here, this is for you.'

Kathleen unwrapped the green plastic contraption and held it aloft. 'Goodness! Now whatever is this for? Taking the stones out of horses' hooves?'

'It's an avocado tool. You cut the avocado open with this so it doesn't discolour,' and she unfolded a white plastic blade from the handle, 'then you take out the pit with this gizmo in the middle—' she pressed the saw-toothed circle down on an imaginary avocado stone, 'and you scoop out the flesh with this paddle thing.'

'Well, isn't that ingenious,' Kathleen said doubtfully. 'Thanks, honey. I'm sure I'll wonder how I ever managed without it.'

'There have to be some perks to running a kitchen-ware store.' Ellie wondered fleetingly how many of the gadgets she sold lay unused in drawers until their owners forgot what they were for and threw them away. She looked around. 'Where is everyone?'

'Dan and Lisa can't make it,' John said. 'There's been some crisis at the hospital so Lisa had to work and Dan's dealing with the builders. At Thanksgiving! The Sistine Chapel was painted with less drama than their kitchen. But Beth's in the den with Morgan. Why don't you go on through?' He pressed a glass of red wine into her hand. 'She can't wait to see you.'

Ellie walked down the familiar corridor, feeling the warmth seep back into her bones. This house had been a constant presence in her life as far back as she could remember, and had become even more important once her own childhood home had been sold after her father died. It hardly seemed a minute since she and Beth had been getting ready for parties and prom nights together in the bedroom upstairs, or hatching plans to sneak into bars with fake IDs. No one had asked to see Ellie's ID for about fifteen years though, and now here was Beth with a baby of her own. How was that possible?

'Hey, you,' she said as they hugged, inhaling the clotted milk and baby-powder smell that clung around her friend these days. 'How's it going?'

Beth sighed. 'Apart from the fact Morgan's sleeping all day and partying all night, just fine.'

The baby was sprawled fast asleep in the middle of her activity mat, surrounded by squeakers to press and Velcro tabs to pull. A mobile of brightly coloured ducklings dangled over her head and a padded book lay close at hand, ready to have its cloth pages turned.

'She's getting so big,' Ellie said. 'All that hair! Do you think we should wake her up so she'll sleep later?'

'Let's chat first while we have the chance.' Beth eyed Ellie's glass avidly. 'I'd kill for a drink. Can I have a sip of yours? One mouthful won't hurt.'

Ellie handed it over. 'You look great.'

Beth laughed. 'Oh, sure. I haven't washed my hair in days and you could pack your groceries in the bags under my eyes.'

'No, I mean it. Motherhood suits you.' Beth had put on weight and she was dressed in a pair of baggy sweat pants but she radiated peace and contentment. She'd lost that nervy, strained expression that had hung over her the past couple of years.

'Are you OK with this whole baby business?' she asked Ellie in a rush, as though she might lose her nerve. 'It doesn't have to change anything between us, not really.'

'Oh, Bee!' Ellie flushed. 'How could I be anything but happy for you and Michael? Besides, now you've given me someone else to love.'

Life had had a habit of falling into place for Beth Scardino: she'd sailed through school and college, played basketball, qualified as an attorney and married her childhood sweetheart on a beach in South Carolina. The only thing that hadn't come so easily was having a baby. Ellie was ashamed to admit it, even to herself, but at first she couldn't help feeling – not pleased exactly, but reassured somehow, that for once Beth might have to struggle rather than getting whatever she wanted at the click of a finger. Ellie had been a gawky teenager with skinny legs, big clumsy feet and braces on her teeth, while Beth had sailed through adolescence with hardly a spot. Her dark blonde hair streaked with gold in the summer and her olive skin tanned without burning, but you couldn't hate her for that because she was funny and didn't take herself too seriously.

Despite her annoying perfection, she was a great friend to have. When Ellie's father died, Beth was always there at the end of the phone, ready to listen and drop everything to come around if required. Yet over the past couple of years, it had been Ellie's turn to console her, as weeks and then months had gone by without the longed-for pregnancy. Several of their friends were starting families, and Ellie could see what torture it was for Beth and Michael to congratulate them. Ellie had only asked Fate for a temporary hiccup in the effortless trajectory of her best friend's life, not this terrible, gnawing grief which was renewed every twenty-eight days with heartless regularity. When Beth had at last conceived, Ellie was almost as excited as if she'd become pregnant herself. The first few months had been an anxious time but now that Morgan had arrived, safe and well, those dark days seemed part of another existence.

'It'll be your turn next.' Beth passed her back the wine. 'Maybe sooner than you think.'

'Oh, I think that ship has sailed. But actually, I'm fine with the way things are.' Ellie meant what she said. She was too rootless, too unsettled, to imagine bringing another life into the world. 'Just as long as you promise to visit me in the old folks' home.'

Beth pretended to think about it, then shook her head. 'Nah.'

At that moment, Morgan opened her eyes and started to cry. 'Let's leave her for a while,' Beth said. 'Sometimes she goes back off by herself.'

'Where is Michael, anyway?' Ellie asked, looking round the room as though he might have been hiding behind the couch.

'He has the flu, or so he says. I think he just wants a rest. He was up with Morgan half the night.' The baby started to wail, so Beth reached under the mobile to soothe her. 'Now, quick. Tell me about your love life. Anyone promising on the scene? There's a new copywriter in Michael's office who's just your type.'

Ellie groaned. 'No, seriously,' Beth assured her. 'He's cute. The right amount of stubble, glasses, great taste in clothes, kind to his mother.'

'You mean he's gay.' Ellie took another sip of wine. 'It's OK, I'm taking a break from dating. So much effort and it never goes anywhere.'

For the past few years, she'd been drifting into relationships and falling out of them equally casually. 'You have a problem with intimacy,' one boyfriend told her as they were breaking up. 'I know less about you now than I did when we first met. You should find a therapist and work through your issues.' But Ellie must have been the only person in Manhattan to feel self-conscious talking about her feelings. When the latest man had dumped her that summer, all she'd felt was an overwhelming sense of relief. She couldn't summon the energy to squeeze into tummy-control pants and plaster on make-up, choose an alluring but tasteful outfit and listen to some unshaven guy talk about the top speed of his car or moose-hunting or once, God help her, the effect of carbs on his colon. Now she was thirty-eight and single, living in a rental apartment and working seven days a week. That morning, she'd discovered a hair growing out of a mole under her chin.

Morgan was crying in earnest now so Beth picked her up for a feed. 'How's your mom doing?' she asked. 'Still not back in her apartment?'

'She seems much happier in the home, though who knows how long she can afford to stay there.' Ellie sighed. 'I'm kind of worried about her, truth be told. She's forgetting all kinds of stuff – it's like she's losing sight of who she is, and there's nothing to remind her.' She glanced around the room, its walls and shelves crowded with family photographs and mementoes; even a framed copy of a record showing the exact day

Emilio Scardino, Beth's great grandfather, had arrived from Italy at Ellis Island. 'Did I ever tell you that my biological grandmother – my mom's real mom – died when she was a baby?'

'That's so sad,' Beth said. 'Here, why don't you cuddle Morgan for a while.'

The baby was handed over, her eyes round in surprise. She looked like a small indignant coconut. 'How's my favourite god-daughter?' Ellie asked, tickling her under the chin. Morgan fixed her with an intent gaze, as though considering the question, then screwed up her face and began to cry.

'Sorry, she's getting super clingy,' Beth said. 'Hand her back if you like.'

'No, it's fine. We'll go for a little stroll.'

Ellie walked around the room, humming softly until the baby quietened down. 'Can I ask you a favour?' she said, turning to Beth. 'Could we swing by Mom's apartment on the way to the station? She mentioned some photographs in a hatbox I'd like to find. If you're going to give me a lift, that is. I can always take a cab and ask the driver to wait.'

'Of course I'm giving you a lift to the station! It's on my way home.' Beth took another cheeky sip of wine. 'And sure, we can look for these photos.' She smiled. 'You have the magic touch. Look, Morgan's asleep. Sit down and we can have a proper talk. How are things at work?'

'Not so great,' Ellie confessed. 'Business is kind of slow.'

Those early days when she'd had such high hopes for the store seemed a long time ago, and recently she'd caught herself wondering why she'd opened it in the first place. She'd always been more interested in cooking than Beth, so Kathleen had taught her how to make pastry, cakes and fresh pasta, how to fillet fish and roast a leg of lamb. As much as cooking, though, Ellie loved kitchens: clusters of saucepans hanging from racks like shiny silver fruit, dressers full of colourful china and pots crammed with strange utensils. She was fascinated by meat tenderisers, garlic crushers, potato mashers, sieves, spatulas, fish slices, egg timers in assorted shapes and sizes, chopping boards of olive wood or slate. And whisks! Who knew there could be so many different types? Airy balloon whisks, whisks with revolving handles like tiny unicycles, whisks made from tunnels of coiled wire. Seeing customers browsing these utensils gave her a sense of security and purpose.

Of course she wanted to make a profit, but she also wanted to sell things that were useful. No one who lived in the Village seemed to cook anymore, though; instead, the winding streets were crowded with bikes and mopeds, delivering takeout meals in recycled cardboard containers. People who still used their kitchens must have been living on protein shakes and smoothies; she hadn't sold a potato peeler or a carving knife in years, while sales of blenders had gone through the roof. It was dispiriting. And now, after Thanksgiving, would come the horror of Black Friday, when customers would desert her store and descend on the malls like a herd of disgruntled bison, fighting each other for bargains.

'Maybe it's time for a change,' she told Beth.

Yet the thought of starting again made her stomach churn with nerves. How would she make a living, for a start? Her father had left her some money, which she'd invested, and although she'd dipped into the pot occasionally, about half still remained. That would keep her going for a while, but she would have to earn something. Her outgoings were small: she was lucky enough to live in a rent-controlled apartment and didn't have a car or a taste for expensive clothes, which was just as well. Going back to work in a professional kitchen was one option, yet she was too old now to put up with the long hours and stress, the humiliation of being yelled at by someone nearly half her age.

Looking back, it seemed her life so far had been a series of impulsive wrong decisions about almost everything, from her choice of career to her taste in men. She had ricocheted from one near-disaster to another, like the pinball in a slot machine. Her first boyfriend, Jake, had been charming and funny, but lazy, stumbling around in a haze of weed and alcohol while she studied and waited tables to pay the rent. She'd wasted five years on him, only to end up with Elliott – charming and funny, but a compulsive liar – then Wilf, who had too many faults to list and wasn't even charming. Or funny, come to that. All these men had seemed to end up disliking her, no matter how hard she worked or how many times she forgave them. What was wrong with her?

'Maybe you just need a vacation,' Beth said. 'You haven't had a proper break in years. That assistant of yours can look after the store, can't she? What's her name again?'

'Shania,' Ellie replied, absent-mindedly. The idea had come to her in a blinding, unwelcome flash that a possible option – one that might even be expected of her – would be to look after her mother. Alice might feel differently about going back to her apartment if Ellie were installed in the spare room. It might not be so bad. Life was peaceful in the suburbs, Beth would be closer at hand and she'd probably make new friends one way or another. She could get a dog, perhaps, or join a book club. She'd miss her runs along the Hudson River in the misty early morning, her yoga classes and late-night dinners in pop-up bars, but there would be other compensations. Wouldn't there?

'You'd go mad!' Beth said, when Ellie told her what she'd been thinking. 'And so would Alice. Cooped up in that tiny apartment? You'd be at each other's throats by the end of the week.'

She was right, of course. 'But I have to do something,' Ellie sighed. 'Mom's so alone and I can't bear it.'

It was a wonderful Thanksgiving dinner, they all decided, one of the best – although Kathleen had cooked for an army and the four of them plus a baby had hardly made a dent in the turkey. 'Plenty of leftovers for the sandwiches tomorrow,' Kathleen said, wrapping chunks of meat in foil for the girls to take home. 'I might drop some off to Dan and Lisa.'

'Give them a ring first,' John said, with a significant look. 'Just to check it's convenient.'

'What was that all about?' Ellie asked, after they had made their farewells and strapped Morgan into her car seat.

Beth started the engine. 'Mom and Dad are worried about Dan. They think he and Lisa are going through a sticky patch, and them not turning up for Thanksgiving is a bad sign.'

'Maybe.' Ellie fastened her safety belt. 'But things are usually pretty tense between those two, aren't they? That seems to be how their relationship works.'

'Or doesn't,' Beth replied. 'I don't know how Dan puts up with it.'

They waved goodbye to John and Kathleen, standing on the doorstep, and Beth pulled the car away. 'Give Michael my love,' Ellie said. 'I was sorry not to see him but it was great, wasn't it, just the two of us? Like old times. Coming to your house makes me feel like a kid again.'

'Me too. A kid and a mom at the same time, which is confusing.' Beth looked at Morgan in the rear-view mirror. 'Family is everything.' She patted Ellie's knee. 'That includes you, of course.'

'Sure you don't mind the detour?' Ellie asked, looking at the roads they used to travel by school bus. Beth lived forty minutes' drive from her parents now. Just the right distance: close enough to drop by, but not so close they were in each other's pockets.

'Are you kidding?' she replied. 'You know how I love a treasure hunt.'

Alice's apartment was only a mile or so away. The hall smelt musty when they unlocked the front door, and the place was deathly cold.

'Feels like we're intruding, doesn't it?' Beth whispered, setting the baby down in her car seat. 'As though your mom is going to appear all of a sudden and ask what we're doing.'

Although Alice had done her best to make the place homely with cushions, plants and throws, it had never had a particularly welcoming feel. The rooms were blank and characterless, rugs skidded over the laminate floor and the bathroom suite was a dingy pink, the colour of liver sausage. Ellie knew she should have decorated the apartment or arranged for someone else to do the work, but Alice had insisted it wasn't worth the effort. 'I don't want the upheaval and besides, who knows how long I'll be here?' She'd always had a gloomy streak.

There was no mahogany wardrobe, of course; when she thought about it, Ellie knew her mother's closets were fitted, with white louvred doors that had never closed properly. Alice's few clothes hung in mute reproach. A 'capsule wardrobe', as the magazines called it. Her shoes were even more poignant, waiting in pairs with matching handbags arranged beside them.

A couple of baskets on the bottom shelf contained gloves, neatly-rolled scarves and berets, but they couldn't find a hatbox anywhere.

'Let's go,' Ellie said. 'This box must be a figment of Mom's imagination.'

'I'm not giving up yet, not if there's a chance of finding some photos of your mysterious grandmother. You go check on Morgan.' Beth pushed her out of the room. 'I'll have one last sweep on my own.'

Which, amazingly enough, was successful. Ellie was sneaking a last cuddle with the baby when Beth emerged from the bedroom. In her arms was a round brown-leather box, about the size of a large cake tin. 'Tada!' she announced. 'I found it under the bed, just where we were sitting.' She laid the box on the hall chair and took Morgan from Ellie's arms. 'You should have first look.'

It's only a hatbox, Ellie said to herself. Yet for some reason her heart was pounding as she prised off the tightly-fitting lid. Inside, she found – a hat. Which for some reason, felt like an anti-climax. The hat must have once been elegant, with its broad ribbon band and sweeping brim, but now it was misshapen, the felt faded and discoloured like an overripe plum. 'Try it on,' Beth urged, yet Ellie was reluctant. She examined the hat for clues – a hair, maybe, caught under the band – but found nothing, only the faint smell of mothballs. She reached into the box again. Beneath the hat lay a brown-leather handbag with long double handles. This was surely more promising. The metal clasp had rusted shut but eventually she managed to force it open. The bag contained a small, thick envelope and a mustard-yellow bus ticket, marked '2d' on one side and 'London Transport Buses' on the other. There was a hip flask, too, black with tarnish but possibly silver underneath, and a silver St Christopher medal that also needed a polish. Her fingers shaking a little, Ellie opened the envelope and took out a buff-coloured booklet with the word 'National Registration Identity Card' on the front, in the name of Eleanor Spelman.

'My grandmother,' Ellie said, showing Beth. Even saying the words made her shiver.

There were also three photographs of the same woman. The largest was a studio shot in which she was posing in pearls and a strapless evening gown, looking fixedly into the distance with her hands clasped as if in prayer. The other two snaps were more natural. One showed her sitting on the top rung of a gate, smiling as she squinted into the camera, both hands around her slim knees. She was wearing a rose-printed sundress with a boned bodice and narrow shoelace straps. Behind her stretched a field dotted with conical haystacks like tiny cottages. In the third photograph, Eleanor was holding a child of around six months old who must have been Alice. The baby was bundled up in a knitted jacket and bonnet, while Eleanor wore the hat, tipped stylishly over her dark curly hair. She looked excited and happy, blissfully unaware of what was to come.

Beth craned over Ellie's shoulder. 'Oh my God, you

look so like her. See? She has your family dimple. Or rather, you have hers.'

Both Ellie and her mother had a single dimple on their left cheek: another thing for Ellie to feel self-conscious about when she was younger. She thought it made her face lopsided. The sight of her grand-mother's dimple now, though, was extraordinarily moving. She took the picture back from Beth and sank into a chair. Eleanor was a real person; her blood ran in Ellie's veins. What else had been passed down through the generations?

'By the way, there was a box under the bed, too,' Beth said. 'Let me fetch it. This is so exciting!'

She came back carrying a cardboard box, battered and torn at the corners. A name and address had been written on the front: Mrs F Roberts, Orchard House, Millbury, Oxfordshire. It was lined with yellowing British newspapers from the 1950s, and a collection of baby clothes had been packed inside. Beth hung back, tactfully, to let Ellie examine them first.

'Oh dear. The moths have been having a party.' The first cardigan she held fell apart in her fingers, and it turned out that none of the knitted sweaters, leggings or mittens had survived. Yet a couple of cotton dresses were unscathed: creased, but still wearable. Ellie held one up. 'Look at the smocking! So beautiful.' She examined the seams more closely. 'This dress is hand-sewn. Do you think it would fit Morgan?'

'Are you kidding?' Beth was horrified. 'That's a precious heirloom. Morgan would ruin it in a heartbeat.' Unable to resist, she dived into the box. 'Oh, my Lord. Take a look at this.' And she shook out an armful of yellowing white fabric: a long christening gown with a scalloped hem, decorated on the bodice and sleeves with delicate cut work and trails of embroidered flowers. They stared at it for a moment in silence.

Ellie held the gown up to her face and inhaled, breathing in the past. She turned to Beth. 'That settles it. I know what I'm going to do next. I'm going to England, to find my family. I want to tell Mom where she came from before it's too late.'

Chapter Six

Westchester County/New York/London, December 2021

All the Scardinos thought Ellie's trip to London was a great idea. They were so enthusiastic it occurred to her that being her surrogate family was a burden they might have been ready to share for some time. Perhaps they were hoping a few English relatives would lighten the load. With their encouragement, she took the plunge: booking her plane tickets and an Airbnb for two weeks. Shania, her assistant, was more than happy to look after the store while Ellie was away; she'd decided to go just after Christmas, when things were usually quiet, and her mom was being cared for at the Willows. Turned out she wasn't indispensable, after all.

'Did my brother give you a call?' Beth asked. 'If you need someone to water your plants, I think he'd be interested.'

'Dan?' Ellie said. 'Why would he want to house sit?'

Because Kathleen had been right: he and Lisa definitely were going through a rough patch. 'We just need some breathing space,' Dan explained on the phone, sounding mortified. 'A couple of weeks to get our heads straight would be perfect, if you don't mind.'

'Of course not. It would be great to have you looking after my place. I'm sorry, though – hope you two can work things out.'

'Oh, I'm sure we will.' He gave an awkward laugh. 'One way or another.'

Later, Beth filled Ellie in on the details to spare her brother the embarrassment. 'Turns out Lisa's been having an affair with a trauma surgeon for the past year. Can you imagine it? The ice queen herself! Dan's putting on a brave face but he must be devastated.'

'I'm really sorry,' Ellie said. 'Poor guy.'

She'd had a secret crush on Dan when she was thirteen. It had lasted a year until one morning she'd woken up and realised Beth was right: he really was the most obnoxious boy in the universe. Over the years, their relationship had weathered those two extremes and come to settle somewhere in the middle. She liked Dan and enjoyed seeing him whenever their paths crossed, which wasn't often – and occasionally, she caught a glimpse of the boy who used to give her butterflies. His wife Lisa, however, was tricky. She had *moods*, and let everyone know about them.

'Maybe we won't have to put up with Lisa for much longer,' Beth said, echoing Ellie's thoughts. 'Must admit, I wouldn't be too upset.'

Kathleen had invited Ellie and her mom to spend Christmas with them, but Alice didn't feel up to it. Ellie didn't mind; she was happy to sit quietly with her mother, concentrating on Alice and preparing for her trip. The Scardinos always had their extended family to stay for the holidays and the house was noisier and more chaotic than ever. Alice would have been lost in the crowd. So Ellie spent a peaceful – if somewhat surreal – Christmas Day at the Willows, playing Scrabble with a ninety-year-old man who never spoke a word and his son who talked all the time, before being entertained by the stony-faced Irish-dancing twins and their bouncing wigs. Alice had moved upstairs to a recently vacated suite ('I think somebody's died,' she'd whispered, 'but they don't like to say so,') with a view of the gardens and a larger bathroom, and extended her stay for another four weeks. That was probably as much as she could afford; Ellie didn't like to think what would happen after the month was up. For the moment, Alice seemed perfectly content, although she missed watching people come and go in the car park. She was delighted with the photographs of her mother, which were now framed and lined up along the windowsill.

'You never know, I might come back with some more,' Ellie said.

'I doubt it.' Alice pursed her lips. 'Gillian won't have kept any.'

It had taken a while to track Aunt Gillian down. Ellie had found her postal address on her mother's

Christmas card list but she had no idea whether it was current. Eventually, the internet had revealed a tour guide named Gillian Spelman, living in London, who seemed to be the right sort of age. Alice had taken a look at the photograph on her website and said it might be her half-sister – and then again, it might not. So Ellie took a chance, which paid off: tour-guide Gillian replied to her email saying she was 'so pleased' to hear Ellie was planning a visit to London. Unfortunately, she was having work done in her house and January was always such a difficult month. (In what way? Ellie wondered.) She was sure Ellie would be busy too, seeing the sights etcetera, but perhaps they could meet one morning for coffee. She had signed off, 'Warmest wishes, Gillian Spelman'. It wasn't the most encouraging of responses. Ellie had been hoping for a personal tour around the city's hidden nooks and crannies, ending up at the Palace of Westminster and Big Ben itself.

'What's Aunt Gillian like?' she asked her mother now.

'I have no idea,' Alice replied. 'I left home when she was eight and haven't seen her since. She was a whiny child, as I remember, with a runny nose. Adenoidal. Why are you interested?'

'Because she's part of our family. You have the same father. Doesn't that mean anything?'

'My father changed when he married Mavis.' Alice folded her hands together. 'She didn't make him happy and things only got worse once Gillian arrived. I couldn't wait to escape, frankly. But do send her my kind regards.'

Kind regards and warm wishes: Ellie was already travelling in another land. She had chosen a pair of olive-wood salad servers to give Gillian and written defiantly in the accompanying card – a shot of the New York skyline – 'With much love, Alice and Ellie'.

'So you've left that girl with the tattoos in charge of your shop?' her mother asked. 'Well, let's hope it's still there when you get back.'

'Mom!' Ellie protested. 'Shania's the best assistant I've ever had. All the customers love her.'

Alice pursed her lips. She disapproved of the store, finding the range of goods on display extravagant and pointless. Any sort of excess offended her. 'Waste not, want not,' she always said. 'It's because I'm a war child. If you've grown up with rationing, you can't bear to throw anything away.' Christmas cards were sliced in half to become postcards, vegetable peelings were composted or boiled for stock, socks were darned, tight shoes had their toes cut out for wearing at the beach, bedsheets had an uncomfortable seam running down the centre where her mother had turned them sides to middle to disguise a worn patch.

'I'll be back before you know it.' Ellie kissed her mother goodbye. 'Are you sure you won't write Gillian a card?'

'Quite sure. I mean, really, what is there to say?' Alice laughed, lifting up her hands in a gesture of resignation, and Ellie laughed too, although she wasn't sure why.

And then Alice's face had fallen. 'I hope this jaunt isn't a mistake,' she'd said, frowning. 'You might find out more than you bargained for.'

She couldn't explain what she meant, although Ellie pressed her. All she would say was that some secrets were meant to be kept. 'We can't change the past, it's dead and gone. There's no point bringing up that old misery.'

'But there must have been love, too,' Ellie said. 'Isn't that worth looking for?'

Alice had only turned her face to the window, rubbing her thumb against her forefinger, and wouldn't reply.

The night before Ellie was due to leave for England, Dan came around to see how everything worked in the apartment and collect a set of keys. She felt a sudden pang at the thought of leaving her refuge, the home that wrapped its walls around her when the world seemed a harsh place. The apartment was small but cosy, with one bedroom, a galley kitchen and a couch in the living room for when anyone who wasn't a boyfriend needed to stay overnight – although guests made her feel as though her sanctuary were being invaded. She had lived there for the past nine years and still felt a jolt of pleasure when she walked through the front door. Why was she abandoning comfort and security to head off on a wild-goose chase?

'Don't worry,' Dan said, 'I'll take good care of the place while you're away.'

'I'm sure you will. Don't spend too much time cleaning, though.' Dan was famously neat and tidy. 'And make the most of Manhattan.' She could imagine him putting a frozen meal in the microwave and eating it by himself in front of the television.

'I'll be fine. I'm looking forward to some time by myself. Lisa and I were meant to be going on holiday but that's not happening, so I have ten whole days off work to do what I want. I can't remember the last time that happened.' He raised his glass. 'Here's to the new year, and a fresh start. We've decided to get divorced.'

'Oh, Dan, I'm so sorry. Still, maybe it's for the best. Let's drink to new beginnings and happier times to come.' Ellie chinked her glass against his.

He'd brought a bottle of wine and they were finishing up the leftovers in Ellie's fridge to go with it: mushroom risotto, ravioli with tomato sauce, half a stuffed pepper, the remnants of three different kinds of cheese and a stale baguette she'd sprinkled with water and warmed up in the oven. It was a strange sort of supper but one that felt appropriate somehow, and she was glad to be sharing it with Dan; on his own, hooray. He didn't seem sad about the end of his marriage, quite the opposite.

'I'm weirdly OK about the whole thing.' He scratched his head. 'It explains a lot of things I'd been thinking were all my fault. I can't blame Lisa, frankly.

We're not right for each other – God only knows why we got together in the first place – and it's a relief to admit that. Besides, I'm the innocent party and she feels guilty so she's being nice to me. We're getting along better now than we have done in years.'

Ellie bit her tongue. She knew the dangers of criticising an ex, only for him or her to come back on the scene; once those words were spoken, they could never be forgotten. 'I'm sorry, anyway,' she repeated. 'Finding out must have been a shock.'

He smiled. 'Come on, I know you and Beth never liked Lisa. At least I don't have to apologise for her anymore.'

Ellie couldn't deny it. There had always been a gulf between herself and Dan's wife which, it had to be said, neither of them had tried particularly hard to bridge. She found Lisa humourless and driven, while Lisa, she suspected, thought Ellie was frivolous. Lisa saved lives every day: she was an emergency-room doctor and brilliant at her job, Ellie imagined, although not someone you'd choose to sit next to on a night out. Whenever Lisa asked what was new in the world of ceramics, she put on a patronising tone of voice that made Ellie's skin prickle with irritation.

'I don't like what she's done to you,' she said diplomatically.

Dan pushed his chair away from the table and crossed his legs. 'Enough about me, I want to hear your plans. Are you excited about the trip?'

'Oh, sure. It'll be great to have a break. No more

chasing up orders or worrying about the inventory for a while.'

Yet some doubt must have shown on her face. 'What is it?' Dan asked. 'Come on, you can tell me.'

There was no point pretending with him; they'd known each other too long. 'Well, I'm not sure Mom really wants me to go. She said something about digging up the past that made me think she's worried I might uncover some dreadful family secret. And it's clear my English aunt doesn't want anything to do with me. And as for my grandmother—' She shook her head.

'As for your grandmother?' Dan prompted. 'Don't leave me hanging.'

'Here she is.' Ellie showed him the photographs she'd copied onto her phone. 'Eleanor Spelman.'

Dan whistled. 'That's amazing! You two look so alike.'

Ellie got up and went to rummage in her carry-on tote, returning with a padded envelope. Inside was a creased sheet of yellowing paper which she laid gingerly on the table, as though it were dirty. 'I found this earlier on, while I was packing. It had been slipped inside the lining of her purse.'

Dan unfolded the leaflet. *'A Last Appeal to Reason*, by Adolf Hitler,' he read aloud. 'Well, I can see why you'd want to keep that hidden.'

'I know, it's awful,' Ellie said. 'You don't have to wade through the whole thing. Basically, it's a speech Hitler made to the German Parliament in 1940, saying the war was all Britain and France's fault in the first place, and since Germany had pretty much won already, why didn't England just surrender now rather than letting it drag on.'

'And why's it been translated into English? For propaganda, d'you think?'

'I guess so.' She folded the paper up again and put it back in the envelope. 'I don't like carrying this kind of thing around with me, but maybe someone in the family can explain why my grandmother might have kept it. Apart from the fact she was a Fascist, that is.'

'Perhaps she just picked up the leaflet randomly and didn't realise she had it.'

'Perhaps. But I found this in her bag, too.' Ellie shook the envelope and a small metal badge fell out, landing on the table with a chink.

Dan examined it. 'What's this, a bunch of wheat? Did she belong to the Guild of Master Bakers or something?'

'It's a bundle of sticks, bound together: a symbol of the Fascist party, apparently. Maybe both my grand-parents were members. My grandfather's parents were German. Who knows what he did during the war?'

Dan shrugged. 'Do you really want to find out?'

'I think so. It's hard to know where to start, though. I have these photos and Eleanor's identity card, and that's about it.' She passed the card across the table.

Dan examined it, squinting at the handwritten addresses. 'So she'd been living in London, at 25 Hathaway Road, and then she moved to Oxfordshire.'

Ellie nodded. 'That Oxfordshire address was written on the box of baby clothes we found in Mom's apartment. Maybe Eleanor and Alice were evacuated to the country because London was too dangerous. Mom said she was killed during the Blitz so I assumed she died in the city, but maybe that wasn't the case.'

'Well, it's something to go on.' Dan stood, starting to stack the dirty plates and cutlery. 'And I guess if you end up finding some murky family secrets, your mom doesn't need to know.'

But Ellie would know, and maybe she would feel differently about herself, and about her mother, too. Maybe she would discover why Alice had left England all those years ago and never once gone back, and maybe she would wish she'd left the past alone. She glanced at Dan. 'Do you think I'm stirring up trouble?'

'It's only a holiday,' he said, smiling, 'and you can always come home early if it doesn't work out. I'd tread carefully, though. Other people might not be as keen to uncover the truth as you are.'

He left soon after, so Ellie could get a good night's sleep. 'Promise me you'll keep in touch. I shall expect daily updates, OK?' he said, giving her a long hug that left her unexpectedly breathless, her knees weak. 'And try not to worry.'

Dear Lord, she thought, closing the door and leaning against it for a moment, I need to get a grip. This is Dan, remember, the brother of your best friend? Who's still technically married and has only just decided to divorce his wife? The last man she should be developing feelings for. Her talent for screwing things up was truly remarkable.

* * *

Sitting on the plane early the next morning, Ellie wondered again whether she was doing the right thing. Well, it was too late to turn back now; in around seven hours, she would be in London. She'd visited the city once before during the bad days with Wilf, but had been so preoccupied with his tantrums that she hadn't thought to contact her aunt and cousins. Her mother hadn't suggested it, either. *I don't have to spend any time with the family*, she told herself, *I'll just meet Gillian once and see how it goes*.

She was renting an apartment on the second floor of a mansion block in a long, sweeping road overlooking Battersea Park. Beyond the park lay the river, and beyond the river were the high-end shops and restaurants of Chelsea and Pimlico. Half an hour's walk in the other direction would take her to Gillian's house in Clapham; close enough for convenience, but not so close that her aunt would feel she was being stalked. The place was fine: clean and light, with a balcony off the living room that would give a wonderful view across the river when the mist cleared. If the blank rooms were a little impersonal, what did she expect? The location was perfect. An hour's walk along the river would take her to the London Eye, where the Houses of Parliament, Big Ben and Westminster Abbey stood just across the bridge.

She was due to arrive in London around lunchtime, the day before New Year's Eve. 'Are you sure you won't be lonely?' Beth had asked. 'All on your own at midnight?'

'I'll be OK,' Ellie had reassured her. 'I have to record Big Ben ringing in the new year for Mom.'

The guy who owned the apartment showed her around and left his phone number in case of any problems. He was a world-weary fifty-something, who was clearly hoping she'd leave him well alone. Ellie sat on the bed after he'd gone, her head thumping. She hadn't slept for long on the plane but if she took a nap now, she'd never adjust. Some fresh air and a pit stop for coffee would wake her up. She decided to walk around the edge of Battersea Park, cross Chelsea Bridge and do the tourist thing: take a sightseeing tour around London from Victoria Station. It was a cold, sunny day. Sitting on the upper deck of the open-topped bus, she drank in the city, wide-eyed and glad to be alone. She could jump on and off the bus whenever she wanted to explore the narrow, crooked streets or wide avenues, with no one to please but herself.

The juxtaposition of old and new entranced her. The Shard rose up on one side of the river, a gleaming vision of chrome and glass; on the other stood St Paul's Cathedral, built over three hundred years before to replace an even more ancient church that had been destroyed in the Great Fire of London. She gazed at the fabulous Christmas window displays of Fortnum & Mason, the store that had sent hampers to the suffragettes imprisoned for smashing its windows, strolled through Green Park and took a selfie at the railings of Buckingham Palace, with the guardsmen in their red jackets and bearskins marching up and down behind her. The marks of history lay everywhere: on the blue plaques set into house walls commemorating the famous people who'd lived there; in the beams of Tudor buildings and the signs and store fronts of St James's, selling hats and boots and shaving brushes to the gentry since Victorian times; even in the sudden appearance of a single modern building standing out among its neighbours which, according to the recorded tour commentary, was a sign of a gap being filled after bomb damage from the Second World War.

Her grandparents must have walked these streets, although no doubt they would have looked very different then. Ellie ended her tour at the Houses of Parliament and Big Ben, which she was saving for last. She'd explore them on foot, then walk across Westminster Bridge and back to her apartment. Her head was buzzing by this point with too many facts she was struggling to remember. This huge building stretching along the bank of the Thames, its sandy-coloured stonework seeming to rise straight out of the water, was home to the Houses of Parliament. It was also known as the Palace of Westminster, but could only be called that when Parliament was sitting – or had she got that the wrong way round? And the name Big Ben referred to the great bell that chimed the hours, not the clock itself or the tower, although most people called the clock Big Ben anyway.

She craned her neck to look up at the huge clock face, its paintwork restored to the original Prussian blue after recent renovation work, the gold leaf dazzling in the bright winter sun. Could her grandfather really have been responsible for keeping it running? Both he and Eleanor seemed very far away, lost in the past. Walking across the bridge, she had to elbow her way through the milling crowds: teenagers with backpacks, harassed parents shepherding fractious kids, tour guides holding up umbrellas for their meandering groups to follow. When she stopped on the other side to look upward for a better view of the Elizabeth Tower, she was jostled off the pavement. Exhausted, she decided to take a cab back to the apartment. Things would be different tomorrow, once she'd had a proper meal and some sleep.

After an early night, Ellie woke before dawn the next morning, full of energy; she had a plan and it was time to put it into action. She put on her running shoes and jogged along the deserted streets, skirting the park and heading for the river. The rising sun set the water gleaming with a fiery glow. She ran on, trying to imagine a time when the city had truly been on fire, the air full of smoke and panic, and the sky crimson not with the promise of a new day, as some had thought, but from flames as the docks burned. Catching sight of Westminster Bridge in the distance, she found it reassuring to gaze across at the clock tower, so solid and unchanging; already she was beginning to think of it as a familiar landmark. Then, following the map on her phone, she turned away from the river and headed south towards Hathaway Road, constructing a story in her head as she ran. Number 25 would turn out to be a quaint Victorian house, owned by a charming couple with an interest in local history. They would invite her inside, once she had shown them Eleanor's identity card, and tell her that in the course of their sympathetic renovation work, they'd happened to discover a suitcase full of possessions – or, better still, a diary – and over a pot of tea and maybe a full English breakfast (by now she was hungry again), she would come to know her grandmother.

There were quaint Victorian houses in Hathaway Road, but the gap between numbers 21 and 27 was filled by a dilapidated modern apartment block, its paint peeling and the featureless windows obscured by net curtains. She stared at it, one hand on her heaving chest. What could have happened? Had the houses been demolished by a developer to make way for apartments, or was she looking at an example of bomb damage from the war? Perhaps this was the reason Eleanor had moved to Oxfordshire. Gillian might possibly know. If not, there had to be records somewhere that could tell her which streets had been bombed in the Blitz. She'd already tried browsing the internet, but it was hard to find a way through the mass of information. She needed someone to point her in the right direction.

Ellie jogged slowly back to her apartment, taking the time to notice everything that struck her as different and exotic: rows of chimney pots on the tiled roofs of terraced houses, bright red letterboxes set in the wall, double-decker buses and the odd black taxi driving past.

Before she could lose courage, she dialled her aunt's number and left a message on the answerphone, inviting Gillian to lunch the next day at a pub of her choice. A long shower cleared her head and by the time she emerged, there was a message in reply on her phone, requesting that Ellie come instead to Gillian's house for lunch, at one o'clock. So that was progress. After a couple of hours' wandering around the antique stores in her new neighbourhood, and brunch in a nearby pub, she was sitting on a bench in Battersea Park when her phone rang. It was Dan, calling to see how she was and pass on some news.

'Hope you don't mind, but I've been doing some investigating myself.' She could hear the excitement fizzing in his voice. 'So, I joined this family history website – you get a month's trial for free, and it's amazing what you can learn. Anyway, I've found out something. About Eleanor.' He paused.

'What?' she demanded. 'Come on, Dan, don't keep me in suspense.'

'Look, I want to tell you but I'm also worried I might have overstepped the mark. This is a sad thing to hear, and you're all alone and miles away.'

'Just tell me! I can deal with it, whatever.'

'OK.' He took a breath. 'I found out where and when your grandmother passed away. She died in Westminster, on the 31st of December, 1940. So today is the anniversary of her death, eighty-one years later. Ellie? Are you OK?'

'Of course,' she said slowly. 'Thanks, Dan. It's good to know – makes her more real, somehow. And now I need to think things over. Talk to you later.'

She walked back to her apartment in a daze and lay on the bed, holding the watch with the cracked face that Alice had given her for luck, thinking about the woman in the photographs on her phone. Might she have been a Nazi sympathiser, working against the government? A beautiful spy, perhaps – a Mata Hari whose husband had links with Germany and worked in the heart of the British establishment. She and Arthur might both have been traitors. Maybe that's why Alice had been worried about Ellie digging up the past. She drifted into sleep, waking hours later from confused dreams: her grandmother strolling arm in arm with Hitler down an English country lane; passing her a gun from the brown-leather handbag and telling her she must protect Alice at all costs; climbing up the outside of the clock tower in that elegant hat and high heels, then slipping and falling down, down, towards the river—

She woke up with a gasp, her heart pounding. It was a while before she could calm down and tell herself not to be so ridiculous; she was taking a few facts and letting her imagination turn them into a story. She had a sudden craving for a cup of tea – must be some strange kind of auto-suggestion, but she'd been longing for tea ever since she'd touched down in England –

and after she'd made a pot and drunk it, with sugar, even, she did indeed feel more like herself. No matter what Eleanor might or might not have done, she was Ellie's blood relative; probably younger than Ellie was now when she'd died, with a baby who would never know her mother. It was desperately sad, and all she could feel was compassion. She also felt that Eleanor was reaching out, calling to her down the years. It was a call she had to answer.

Hours later, Ellie was still thinking about her grandmother as she joined the crowds near Westminster Bridge. She was too emotional to risk calling her mother; besides, getting through to Alice on her antiquated cell phone was tricky, since she was always forgetting to switch it on, let alone charge it. She looked up at the glowing clock face on her right, unchanging and mysterious. It had witnessed history for over a hundred and sixty years, from epic catastrophes to the smallest personal tragedies, and Ellie felt a connection to the past, simply by standing in its shadow. The faces around her were flushed with alcohol and excitement. Music blared from nearby cafés and bars, while a man on the balcony of an apartment across the river was playing wistful jazz on a saxophone. Her grandmother had died somewhere near here, on a very different New Year's Eve at the height of the war. Ellie felt as though she could reach out, pierce the skin of history and touch her. The clock's vast minute hand edged towards midnight. She popped the cork of her mini champagne bottle, slipped in a straw and waited for the famous sound of Big Ben striking midnight. How powerfully those chimes would have resonated in December 1940, when London was being torn apart in the Blitz and the whole country's future lay in the balance. Her grandmother had died on the final day of the year, not knowing how or when the war would end.

Ellie held her breath – until the notes of the great bell rang out, and fireworks exploded over the water, and the crowds burst into wild cheers and applause. A kind man nearby gave her a pity hug, but she didn't feel sorry for herself. The women in her family were made of strong stuff. She was thinking of the courage it must have taken for her mother to leave England at the age of twenty-two and embark on a new life in a foreign country. It struck Ellie suddenly that it wasn't only Eleanor she had come here to find: she was also looking for Alice. Her mother, the beloved stranger.

Chapter Seven

London, January 2022

Aunt Gillian in person didn't look much like the photograph on her website. She had jet-black hair cut in a bob, perfectly-arched eyebrows that gave her a permanent look of surprise, startlingly blue eyes, pale skin and a beaky nose. She was so thin that her clavicles stood out like the bones of a gnawed chicken leg.

'Hello, there,' she said, looking Ellie up and down. 'You made it, then.' As though she had come from deepest Africa by canoe, rather than on the bus from Battersea.

Gillian was wearing a pair of wide black trousers with a grey silk shirt, and Ellie immediately felt at a disadvantage in her skinny jeans and roll-neck sweater. There was an awkward moment on the doorstep as they decided whether to hug or shake hands, but the greetings were fumbled through somehow and her aunt stood back to let her inside.

'You'd better come on through. Filthy day, isn't it?'

The terraced house was a handsome red-brick building with white-framed bay windows and an ornate fretwork porch. The front yard, paved in grey slate and enclosed by black railings, was laid out with a rose bed and neatly-clipped bay trees marking each corner. A black-and-white tiled path led to the front door, which was inlaid with stained glass in intricate patterns: flowers and leaves, and birds hidden among the twining foliage. From the outside, it could have been the home of a Victorian bank manager, or a shop owner whose business was doing well. Inside, however, everything was plain and minimal. The hall floor was made of pale wood and the walls were dazzlingly white, decorated only by a few artistic black-and-white photographs of sand dunes, a spiky plant, a derelict warehouse in the snow. The only splash of colour came in the shape of a grandfather clock standing in the far corner, its golden-brown oak case and brass dial gleaming in the stark surroundings.

'What a beautiful thing!' Ellie laid her hand on the smooth polished wood. She could hear the quiet, steady tick-tock of the pendulum inside: a reassuring sound that reminded her why she was here, and that she shared a connection with Gillian, even though they might not initially seem to be kindred spirits.

'It is, isn't it?' her aunt agreed. 'High-maintenance, though. My father was always tinkering about with it.'

'Was he?' Ellie's heart leapt. 'You must tell me more.'

'Must I?' Gillian gave a short laugh. 'Well, the feet have to be absolutely level otherwise the pendulum won't swing evenly, and you have to wind the clock up with a key which is always getting lost. Rather a nuisance, really, but I'm fond of the old thing. Come into the kitchen and let's have a drink.'

Thc kitchen was all white, and clean as an operating room. There was no sign of any work being done here, or anywhere else in the house that Ellie could see. She handed over a bottle of wine and the olive-wood salad servers. 'Oh, these are rather nice!' Gillian exclaimed in surprise. 'Thanks. You shouldn't have, though.'

'I run a kitchenware business,' Ellie said, by way of an apology.

'Fancy that.' Gillian opened a drawer and stowed the salad servers inside. 'Now, wine, beer or gin and tonic? It's the simplest of meals, afraid I don't have much time for cooking. My son and his partner will be joining us. You'll like them, they're more your sort of age. Well, Max is, anyway.'

She rattled out the sentences without waiting for a reply: the verbal equivalent of a 'Keep Out' sign, Ellie thought. She sat on a chrome stool at the marble-topped kitchen island, drinking white wine and eating pistachio nuts, looking for a chance to break through Gillian's defences.

'Are those your children?' she asked when her aunt paused for breath, nodding at the only personal photograph she'd spotted so far on the wall: a brother and sister, clearly, with the same dark hair and dramatic eyebrows. The girl was looking into the camera with a truculent expression as if to say, 'And what are you staring at?' while the guy standing at her shoulder had an easy, ironic smile. Great teeth, Ellie noticed, especially for an Englishman. They both seemed aware of how very good-looking they were.

'That's right. Max and Lucy, taken a few years ago. I'm afraid Lucy's in South Africa at the moment, catching some winter sun, but Max should be here any minute. With Nathan.' She glanced at her watch, the mask slipping for a moment. 'Where on earth are they?'

'I'm so excited to meet everyone,' Ellie said. 'Thanks for inviting me, Aunt Gillian. I really appreciate it. You see, I'm trying to find out about—'

But she didn't get the chance to continue, because at that moment they heard the front door opening and footsteps coming down the hall. 'At last!' Gillian said, with evident relief. 'Now we can make a start on lunch.' She obviously wanted to get the meal over and done with as soon as possible.

Max was every bit as charming as Ellie had anticipated. He was in his early thirties, she guessed, immaculately dressed in jeans, a cashmere sweater and suede loafers. He was still handsome but no longer as striking as the young man in the photograph: his face a little more puffy around the eyes, his hair thinner, his jaw less well-defined.

'A mystery cousin from America,' he said, taking Ellie's hands. 'What a wonderful start to the new year!'

'All right, darling,' Gillian said. 'Don't overdo it.'

'Play nicely, Mother,' he replied, with an edge to his voice. 'We shouldn't frighten our guest when she's only just arrived.' He sat at the table and pulled out a chair for Ellie. 'So tell me everything. I want to know what brings you to London and why it's taken so long for us to meet.'

'Gosh, Nathan, champagne!' Gillian exclaimed as he handed her a bottle. 'What a treat. Would you be a love and open it?'

'As a matter of fact,' Ellie began, taking the seat next to Max, 'this isn't just a sight-seeing trip. I'm looking into my family history, and—'

Gillian groaned. 'Isn't everyone these days? I blame these television programmes with weeping celebrities discovering their great-great-grannies were kitchen maids. Didn't you work on one of those once, Nathan?'

'That's right,' he said, twisting the champagne bottle while holding on to the cork – the correct method, Ellie noticed with approval – 'only we had ordinary people on the show instead of celebrities.'

Gillian wasn't listening. 'I'll fetch some proper glasses. Flutes or coupes, Ellie? Which would you recommend, with your kitchenware experience?'

'Kitchenware?' Max's face lit up. 'How intriguing.'

Were they making fun of her? Probably, but then perhaps she deserved it, interrogating her relatives rather than getting to know them and teasing out whatever information they might have. She tried to act less like a crazy person for the rest of the meal, which was delicious in an elegant, understated way: sourdough baguette, smoked salmon, a green salad, French cheeses and the most amazing zucchini soup.

'Brown butter, added at the last minute,' her aunt replied when Ellie asked what was the secret. 'Deepens the flavour.' She had hardly eaten anything, just picked at a sliver of cheese and torn some bread into pieces, most of which she left on her plate.

'Gillian's an excellent cook,' Nathan said. 'I'd eat here every day if I could.'

Ellie liked him immediately. He was shorter and stockier than Max, not so obviously good-looking but with a benevolent, amused expression that made him just as attractive. He worked in television, producing documentaries, while Max was a garden designer. Ellie sat back, listening to the conversation and trying to work out the dynamic between Gillian and her son. There seemed to be some resentment about Christmas, which Gillian had spent with 'great friends' in the country, while Max had stayed with Gillian's ex-husband and his second wife. Max's sister, Lucy, had escaped the drama by going to South Africa.

'And how is your father?' Gillian asked her son. 'Still pretending to be twenty?'

'Much as ever,' he replied. 'You'll be glad to hear he's suffering from gout.'

'Oh yes, that is rather gratifying,' she said, with a

thin-lipped smile. 'Such an old man's affliction! He must hate it.'

'Families, eh?' Max turned to Ellie. 'So tell us about yours. Your mother Alice is my ma's half-sister, is that right? Did she not want to come over here with you?'

'She's in her eighties,' Ellie said. 'And she broke her hip not that long ago, so the journey would have been a bit much. She sends her love, though.'

She found herself looking at Gillian. 'Do send ours back,' her aunt said stiffly. 'And best wishes for a speedy recovery.'

Max frowned. 'Come on, Mother! You can do better than that. Why don't we Skype her right now?'

'Mom's not up to Skyping,' Ellie said. 'New technology's not really her thing. But it would be amazing if you had any photographs that I could share with her.' She hesitated. 'I don't know anything about my English grandparents, so whatever you could tell me would be much appreciated. I know my grandfather was a clockmaker. Is it true he looked after Big Ben during the war?' She corrected herself. 'The clock at the Palace of Westminster, I mean.'

'Really? First I've heard of it.' Max turned to his mother, raising an eyebrow.

Gillian frowned. 'That might have been just a family myth. When I was growing up, he had a clock repair shop. He used to restore long-case clocks, that was his passion, but he could never bear to sell them once he'd finished. There were about twenty in his workshop when he died. My mother got rid of them all, apart from the one I managed to rescue.'

'I was hoping to go up the clock tower,' Ellie said.

'Then I'm afraid you'll be disappointed,' Gillian replied. 'You have to be resident here and arrange the visit through your MP, well in advance.'

So that was that. 'I don't suppose you know anything about Arthur's first wife?' Ellie hazarded. It was worth a try, surely.

'You suppose right,' Gillian said, snatching up their empty bowls and stacking them with a clatter. 'I can't recall my father even mentioning her name. I suppose he didn't want to upset my mother. Anyway, she died several years before I was born.'

'Do you know how she died?' Ellie asked.

'Haven't the faintest idea, I'm afraid.' She dumped the bowls in the sink and stood there for a moment with her head lowered, staring at them.

'But what about photographs?' Max reminded her. 'I seem to remember once looking through an album with you.'

'God knows where that is.' Gillian gave a brittle laugh. 'I had to tidy everything away before the decorators came and what with Christmas, I still haven't had a moment to sort myself out.'

'Come on, surely you can find it somewhere?' Max said. 'Ellie's come all this way to see us. There must be something you can show the poor girl.'

'Dear God! Will you let the matter drop?' Gillian snapped. Bright spots of colour burned in her pale cheeks and her eyes were unnaturally bright. She seemed on the verge of hysteria.

Even Max looked startled. 'All right, all right. There's no need to throw a hissy fit.'

'Stay out of things you don't understand.' Then Gillian turned to Ellie and said abruptly, spitting out the words like bullets, 'I know why you're really here. Quite frankly, I'd have respected you far more if you'd told the truth, rather than faking some spurious interest in genealogy.'

There was an appalled silence. 'I-I'm not sure what you mean,' Ellie stammered at last, hot with embarrassment. 'I don't have any ulterior motive, I promise. I just wanted to meet you, that's all.'

Max pushed back his chair. 'Mother! What's going on?'

'I'm sorry,' Gillian said, not sounding sorry in the slightest, 'but I felt it was time to confront the issue rather than dancing around it.' She leant against the kitchen island. 'I have a migraine coming on, as a matter of fact, and I've said all I have to say on the matter. Would you excuse me? I want to go upstairs for a lie-down. You can let yourselves out.' Without waiting for a reply, she marched out of the room.

Max, Ellie and Nathan were left staring at each other in dismay. 'I'm so sorry,' Ellie said, her cheeks burning. 'I feel awful, but I honestly have no idea what all that was about.'

'She's the one who should be apologising,' Max said. 'She's behaved disgracefully, inviting you here and then treating you so rudely. I would never have suggested—' He broke off abruptly.

So that explained Gillian's apparent change of heart; the lunch had been Max's idea, not hers.

'But it's not like her to be quite so . . . outspoken,' Nathan said. 'I wonder what's really the matter? Something must have brought this on.'

'Well, it can't be the menopause. We went through that particular hell ten years ago,' Max said as he stood. 'Come on, Ellie. We'll take you for coffee in our favourite pub to make up for the histrionics.'

'Let's clear up the kitchen first.' Nathan began collecting their glasses. 'It's not fair to leave Gillian with all the mess. And maybe you should invite her out for lunch some time, Max, and get to the bottom of all this. You know how much she'd like it.'

Max sighed. 'Do I have to? Things are so busy at the moment, and she'll only spend the whole time nagging me about getting a proper job.'

'Things aren't busy, though, are they?' Nathan said mildly. 'It's the middle of winter and nothing's growing.'

'All right, all right,' Max muttered, grabbing the cheese board so clumsily that a wedge of Brie fell on the floor. 'You win. I'll be a good son, although she doesn't deserve it.'

'You need to relax and stop grovelling,' Max said to Ellie as they walked to the pub. 'Ma has her moods, that's all, though today's was particularly extreme. She'll come around to you in time.'

'Not if she thinks I have some hidden agenda. Anyway, I might only be here for a couple of weeks,' Ellie replied, shoving her hands in her pockets so she wouldn't be tempted to chew her fingernails.

'Not nearly long enough.' He smiled. 'Cheer up, though – at least you have us.'

The Feathers could have doubled as a junk shop, it was crammed with so much bric-a-brac. The bar was a lofty room, double the usual ceiling height, with a strange assortment of objects hanging from its wooden beams: a painted fairground pony galloping next to an old-fashioned bicycle, its wicker basket crammed with flowers, flags and Chinese lanterns jostling for space with a huge model aeroplane, a Victorian birdcage, a single hunting boot and a dried-up leathery alligator that Ellie could only hope was plastic. A shaggy-haired terrier lay asleep in a basket, adding to the homely atmosphere. She would have to find her way back here again; it was the sort of place you could visit alone with a book or a laptop and feel comfortable. Nathan ordered drinks at the bar while she and Max sat in slouchy armchairs by the wood burning stove. Ellie felt herself gradually relax. Max was easy company and at least he seemed to take her at face value.

'So you don't remember our grandfather?' she asked him.

'No, he died when I was three or four. Must be coming up for thirty years ago.' He stretched out his legs. 'I can tell you about my grandmother but I suppose you're not so interested in her. Now she was a piece of work, as the saying goes. She and my ma used to have the most almighty rows. Mavis went in for feuds; she was always fighting with somebody. Literally, sometimes. Ah, here's Nathan.'

Ellie didn't normally take sugar in her coffee but she was still a little shaky. 'I don't think my mother had a great relationship with Mavis, that's for sure,' she said, stirring up the froth. 'Then again, she's not the most diplomatic person in the world, either. Funnily enough, there's something about Gillian that reminds me of Alice. It's sad, isn't it, that the two of them have lost touch.'

'So how come your mother ended up living in America?' Nathan asked.

'Because she fell in love with my dad. He came to the UK on a scholarship and they met on a peace march in 1961.' Ellie smiled. 'You should see the photographs. They were the original hippie couple: all long hair, beads and flower power.'

Max snorted. 'That doesn't sound much like Gillian to me.'

'No, but she's forthright in the way my mother is. And they have a similar turn of phrase.' Ellie frowned. 'Why does she think I came here? Unless—'

'Unless what?' Max asked sharply.

Ellie took the badge from her purse and laid it on the table. 'I found this in my grandmother's things.'

'Ah,' Nathan said, after a quick glance. 'I can see why that might give you pause for thought.'

'What is this?' Max asked, picking it up.

'The emblem of the Fascist party. Didn't you learn anything at that posh school?' Nathan turned to Ellie. 'My family are Jewish and my gran was constantly lecturing me about the evils of Fascism. Her father fought in the Battle of Cable Street.'

'As if Ellie's going to have heard of that,' Max said. She guessed he was none too certain either.

'It kicked off when Oswald Mosley and his followers, the Blackshirts, went on one of their marches through the East End of London,' Nathan explained. 'In 1936, I think it was. Hundreds of Communists and Jews turned up to protest and there was a massive brawl in the streets, with the local women joining in as well. Gran emptied her chamber pot out of an upstairs window over a Blackshirt's head. She always claimed it was her proudest moment.'

'So she was one of the good guys.' Ellie put the badge away. 'What if my grandmother was a Fascist, though? And what if our grandfather was, too? His parents were German, after all. Maybe Gillian thinks I've come here to dig up the dirt on our family.'

'To be honest, I'm not sure my mother would care that much if her father *was* a Fascist,' Max said. 'She's very right wing.'

'You should be able to do some research,' Nathan said. 'The British Union of Fascists might have a list of members. What do you know about your grandmother?'

'Not much. Her name – Eleanor Spelman – and that's about it. She lived for a while at an address in

South London but I went there yesterday and the house doesn't exist anymore. I guess it was bombed. She moved to somewhere in Oxfordshire after that so maybe I should try going there, too, though I'm not sure what good it will do.' She sighed. 'The family name was originally Spielmann, I think. That's right, isn't it, Max? Our grandfather's parents came to England from Berlin in the early 1900s, and they were watch- and clockmakers.'

'So far as I know.' Max drained his cup. 'Well, this is all very interesting but unfortunately I have a few phone calls to make. Ellie, it's been a joy to meet you, despite the drama, and I hope we'll see you again soon. Coming, Nat?'

'In a minute,' Nathan said. 'We haven't finished our coffee and anyway, I want to talk to Ellie some more.'

'OK, see you at home. Bye, folks.' Max shrugged on his leather jacket and sauntered off, checking himself in the mirror as he passed.

'You must be so proud of your family,' Ellie told Nathan. 'I can't fathom the thought of being descended from Hitler supporters.'

'I wouldn't jump to conclusions until you know more,' he advised. 'Why don't you check out the Imperial War Museum? It's not far from your apartment. They have some great exhibitions and a research room where the staff are really helpful. I could start digging, too, if you like.'

'Oh, would you?' Ellie beamed. 'That would be amazing, thank you.'

Nathan smiled back. 'As Gillian kindly pointed out, I used to work on a family history show so I've picked up a few shortcuts. If Max can find out his grandfather's date of birth, that would be a help.'

'I don't want to risk upsetting Gillian any more, so maybe we should leave Max out of this. Thanks, though, Nathan. I owe you.'

Lunch with her aunt could hardly have gone any worse, Ellie thought as she walked home. She could make a story out of their meeting to amuse her mother, but Gillian clearly wasn't going to be taking her on a personal tour around London any time soon.

Chapter Eight

Oxfordshire, November 1940

Nell lay back on her bed and stared up at the ceiling, as she had done countless times over the years. When she was young, she used to imagine the crack snaking across it was a river along which she could sail to the open sea and then far away. She was always dreaming of escape, of travelling to some distant town or city where nobody knew her and she could live exactly as she pleased. Yet now here she was, back in her childhood home with a baby in tow.

She glanced at the watch Arthur had given her. There was another half hour till the evening news, when Big Ben would strike and they would be thinking of each other. People all over the country were encouraged to pray for loved ones as the notes rang out; the Silent Minute, it was called, and Arthur was prouder than ever.

It had been a long and stressful day. Her mother had instructed her to arrive before dark in case a bombing raid left them stuck in a railway siding overnight, and although she and Alice had set off for Paddington Station first thing that morning, for a while it had looked as though they might not make the deadline. Her insistence on bringing the pram complicated matters, but she refused to leave the Ambassador behind. She had said a brief goodbye to Arthur in Westminster, then pushed her daughter through the parks and along the shabby, ruined streets to Paddington Station, where she'd had to tip the guard half a crown to have the pram stowed in the goods' van. The train had been crowded and she'd spent the journey sitting on a soldier's kitbag in the corridor with Alice on her lap. The baby was fussed over and handed from hand to hand like a good luck charm. Who could resist Alice, with her round, solemn face and inscrutable expression? She was unbearably precious. A squaddie's eyes had softened as he looked at her and he'd had to turn away. Nell pretended she hadn't seen.

She'd retrieved the pram at Didcot station and they waited an hour or so in the café for the connecting train to arrive. Nell had felt numb, in limbo, and Alice was irritable, crying at the slightest provocation. Her cheeks were flushed despite the cold; either she was still teething or she had a temperature. Please don't fall ill, Nell had prayed, wheeling her baby up and down the platform. Don't make me a worse mother than I already am. By the time they were beginning the second leg of the journey, along the smaller branch line, she was unbearably tense. A couple of Land Girls – Dot and Marjorie, she discovered later – took pity on her and heaved the pram up into the carriage with an astonished Alice still sitting in it. Although their broad shoulders, muscular arms and capable hands made them pass for country folk, Nell could hear from their accents that they were Londoners. They came from Bethnal Green, they said, and used to work on the sweet counter in Woolworths. They'd thought helping out on a farm would be a lark but getting up early on these freezing mornings was torture and their nails were ruined. Still, at least there was plenty of food to be had. When they asked Nell how things were in London, she didn't know what to say. Her life there already seemed unreal: a jittery, fragmented dream, its long, monotonous hours punctuated by moments of terror or wild elation. She couldn't put any of that into words for Dot and Marjorie, though, so she simply told them everyone was doing their best and that she would be glad of some uninterrupted sleep. There was an aerodrome several miles away from her parents' house so they'd had the odd raid or two, her mother had reported, but nothing like the nightly bombardment London had suffered.

The girls were travelling a few stops further along the line so when it was time for Nell and Alice to disembark, Dot jumped onto the platform and Marjorie lifted the pram down to her. They waved goodbye, giving cheery thumbs up signs before slamming the carriage door shut. Nell felt a curious sense of abandonment as the train drew away. There were still a couple of miles to walk but as luck would have it, a passing lorry full of Air Training cadets gave her and the baby a lift almost all the way, dropping them at the bottom of the lane that led to Orchard House, her childhood home. Dusk was falling as Nell hauled the Ambassador backwards over the gravelled drive with the last of her strength. Rose had opened the front door as soon as she approached, wiping her hands on a corner of her apron. 'There you are,' she'd said. 'Just in time for tea.'

Nell had felt both an immense weight dropping from her shoulders and a sense of disappointment in its place: as though she were returning from a thrilling, arduous adventure that had ended in failure. 'Here we are indeed,' she'd said, unstrapping Alice from the pram. 'Thanks for having us, Ma.'

It was a relief to hand the baby over, to have her mother lick her thumb and wipe the smuts from Alice's face. 'Oh, it's so lovely to see you,' Rose said. 'I was only worried in case – well, you know.' She gave a nervous smile. 'Your father's in the sitting room.'

Frank was installed in his usual chair by the fire, reading a newspaper. 'Have a seat,' he said, indicating a chair as though Nell were coming for an interview. 'Good journey?'

'Not too bad.' She took off her hat and leaned back, suddenly weary. 'I met some Land Girls on the train.'

'Land Girls!' Her father snorted. 'They're all over

the place these days, leaving gates open and generally causing havoc. I pity the poor farmers, having to keep that lot under control.'

Nell hadn't the energy to defend Dot and Marjorie, so she merely said, 'How are you keeping? Still busy with the Home Guard?'

'Absolutely. Lord Winthrop and I are whipping the men into shape.' Frank gave her his usual look whenever that name was mentioned: a blend of hostility and reproach. 'At least there are two of us who've seen active service. You can't beat experience.'

'I'm sure.' Nell stood. 'Well, I'd better go and settle in.'

'We've put you in your old room,' her father said. 'Is your luggage coming separately?'

'There isn't any luggage,' Nell replied. 'Only some baby clothes my neighbour gave us. We've lost everything, pretty much.'

Her father shook his head. 'You should have left London a long time ago. I can't imagine what your husband was thinking.'

'It's not Arthur's fault. He's been telling me to take Alice away for weeks, but I didn't want to go.' Nell had to blink away the shameful tears from her eyes.

'There, there.' Frank smiled at her indulgently. 'Don't upset yourself. You have to understand, Nella, I've handed my most precious possession to Arthur for safekeeping. It pains me to think he isn't taking proper care of you. Still, at least you're here now.' He shook his head. 'But when I think of what you—'

Nell heard the gong in the hall being struck just then, thank goodness. 'Tea's ready, better dash,' she said, making for the door. Her father wouldn't be joining them: he preferred to eat separately if children were present at the table.

Frank hadn't quite finished with her, though. 'You could have had a very different life, you know,' he said, looking at her over the top of his spectacles. 'I hope you're happy with the choice you made.'

Nell chose not to reply. And so it begins, she thought, closing the door behind her.

There were boiled eggs for tea, and bread spread thickly with yellow butter instead of a scrape of margarine.

'Don't think we have shell eggs every day,' Rose said. 'This is a special occasion.'

The evacuees were already sitting at the table by the time Nell took her place. Four of them came from the same family, the Potts: Susan, a stolid girl of thirteen; Brenda, aged ten with flaming ginger hair; and the twins, Timothy and Janet, who were eight. The gang was completed by Malcolm Parsons, a tiny, miserable boy of six, whose eyes swam behind thick-lensed glasses.

'You should have seen the Potts brood when they first arrived,' Rose told Nell when the meal was over and they were having a cup of tea together in the kitchen. 'They couldn't have had a bath for weeks, and they all had nits. And as for their clothes! Filthy dirty, full of holes, and Susan's shoes two sizes too small. The poor girl could hardly walk. She'll be a martyr to bunions when she's older.'

The evacuees had cleared the table and were currently doing the washing-up in the scullery under Brenda's direction, apart from her older sister Susan, who had loaded Alice back into the pram and was pushing her up and down the hall. She was the motherly type, Rose said approvingly.

'So tell me about Harry,' Nell said. 'Do you know where he's being held?'

Her mother took a crumpled postcard out of her apron pocket. 'Am safe, a prisoner of war in Germany,' Harry had written. 'Do not worry. My address will follow shortly and then you can write to me. Love to all.'

'Good news, isn't it?' Rose's face had lit up. 'I always thought he'd come through, though one never likes to say so. We'll be able to send him packages through the Red Cross. I'm busy knitting socks.'

'It's wonderful,' Nell agreed. Her brother was tough and resilient: if anyone could survive, it would be him. The two of them were only eighteen months apart and had been close throughout their childhood, and beyond. As soon as Harry had learned to ride a bicycle or swim in the lake, she'd wanted to follow him, and he was prepared to teach her. Their parents thought girls shouldn't climb trees or play football but luckily for her, Harry didn't agree. They'd spent hours together outdoors in the holidays and during long summer evenings. Sometimes she was left out when a gang of boys tore off on their bikes – Harry wasn't a saint – but he would usually make it up to her later. When they were younger, they'd build go-karts and make dens; later he'd taught her how to shoot rabbits with an air rifle, and skin and gut them ready for the pot. They would practise shooting tin cans off tree stumps and at fifteen she became a better shot than he was. 'Whatever have you been up to?' their mother would complain, looking at the state of Nell's shorts (she was allowed to wear them for running about in the woods). 'People in the village are making remarks.'

Nell took a surreptitious glance at her mother across the table. Rose's hair was drooping out of its curl and her cheeks were flushed. 'I hope it won't be too much for you, Ma,' she said, patting Rose's hand. 'Taking care of us as well as the evacuees.'

'I'm sure you'll pull your weight,' her mother replied. 'Anyway, it's lovely to have the house full. Reminds me of when you and Harry were little. Those were the happiest days of my life, you know.'

'Pa seems on good form,' Nell said carefully. 'How's he been?'

'Oh, he's in fine fettle. Parading about in the Home Guard with Lord Winthrop – what more could he ask?' They exchanged knowing smiles. 'Daft, isn't it? Three rifles between the lot of them and if one goes off, he'll fall down in a faint. Still, it keeps him busy so I'm not complaining.'

Her father's moods had been a constant preoccupation for as long as Nell could remember. Frank Roberts had gone away to fight in 1915 and come back a changed man. He'd been an assistant bank manager before the war and tipped for promotion, but being wounded at the battle of the Somme brought his career to an abrupt end. Apart from his physical injuries, which were never spelt out, his nerves had gone. He still suffered from headaches and bad dreams, and would sometimes wake the household up at night with his shouting. Their father had seen terrible things in France, Rose had told the children when they were (almost) old enough to understand, and he couldn't get those pictures out of his head. That's what made him angry sometimes. It wasn't their fault but it wasn't necessarily his, either. Nell felt as though she hardly knew her father, although he was always around the house: sitting in his chair by the fire, reading a newspaper at the kitchen table, cleaning his shoes in the scullery. She'd learned early on that it was wisest to keep out of his way and the habit had persisted.

They had tolerated each other well enough until Nell had been unfortunate enough to catch the eye of Lord Winthrop's only son, Hugo. The Winthrops lived in Millbury Manor, a couple of fields away, and were the nearest thing the village had to a squire and his lady. Lord Winthrop had served with distinction in the Royal Engineers during the Great War and gone on to make a fortune in the automobile industry – much of which, it was rumoured, he'd given to the Conservative party. At any rate, he'd been rewarded with a title and a seat in the House of Lords. He was a moody man, often to be seen stomping along the lanes, swiping at nettles in the verge with his shooting stick. He was keen on flying and kept a private plane at Hatfield aerodrome, but cars were his passion: he had a fleet of five or six in the garage, and a manservant called – rather confusingly – Cooke, to drive him. Nell lived in hope the Winthrops would employ a cook called Driver, but life was rarely so perfect. It was Cooke who dressed up as Father Christmas at the Winthrops' annual party and handed out presents to the overexcited children. Lord Winthrop would have been better suited to the role, with his thick white hair and ruddy complexion, if only he could have been persuaded to smile.

The Winthrops also opened their garden for the church fête each summer, which was when Hugo Winthrop, just down from Cambridge for the Long Vacation, had noticed Nell. He'd struck up a conversation that quickly revealed his arrogance, and a condescending streak she couldn't abide. From that day on, he wouldn't leave her alone: was always bumping into her whenever she walked into the village or singling her out after church.

Frank was delighted. 'What a match,' Nell overheard him say to Rose one evening. 'She could end up Lady of the Manor. Our little Nella!'

'But I can't bear Hugo,' Nell told her mother as soon as she got the chance. 'He makes my flesh creep. He doesn't want to marry me, anyway; he's got other things on his mind.'

Rose's lips had set in a thin line. 'Don't worry,' she'd said. 'No one's going to make you do anything against your will. Leave your father to me.'

For days, the house had simmered with tension. Frank went about glowering and slamming doors, while Rose watched him with nervous eyes, jumping at every sound. Nell would lie awake, listening to them argue long into the night. She knew the effort it took for Rose to stand up to her husband.

Things came to a head when Hugo waylaid Nell up on the hills one afternoon, as she was walking the neighbour's dog, and kissed her, pressing his bristly moustache against her lips and forcing his tongue into her mouth. It had taken all of her strength to push him off. He had looked at her with cold eyes, wiping his mouth with the back of his hand, and called her a provoking little bitch. When he came for her again, she was ready. She'd wrapped the dog lead around her fist and hit him hard: an uppercut to the jaw that sent him sprawling back on the grass, stunned. Harry would have been proud. And then she walked to Millbury Manor, asked to see Lord Winthrop and told him what had happened.

'I don't believe you,' he'd said, but she knew from his expression that he did, and that she would have no more trouble from Hugo.

That evening, Lord Winthrop had telephoned her father. She had no idea what was said, but Frank locked himself away in his study after the conversation and refused to speak to anyone for days. That was when

Nell decided that she would train as a teacher in London, rather than at the local college, and live in digs there. She'd had enough; the atmosphere at home was intolerable.

'Are you sure you'll be all right?' she'd asked her mother, the night before she left.

'Don't you worry about me,' Rose had said, hugging her. 'I've made my bed and it's not such a hard one, really. I can manage him better on my own. You look out for yourself.'

So Nell had looked out for herself, and found Arthur. She'd kept him a secret at first, but after he'd proposed, introducing him to her family was unavoidable. Her parents came up from Oxfordshire on the train and the four of them had had tea together in a grand hotel near Paddington Station. The conversation had been flowing reasonably smoothly until Arthur had mentioned that his parents were German, and he'd grown up speaking that language at home. One would never have guessed, Rose had complimented him, after a short, stunned silence; he hadn't the trace of an accent.

'But I was born here,' he'd reassured her. 'I love everything English as much as you do – probably more! Afternoon tea,' he indicated the cucumber sandwiches, the plate of scones and little pots of jam and cream, 'and thatched cottages, and our marvellous Royal Family.' Who were half German anyway, Nell thought. 'And Charles Dickens,' Arthur had added desperately, looking to her for support. 'Little Nell! From *The Old Curiosity Shop*, as of course you know.'

Little Nell was his pet name for her – although with her shoes on, she was only an inch shorter than he was. He was trying so hard, and she loved him for making such an effort to please. The atmosphere changed from that moment on, however. Her father became silent, leaving Rose to chatter nervously. When Nell was saying goodbye to her parents at the station, Arthur having already left, Frank had stepped away from her and said over his shoulder in a cold, flat voice, 'A blasted German! Eleanor, how could you?' And her mother had simply looked from one to the other of them with that cowed, anxious expression on her face.

Both sets of parents came to their wedding – a rushed affair in the town hall, hastily arranged because of the looming war – but her father wouldn't shake Arthur's hand and pretended not to understand a word Mr Spelman said. Harry would have cheered up the proceedings, but he was away training with the British Expeditionary Force by then and wasn't given leave to attend, so Nell had to make do with a distant cousin and two friends from teacher-training college to oil the social wheels. They had cake and sandwiches in an ante room upstairs, along with the half dozen bottles of champagne Mr and Mrs Spelman had brought to the reception.

'Ostentatious,' her father had remarked later, although he'd condescended to drink three glasses.

Nell had liked Arthur's father, Henry (or Heinrich, as Arthur's mother, Frieda, called him), straight away. He was a short, bald man with a ready smile and polished old-world manners. He had kissed Nell's hand and congratulated his son on marrying the most beautiful girl in England so charmingly that she almost believed him. He spoke English with a heavy German accent, admittedly, but his warmth and humour shone through. Eventually he and Frieda gave up the effort to make conversation and talked quietly to each other, or to Arthur. Nell was ashamed of her father, who took no interest in his new son-in-law and couldn't even pretend to look happy on his daughter's wedding day.

She had apologised to Arthur later. 'It's all right,' he said. 'My parents are used to it. Every window of my father's shop was smashed after the *Lusitania* was sunk in the last war. The sound of breaking glass is one of my earliest memories.'

Up in the loft room, the evacuees were meant to be settling down for the night. Nell could hear the odd thump, and then a scraping sound as something heavy was dragged across the floor. She hoped it wasn't Malcolm Parsons. Alice cried briefly a few times in the makeshift cot Rose had devised for her – a blanket box lined with an eiderdown – but without much conviction. The sound of Tommy Dorsey and his orchestra drifted upstairs from the gramophone player in the sitting room.

Nell had begun composing a letter to Arthur in her head – 'quite a journey but we're settling down now, Mother's so pleased to see us and the evacuees are certainly good value' – when a sudden thought sent her sitting bolt upright. Swinging down her legs, she went over to the fireplace and kicked aside the rug in front of it, running her fingers over the floorboard beneath. She had forgotten how smoothly the plank fitted and initially wasn't sure how she would lever it up, but eventually she managed with the help of a metal-handled comb from her dressing table. Alice turned over, coughed, then settled back into sleep. Nell reached down into the cavity between the floor joists and felt around for the gun she had hidden there, wrapped in a canvas haversack: the pistol Harry had given her.

They had both come home for the weekend to say goodbye before he left for training camp and the two of them had gone for a walk together. The woods had looked spectacular that morning, the spring sunshine slanting through a canopy of acid-green leaves to fall on a sea of bluebells, stretching away to the horizon. The light was so clear, the colours almost painfully intense. She wondered whether such beauty had made it harder for Harry to leave, and whether the memory was a consolation or torture to him now.

'I've been issued with a service revolver,' he'd said, handing her the haversack, 'so I want you to have my old Beretta. We might not win this war, Nella. The top brass can say what they like but we're not prepared for what's coming.' His eyes had been serious. 'Things could get nasty. If the Germans invade, I should like to think of you having options.'

Nell had left the pistol behind at Orchard House when she went back to London. War hadn't seemed inevitable then, let alone an enemy invasion, and although she and Arthur weren't yet engaged, he might have found the gun by chance and wondered why she should have had it. Holding the Beretta now made her feel calm and powerful for the first time in a while. She checked the magazine – seven cartridges, which should provide enough options for her immediate family, should the worst come to the worst, with a few shots left over – put the pistol back in its bag and stowed it under the floorboard once more.

Chapter Nine

Oxfordshire, November/December 1940

Nell loaded her father's breakfast things onto a tray and walked into the hall, where she found Susan Potts fussing over Alice in the pram and Brenda Potts sitting on the stairs, her bright hair glowing like a beacon in the gloom. Brenda followed Nell through to the kitchen, watching her closely.

'What is it?' Nell said, when she couldn't bear the scrutiny any longer.

'Is your husband really a spy?' Brenda asked.

'Of course not. Why would you think that?'

Brenda narrowed her eyes craftily. 'Because I heard you and your mum talking about it this morning. About him being German and that.'

Nell put the tray down on the kitchen table. 'My husband isn't German. He was born in London, and he's as English as you or me.' More or less.

'Don't tell anyone about Arthur's parents,' Rose had said to her. 'If by any chance it should come up. You know what people are like in this village for gossip.'

'You shouldn't eavesdrop,' Nell told Brenda. 'You know what they say: listeners never hear any good of themselves.'

'I did once,' Brenda remarked nonchalantly. 'I heard my teacher say I was grammar-school material. She's thinking of putting me in for the scholarship exam.'

'Bully for you,' Nell said. Brenda didn't seem to care; she was evidently a tough nut. Nell put the crockery into the washing-up bowl and turned on the tap.

'I'll do that.' Brenda nudged her out of the way towards the kitchen table. 'Have a sit-down and take the weight off your poor feet for a minute.'

Nell couldn't help smiling at the phrase and Brenda grinned back. 'Your husband's not Lord Haw Haw, is he?' she asked chummily over her shoulder. 'You know, that man on the wireless who keeps saying we're going to lose the war? You can tell me, I won't pass it on.'

'I'll tell you something for nothing,' Nell said, as Brenda's eyes widened in anticipation, 'if you start spreading rumours, you and your brother and sisters will be back where you came from faster than you can spit. Is that clear?'

'Don't take the hump.' Brenda turned back to the sink and began splashing about. 'I didn't mean anything bad.'

'It doesn't matter what you meant. A girl who's

grammar-school material should understand how dangerous careless talk can be.'

'Fair enough,' Brenda said. 'I'll keep my mouth shut.'

She was incorrigible, but actually, who would believe a girl like her telling a story like that? 'Where *do* you come from, out of interest?' Nell asked.

'Coventry,' Brenda replied.

'Oh, dear. I'm sorry. I suppose you won't be going back there, then.' Poor Coventry had suffered a terrible raid the month before, with hundreds of people killed and the ancient cathedral destroyed.

Brenda emptied the water out of the washing-up bowl and seized a tea towel. 'Not any time soon, but that's all right. I like it here. There's enough to eat and plenty to do.'

'Like what?' Nell asked, intrigued.

Brenda shrugged. 'Help at the farm, look after the hens, do our chores and homework and stuff.' She glanced at Nell as though wondering how much information to share. 'And physical jerks. You know, training exercises.'

'Training for what?'

'For all eventualities.' Brenda put the cups and saucers back in the dresser and hung the tea towel on its hook by the Aga. 'I can't say any more.'

'All right.' Nell yawned and stretched. 'Well, time for Alice to have some fresh air, I suppose.'

'Susan will take care of that,' Brenda said. 'She couldn't wait to get her hands on a proper baby. She's been making do with Malcolm but it's not the same.'

Susan was indeed reluctant to hand Alice over. 'Please let me push the pram,' she said. 'I'll be careful, honest.' She ran a hand over the Ambassador as though it were Cinderella's enchanted carriage.

'Maybe tomorrow,' Nell promised. She had to reclaim her daughter before she became an honorary member of the Potts clan. Alice was hers, after all, and she had little else.

It didn't take long for Nell to fall into a routine at Orchard House. Each morning she'd wait until her parents had finished in the bathroom, then she would slip in there with Alice before the evacuees came clattering down from the loft room for a quick wash. They would eat breakfast in the kitchen under Nell's supervision while Rose and Frank had theirs in the dining room, Frank being unable to tolerate the slightest noise so early in the day. He would then retreat to the downstairs cloakroom with his pipe and newspaper while Rose pottered about the house and the evacuees set off for school. Nell would clear the breakfast things, feed the chickens and make the beds, before loading Alice into the pram and setting off for the shops. There were two pubs in Millbury now, and a draper's shop alongside the baker, butcher, greengrocer and chemist in the high street.

She would usually have to wait in a long line of other women for whatever supplies were available. Bread and vegetables weren't rationed, but there was often little or none left by the time she reached the head of the queue. Outside the shop, there might be friendly gossip and clucking over Alice in her magnificent carriage; inside, the atmosphere changed. Everyone watched each other, on the alert for special treatment: maybe a slice extra for a favourite, or half an ounce under for an enemy. Nell had a generous number of coupons to hand over, now that her rations were added to her parents' and the evacuees' allowance, and had to put up with dirty looks and muttered remarks about shopping for an army. She was back among people who'd known her since she was a baby. They would soon knock her down to size if she put on any airs; she couldn't waltz into their shops as if she had a God-given right to be there.

She'd walk out with a laden basket and her head held high but it was a relief to come home again, back to the quiet house and her father closeted away in his study. She'd put Alice down for a nap and read or write to Arthur, take up her knitting or sewing (she was attempting to make a new wardrobe from the odds and ends of fabric her mother had produced), or knuckle down to some half-hearted cleaning to the sound of 'Music While You Work' on the wireless. Rooting through her wardrobe, she found her old sketchpad, pen and inks, and set about drawing Alice while she slept. She used to draw all the time, and had even wondered about going to art college and making a career out of painting or design. She knew Frank wouldn't support her, though; in his world, men worked and women stayed at home, looking after them. It was

Rose who'd used her savings to pay for Nell's course at teacher training college.

Sometimes Nell would find herself simply sitting and staring out of the window, becalmed. She was lonely. Her parents were absorbed in their own little world and the few friends she still had in the village were mostly away on military service. She felt guilty, too, because she was doing nothing for the war effort except making do and mending, and trying not to give way to melancholy. She had volunteered with the Red Cross after she'd given up teaching on her marriage, and learned how to drive ambulances. Arthur had not been at all keen on her doing anything so dangerous, and of course once she had become pregnant, she'd had to abandon the idea. She supposed he was right. She longed for Arthur so deeply that it left a physical ache in her chest; especially at night, when the outside world used to fade away to leave just the two of them, so happy in each other's company and very much in love. He wrote to say he was getting along well, although missing her and Alice terribly, of course. There had been a couple of hairy raids recently but he felt safe in the crypt, and he'd discovered a mobile washing van that would take care of his laundry for free! The other good news was that Bill Talbot seemed to have turned over a new leaf. Maybe the Keeper of the Clock had had a word with him, because he certainly seemed to be taking more of an interest in his work. Arthur felt Talbot might be up to something, but he couldn't work out what.

Nell wished the laundry van would call at Orchard House, she wrote in reply, because Malcolm Parsons was still having 'accidents' two or three nights a week. Rather than lugging his sheets to the outside wash house and lighting the copper to boil them, she had taken to washing the damp patches in the bath under a trickle of hot water from the geyser, and sponging off the mattress as best she could. The loft room had its own fetid atmosphere and required daily airing, although the evacuees kept it neat and tidy. They slept on a row of lumpy mattresses along the floor, and hung what few clothes they had on an ingenious indoor washing line they'd rigged up, stretching from one end of the room to the other.

It was extraordinary how clearly the children's personalities emerged in each of their sleeping spaces. Susan had tacked a display of torn-out magazine photographs of the princesses, Elizabeth and Margaret Rose, on the wall behind her mattress, and a doll with a vacant china face lay waiting on the pillow for her return each night. Brenda had pinned up a dog-eared copy of that ridiculous leaflet they'd all been sent in the summer, detailing what to do in case of invasion. Various sentences had been underlined: 'Keep watch. If you see anything suspicious, note it carefully and go at once to the nearest police officer . . . Do not give any German anything' – this was underlined three times, with a star in the margin – 'do not tell him anything. Hide your food and your bicycles . . . Think before you act. But think always of your country before you think of yourself.' She kept a catapult beside the mattress and Nell had found an exercise book entitled 'Observations' tucked underneath it, which she was resisting the temptation to read.

Timothy's section of the wall was decorated with meticulous drawings of German and Allied aircraft, labelled in minute writing, and a model aeroplane made of balsa wood hung from the washing line above his mattress. Janet had laid out a gallery of horse pictures and a homegrown nature table in the lid of a cardboard box: a bird's nest containing half a robin's egg shell, a horseshoe, a rabbit's ear, and a brown lump of something dried that Nell didn't like to examine too closely. She slept with a stuffed grey animal of indeterminate species. Lastly, Malcolm's quarters by the eaves window were bare except for a photograph of his mother, a toothy woman with an eager smile and the same milk-bottle bottom glasses, which brought tears to Nell's eyes. She could forgive him the accidents.

Strangely, her father seemed invigorated. He'd never had many friends but the Home Guard gave him a circle of acquaintances whose company he seemed to tolerate, and maybe even grudgingly enjoyed. They'd recently been issued with caps and uniforms which made them look like a proper fighting force, he told Nell proudly, and he'd resurrected his army service boots from the last war. Nell wondered what memories had come back when he'd first cleaned them, chipping away dried mud from the banks of the

Somme. Surely he couldn't have borne to wear khaki again, yet there he was, whistling as he adjusted his cap in front of the hall mirror. He left the house with his shoulders back and a spring in his step; if she'd seen his figure in the distance, she wouldn't have known who it was.

Lord Winthrop was often away in London so her father was left in charge. He went out on patrol three evenings a week, and there was a parade every Saturday afternoon around the recreation ground. People had made fun of them at first, he told her, marching with golf clubs and broom handles instead of guns, but they weren't laughing now, oh no. And if the Germans landed – Nell had the impression he was rather hoping they would – then the Home Guard would come into its own. Preparations were being made. There was an Invasion Committee – of which he was a member, naturally – primed to set a chain of events in motion from the second the church bells rang out in warning. He couldn't go into detail but she should be aware that Millbury had its own food reserves, held in three separate locations around the village, one of which— But no, that was classified information.

Goodness, it was probably the longest conversation they'd ever had. 'Pa, could I borrow the air rifle tomorrow?' she asked, when he drew breath. 'The forecast is good and I'd like to try bagging a rabbit.'

'At this time of year? You'll be lucky.' Yet he unlocked the cupboard and let her take the gun – a little shamefaced, as though she were trying to catch him out. He would have been mortified if he ever found out that Harry had given the Beretta to her.

She got up early the next morning, a Saturday, and having left Alice in her mother's care, took the oilcloth mackintosh from its hook and headed for the field of winter wheat where she'd seen rabbits sunning themselves in the distance a few days before. It had rained for much of the previous night so they wouldn't have come out to feed and would be hungry now. She climbed over the gate and walked along the edge of the field, keeping close to the hedge, then dropped to her knees and edged forward on her elbows and stomach. Small black droppings were sprinkled over the grass like raisins. When she was in pole position, downwind of the warren but close enough to get a good view, she primed and loaded the rifle, adjusted the sights and settled down on the damp ground to wait.

There was something to be said for being out in the fresh air, caught between the brown earth and the iron-grey sky, with only the sound of the wind itself blowing towards her across the open field. She concentrated on keeping so still that she merged into the landscape, occasionally relieving the crick in her neck by laying her cheek flat against the turf. One solitary aeroplane flew overhead, heading for the nearby aerodrome perhaps. She closed her eyes and listened to the thud of her heart, exulting in the joy of independence.

A faint warmth on the back of her neck told her the sun had broken through. Shortly afterwards, the first rabbits emerged from the warren: young ones, a little timid at first, then gaining in confidence as they advanced towards the tender green shoots. Nell ignored them. She was interested in animals with more flesh on their bones. Eventually, three plumper specimens appeared, twitching their noses. She raised the gun slowly to her cheek, holding out for a clearer view. The leader of the trio hopped forward, the skin of its ears shining a translucent pink against the light. Nell thought of the rabbit's ear on Janet Potts' nature table. Janet wouldn't approve of what she was doing now, but the creatures were pests who could decimate a growing crop. The second rabbit came lolloping to join the first and the pair sat obligingly still. With a bit of luck, she might be able to get them both. She steadied the gun and gently, smoothly squeezed the trigger. One rabbit flipped over immediately, its paws beating a frantic tattoo of death, while the other bolted for the shelter of a nearby tree trunk, as Nell had predicted. She was already aiming ahead and shot it cleanly through the neck.

The rest of the colony had scattered so no chance of another kill but she was pleased with her haul. She broke the rifle open, hooked it over her shoulder and went to retrieve the rabbits, tying them together by their hind paws with twine and hanging them inside her coat in true poacher fashion. Only then did she realise that she was being watched. Someone was staring at her from the other side of the gate. She felt guilty for a moment, although she'd committed no crime;

she'd kept to the edge of the field and done the farmer a favour. As she grew nearer, she saw that it was Lord Winthrop – which was odd, because he usually avoided social contact, and she was surely the last person he'd want to encounter. He was wearing a baggy tweed jacket and cavalry twill trousers, with a cap pulled low over his forehead. He didn't move as she approached, just stood there, staring at her. Well, she had to meet him some time.

'Good morning, Lord Winthrop,' she said, trying to keep her voice steady.

He nodded at her. 'Miss Roberts.'

'Actually, it's Mrs Spelman now.' She nerved herself to carry on. 'I was very sorry to learn about . . . your son.'

He nodded again. 'Thank you. A great loss. To his country, as well as his family.'

Hugo Winthrop's plane had been shot down over the English Channel shortly after the start of the war. At first, little was known about the precise circumstances of his death, but the Winthrops' housekeeper happened to overhear telephone conversations and soon rumours were circulating around the village. It seemed that faulty radar had led to a false report of enemy aircraft in the area, resulting in a unit of Hawker Hurricanes from a nearby RAF base being scrambled to hunt Hugo down. The episode had been a tragic fiasco. There'd been a failure of communication between ground control and the pilots, apparently, and procedures for distinguishing between German and British aircraft had been rudimentary back then. This version of events had never been officially confirmed, but that was only to be expected, and no alternative account had been offered.

Nell could still see Hugo's cold, angry eyes, feel the prickles of his nasty little moustache against her lips. 'He was . . .' *What could she say?* '. . . Very brave.'

'He was indeed.' Lord Winthrop fixed his eyes on the horizon. 'A brilliant young man, of whom I was extremely proud.'

Nell nodded, shifting the gun on her shoulder.

'I heard from your father that you were back in the neighbourhood,' His Lordship went on. 'Bombed out, I gather?' He shook his head. 'The waste of it. All this could have been avoided, you know.'

Nell wasn't sure what he meant, so she merely replied uncertainly they were lucky to be alive.

'Quite so.' He gave her a long, hard look. 'And what about this husband of yours? Your father mentioned that he worked in the Palace of Westminster, my neck of the woods. Is that right?'

'He's in charge of the Great Clock,' Nell said, with a flush of pride. 'And all the other clocks, of course.'

Lord Winthrop frowned. 'I thought a chap called Talbot was responsible? Know a bit about horology, you see. Had a long chat with him the other day.'

'Well, in fact there's a team of three,' Nell clarified. 'Arthur, Bill Talbot and Ralph Watkinson, plus an apprentice, although Mr Watkinson's ill at the moment so they're down to two.' She was gabbling, she realised, and made an effort to stop talking.

'Well, well, well.' Lord Winthrop inspected Nell with his head on one side, as though he were going to bid for her at auction. 'Arthur Spelman, that's your husband's name? I shall have to look out for him on my next visit to the Lords. Important to know how the place runs, who keeps it ticking over, and so on. If you'll pardon the pun.' He smoothed his yellowing walrus moustache. 'Had a mechanic once called Spielmann. Does he have German blood, by any chance?'

Nell braced herself. 'Arthur's parents are German but he was born in London. He's lived in this country all his life.'

'It's all right, I'm not questioning his loyalty.'

Nell became aware the rabbits were dripping blood onto her boot. 'I'm awfully sorry, Lord Winthrop, but I have to be getting home.' She put her foot on the bottom rung of the gate. 'My mother's looking after the baby and I'd better not test her patience. So nice to talk to you, though.'

He stepped back to let her pass. 'Goodbye, then, Mrs Spelman. Give my regards to your father.'

It had been an odd, unsatisfactory conversation, but Nell had recovered her spirits by the time she'd walked home. She entered the house through the back door to find her father in the scullery, polishing the buttons on his tunic and muttering to himself in what sounded like German.

He broke off when he saw her, embarrassed. 'There

you are. Goodness, a brace of rabbits? Well done.' She welcomed the praise, although she knew he'd been hoping she would have come back empty-handed.

'What are you up to, Pa?' she asked, a flicker of affection softening the usual sense of unease she felt at the sight of him. His sparse grey hair was neatly parted at the side, and his navy-blue cardigan had been darned by Rose at the elbows with black wool.

'Just practising my phrases.' He laid down the cloth. '*Halt! Hande hoch!* Do you know what that means?'

Nell hazarded a guess. 'Stop, hands up?'

'Yes, well, I suppose you're already familiar with the language,' he replied, shaking the tin of Brasso, 'given your husband's background. But if the enemy is shot down somewhere in this vicinity, I like to think we'll be ready for him.'

'I met Lord Winthrop this morning.' She edged past him and laid the rabbits on the draining board. 'He sends you his regards.'

'Does he?' Frank smiled, dipping his cloth in the polish. 'Wonder what he was doing out and about so early. Off on one of his wild-goose chases, I expect – bird-watching, or hunting for Roman coins. If it was up to him, we wouldn't be on parade till supper time.'

'Just as well he has you to organise things,' Nell said, retreating.

She could hear Alice squawking indignantly as she ran upstairs. 'All right,' she said, lifting her out of the cot. 'Come and help me tidy the loft room.'

Upstairs, she sat the baby down with the wooden rattle that was currently her favourite toy, barricading her in place with a couple of pillows since she was crawling now and becoming increasingly adventurous. Malcolm had had a good night, Nell was pleased to discover; perhaps he was finally settling down. She smoothed his blanket and tucked in the sheets, then stood for a moment to look out of the small window set in the eaves. She could see as far as the High Street in one direction and the recreation ground in the other, with the church halfway in between. A gang of children were running around the rec; she could make out a flash of ginger hair among them. Nell opened the window and leaned out to look more closely. There seemed to be some sort of scrum with Brenda at the centre of it, alternately swallowed up by the group and spat out again as they streamed over the pitch, splitting and re-forming in a complicated pattern like a shoal of minnows. It didn't seem long since she and Harry had been absorbed by those secret games, Nell thought nostalgically, drawing in her head and shutting the window.

She turned around to check on Alice – to discover that Alice had disappeared.

The pillow barricade had been pushed aside and her baby was gone.

Nell looked around the room, her heart beating wildly. Alice couldn't have vanished into thin air; the bedroom door was closed and if someone had come in to snatch her, she would have heard. Frantically, she tossed away pillows, pulled over mattresses, kicked through a heap of clothes. The contents of Janet's nature table went skittering across the floor and, to add to the chaos, the indoor washing line collapsed, sending an array of vests, pants, skirts and trousers tumbling around her.

'Alice?' she called in despair amid the wreckage. 'Where are you?'

And then her ear caught a faint sound which seemed to be coming from somewhere deep in the loft. The low door leading to a storage area under the slope of the rafters was standing ajar. Damping down a rising sense of panic, she bent double to crawl through it and into the confined space beyond, jammed with packing crates and cardboard boxes. There, in the darkness, her daughter was burbling away to herself.

'Alice, darling?' she called, her voice catching in her throat as she fumbled for the light switch.

A naked bulb hung from the rafters. Blinking in its glare, Nell saw Alice sitting a few feet away on the plank between two wooden joists. She was holding something which she waved at her mother, bouncing on her padded bottom with the particular chirrup she made when she was excited, like a small engine revving up. In her hand was a cylindrical metal object, rather like a pineapple, with a ring at the top. Nell had only seen one in a photograph but she recognised it instantly. Her heart lurched in terror.

'Rur, rur!' Alice chirped, raising the grenade to her mouth.

Chapter Ten

Oxfordshire, December 1940

Nell kept her eyes fixed on Alice as she dropped to all fours and crawled clumsily along the joist. Later, she would find a rash of tiny splinters embedded in her knees and the palms of her hands.

'What have you got there?' she asked, trying to keep her voice calm. 'Give it to Mummy.'

Alice laughed and bounced again, holding up the hand grenade. At that moment she caught sight of the ring at the top; perhaps it reminded her of the ring on the dummy she was no longer allowed to have, because Rose thought pacifiers were common. She stared at it for a few seconds, flipped it back and forth, then clamped her gums around the knob holding the pin in place and gave it an experimental bite.

'No!' Nell shouted. 'Stop that, right now!'

Alice stared defiantly back at her. Looking down, she threaded her tiny fingers through the ring—

'No!' Nell shrieked, paralysed with horror.

Startled, Alice dropped the grenade and screamed too as it rolled away. She set off immediately after her exciting new toy but Nell lunged forward and managed to grab her by the waistband of her nappy before she crawled out of reach. Clutching a wailing Alice with one arm, she edged backwards along the joist as fast as possible and backed through the doorway into the comparative safety of the loft room. For a second, she knelt there, her legs weak. Then, pulling herself together, she scrambled to her feet, ran downstairs with Alice and dumped the baby in her cot, closing their bedroom door firmly behind her. If she didn't go back to the loft immediately, before she had time to think how dangerous it was, she'd lose her nerve.

Edging along the joist a second time, she noticed in passing that various odds and ends were piled in the gaps on either side: dozens of spent cartridge casings, a grappling hook, lumps of shrapnel, various tins, a pair of what looked like wire cutters. She would have to think about this collection later. Retrieving the grenade from where it had come to rest against Harry's old school trunk, she laid it gingerly in an upturned tin helmet lying nearby, crawled out of the loft, then down both flights of stairs, straight out of the front door and along the lane. She kept her eyes fixed on the helmet, not looking up until she had reached the Air Raid Precautions post next to the pub.

The warden was sitting on a pile of sandbags, drinking tea.

'Good God!' he spluttered, leaping to his feet and spilling half the mug when he saw what she had brought. 'Where the hell did you find that?'

'In the wheat field up on the ridge behind the Manor.' Nell laid the helmet carefully on the ground and stood back, one hand at her throat. 'Can you deal with it now? I have to go, I've left my baby at home.'

Without waiting for a reply, she turned and ran back the way she'd come. Brenda would have a few questions to answer when she came back from whatever mayhem she was causing elsewhere.

When the Potts children trailed into the house that afternoon for their tea, Nell took Brenda into her father's study. Frank was out on parade and it seemed the right place for a serious talk.

'Where did you get a hand grenade?' She gripped the girl by her shoulders. 'Come on, I need to know.'

'Why?'

'Because if there are any more lying around, we should alert the police.' She gave Brenda a shake. 'Don't you realise the risk you were running? Children have been killed playing with live ammunition!'

'We weren't playing with it.' Brenda wriggled out of Nell's grasp. 'We were keeping it safe. I wasn't to know you'd go poking around up there.' To give her credit, she was holding up well under interrogation.

'If my mother had found that thing, you'd be packing your bags by now.'

'Are you going to tell her?'

'I haven't decided yet.' Nell should probably have talked to Rose already but she knew the trouble it would cause, and where would the Potts children go if they couldn't stay at Orchard House? Besides, she was growing strangely fond of Brenda: an unprepossessing girl in so many ways, with her pale face splotched with freckles and that mop of flaming hair, her shifty eyes and truculent expression. Yet one couldn't help admiring her sense of responsibility as head of the Potts clan. The others all deferred to her, including Susan, who was older, and Timothy, who was taller and broader; if they were asked a question collectively, they would wait for Brenda to answer. None of the village children would pick on the evacuees with her around. She'd taken Malcolm under her wing, too, and Nell knew only too well that he was the sort of child who'd have been bullied otherwise. Brenda was stubbornly and uncompromisingly herself, unhampered by any sense of obligation or guilt.

All the same, the girl had to accept there were limits. 'I need to know exactly what you're up to, so you'd better come clean.' Nell waved the exercise book. 'About everything, including this.'

'That's private property,' Brenda began, but she quailed at Nell's expression. 'All right,' she conceded. 'I'm keeping an eye on the people round here in case anyone's passing information to the enemy. Then when the Germans come—'

'*If* the Germans come,' Nell corrected.

'—then, if the Germans come, we'll know who to trust and we'll be ready.'

'Ready for what?'

'Resistance,' Brenda replied, as though the answer were obvious. 'We're going to hole up in the loft and carry out acts of sabotage.' She gave Nell a sideways look, daring her to mock.

'Look, I understand why you want to be involved,' Nell said carefully, 'but fighting the Germans isn't your responsibility. You must leave that to others.'

'What others? Mr Roberts and that lot are doing their best but they're far too old. We watched one of their training sessions and it was a shambles. Lord Drip Drop's got no authority.'

'Did you steal the grenade from the Home Guard?'

'We didn't steal it. We found it.'

Nell opened the Observations book, turned to a particular spread and held it up. 'In Dead Animal Wood, by any chance?'

Most of the pages were filled with reports of the comings and goings in various streets but there were also a few hand-drawn maps, with landmarks identified by cryptic references: Angry Man's House, Green Pond, Rusty Dump Field . . . Dead Animal Wood was labelled with arrows in various places pointing to smaller pictures, one of which looked like a small leafless pineapple.

Brenda took a cursory glance and nodded, reluctantly.

'It's getting dark,' Nell said, looking out of the window. 'You can show me this wood tomorrow morning. Now go and wash your hands before tea.'

Brenda stood her ground. 'I know you think we're just children, but there are things we can do and you ought to let us do them. We're not going to sit back while a load of Germans march in and take over.'

Nell could imagine herself and Harry taking the same attitude at Brenda's age. She suddenly remembered her gun, lying hidden upstairs; it would be as well to store the ammunition separately in case Brenda stumbled across it. 'I understand how you feel,' she said, 'but stay away from weapons, they're too dangerous. If you find any more, you must leave them alone and tell the warden.'

'All right.' Brenda held out her hand for the exercise book, took it with averted eyes and sidled out of the room. Nell was left with the distinct feeling she had come off second best in the encounter.

Frank came back from parade later that afternoon in a state of some agitation. Lord Winthrop had asked them all over for drinks the following morning after church – including Nell. 'He specifically asked for you to be there. He must have decided to let bygones be bygones, which is jolly good of him.' It was, indeed, a surprising invitation.

'Oh my goodness,' Rose said, jumping to her feet and then sitting down again to consider the implications.

'What on earth can we give them? I've just made some apple chutney but it won't be ready for eating yet. Nell, you can't bring the baby. Susan will have to look after her.'

A trip to Millbury Manor was not to be sneezed at. To set against Lord Winthrop's lugubrious presence, there was always the thrill of seeing what Lady Winthrop was wearing, and what could be glimpsed of their unusual lives. Hermione Winthrop was as different from her husband as it was possible for a person to be. She wore brightly coloured stockings, embroidered Chinese jackets and voluminous frocks gathered at the hip in an old-fashioned style, and her long hennaed hair was constantly escaping from the combs and pins she jammed haphazardly into it. On fine summer evenings, she could be seen dancing barefoot over the lawn in the style of Isadora Duncan and rumour had it she swam naked in the river at the bottom of their garden. There were often artistic friends of Her Ladyship's staying at the Manor, or fellow motor-car enthusiasts and pilots; they had even once entertained an entire troupe of Bavarian folk singers. Lady Winthrop kept goats and a parrot called Algy which flew about the house, shrieking like a banshee and often, according to the housekeeper, making messes on the furniture.

Nell briefed Susan to take care of Alice the whole of Sunday morning, since she and Brenda had another important assignment to keep before the drinks party. They left the house early and walked down the lane, away from the village and past the Manor, then skirted round the edge of the field beyond and climbed over a gate. Nell vaguely remembered the coppice on the other side from her childhood. Brenda led the way along a narrow track, walking quickly over the frozen rutted ground, alert to every rustle in the undergrowth. No longer Brenda Potts, she was now a scout in enemy terrain. A member of the Maquis, perhaps, stealing through a French forest to bring news to her friends in the Resistance. Nell smiled to herself; she and Harry had played similar games.

'Do the others come with you on these reconnaissance trips?' she asked, when they had stopped so she could catch her breath.

'Only Timothy,' Brenda replied. 'Sometimes we take Malcolm as a lookout but he's not reliable.'

They seemed to be heading back the way they'd come. When they had been walking for another fifteen minutes or so, Brenda turned and said over her shoulder, 'Here we are. This is the place.'

The path opened out into a large clearing about the size of a football pitch. Brenda was already crouching down to poke among the fallen leaves and branches; looking for more treasure, presumably. The place was deserted yet some kind of activity had been taking place recently: a row of rusty tin cans had been arranged on tree stumps, which explained the spent cartridge cases, and cigarette butts littered the ground beneath a rusty metal bench nearby.

'Have you seen the animals?' Brenda asked.

Nell nodded. Several trees around the edge of the clearing were festooned with corpses: mostly crows and rabbits, but a couple of pathetically tiny moles and a huge decaying badger had also been strung up from the branches.

Brenda walked over to join her. 'Who's done this?' she whispered. 'What are they for?'

'It's a gamekeeper's gibbet. To prove to the landlord he's doing a good job.' Nell shivered, rubbing her arms. 'I've heard about them but I've never seen one before.'

'Who is the landlord?'

'I'm not sure. Everything's changed around here since I was a girl.'

A wooden hut stood opposite, its door secured with a padlock. Nell walked over and peered through the cobwebby windows but she couldn't make out much inside. It seemed a strange place to store supplies.

'That's where we found the grenade.' Brenda pointed to a clump of grass beside the shed door. 'It was just lying there.'

The flicker of apprehension in Nell's stomach was hardening to fear. She put her arm around Brenda's shoulders. 'You mustn't come here again. You could get hurt or end up in serious trouble. The keeper might have set traps, for one thing. Will you promise to stay away?'

Brenda's face was paler than usual under its rash of freckles and her eyes were wide; she looked like one of Peter Pan's lost boys. Nell bent down to her level. 'I mean it. You must keep safe. If anything happened to one of you children, I don't think we would ever get over it.'

Brenda's mouth dropped open. Clearly, this was such a startling idea that it needed mulling over. At last she gave a secret, crooked smile, as though it had been forced out of her, and said, 'All right. We'll steer clear, I promise.'

'Good girl. Now let's go.' Nell took a last look around the desolate spot. It reeked of menace, of sadness and death. 'You've never brought Janet here, have you?'

'Not likely. She'd have nightmares.' Brenda plunged ahead into the trees. 'Come on, I'll show you a different way home.'

Nell glanced over her shoulder, unable to shake off the feeling they were being watched, but only the trees with their grisly offerings stared back. She and Brenda walked on, emerging eventually on the far side of the stream that ran along the bottom of the Manor house garden. The rolling lawn sloped downhill. Looking up, they could see the edge of a stone balustrade that bordered the terrace, although anyone sitting there would have been shielded from view.

'Nice house,' Brenda said, back to her solid Potts persona. 'I like the towers.'

Millbury Manor had been extended over the years without much of a plan, ending up as a rambling hotch-potch of chimneys, gables, Gothic arched windows, turrets and balconies that somehow suited its current owners. Did the Winthrops know what lay on their doorstep? Nell couldn't imagine they'd approve.

'Is that where you're going later?' Brenda asked. 'Can I come with you?'

'No, it's adults only. But you'll get to see inside it soon, with a bit of luck. There's a Christmas party every year for the village children. I expect you'll be included.'

Brenda nodded, satisfied. She took Nell's hand and pulled her along. 'Let's get home. I'll show you where to cross the stream. There's stepping stones around the bend.'

Arthur would laugh if he could see me being told what to do by a ten-year-old, Nell thought – and there it was again, the dreadful ache of missing him. She wanted to ask his advice about what she'd just seen, and the right way of dealing with Brenda. Letters weren't much good; it was so hard to convey what she meant, and by the time he'd written in reply, she was usually preoccupied with something else entirely. He had rung the house a few times but their conversation had been stilted; her parents' telephone was on the hall table and everyone could hear what she was saying. Still, it would be Christmas in a fortnight and while he might not be able to get away for the day itself, he was hoping to join them on Boxing Day and stay until New Year's Eve. Surely she could last until then? Stop being so feeble, she told herself. Think what other women have to put up with and count yourself lucky.

Chapter Eleven

Oxfordshire, December 1940

Nell and her parents drove to Millbury Manor, although it would only have taken them fifteen minutes to walk. It was important to make the right impression, despite the fact that the family car was a shabby Austin 7 and petrol was in short supply.

Lady Winthrop herself opened the door, resplendent in a full-length crimson gown and a fringed Chinese shawl. 'The Roberts family!' she exclaimed in her deep, melodious voice. 'How lovely to see you. Welcome to the Manor.'

She looked startled at the sight of Nell, which was disconcerting. Nell had made her outfit from a length of blue-and-white flowered cotton her mother had bought in the latest village jumble sale: an empire-line frock and matching bolero jacket which she'd pinned with a brooch to hide the uneven neckline. She tugged discreetly at the hem, in case by some awful chance she'd tucked it into her knickers, and ran her tongue over her teeth. Yet who knew what unconventional thoughts might be running through Lady Winthrop's mind. They were ushered through to the drawing room, where the vicar and his wife were talking to His Lordship. A small fire burned in the huge hearth, large enough to seat two people on each side – the only spot they might have conceivably felt any warmth – and the furniture was all heavy oak and fusty cretonne. Still, the sherry decanter was full and the cigarette boxes well-stocked.

'And how is your merry band of evacuees?' Lady Winthrop asked. 'I see the plump red-headed one running about in the wood sometimes.'

Poor Brenda: she was far too conspicuous to be a decent spy. 'That would be Brenda,' Nell said. 'I hope she isn't trespassing on your land.'

Lady Winthrop looked puzzled. 'Is that our land? I'm not entirely sure. I shall have to ask Lionel, he'll know.'

Lord Winthrop was handing round glasses of sherry. 'The wood, darling,' said his wife. 'Does it belong to us?'

'We rent it out,' he replied briefly. Nell would have liked to ask to whom, but he took her by the elbow and drew her aside.

'I've been thinking about this husband of yours. Tell me about his duties, Mrs Spelman. On a day-to-day basis, I mean.'

What a strange man he was; Nell would far sooner have been talking to Lady Winthrop. She wasn't sure whether Hermione Winthrop knew what had taken place between Hugo and herself; Her Ladyship had always treated her with absent-minded good manners.

She tried to recall Arthur's routine. 'Well, the clocks have to be wound first thing every morning and checked for accuracy. There's a workshop at the Palace for running repairs, and the men can take away the clocks that need more complicated restoration at their company workshop. Of course, the Great Clock occupies most of their attention. They have to make sure the mechanism is running smoothly, oiling it and so on, and checking that it keeps perfect time.'

Was this really the sort of information Lord Winthrop was after? Apparently not: she was losing his attention. 'I was certain Talbot ran the show. He never mentioned anything about colleagues *in situ* at the Palace.'

He wouldn't though, would he? Nell thought. Talbot had locked horns with Arthur from the moment he had started work at Saunders and caught the boss's eye because he was so conscientious and patient. When he'd managed to fix a clock that Bill Talbot had claimed was beyond repair, he'd made an enemy for life. Talbot was one of those sour people who like to feel hard-done-by, and Arthur seemed to have become the focus of his resentment.

'Mr Talbot might not be quite as important as he thinks he is,' Nell said – and immediately regretted her indiscretion. Arthur would have been appalled.

Lady Winthrop called over, 'Lionel, please offer that poor girl a drink before she dies of thirst.'

'Oh, how remiss of me. Do have a sherry.' He splashed some into a glass. 'I'd like to meet your husband, Mrs Spelman, and talk clocks with him. As a matter of fact, the House is sitting this week and I'm off to Westminster tomorrow. I could look him up.'

Poor Arthur, Nell thought. Could she really inflict Lord Winthrop on him? And yet she'd just finished knitting a balaclava, and the post was so unreliable. She could parcel up some bacon, too, and perhaps a jar of honey; it was draughty up in the belfry and Arthur usually had a cold at this time of year.

'Actually, you could do me the most enormous favour,' she said. 'Would you mind taking him a small package?'

'I suppose not.' Lord Winthrop looked surprised. 'But I'm leaving at nine o'clock sharp. You'll need to drop it off here by then.' He seized the decanter and left her alone at last.

'You two were deep in conversation.' Rose had come to stand beside her. 'What was that all about?'

'I'm not entirely sure.' Nell took a long-overdue sip of sherry. 'But His Lordship's going to meet Arthur at the Houses of Parliament and deliver his balaclava.'

'Is he, indeed? Well, I wonder what they'll make of each other.' Rose looked around, ill at ease in her tweed costume and best shoes. 'At least that blessed parrot's been shut up somewhere.'

'Are my clothes all right?' Nell whispered. Lady Winthrop was staring at her again.

Rose took a quick glance. 'As far as I can see. You look very smart.'

And now Lady Winthrop was bearing down on them. 'Ladies, do you know about my classes in the village hall?' She was an enthusiastic member of the Women's League for Health and Beauty. 'Tuesday evenings, at seven o'clock. We love to have mothers and daughters exercising together. Our oldest member is seventy-four!'

Nell and Rose stared at her, equally appalled. 'Well, bear it in mind,' she said. 'Exercise is so tremendously invigorating. By the way, my dear' – she turned to Nell – 'your frock is so pretty. The pattern seems familiar somehow but I can't think why.'

It was the most ridiculous thing, Nell wrote to Arthur the following week. *When I called at the Manor to drop off your parcel (so glad the balaclava's coming in handy, by the way), nobody answered the front door so I went around to the back, and would you believe it – I saw through the window that their kitchen curtains are made from the same material as my frock! Lady Winthrop's housekeeper must have given the leftover fabric to the jumble sale, where Mother bought it. I nearly died when I found out.*

Hardly the most thrilling anecdote. She sucked the top of her pen, hoping for inspiration. She could hardly tell him about Alice and the hand grenade; he'd have had forty fits. Ah, yes. *The other splendid news is that we've had a letter from Harry, giving us his address. Apparently he's safe and in good shape. The Red Cross are delivering parcels to the camp and we can also send supplies, although they may take a while to get through. So now I'm busy knitting another balaclava!*

How trivial her life had become. Of course, it was wonderful to get a good night's sleep and see Alice so settled and happy, but she couldn't help missing the excitement of London, the sense she was living at the very heart of things, at a time when history was being made.

Well, not much more to report, she wrote. *And it's nearly time for the highlight of our social diary, the children's Christmas party. I'm in charge of the evacuees, plus Alice, of course, and hoping they won't let the side down. It's good of Lady Winthrop to carry on with the tradition, especially since now she won't have any grandchildren of her own.* (Nell had never managed to tell Arthur about her encounter with Hugo Winthrop; it was too shameful, somehow.) *Sad, isn't it? Although after a couple of hours with the rampaging hordes, she may count herself lucky. Sorry to hear His Lordship took up so much of your time, he is rather a bore. Can't wait to see you, dearest. Only another week to go! Mother has hopes of a goose for Christmas and we shall make sure there are plenty of leftovers on Boxing Day.*

'Nell?' her mother called, from the kitchen. 'Are you ready? You'd better not be late.'

'Coming.' She signed off with the customary kisses and sealed her letter, scooped Alice out of the playpen and went to call the other children, who were meant to have been resting upstairs after an early lunch to prepare for the excitement ahead. The telephone rang almost as soon as she passed it, making her jump. When she picked up the receiver, Arthur himself spoke to her.

'Hello, darling!' she said, her heart leaping. 'I've just written to you.'

'Listen carefully, I haven't got long.' His voice was high-pitched and breathless, the words tumbling over themselves. 'There's been some ridiculous misunderstanding. I can't explain now but they want me to answer some questions, and there's a chance I may be—' A crackle and splutter on the line muffled his next few words.

'What sort of misunderstanding?' she asked sharply, his fear infecting her. 'And who's "they"?'

'Just listen, darling,' he repeated urgently. 'I might have to go away for a little while, so don't worry if you can't get hold of me for a few days. But everything will be all right, I promise.'

He wasn't making any sense. 'Go away where? And what about Christmas?' was all she could think of to say, sinking into the chair with Alice on her lap.

'I'll try—' He broke off, adding abruptly, 'Sorry, I can't say any more. I shouldn't even be—' There was some sort of commotion in the background and then she heard a clatter, as though he had dropped the telephone receiver.

'Arthur?' But there was no reply, only the sound of

scuffling footsteps, followed by a thump and voices raised in some sort of altercation. She heard Arthur say, in the same panicky tone, 'There's no need for that sort of—' And then a click as the call was ended.

'Who was that?' Rose asked, coming out of the kitchen with her hands covered in flour.

'Only Arthur,' Nell replied, as calmly as she was able. 'Such a terrible line, I could hardly make out a word he was saying before we were cut off.'

The evacuees were assembling by the front door, fizzing with excitement. 'Can I push the pram?' Susan asked. 'Please, I'll be ever so careful.'

Nell busied herself strapping Alice into the Ambassador. There was nothing she could do immediately; she needed time to think, and she didn't want to worry her mother until she knew more. Nell put on her hat in front of the mirror, her fingers shaking, and unhooked her coat from the stand by the door.

'If there's the slightest misbehaviour from anyone, I'm taking you all straight home,' she warned the children, and there must have been a new note of authority in her voice because they nodded meekly, even Brenda.

She ran through the telephone call in her mind as they walked to Millbury Manor. Something was terribly wrong; she'd never heard Arthur sound so flustered. Yet what could she do from a distance? She would just have to wait in the hope he'd ring again, or maybe that he'd send a telegram as soon as the misunderstanding – whatever it was – had been resolved. Unless she could telephone the workroom herself to find out what had happened? Ralph Watkinson was back at work; with a bit of luck, he might answer, and be able to tell her more. If Talbot picked up the phone, she could make an excuse. She would wait till the party was over and sneak out to the telephone box on the village green for privacy – except there was little of that in the centre of Millbury. Better to ring from home and choose her words carefully so as not to cause alarm. Until then, she would just have to think about something else.

Other groups of women and children were walking up the drive towards the Manor. Nell pulled her small party to one side and went over their orders one last time. 'No pushing or shoving, absolutely no swearing, only speak if you're spoken to and remember to say please and thank you. Understood? Timothy, stop picking your nose and Malcolm, tell me at once if you need the lavatory.' The village mothers would be watching the evacuees closely in the hope of misbehaviour.

A holly wreath tied with red velvet ribbon adorned the front door, and the hall was festooned with paper chains made out of newspaper. A tall spruce tree leaned in its pot, decorated with more holly berries and brightly painted wooden ornaments.

'Bloody hell.' Brenda whistled, gazing up in awe. 'Did you ever see anything like it?'

Nell gave her a swift thump.

'Mrs Spelman, how lovely!' Lady Winthrop was

advancing towards them. 'And this must be your troupe of waifs and strays.' She smiled encouragingly at Malcolm, who was blinking behind his glasses. 'Don't be afraid, little boy. We're all going to have the most splendid time.'

Alice had fallen asleep in the pram so Nell parked her beside the Christmas tree and took her charges through to the dining room, cleared of its table, where the games of Pass the Parcel and Musical Chairs would take place. The vicar's wife was already sitting at the piano behind a screen. A circle of chairs had been arranged in the middle of the room while the mothers and grandmothers were sitting on stools and benches against the wall, ready to pounce at the first sign of naughtiness. When the room was full, Lady Winthrop clapped her hands, told a story about a Christmas mouse looking for crumbs – Brenda shot Nell a sardonic look over her shoulder – before announcing the fun would begin as soon as photographs had been taken. A reporter from the local newspaper was there to record the festivities and he spent some time arranging the children (by now virtually hysterical) into rows, their parents standing at the back and Lady Winthrop smiling benevolently from a chair in the middle.

Nell was desperate for the party to be over; sitting still with nothing to do but think made her more tense than ever. She couldn't bear to think of Arthur in trouble. He hated any sort of conflict or rudeness, couldn't bear even to raise his voice in an argument. What could have happened? Suddenly tearful, she got up and hurried out of the room under the pretext of checking on Alice. The baby was still fast asleep, her cheeks flushed. Nell tugged off her pixie hat, hoping she'd wake up, but Alice didn't stir.

'Such a dear little thing.' Lady Winthrop had appeared from nowhere and was standing beside her, looking into the pram. Nell nodded and tried to smile. 'My dear, are you all right?' Lady Winthrop asked. 'Has something upset you?'

Her long, powdery face was creased with such concern that Nell found herself unable to speak. 'Come through to the kitchen.' Lady Winthrop put an arm around her shoulders. 'The kettle's just boiled. Things always look brighter after a cup of tea, especially with a drop of something fortifying in it.'

The housekeeper was filling beakers with lemon barley water, and tea had just been made in a giant urn. Nell noticed the curtains but hardly registered them; it seemed ridiculous to have spent a moment worrying about something so trivial. And how could she inflict her fears on a woman who'd recently lost her only child?

Lady Winthrop poured the tea and produced a silver flask from the folds of her smock. 'Care for a splash of brandy?' She added a slug to both cups without waiting for an answer, and Nell was glad, because she'd have felt she ought to refuse. She began to stammer her condolences but Hermione Winthrop cut her short. 'Please, my dear. We shan't speak of such things now. Tell me what's troubling you.'

'I'm a little concerned for my husband, that's all. It's hard when we're so far apart.' Nell took a sip from her cup and let the brandy warm her. 'He's still in London, you see, and I can't help but worry.'

'Of course. London is a dangerous place at the moment. I'm always relieved to see Lionel home in one piece from the House of Lords. The Palace of Westminster is such an obvious target. All the Germans have to do is fly along the Thames to find it.'

'I know.' Nell bit her lip.

'But of course, your husband works there, too. How tactless of me.' Lady Winthrop poured some more brandy into their cups, to make up for it. 'The barrage balloons will stop any bombers getting through, never fear.'

Neither of them mentioned the fact that the Palace had suffered already, although they were both probably thinking about it. In September, a high-explosive bomb had fallen in Old Palace Yard, causing the statue of Richard the Lionheart to be lifted bodily from its pedestal and then dropped back into place. Extraordinarily enough, only the King's sword had been bent. Several Palace staff had been injured, however, and it was sheer luck no one had been killed.

Lady Winthrop patted Nell's hand. 'I gather Lionel met your husband the other day, and they had a most interesting talk.'

'So I hear.' Nell did her best to smile. According to Arthur, Lord Winthrop had bearded him in the clockmakers' room and insisted on being shown around the clock tower. He'd been particularly interested in the Ayrton light, for some reason, even though it had been switched off since the start of the war.

Lady Winthrop drained her tea and splashed another slug of brandy into the empty cup. 'As a matter of fact, Lionel's off to Westminster this afternoon – against my advice, I might add. Cooke's driving him there once our festivities are over. Perhaps he could take Mr Spelman a quick note from you, or even a small parcel? Some mince pies and a slice of cake might be cheering.'

Nell's heart had begun to thud. 'What a kind gesture. His Lordship was good enough to bring Arthur a balaclava the other week. I wonder—' she hesitated, then continued in a rush, 'Do you think he might consider giving me a lift to London? You see, I need to talk to Arthur urgently and I'm having trouble contacting him by telephone.' She paused, half-appalled by her own cheek. 'Forgive me, Lady Winthrop. I wouldn't ask if it weren't important.'

She shrugged. 'Why shouldn't he take you? He's going there anyway and it's a crime to waste petrol. He's off to London at the drop of a hat these days – no sooner home than he's tearing back there again, whether the House is sitting or not.' Her eyes focused blearily on Nell for a moment. 'Anyone would think he was trying to avoid me.'

Nell laughed nervously. 'I'm sure he's a busy man.'

'Oh, yes. My husband has his finger in all sorts of pies.' Lady Winthrop rose, a little unsteadily, to her feet.

'Let's go and beard the ogre in his study. You never know, he might be glad of some company on the journey.'

I doubt that very much, Nell thought, following Lady Winthrop upstairs. She was probably the last person Lord Winthrop would have chosen as a companion. The door to his study was ajar and Nell could hear him talking as they approached.

'Yes, Handle's going ahead,' he said. 'Definitely.' Followed by a clunk as he replaced the telephone receiver. By the time Lady Winthrop had knocked and entered the room, he was stuffing papers into a brief-case. He looked startled and not exactly overjoyed to see them, and listened to his wife's rambling request with a deepening frown.

'I'm afraid there's no time to take passengers on board,' he growled. 'We shall be leaving the minute Cooke's finished his stint as Father Christmas. I have to reach the city before nightfall.'

'That won't be a problem,' Nell assured him. 'I'll just run home to grab a few things and be back before you know it. I need to contact Arthur urgently, you see.'

He glared at her. 'Can't you go by train in the morning?'

'Don't be so disobliging, Lionel.' Lady Winthrop's face was flushed. 'No skin off your nose, is it? You don't have to drive. You just sit in the back, reading your papers and not talking to anyone. Not even your wife.'

'All right, all right,' Lord Winthrop snapped. 'I see I won't get any peace until I agree. Just don't be late, Mrs Spelman. If you're not back here in an hour, we won't wait.'

'Thank you so much,' Nell replied humbly. 'I do appreciate it.'

When they were alone in the hall, Lady Winthrop took Nell's hands in hers and pressed them to her ample chest. 'Don't pay that old grump any attention. Your place is with your husband,' she murmured, in a gust of alcohol-laced breath. 'Fly to him and bring succour.'

Nell could hardly believe her impulsive request had been granted. Of course, there was Alice to think of, but her mother and Susan Potts wouldn't mind looking after the baby between them. It was the school holidays now and Nell wouldn't be away for long. She had to hurry, though, and keep her head. Firstly, she ran back into the dining room, where the game of musical chairs was reaching its conclusion. Susan and Janet were watching Timothy, one of the final few still clinging to a chair; apparently Brenda had taken Malcolm to the toilet. Nell asked Susan to take the other children home after the party, and to help Rose take care of Alice for a day or so. Then she slipped out of the room, seized the pram and pushed it hurriedly back to Orchard House, planning what she should pack and how she could explain the situation to her mother.

In the end, she opted for simplicity. 'Ma, I need to go to London for a couple of days, to sort something out for Arthur. Lord Winthrop's offered me a lift in his car. Would you mind looking after Alice while I'm gone? Susan will help.'

Rose's hand fluttered to her chest. 'You want to go to London? At a time like this? Whatever for?'

'Please,' Nell begged, dancing from foot to foot with impatience. 'I haven't time to explain but I'll be careful, I promise.'

Rose glanced at the clock. 'Your father's taking a nap. He'll be in a terrible mood if I wake him up.'

'No, don't do that,' Nell said quickly. She improvised, crossing her fingers behind her back. 'I told him the other day I might have to go back at some point and he didn't object.'

'Oh, all right, then,' Rose sighed eventually. 'If you're set on going, suppose I can't stop you. But please come home the minute you can. You know how I'll worry while you're away.'

Nell ran upstairs, threw some clothes into a haversack and changed into more sensible shoes, suitable for dashing about. Then she levered up the floorboard to retrieve the Beretta; she daren't risk leaving a gun for Brenda to find. Her identity card and enough money for the return train fare were in her handbag, and the watch Arthur had given her was around her neck, as always. She fished it out: with a bit of luck, she'd make it back to the Manor in plenty of time. First, though, she had to say her goodbyes.

'Be a good girl for Granny,' she whispered, holding Alice so tightly she squawked in protest and burying her face in the warm, soft folds of baby skin. 'I'll be back before you know it.' For the briefest of moments, she wondered whether she were doing the right thing, until she remembered the fear in Arthur's voice.

Rose held out her arms for the baby and Nell passed her over. 'Thanks, I'm truly grateful. Say goodbye to Pa for me.' And then she was gone, hurrying up the lane with the haversack bumping on her shoulder and the breath tearing at her throat. How long would it take to drive to London? An uncomfortable couple of hours, maybe, but she could put up with that.

When she rounded the last corner of the drive, Lord Winthrop was already standing on the doorstep and the smooth, shiny bulk of the Bentley was nosing its way out of the garage to pick him up. She might have guessed he would try to give her the slip. Running the last few yards, she arrived panting and flustered as Cooke was opening the rear passenger door for His Lordship to climb in.

'Oh, there you are,' he said, peering out at her from the back seat. 'In the nick of time. Would you mind sitting in the front? I have papers to read.'

Cooke held the door open for Nell, staring impassively into the distance. She was just stowing her handbag in the footwell and settling herself down for the journey when Brenda's face loomed up at the car window.

'Goodbye,' Nell mouthed, giving her a thumb's up. 'See you soon. Behave yourself!'

Brenda looked agitated, hopping from foot to foot. She signalled that Nell should wind down the window, but its handle was stiff and wouldn't move. Cooke started the engine and the Bentley began to crunch forward over the gravel. Brenda said something Nell couldn't make out and rapped on the window, trotting along beside the car.

'Drive on!' Lord Winthrop commanded from the rear seat. 'Who is that ghastly child?'

Nell raised her hands in mock surrender as the Bentley drew away. 'I do believe she's chasing us,' Lord Winthrop grunted, craning around. 'What infernal cheek.'

Nell felt a pang of disquiet as the car gathered speed and Brenda's running figure receded into the distance. What had she been trying to say? Nothing important, most probably, but she wished they could have spoken nevertheless. Glancing in the wing mirror, she saw Lord Winthrop clasp his hands over his stomach and close his eyes, frowning. Cooke still seemed determined to ignore her so she stared out of the window, watching the countryside roll by as they drove through the gathering dusk towards London. For some reason, she remembered the phrase, 'Handle's going ahead,' spoken so urgently and distinctly. Which particular pie of His Lordship's was that?

Chapter Twelve

London, January 2022

Ellie and Dan had fallen into the habit of speaking on the phone almost every night. Whenever she'd tried calling Beth, it always seemed to be the wrong time: Morgan was either taking a nap so Beth was busy with chores, or needing a feed or to have her nappy changed. But Dan had time to talk and he usually had some news to report – her cactus had flowered, a new tenant had moved into the apartment downstairs, there'd been a fire at the Italian restaurant on the corner, her dishwasher had broken but he'd managed to fix it – and he was interested in what she had to say. She caught the loneliness in his voice, the sense of dislocation. Perhaps she was especially glad to hear from him because that's how she was feeling, too, navigating her way through a strange city. It didn't sound like he was living the bachelor in

Manhattan dream. When she asked him what he'd been up to, it mainly seemed to consist of running along the Hudson River Park and watching old movies on Netflix. 'Same old, same old,' he'd say. 'So come on, tell me what you've discovered.'

Not a great deal, Ellie had to admit. She'd visited the Palace of Westminster, home to the Houses of Parliament, and although the buildings were magnificent, they hadn't given her the instant connection to her family that she'd been hoping to find. Her grandfather hadn't been a politician or a peer, he'd been a craftsman. She couldn't sense his presence in the echoing Westminster Hall, with its timber roof like the hulk of an upturned boat so high above her head, nor in the long corridors, where light fell through stained-glass windows to scatter jewels over the marble floors. History unfurled before her in a gorgeous tapestry of statues, paintings, robing rooms and thrones: remote and academic. She'd spent a long afternoon at the Imperial War Museum, she told Dan, looking at cases of Second World War stirrup pumps, ration books and gas masks, and sitting in a replica Anderson shelter while an air raid exploded outside.

'Terrifying, and so claustrophobic – I could only stand it for ten minutes.'

She told him how she'd booked a session in the research room, to read up on Fascism.

'Should be interesting,' Dan said. 'I'm jealous.'

He sounded sorry for himself. For some reason a memory flashed into Ellie's head: red party cups, kegs of beer, teenage boys throwing up in the Scardinos' back yard. 'Wait a minute! Isn't it your birthday sometime soon?'

'That's right, in a few days. How did you remember?' She could tell he was touched.

A dreadful thought struck her. 'It's not your fortieth, is it?'

'That's next year. I'm going to pretend this one isn't happening. Or maybe treat myself to extra pepperoni on my pizza.'

'Oh, Dan.' She tried to think of something to cheer him up. 'Well, if you're at a loose end, you can always jump on a plane and come to London. There's a couch in my living room.'

As soon as the words were out of her mouth, she regretted them. Sure, it would be great to have company, but Dan might think she was hitting on him, and she had enough emotional drama to deal with as it was. Luckily, Dan wasn't the impulsive type. He only laughed nervously and said it was a kind offer that he would think about. 'So, have you patched things up with your aunt?' he asked, clearly wanting to change the subject.

Ellie groaned. 'Not yet. I will, though. Soon.'

'You've been saying that for days. Go tomorrow, then you won't have it hanging over you anymore. I'll call in the evening to hear how it went.'

The next afternoon, Ellie found herself standing on Gillian's doorstep, with a bunch of flowers this time. What was the worst that could happen? If Gillian slammed the door in her face, that would prove she was mad and Ellie wouldn't have to worry about her anymore. She'd have done all she could. She pressed the bell, her heart thumping. Through the stained-glass panels of the front door, she saw the slender outline of her aunt approaching and braced herself.

'Oh. I thought it was my supermarket delivery.' Gillian was wearing a pair of dark glasses; it was impossible to read her expression behind them.

Ellie thrust the flowers towards her. 'I brought you these. To apologise for the other day.'

Gillian hesitated, then reached forward. 'Thank you. They're very nice.'

They stood looking at each other. 'May I come in?' Ellie asked.

Gillian turned without a word and Ellie followed her down the hall to the kitchen, rehearsing what she might say. When she faced her aunt, though, it was Gillian who spoke. 'I should be the one bringing you flowers. I wasn't on very good form the other day.'

That was an understatement. 'You weren't feeling well,' Ellie said. 'And having to entertain me was too much of a strain. When you're better, maybe I could take you out for tea or something, and we could start over again.'

'Maybe. Although actually, I might not be feeling better for a while.' Gillian laid the flowers on the counter and took down a vase from one of the cupboards. 'How lovely. White lilies remind some people of funerals but

I rather like them, and they do suit this room.' Propping her glasses on top of her head, she filled the vase with water, tore the cellophane from the flowers, trimmed the stems and began to arrange them. Her eyes looked pink and swollen.

'Is it the flu?' Ellie asked tentatively.

Gillian looked at her directly for the first time. 'No, I'm afraid it's cancer.'

Her words hung in the air like smoke from an explosion. Ellie racked her brain for some kind of response but all she could do was stare at her aunt, speechless.

'That's the first time I've said it out loud.' Gillian stood back from the vase and tweaked one of the stems, frowning. 'Perhaps the telling will get easier with practice. I'd found a lump in my breast before Christmas, you see, and was waiting for the biopsy results when we met. Not very good timing, was it? But you couldn't have had any idea about that. Anyway, I heard yesterday the tumour's malignant. I have breast cancer. You're the only other person who knows, apart from the nurse and my oncologist.'

Ellie sat down with a thump. 'But what about Max? And your daughter?'

'Lucy has another couple of weeks in South Africa and there's no point spoiling her holiday. As for Max – well, you've met him. You've seen what he's like.' She shot Ellie a fierce look. 'You must promise not to tell him. This information is strictly between the two of us.'

At that moment, the doorbell rang. 'That'll be my

shopping.' Gillian put her glasses back on and straightened her shoulders.

Ellie slid off the bar stool. 'Don't worry, I'll bring it in.' She walked down the hall, her head reeling, glad of the chance to digest what she'd just heard.

It took her a couple of trips to bring all the bags through to the kitchen. Gillian was sitting at the kitchen table, gazing out of the window, so Ellie unpacked the groceries, arranging them on the island in groups so they'd be easy for her aunt to put away. She wondered about putting the milk and cheese in the fridge, but that felt like intruding. Fridges were so personal; what if she opened Gillian's to find nothing but a bottle of vodka and a tin of cat food? And Gillian didn't have a cat? When she'd finished, she sat beside her aunt and joined her in looking out at the yard. It was immaculately landscaped, with seats under a pergola at the far end, square flowerbeds surrounded by low box hedges, and a pond full of waterlilies fed by water flowing from pipes set into the wall.

'Max designed my garden,' Gillian said. 'He's a dear boy, really, although rather too easily blown off track. He doesn't like any sort of unpleasantness.'

'You'll have to tell him sooner or later. He's bound to notice something's wrong.'

Gillian laughed. 'You'd be surprised.'

They sat quietly for a little while longer. 'Should I make us a cup of tea?' Ellie offered. She'd have killed for one.

'Actually, that would be rather nice. But you don't know where anything is.'

'I'm sure I can find my way around.'

'All right, then. Do your best. I like mine strong, with plenty of milk and no sugar.'

Gillian resumed her garden vigil while Ellie pottered around the kitchen, opening and closing cupboards in her search for teabags, and a couple of mugs. The design was too stark for her taste but she could appreciate the workmanship and thought behind it: the drawers sliding smoothly to and fro, the doors softly closing, the canisters slotting so neatly into place. Maybe if she had a kitchen like this, she would become a more efficient, purposeful person altogether. She brought Gillian her tea with a packet of ginger thins from the supermarket delivery and they sat together, drinking and nibbling. Ellie was afraid of saying the wrong thing, so she waited for her aunt to break the silence.

Gillian didn't seem in any hurry. Eventually she said, pushing back her chair, 'By the way, I have something for you. Wait here and I'll bring it through.'

She returned with what looked like a thick hardbacked book, which she placed on the table between them. 'The album. Turns out it wasn't so hard to find after all.'

Ellie laid her hands on the faded leather cover, as though she could absorb the past through her skin. Then, reverently, she opened it. The first photograph showed Arthur and Mavis on their wedding day. Ellie guessed it was Mavis who had compiled the album, labelling each picture underneath in small, looped handwriting with the date and any other salient facts. She and Arthur had been married on Friday, 18 March, 1949, at St Luke's Church in Kentish Town. The bride wore a rayon satin gown with a Chantilly lace veil, according to a newspaper clipping on the next page, and was attended by her niece, Miss Marigold Rawlins, and her stepdaughter, Miss Alice Spelman. Mavis was short and plump, her blonde hair set in frantic waves and an expression of joyful triumph on her face. She had a weak chin and small pointed teeth, and looked as though she would be more inclined to fussiness and nit-picking than coarseness. Arthur was solemn and resolute, stooping next to his new wife as though to minimise their height difference. There were several pictures of the bride and groom: on the church steps, climbing into a car, flanked by Arthur's mother and both Mavis's parents – Ellie was interested to see the bride's father, a bespectacled man in a top hat whom she wouldn't necessarily have taken for a butcher – and then, at last, a photograph of the bridal party, with an awkward, glowering Alice on the end of the row, beside a fair-haired cherub of five or so. She must have been about nine, already tall for her age and not at all flattered by the frilly bridesmaid's dress that looked adorable on little Marigold.

'Oh dear.' Ellie couldn't help smiling. 'Mom isn't very happy.'

Gillian leaned over to see the picture. 'That's how I remember her. Always rubbing against the grain.'

'So you two didn't get along?'

'Oh no, I worshipped Alice. She seemed so glamorous and exciting. I probably drove her mad, trailing around after her all the time.' Gillian sipped her tea. 'Although I was a little afraid of her, too. She used to have the most furious rows with my mother. Neither of them would back down and my father would always take my mother's side. Alice was a radical, always going off on marches to protest about something or other – banning the bomb, or the Vietnam war, or factory farming – and my parents took it personally. Why couldn't she be grateful for the sacrifices their generation had made? I used to think Alice caused all the trouble in our family, until she left.' She hesitated. 'Has she been happy, do you think?'

'By and large, I guess,' Ellie replied. 'She and my dad had a good marriage, so far as I knew. We were never rich, yet there was always food on the table and enough money to get by. It's been tougher for Mom since he died but I don't think she has any regrets. Did you ever meet my father?'

Gillian shook her head. 'My parents wouldn't have him in the house till he got his hair cut, so he never came.'

Ellie laughed. 'That sounds like Dad.' She went back to the album, turning over the thick card pages to see the Spelman family history playing out. They had moved from Kentish Town to St Albans, Gillian told her, where Arthur and Mavis had lived until they died; Arthur first, and Mavis five years later. There were various photographs of the new house in the suburbs: Arthur mowing the lawn and Mavis picking raspberries in a fruit cage, and the Morris Minor they had bought in 1952 parked proudly in the drive. Alice hardly ever featured. An elbow or foot that might have belonged to her was sometimes included at the edge of the shot, but she was never centre stage. One picture showed Arthur beaming as he washed the car; above him, Alice's small, wan face looked out from an upstairs window.

Arthur grew leaner and greyer year by year, while Mavis became steadily plumper. She was almost spherical by 1954, and then Gillian was born. From then on, Alice made a more frequent appearance: pushing the pram, helping to bath her baby sister in the sink, pulling Gillian along in a toy cart. Much later, there was even a photograph of Alice and her father alone. She must have been about seventeen or eighteen, showing a first hint of the beauty she'd become: dark slanting eyes, high cheekbones and dazzling skin. Her face wore the mischievous, defiant expression that Ellie knew well. Arthur was looking back at her warily, as though anticipating her next move.

'Can I take a picture of this one on my phone?' Ellie asked.

'You can have it.' Gillian slipped the photograph out of its triangular corners, studying it for a few seconds before handing it over. 'Alice meant everything to my father. He loved her far more than he ever did my mother or me. It broke his heart when she moved to America. And she never came back, not even for his funeral.'

'My mother isn't cruel,' Ellie said, her blood rising. 'She must have had a reason for behaving that way.'

'Well, I suppose it doesn't matter now.' Gillian took another biscuit and snapped it in half. 'All water under the bridge, as they say.'

'What was Arthur like?' Ellie asked, turning over the album pages.

'Very much a man of his time. Saw himself as head of the family, didn't like talking about his feelings, believed expressing any sort of emotion was a sign of weakness. I don't know whether he'd always been like that, or if it was a result of losing his first wife in the war.'

Ellie found a folded sheet of card at the back of the album: an order of service for the funeral Alice hadn't attended. A photograph of Arthur on the front showed his hair still thick but completely white, his heavy-lidded eyes sombre behind black-rimmed glasses. Dates were printed under the picture: 3 June, 1910 – 12 January, 1992. He'd had a long life, although maybe not a happy one.

'Why are you looking at that?' Gillian reached forward to snatch the sheet out of Ellie's hands.

'I'm sorry,' she said. 'I thought – I mean, I didn't realise it was private.'

'That's enough ancient history for one day.' Now Gillian was cross again, her jaw set and her lips clamped in a tight line. She put the order of service back in the album and hugged it against her chest.

'Of course,' Ellie said. 'Sorry.' Although why was she apologising? Arthur was her grandfather; why shouldn't she know about his funeral? But Gillian was ill, she reminded herself, and obviously the slightest thing would set her off.

Her aunt stood up. 'Well, I mustn't keep you. I'm sure you've heard enough of my tale of woe.'

Ellie pushed back her chair. 'If you're really not going to tell your kids for the time being – about the cancer, I mean – maybe I could help. Do you have a treatment plan? If you like, I could come with you to the hospital.'

'Oh, there's really no need for that,' Gillian said quickly. 'I wouldn't dream of putting you to any trouble.'

Two steps forward and one back, Ellie thought, but still, this was an improvement on their last meeting.

'And you promise not to say a word to Max about all this?' her aunt said, walking her to the front door.

'Of course not. I won't tell anyone. You have my number – just text me if you need anything and I'll come over right away.'

'Thank you, but I'll be fine.' Behind the glasses, Gillian was retreating into her shell. 'I don't know why I burdened you with my story in the first place. Obviously, I'll be taken up with medical appointments and so on for the next little while, but do give me a ring before you leave.'

Ellie stopped once she'd walked around the corner,

to text Nathan her grandfather's date of birth before she forgot it. She would call her mother that evening. The image of Alice staring out of an upstairs window like a pale, unhappy ghost would stay with her for a long time.

'Aunt Gillian's highly strung. You have to be careful not to say the wrong thing, and you have no idea what that wrong thing might be until you've said it, so it's all pretty difficult.'

Alice snorted. 'Neurotic. I could have told you she'd turn out like that.'

'She said she worshipped you.'

'Well, she had a funny way of showing it, always running to Mavis if I so much as looked at her the wrong way. When are you coming home, dear?'

'In another week. Not too much longer.' Ellie was talking to her mother as though Alice were a child, she realised. 'How are you, Mom? I miss you. It was great, seeing all those photos of you growing up. You were quite the looker.'

'I was, wasn't I?' Alice agreed. 'Your father said I had the most beautiful breasts he'd ever seen, and he'd seen plenty. We used to take off our tops at the drop of a hat back then.'

Ellie tried hard to dismiss that image from her mind. 'Mom, Aunt Gillian mentioned your father's funeral. Didn't you want to be there?'

'Oh, I would have gone,' Alice replied, 'but Mavis made it clear I wasn't welcome.'

'You mean, you weren't invited?'

'Well, she wrote to tell me the date but she didn't put a stamp on the envelope. By the time the letter reached me, it was too late.'

'I guess anyone can make a mistake. She was probably getting forgetful by then.'

'Oh no, it would have been deliberate,' Alice said, very matter-of-fact. 'That's the kind of woman she was.'

Ellie sighed. 'So how's life at the Willows? Beth told me Kathleen called by the other day.'

'Oh, I haven't seen Kathleen for ages,' Alice said cheerfully. 'Do you know, I can hardly remember what she looks like.'

'Mom, I have to go.' Ellie's phone told her Dan was trying to get through. 'Take care of yourself, OK? I'll call again soon.'

Dan cut straight to the chase. 'So, are you and Gillian friends now?'

'It's a long story.' Ellie felt drained. 'Let's wait till I can tell you face to face.'

'Sure. As a matter of fact, that might be sooner than you think.' He sounded pleased with himself. 'I've done it!'

'Done what?'

'Bought a plane ticket to London. I suddenly thought, well, why not? Your plants can manage for a few days and I'm just kicking my heels here. If you're still happy for me to stay, that is.'

'Of course.' What else could she say? 'It'll be great to see you.'

And yet, she thought as she headed for the shower, Dan was a complication she could have done without; entertaining him on his birthday only added to the pressure. He reminded her of the girl she used to be – easy and carefree, with her whole life ahead of her – but she was too old now to bounce back from her mistakes. And definitely too old to make a fool of herself with her best friend's brother. Dan was strictly off limits.

Chapter Thirteen

London, January 2022

Ellie might have been closing in on Alice, but her grandmother hovered tantalisingly out of reach. The few facts she'd discovered so far about Eleanor Spelman only added another veil of confusion. Why had Eleanor been in London at the height of the Blitz? Had she brought her baby or left her behind in Oxfordshire? If so, who was looking after Alice? And Eleanor's political leanings remained a puzzle that might never be solved. In her quest to find some answers, Ellie had made an ally in the Imperial War Museum research rooms. The librarian looked younger than her but dressed like an old fogey in a three-piece suit with a collar and tie; he'd waxed the ends of his moustache into tiny points. 'Grant Collins,' announced his name badge. 'How may I help?'

Ellie had looked on the museum's website and

located some files relating to the British Fascist movement: letters, photographs and transcripts of interviews with suspected Fascist agitators. That seemed as good a place to start as any. She'd given the reference numbers to Grant Collins, who'd brought her stacks of dusty folders to look through, but she needed someone to give her an overall picture. So, taking Grant up on his offer of help, she told him the reason for her investigation and showed him the photographs of Eleanor on her phone, followed by the disturbing contents of her grandmother's handbag. His eyes lit up behind the horn-rimmed glasses. It was a romantic story, if you were that way inclined: the grandmother who looked so like Ellie, tragically killed in the war, and her own elderly mother waiting thousands of miles away for news. Except for the fact Eleanor might have been a Fascist – which was unfortunate, to say the least.

Grant held the badge carefully, as though it might burn his fingers. 'Of course, the British Union of Fascists had been disbanded in May 1940 and their leader, Oswald Mosley, thrown into jail.' He had a precise, pedantic turn of phrase. 'No one would dare wear an emblem like this in public, but there was still plenty of Fascist activity going on under the radar. A lot of people thought it was only a matter of time before the Germans invaded England, and some home-grown Fascists were jockeying for position, so to speak, waiting for their day to come.'

'And what about the leaflet?'

'Fairly standard propaganda. German planes would

drop these alongside their bombs.' He smiled encouragingly. 'Not every Fascist was a pantomime villain, you know. Someone who'd lived through the previous war might have been desperate to avoid another one.'

'You're not reassuring me,' Ellie said. 'People must have known by then what Hitler was like. They could see the way that Jewish people were being treated.'

'Oh, yes. But anti-Semitism was rife, remember, in all sections of society. "The Jew problem" was a commonly accepted phrase.'

'How awful.' Ellie gathered her shameful memorabilia. 'Oh well, I guess I'll never find out.'

'Keep looking, you never know what might turn up.' He picked up the file she'd returned to his desk. 'Are you ready for the next one?'

Ellie glanced at the clock. 'I guess so. But that had better be the last.'

She'd spent so long looking at page after page of close-typed transcripts that her head rang with disjointed, meaningless sentences. According to the files' cover note, an undercover MI5 agent was pumping suspected Fascists for information. As far as she could make out, he wasn't getting anything particularly interesting.

For heaven's sake don't tell them it's gone there yet, you see, wait until they've . . . gone (?) . . . (2 words). I'll tell you, I promise . . . You can trust me by now, can't you?

There'd been a lot of inconsequential chatter and references to places in England and Germany that she'd never heard of. It took her a while to work out which set of initials belonged to the agent, as everyone seemed to be asking questions and the dialogue was full of ellipses and indistinct words. Eventually, she decided K was in charge of the proceedings. The person referred to as EP seemed quite mad, going off at a tangent on rambling anecdotes that seemed to bore even the transcriber:

discussion of Goldman's black-market business and properties, '5 beastly houses, living in absolute squalor he is . . . Whitechapel or somewhere . . . and a girlfriend in Austria . . . Yes, and his wife . . . (3 words, inaudible). Horrid little man, waving his legs about like a spider . . . He ought to be exterminated.' (laughter)

She was looking through the last file without any great expectations when a name jumped off the page to make her sit bolt upright, as though a bucket of cold water had been emptied over her head.

Mrs SPELMAN arrived at 3.20 p.m. and was introduced. She stated that BT had told her to come and that she was looking forward to 'meeting like-minded souls'.

K: So tell us about yourself, Mrs Spelman. What brings you here?

ES: Well, I suppose you could call me disappointed, really. I'm a disappointed woman. You see, I married my husband and his parents are German. I thought we were going to live in Germany and I should have liked that. I like the way they do things over there. But he wasn't what I expected, not at all. He'll lie down and let anyone walk over him. Now he's been arrested so I can do as I please, and I got talking to Mr Talbot in the pub and he said I should come and see you, to offer my services.

CD: My husband's been interned, he's in Brixton. They might take your husband there too. That's where Mosley is, you know, but he doesn't fraternise with everyone . . . seems to think . . . (they all speak at once).

They went on to talk about Mrs Spelman's father who'd worked in a bank and had been passed over for promotion . . .

ES: Because his name wasn't Rothschild or Sachs, that's why. The Jews have got everything wrapped up. They're the ones who started this war in the first place, after all, to make money. There are no prospects for honest hard-working people in this country and I want to do something about it.

K: In what way? What do you mean, exactly?

ES: Well, I'm not sure what action you have in mind but I can keep my eyes open and pass on any information I pick up. You see, I have access to the Houses of Parliament. If you have plans in that direction, which Mr Talbot seemed to think, then I could help.

EP: Where is Bill, anyway? I haven't seen him for ages. No offence, Mrs Spelman, but I can't imagine why he should be saying these things to you in a pub, you being a virtual stranger. How do we know you can be trusted?

ES: Oh no, Mr Talbot worked with my husband. So I knew of him, and he knew of me.

K: Well, that's very interesting, Mrs Spelman. Thank you, and welcome.

The discussion went on for another few pages but *ES* didn't have much more to say; *EP* dominated the conversation until the meeting ended with vague promises to meet again after Christmas.

Ellie closed the file and leaned back in her chair. Too late now to wish she'd never started digging into the past. No matter how widespread anti-Semitism might have been, it was depressing to see her grandmother, her own flesh and blood, revealed as a mean-minded bigot. Lovely Eleanor was ugly underneath, trotting out the old prejudices that had never gone away, and she had died with those beliefs still intact. Ellie was disappointed, too. Thanking Grant Collins for his help, she picked up her coat and headed outside. She had an appointment to keep: Aunt Gillian had managed to find her a place on a trip up the clock tower to see Big Ben. The tour guide was a friend who owed Gillian a favour and, following a last-minute cancellation, had agreed to squeeze Ellie in.

'Just give my address if you're asked and everything

should be fine,' Gillian had said on the phone. 'It's a little irregular but, given our family history, they made an exception.'

Ellie was ashamed of her family history now; it felt like a dirty secret. Her grandmother had been a Fascist and her grandfather must have been, too, otherwise why would he have been arrested? He had worked at the Houses of Parliament but he had been a traitor – although, of course, she could never tell her aunt about her father having been arrested. Regardless, she had to take up her place on the tour, given the trouble Gillian had taken to arrange it. Renovation work on the clock tower and the clock itself had recently been completed, so that was worth a look, and she might get a good view of London from the top. She would forget about Arthur Spelman and tell herself this was just another sightseeing trip. All the same, it was hard not to imagine her grandfather climbing the spiralling limestone steps beside her – over three hundred of them leading up to the belfry – his hand grasping the iron banister she held now.

She was part of a group of ten or so. The tour guide was a cheerful woman with a seemingly inexhaustible fund of information and the enthusiasm to match, although she must have given the same talk hundreds of times before. She took them first into the clock room, home to the original Victorian machinery. The clock ran by gravity, the guide explained: the clock hands, the bells and the clock mechanism itself being controlled by three weights which dropped down the tower's central shaft. These weights would have to be wound up again; two by means of an electric motor but one by hand, even today. Two clockmakers still had to wind the going train, as it was called, three times a week.

There was something delightfully eccentric and old-fashioned about the system. A pile of old pennies on the pendulum tray kept the clock accurate; the clockmaker would add a coin to speed things up, or take one away to slow them down. The guide was in the middle of her explanation when a tremendous racket started: cogs and ratchets whirred and the fly fans high above their heads clattered into life as the minor bells rang out the Westminster Chimes, announcing the quarter hour. It was extraordinary to think the mechanism had been operating for over a hundred and sixty years, virtually unchanged. In the gallery that ran behind the four huge dials, they could see the original gas mantels that had first illuminated the clock, and the metal rungs which had let a workman scramble up to light them. And then at last they had climbed up to the belfry to see where Big Ben hung in state, with the smaller quarter bells arranged around him. Ellie found herself unexpectedly moved. Wars had been fought, fires had raged and people had died in the streets below, but these bells had carried on striking and the vast clock had counted the minutes through it all.

The belfry was open to the elements, its arched Gothic windows covered only by a metal grille so the wind howled through and occasional squalls of rain splattered the bells.

She wandered over to gaze across the river. Dusk was falling quickly, and the dark sprawl of London was pierced by a thousand pinpricks of light. She could glimpse the glowing Ferris wheel of the London Eye across the river, see the tip of the Shard.

'Everyone got their ear defenders on?' called the guide. 'Big Ben's about to strike.'

They waited a little nervously as the quarter bells sounded, waiting for the seconds of silence before the great hammer, all two hundred kilos of it, dropped down to strike the bell. Ellie turned back towards the view. Someone was calling her, or so it seemed, in that quiet moment as the Westminster Chimes faded away. She sensed a distinct presence at her shoulder, so real that she might have leaned back and found herself supported, and a tremendous sense of peace washed over her. It was as though she had found something that had been missing for a long time, without her having even noticed it was gone. Her heart was full to bursting. She heard the voices of her family, in all of their complexity, and could only be grateful for the life they had given her, could think of them with nothing but love and acceptance.

And then as abruptly as the sensation had come, it was gone. A gust of wind drove stinging raindrops into her face and she leaned back against the wall. Her ears rang as the bell's vibrations died away and she returned to normality: faint and dizzy, and quite alone.

⋆ ⋆ ⋆

‘I can’t explain,’ Ellie told Beth on the phone that evening. ‘It was as though someone were standing next to me, so close I could reach out and touch them. Perhaps I’m going crazy. It might be just as well Dan’s coming over – he can keep an eye on me.’

‘Sounds weird,’ Beth said, and Ellie could tell she’d only been listening with half an ear. ‘But listen, Morgan’s waking up so I have to go. Have fun! Don’t let my brother cramp your style.’

Ellie couldn’t blame Beth for her lack of interest; she couldn’t put the experience into words without it sounding far-fetched and ridiculous. Describing what had happened made her doubt herself.

‘Honestly, I thought I’d seen a ghost,’ she said to Dan a couple of days later. ‘Or rather, felt one. Do you think there’s something wrong with me?’

‘Not necessarily.’ Dan yawned, still rumpled from the plane. He’d insisted on going out for lunch before he fell asleep, but maybe the beer wasn’t such a great idea. ‘In fact, I understand better than you might imagine.’

‘How come?’ Dan was one of the most logical people she’d ever met. That was partly why she’d confided in him, so he could bring her down to earth with a dose of common sense.

‘Because I have a story like that of my own.’ He ran a hand through his hair, leaving it sticking up in tufts. ‘Do you remember that year Lisa and I went to Europe? No, of course you don’t, but never mind. We were staying in the middle of the countryside in France, and I'd got up early one morning to fetch bread from a bakery in the next village. The croissants were incredible.' He yawned again. 'I remember the road clearly, stretching ahead for miles through lavender fields. There was no one about, only the birds singing and the sun on my back, and this amazing scent blowing towards me on the breeze. And then, all of a sudden, someone was walking beside me. I could sense their footsteps keeping time with mine, feel their breath on the air. And . . . yes – the smell of French cigarettes. I'd forgotten about that! I stopped and looked around a couple of times but there was no sign of anyone nearby. Whenever I set off again, so did they, and we walked all the way to the village together.'

'Were you frightened?'

'Not at all. I felt he didn't wish me any harm. I've always assumed it was a man, for some reason.' He shrugged. 'I've got no idea why he came to me or what he was trying to say – or if he had any message at all. It was just an ordinary road on an ordinary day, with a lonely ghost keeping me company.'

'Dan, that's beautiful!' She looked at him in surprise.

He laughed, embarrassed. 'I've never told anyone else. But since then, I've believed the air is full of echoes. And that sometimes if our minds and ears are open, we get to hear them.' He drained his glass. 'And now I'd better order coffee or your cousin will find me asleep with my head on the table.'

Who would have thought Dan would come up with a story like that? Ellie watched him as he stood at the bar: tall and broad-shouldered, hanging back a little as he waited his turn. Yet she shouldn't have been surprised. Dan might not have been good at small talk but he usually had something original to say when he did speak, because he was interested in so many things. She remembered laughing with Beth about the weird hobbies her brother had had at high school: astronomy, drawing comic-book characters, brewing his own beer. He'd never cared what other people thought, which she could admire now, although it had seemed a little freakish at the time. Somehow, he'd got away with it; perhaps because the guys who would have picked on him all wanted to hang out with Beth. She could imagine him alone on a road in France. He had always walked by himself.

And there was her imagination again, leading her into places it was safer not to go. Thank goodness, Max and Nathan were arriving now. Nathan had suggested they meet as he had some information to give her, and she'd thought Dan might enjoy a Sunday-morning drink at The Feathers. Besides, it would be interesting to get his take on Max. She still wasn't sure what to make of her cousin, although he greeted her so affectionately that she felt ashamed.

'Nathan's found out something rather interesting about our grandfather,' he said. 'You tell her, Nat, since you were the sleuth.'

'Arthur was Jewish,' Nat said. 'Or rather, his grandmother was. Who knows whether he observed the faith but he definitely had Jewish blood, so it was unlikely he'd have been a Fascist. Or married one, come to that. Although stranger things have happened, I suppose.'

What was it Eleanor had said? Her husband 'wasn't what she'd expected, not at all'. Well, it must have been a shock to discover she'd married a man who was partly Jewish. But in that case, why could Arthur have been arrested? Suddenly aware the others were looking at her, Ellie recovered herself. 'I suppose it was just as well the family moved to England when they did.'

'Yup. Arthur would have been classed as a *Mischling* – mixed blood – which was enough to have had him sent to a concentration camp.'

'You'd have thought my mother might have mentioned that fact,' Max said, 'but she claims to have forgotten.'

'Have you taken her out to lunch yet?' Ellie asked, keen to change the subject.

He groaned. 'Don't you start nagging. I get enough grief from Nathan.' He turned to Dan. 'So, tell us what brings you to London, my friend. Have you come chasing after the lovely Ellie?'

Ellie felt herself blushing furiously but Dan only laughed, not at all embarrassed. You see? she told herself. He thinks that's a ridiculous idea. Max's joke broke the ice and conversation was soon flowing. The four of them had plenty to talk about. Dan's work as a health-care journalist overlapped with several documentaries Nathan had produced, and Max, it turned out, was a fairly hilarious hypochondriac. What should have been a quick drink turned into a lazy lunch that stretched well into the afternoon. Still, at least now she knew Dan could fend for himself and wouldn't be relying on her to entertain him all day.

'There's something I have to do tomorrow,' she said as they were walking back to the apartment. 'Will you be OK on your own for a while?'

'Sure. I'm thinking of taking a sightseeing tour around London.' He grinned. 'I'll have to look at your famous clock and see if I feel anything.'

She was grateful he hadn't asked her what she was up to.

'This is going to be an awful waste of your time,' Gillian said, climbing into the cab. 'I told you, I only need someone to be with me when I'm going home. You'll have to hang around for hours.'

She was wearing a military-style coat with epaulettes, frogging and gold buttons, and a white fur hat that turned her head into a giant puffball. As she turned to fasten her seatbelt, the gap between her hat and collar exposed a few inches of skin, pale and powdery as marshmallow.

'It's fine,' Ellie said. 'I brought a book. You don't have to talk to me if you don't want.'

Gillian harrumphed. 'It's not a question of wanting. I might not feel like chatting, that's all. I don't think this will be a particularly pleasant experience.'

She had called Ellie out of the blue a couple of days before, saying that she would like to take advantage of her kind offer of help, if it were still available. 'I'm to have an initial round of chemotherapy to shrink the tumour,' she announced. 'And I've just been informed that someone has to collect me from the hospital after each session. They won't let me go home on my own, which is ridiculous, but there we are.'

Ellie could imagine how much she hated having to ask. It was such an admission of vulnerability and loneliness. Gillian in her immaculate house, with no one to turn to but a niece she hardly knew. 'Of course,' she'd said casually. 'I'd be happy to.'

So now here they were, on their way to the cancer centre near London Bridge. Ellie had scoped out the location and thought she might walk down the riverbank, if Gillian didn't want her around, and cross the Millennium Bridge to St Paul's Cathedral. She'd seen it from the sightseeing bus but hadn't had time for a proper look.

Gillian most definitely didn't want her around. 'I knew this would take forever,' she said crossly, coming back to the waiting room after her initial consultation. 'I have to wait for the results of my blood test before chemo even begins.' She took out her purse and pressed a few coins into Ellie's hand. 'Go and get yourself a coffee, or a bun or something.'

'I have money,' Ellie said. But her aunt wouldn't be dissuaded and it wasn't worth making a fuss. 'OK,' she said at last, 'see you in a couple of hours. But text if you need me to come back sooner.'

St Paul's stood in the ancient City founded by the

Romans, once enclosed by walls that led to the Tower of London. Ellie had learned from her research that a couple of nights before Eleanor died, the Germans had blasted the area with so many incendiary bombs that its narrow streets had been swallowed up in a carpet of fire. It was one of the worst nights, not just of the Blitz, but of the whole war: the second Great Fire of London, a reporter called it later. The firemen's hoses had run dry and the tide was too low in the Thames to supply more water, so all they could do was watch as the flames leapt from one empty building to another. Churches, offices and warehouses had burned to the ground, and St Paul's itself had only been saved by a miracle. Had Eleanor been in London then? She must have been terrified.

The bridge gave a spectacular view of the dome of St Paul's. Ellie walked towards it as though pulled by a magnet. She had seen a photograph of the cathedral on that terrible night, lit up by the blaze and wreathed in smoke like some heavenly temple floating above the clouds. It must have seemed as though the world was coming to an end. Maybe that was why these old buildings were so moving, because of the history they had survived. Yet somehow the cathedral didn't affect her in the way the clock tower had; it was on too grand a scale, marooned among the modern buildings like a holy relic. She pulled her coat more tightly around herself, and wandered on. There were a few pockets of antiquity left in the city's financial district – a church here, an old street sign there – but they were swallowed up in a sea of concrete, steel and mirrored glass.

When she got back to the cancer centre, a nurse told her that Gillian's treatment was under way but she was welcome to join her. 'She'd probably like the company.'

Ellie wasn't so sure. She found Gillian hooked up to a drip in a cubicle with a view over the river. 'How's it going?' She pulled up a chair.

'As well as could be expected, I suppose. Being pumped full of poison isn't how I'd choose to spend my time.' But Gillian sounded resigned. 'Had a good walk?'

'Sure. I went over the bridge to St Paul's and then through the City.'

'I haven't been a very dutiful aunt, have I?' Gillian sighed. 'The least I could have done was show you around London. Especially with my credentials.'

'Come on, it's thanks to you I got to see Big Ben. How cool is that? Anyway, you have a good excuse.' Before she could think better of it, Ellie went on, 'Can I ask you something, though?'

'I suppose so.' Her aunt looked wary.

'When we first met, you said you knew the real reason I'd come to London. What did you mean?'

Gillian frowned, shifting in the reclining chair, then spent a few unnecessary moments untangling the drip line. Eventually she sighed, looked Ellie in the face and said, 'I seem to have misjudged you, for which I apologise. We don't have to go into detail.'

'Although perhaps we should.' Ellie wasn't about to let her off the hook. 'This is the perfect time to get everything out in the open, surely.'

'Now you've got me at your mercy? Perhaps you're right, although I'm afraid you'll change your opinion of us when you find out. My mother and me, I mean.'

'Does that matter?'

'More than I expected. One likes to think of oneself as a decent human being, I suppose. It's easier to find the faults in other people than confront one's own.' Gillian glanced at Ellie, then quickly dropped her eyes. 'And harder to ignore the way we treated Alice with you sitting next to me.'

'You might be relieved to get it off your chest,' Ellie said, without thinking. 'If you'll pardon the expression,' she added hastily.

'Along with the cancer?' Gillian leaned back, closing her eyes. 'You might have a point. All right, then, here goes – for better or worse. You asked for this, remember.'

Chapter Fourteen

London, December 1940

Lord Winthrop instructed Cooke to drop Nell off on the north side of Vauxhall Bridge before they went on to his London residence, wherever that might be. He didn't offer her a return lift or ask whether she had anywhere to stay but that was a relief; all she wanted was to escape the frosty atmosphere inside the Bentley as quickly as possible. It was dark by now, with a wintry sleet falling as she hurried along the damp pavements to the Palace of Westminster. 'I'm coming, Arthur,' she promised silently, catching sight of the clock tower looming above. 'Hold on.' The Great Clock's familiar face was such an agonising reminder of her husband that she broke into a run, desperate to find him. So near and yet so far. Where could he be, if not here?

Picking her way over the uneven, cratered ground

of Old Palace Yard, she glanced up at the statue of Richard the Lionheart, defiantly waving his crooked sword. He represented every Londoner: bloody but unbowed. At the Parliament entrance, however, she came up against one of the bloodiest Londoners of all.

'I don't care who your husband is,' the policeman said. 'You could be married to Winston Churchill and I still wouldn't let you through without proper authorisation. Now clear off before I arrest you for causing a disturbance.'

He was making the most of his authority, staring down at her from under his helmet. Even Nell's usually reliable helpless look – lowered chin, appealing eyes, quivering lip – had failed to work. He was implacable.

'There's no need to be rude,' she muttered, retreating a safe distance while she decided what to do. Catching sight of the tube sign at Westminster underground station, she suddenly remembered the revolving door that Arthur had once shown her. Parliamentary staff could go through it to access the Palace directly from the station, via a passageway under the road. She would position herself by this door and wait to see if anyone she recognised emerged; even a sympathetic stranger might be persuaded to help. It was manned by one of the Home Guard, armed with a machine gun, who looked almost as fierce as the policeman.

An hour or so later, after having seen no one but a couple of officious-looking wardens she was too nervous to approach, her luck changed. The very person she could have hoped to see walked through from the corridors of power into the everyday world: Arthur's colleague, and friend.

'Mr Watkinson?' she cried, abandoning caution. 'Do you remember me? It's Eleanor Spelman, Arthur's wife.'

He pushed back his cap. 'Why, so it is. I thought you were safely in the country, though?'

'I was,' she said hurriedly, 'but Arthur telephoned earlier and I managed to cadge a lift to London. Please, do you have any idea what's happening?'

He glanced at the people rushing past, anxious to get home before the air-raid siren sounded. 'We can't talk here. Come up to the workroom with me.' He took a visitor's pass out of his jacket pocket and handed it to her. 'This'll get you through.'

He shepherded her back through the door, nodding at the guardsman, and down the tunnel into the colonnade, a covered walkway that ran along the side of the building. Nell had to contain her impatience as Mr Watkinson unlocked the door to the clock tower and proceeded to climb the stairs. You couldn't hurry Ralph, Arthur had told her. He was a quiet, deliberate man in his late fifties.

'You were lucky to catch me,' he said, when at last they had reached the door to the clockmakers' room. He unlocked this too, very slowly. 'I've been off sick for a while, and I shall be working back at company headquarters from tomorrow. The stairs are getting too much for me.' He ushered her inside, adding in a lower voice, 'Or so I'm told.'

'But with Arthur gone, there'll only be Mr Talbot left,' Nell exclaimed. 'How can he manage on his own?'

'They're bringing in a couple of outsiders, people I've never heard of. And there's the lad, too, for what he's worth. Not much, in my opinion.' Mr Watkinson sat on a bench, pulling up his trouser legs so they wouldn't crease, and indicated Nell should do the same. He glanced uneasily at the door.

'Where's Mr Talbot now?' Nell asked.

'Over at engineers' control. Spends most of his time there, these days.' He shifted uneasily. 'Something odd's going on, Mrs Spelman, I don't mind admitting.'

'Do you have any idea where my husband is,' Nell begged, 'and why anyone should want to question him?'

'I can't make head nor tail of it, to be honest. Arthur seems to have got himself mixed up in some sort of trouble but I've no idea what it could be. Two men arrived this afternoon and took him away. I don't know how he managed to make a telephone call; they wouldn't even let him change out of his overalls.'

'What sort of men?' Nell asked. 'Police?'

'I'm not sure. They weren't in uniform but I heard them say he was to answer some questions, and that it was a matter of national security.'

A sense of dread had settled in Nell's stomach like a cold, coiled snake. 'Couldn't anybody have stopped them?' she asked. 'If Arthur hadn't telephoned me, I'd have had no idea what had happened to him. People can't just be carted off like that!'

But of course, these days, people could; Mr Watkinson didn't need to point that out. 'Sorry,' she said, rubbing her forehead. 'This isn't your fault. Do you know where he's been taken?'

'Scotland Yard, that's what they said. So I suppose they must have been police, mustn't they?'

Nell dug her fingernails into her palms. 'I'll go there. They have to let me see him.'

'It's worth a try,' Watkinson said doubtfully, 'but I wouldn't get your hopes up. Still, at least it's close by. Won't take you more than ten minutes to walk there along Victoria Embankment.'

Nell tried to think clearly. 'I'd better collect Arthur's things, in case they keep him there a while. He'll need his jacket, for a start.'

'It's in there.' Mr Watkinson nodded towards a metal locker in a corner of the room. 'You'll find the key in that Coronation mug on his bench.' He rose to his feet. 'I'll wait for you outside, give you some privacy. Take your time, I'm not in a rush.'

Arthur's sports coat was hanging on a hook inside the cupboard and the siren suit and tin helmet he wore for fire-watching were rolled into a tidy bundle on the shelf underneath, along with the torch he'd brought from home. She took them, too. For reasons she couldn't explain, or didn't want to acknowledge, she sat on the bench to go through his jacket pockets. Inside she found a set of keys, his security pass and wallet, a clean handkerchief folded into a square, an engagement diary, the fountain pen she'd given him on his last birthday, and a small metal badge in the shape of a bundle of rods. She looked at it for some time before stowing his possessions away in her haversack. Why on earth would her husband be carrying an emblem of the Fascist party?

Arthur in police custody! The very idea was inconceivable. He was the most law-abiding of men, scrupulous in observing every regulation, from drawing the blackout blinds to the level of water in his weekly bath. He'd once found a blank book of clothing coupons in the street and insisted on handing them in. When she arrived at Scotland Yard and told the custody officer she was Mrs Arthur Spelman, he took her to an interview room and told her to wait; somebody would be along shortly to answer her questions. She had ended up being interrogated herself, however, by a detective sergeant in a shabby suit. Had she ever been a member of the Fascist party? Or attended their rallies? Did she agree with their beliefs? Had she lived in Germany for any length of time or travelled there recently? Where could she be contacted if they needed to question her again?

She answered concisely, her anger growing. 'May I ask what my husband is meant to have done?' she asked coldly, when the stream of questions had at last dried up.

'You can ask but I'm not at liberty to tell you,' the detective replied. Davis, his name was. 'Or not in any detail, anyway.'

'This is a travesty,' she burst out. 'You can't lock him up just because his parents are German!'

'We can lock up anyone who's working with the enemy, I'm pleased to say.' He gave her a chilly smile. 'With the minimum of fuss.'

'I've never heard anything so ridiculous! Arthur's completely loyal to this country.'

'Then you've got nothing to worry about,' the policeman replied. It was an exchange he'd probably had many times before. 'He'll be released after questioning and home in a jiffy.'

Still, he had at least allowed her to give Arthur his jacket, after it had been thoroughly checked. The visit was highly irregular, he stressed, only granted as a favour because she had cooperated with enquiries. She and Arthur weren't allowed to touch. They had to keep six feet apart and had ten minutes, at most, in which to talk. And they were strictly forbidden from discussing anything to do with Arthur's 'situation'.

When she saw him, she had to struggle to keep her composure. He was trying so hard to maintain his dignity, too, to keep a straight back as he walked into the interview room beside a uniformed officer, his hands cuffed in front of him. They sat facing each other across a wide table while the constable stood sentry by the door.

'Nell?' he asked, staring at her with desperate eyes. 'What on earth are you doing here?'

'Lord Winthrop gave me a lift. I had to come, Arthur. You mustn't worry, everything will be all right.'

He carried on looking at her without a word, as though he were trying to memorise her face.

'Here's your jacket,' she said, passing it over. 'Just as well I emptied the pockets,' she added, seeing the flash of alarm in his eyes. 'I found that handkerchief you've been on at me to wash.'

A flush crept up his neck. 'Do you need your wallet?' she asked. 'Or anything else?'

He shook his head. 'Is Lord Winthrop taking you back again? I can't bear to think of you here, darling, mixed up in all of this. Please, you must go home. London is far too dangerous.'

'But I had to see you. This has all been a silly mistake, I'm sure.' She longed to take his hands in hers, to smooth back the hair from his forehead and comfort him. 'We'll soon have it straightened out.'

'That might not be possible. You must understand, I only wanted to—' The policeman coughed, pointedly, and Arthur stopped speaking. A muscle worked in his cheek. Then he cleared his throat and said, 'Strange what comes to mind at times like these. Do you remember when my bicycle was stolen?'

'Of course.' Arthur had been extremely proud of his Raleigh with Sturmey-Archer three-speed gears, and a particularly comfortable saddle that he'd customised himself. He'd reported the theft but the police had shown little interest, so he'd scoured the local papers for bicycles advertised for sale, and let it be known at every local market that he wanted to buy one second-hand. Eventually he had been offered his own Raleigh by a weaselly youth on a street corner, and had brought a policeman along with him when he arrived with the cash to buy it back. But what did his bicycle have to do with anything?

'I was thinking about the row we had,' he went on. 'Turns out you were right all along.'

It had been one of their rare arguments. She had been angry with Arthur because of the risk he was running, getting mixed up with the wrong sort of people. 'You should leave criminals to the police,' she had told him.

'But I'm tired of waiting for them to act,' he'd replied. 'If one wants something done, one has to do it oneself.'

Finally, now she understood. 'I'm your wife,' she said, smiling at him. 'Of course I was right. Listen, is there anyone you want me to telephone? Your mother, perhaps?' Arthur's father had died suddenly in the spring, just after Alice was born.

'No, please don't. She mustn't know I'm here, it would only upset her. Go back to the country, darling, take care of Alice and try not to worry about me.' He did his best to smile, too.

'I have your watch.' She pulled it out from under her blouse. 'We'll carry on thinking of each other at nine. Stay strong, my darling.'

There was nothing more to be said; she left the room with her head high.

'There's something odd going on,' Mr Watkinson had said. Arthur was evidently of the same opinion, and had decided to carry out his own investigation. She knew he would have nothing to do with Fascists under normal circumstances. He hated everything they stood for: violence, mob rule, anti-Semitism. Surely the police would realise that, and let him go? Yet she couldn't leave the city until she was certain.

She made her way slowly through the dark, up Haymarket towards Regent Street. She felt safest on foot at night, ever since she'd seen the wreck of a bus that had crashed headlong into a bomb crater. She kept her eyes on the white stripe painted along the pavement's edge and inched along with the help of Arthur's torch, trained downwards. Central London had been badly knocked about; the pavement beneath her feet was fractured and uneven, and fragments of glass that had escaped the street sweepers' brooms glittered in her torch beam. On she went, around the vortex of Piccadilly Circus and up into the sweep of Regent Street. Several of the department stores had shelters in the basement; if Dickins and Jones were full, she might try Liberty's or John Lewis. John Lewis had been hit by incendiaries a couple of months before, when two hundred people had been sleeping in the shelter, but she couldn't waste time worrying about bombs. One would either get you or it wouldn't, and there was no point fretting.

In the basement of Dickins and Jones, mattresses were laid out on the floor like bricks on a herringbone path. She managed to bag one in the corner, with a nail on the wall above to hang up her coat and a shelf for her haversack. It cost sixpence for the privilege but she had enough money. The shelter was filling up fast. A middle-aged couple with a carpet bag took the mattresses next to hers and agreed to guard her place while she queued for tea and a sandwich from the refreshment counter. She ate and drank quickly, standing up, and when she had finished, locked herself in a cubicle of the ladies' lavatory to go through Arthur's things. She took out the badge and stared at it, running her fingers over the smooth enamel, then opened the engagement diary and flicked through. A card had been pushed between the pages. *The Rt Hon Lord Lionel Winthrop, House of Lords, London SW1A* was printed on the front, and on the back was written: *Flat 227, Howard House, Dolphin Square*. She knew they had met, yet it seemed odd that Lord Winthrop should have given Arthur his home address, and odder still that Arthur hadn't mentioned this fact to her.

She flicked through the pages of his engagement diary, but no meeting seemed to have been recorded with an LW. Several days had been marked 'FW', which she assumed stood for Fire Watching. Arthur often stayed overnight, as his shifts might last till the early hours. Apart from those sessions and the odd birthday (including hers, she was glad to see) or dentist's appointment, the diary was virtually empty so one particular entry stood out. The day before, another address had been written down in Arthur's careful script: *173, Park West, Edgware Road, W2*. And a time: *seven p.m.*

Nell leant back against the lavatory cistern, thinking.

The badge was a mystery she would have to put to one side for the time being. The appointment in West London deserved closer attention, though. Was it a coincidence that Arthur should have been taken in for questioning the very next day? She put the diary back in her satchel and took out his wallet, feeling a little disloyal as she went through it. Inside she found three one pound notes, a first-class stamp, a dry-cleaning ticket and a tiny snapshot of her, the first she'd given him. The money would keep her going for a few days, added to the amount she already had.

People came and went from the shelter all night: using the lavatory, returning from work, stepping outside for a smoke. Every couple of hours, someone flashed a torch across the sea of bodies stretched out on the floor. The woman whose head lay only inches away from Nell's muttered and groaned, while her husband snored with a particularly high-pitched whistle. The peace of Orchard House had left Nell unprepared for this mass of strangers in such close proximity. To calm herself, she pictured Alice, warm in her nest of blankets, and the evacuees on the floor above: Susan dreaming of babies to be bathed and fed, Brenda of stealing through the woods to ambush the enemy, Janet of galloping over the fields on horseback, Timothy of gunning his Spitfire through the clouds, Malcolm of running into his mother's arms. She would do anything to keep them safe, she thought, drifting into sleep. Anything at all.

⋆ ⋆ ⋆

Early the next morning, Nell threaded her way through the sleeping figures and out into the iron-grey air. The Lyons Corner House on Piccadilly Circus was just opening, so she treated herself to a breakfast of tea and Spam fritters before heading back towards the river. After almost a month away, she was shocked as daylight revealed the state of the city. London looked dirty and neglected, its streets piled with sandbags and shattered roof tiles. Rounding a corner, she was confronted by a jagged gap in the buildings and a view of barrage balloons in the sky beyond, floating over a wasteland of rubble. How many more people were emerging that morning to find themselves homeless? Yet there was no point crying over spilt milk. The countryside had made Nell softer than she could afford; now it was time to gather up her wits, and use them.

It took her another hour to reach Dolphin Square, a modern block of flats just past Vauxhall Bridge that she knew from her walks along the river with Arthur. She felt certain Lord Winthrop had something to do with his predicament. It was hard to pinpoint what that something was, but she had so few leads to follow that she might as well start with His Lordship – and if he was only paying a brief visit to London, the sooner the better. Feeling suddenly conspicuous as she approached the buildings, she pulled out Arthur's siren suit and helmet from her haversack and dodged behind a telephone box to put them on, scooping up her hair and pulling the helmet low over her eyes. Now she was anonymous.

Dolphin Square was the size of a village all on its own: built out of red brick with various blocks making up a rectangle, it rose ten storeys high. She and Arthur had once looked through the grand arched entrance into the central gardens beyond, but had felt too intimidated to go any further. Now, Nell walked briskly through, looking about as though taking an inventory. There were signs pointing down to an air raid shelter, and a red cross marking what seemed to be a first-aid post. Most of the windows were shuttered; she guessed many of the residents had moved to a safer spot. Howard House lay on the west side of the square, with another central archway that led through to a slip road beyond. Nell could imagine Lord Winthrop gazing down at her from his eyrie as she hugged the side of the building, and felt glad of the tin helmet. What was it about him that made her feel uncomfortable? It seemed strange that he should have been so keen to meet Arthur, husband of the girl who'd spurned his son, and that he should have quizzed him at such length about the clock tower. But he was an eccentric, everyone knew that. Lady Winthrop had too much empathy and he had too little; that's just how they were made.

Emerging onto the slip road, she saw a line of chauffeured cars idling like basking sharks and shrank back. Cooke and the Bentley were probably among them. Hastily retreating, she resumed her patrol around the gardens, keeping an eye on the trickle of people who were filing through the archway and out to the important business of their day. She nearly missed her quarry, but the familiar shambling, flat-footed gait of a portly gentleman in a pinstriped suit caught her eye at the last moment. She had assumed Lord Winthrop would have been alone, yet this person was talking to a younger, thinner man wearing a cloth cap and donkey jacket. Quickening her pace, she managed to catch a glimpse of the pair before they shook hands in parting. It was indeed His Lordship, accompanied by Bill Talbot. She had to look twice to make sure, but there could be no mistake. Arthur had pointed Talbot out to her once from a distance and she'd seen the port-wine birthmark splashed across the left side of his face. Another reason for him to feel angry at the world, Arthur had said.

A car slid forward and Cooke climbed out of it to open the door for his employer. Bill Talbot walked off in the opposite direction, his hands in his pockets and shoulders hunched against the cold. Nell hurried after him, her head full of questions. For one thing, why would Bill Talbot have been meeting Lord Winthrop at his home? Talbot strode on, past Vauxhall Bridge and along the riverbank. As the Houses of Parliament came into view, he stopped for a moment, looking up at the clock tower, and Nell hung back, although he could have had no idea who she was. It was coming up to nine o'clock. She leant against the wall, taking the weight of the haversack off her back for a moment, as the quarter bells began to ring out the Westminster Chimes. Nell repeated the words accompanying the melody that were inscribed on a plaque in the tower as she waited for Big Ben to strike: 'All through this hour, Lord be my guide, That by Thy power, no foot shall slide.'

When she looked again, Talbot had vanished. She rushed on towards the Palace, just in time to catch a glimpse of him disappearing through the street-level entrance. So that was that, as she knew from yesterday's experience – until she remembered Arthur's security pass. It was worth a try, and the helmet and armband would add to her credibility. Her mouth dry, she marched purposefully towards the policeman on duty and flashed him the most dazzling smile she could muster, waving the pass in his general direction. Grinning back, he waved her through. Trying not to break into a run, she followed Talbot through shadowy Westminster Hall, up the steps to St Stephen's Hall and along towards the central lobby separating the House of Commons from the House of Lords. And there, she lost him; for good this time.

He went through a door she remembered Arthur once showing her, which led down to a central vault with passages radiating from it like the spokes of a wheel. Here lay the workshops belonging to the Palace's craftsmen: carpenters and French polishers, electricians and plumbers, stained-glass artists, stone masons and seamstresses. She daren't risk following: there were fewer people around in the workshops and a stranger would be more conspicuous. Instead, she walked slowly back into the lobby and sat on a pile of sandbags. The place felt empty and forlorn, sandbags piled against the walls and most of the beautiful stained-glass windows boarded over or blown out. The niches where statues of kings, queens and saints once stood were empty, and only a few maintenance men walked through the place that should have thronged with life. Parliament was no longer sitting at the Palace of Westminster, Arthur had said; its prominent location was considered too dangerous. Both the House of Lords and the Commons were meeting secretly elsewhere. Well, the location was meant to be a secret but most of the Parliamentary staff knew by now: Church House, close to Westminster Abbey on the other side of the street.

'I say! You there!' With a start, Nell turned to see a warden in ARP uniform marching towards her. She looked around but there was no one else in sight.

'You're the one I want,' the man said. He walked up to Nell and loomed over her, bristling with indignation. 'Unless there are any other firewatchers in the vicinity. What do you mean by leaving the cupboard in such a state?'

Nell got to her feet. 'Um, I don't think that was me.'

'Then who else was responsible? Do you think Herr Hitler sneaked into the Palace and disordered our supplies?'

'Probably not,' Nell replied, smiling.

'This isn't a laughing matter, young lady. You're to come with me this minute and tidy everything away. Hurry up, please. Chop, chop.' The warden turned on his heel and stalked off, not waiting for a response. Nell hurried along behind.

'I know you're tired, but so are we all,' he flung over his shoulder. 'And quite possibly hungry, and a little afraid. That's no excuse for laziness. Once standards start to slip, the effect is contagious. One bad apple spoils the whole barrel.'

He led the way downstairs, Nell following with her head lowered. The door to the engineers' control room was shut, she was relieved to notice as they passed. The cupboard in question stood halfway along one corridor. Nell's guide flung open the door and stood back, waving his arm at the chaos inside. 'Disgraceful! Would your husband tolerate such a muddle in his home?'

Nell shook her head. 'I'm sorry. This is my first shift, you see. I don't know the ropes.'

The warden sighed, and pointed at each section of the cupboard in turn. 'Fire buckets to be stacked, stirrup hoses coiled, axes and shovels leant against the wall, log book initialled after inspection and put on the shelf. Is that clear?' Nell nodded. 'Good. I shall expect to see this cupboard spick and span from now on.' And he strode away, keys jangling.

Arthur would never have left the place in such a shambles, Nell thought, as she began to restore order. In fact, the mess was probably a result of him not being here. She could picture him methodically, uncomplainingly, putting everything to rights, just as she was doing now. And there were his initials in the log book; she felt her heart would burst, looking at them. Apart from AS, there seemed to be only one other regular cupboard-tidier: the initials HC were dotted sporadically through the pages.

When the cupboard was transformed, she stowed her haversack in a dark corner under a shelf at the very back, then sorted through Arthur's keys to find out which one would fit the lock. She needed somewhere to store her things and it might as well be here. A plan was forming in her mind. Her husband was innocent, she knew it in her bones, which meant someone must have led him along a dangerous path for reasons she didn't yet understand. She felt sure Lord Winthrop was involved and that was her fault, because she had introduced Arthur to him, and also – she remembered with a sinking heart – blabbed about Bill Talbot. It was too late for regrets, though. What she had to concentrate on now was finding evidence and presenting it to Detective Sergeant Davis. She hadn't the faintest idea how to set about doing that but one thing, at least, was clear: she had to fight for her husband, because nobody else would.

Chapter Fifteen

London, December 1940

Nell set about establishing a base for herself. She found municipal baths in a street the other side of Westminster Abbey and paid extra for a first-class cubicle, with soap and a towel. She should stay in the area, she decided, as the warmth of the water seeped into her frozen bones: the answer to this mystery lay buried somewhere in the Palace of Westminster, and she should dig here to find it. The siren suit and Arthur's pass would get her into the building; she had used Arthur's pen to add an 'M' to the front of his first name and smudged the final letters with a drop of water to transform herself into Martha Spelman. Provided she kept her head down and stuck to the maintenance areas and other places one might expect to find a firewatcher, she ought to be safe enough. Even if she ran into Bill Talbot, he wouldn't know who she was.

After her bath, she walked past the tall blocks of a housing estate in search of a shelter for the night. She found one in the basement of Caxton Hall, an imposing red-brick building that looked vaguely familiar; she'd come back later that evening and hope to bag a good spot. There was a British restaurant set up in a church hall around the corner where she bought herself lunch for ninepence: mince and mashed potato, followed by steamed jam sponge. Suitably fortified, she rang her mother from a public telephone box to tell her that everything was fine and she'd be back in a few days – probably by the weekend, or Monday at the latest.

'I should hope so,' Rose said, sounding very faint and far away. 'It's Christmas next Wednesday. Are you sure you're all right, dear? Is your business finished?'

'Almost. How's Alice?' Nell asked, gripping the receiver as she strained to hear. 'And everyone else, of course.'

'As well as can be expected. Susan's spoiling the baby to death, lugging her about everywhere. And we're losing Malcolm. His mother's coming to fetch him tomorrow, she says she wants him home for Christmas. I told her—'

But already the pips were sounding. 'Ma, I haven't got any more change,' Nell cried over the frantic beeping. 'I'll ring again soon, I promise.' And with that, the line went dead.

She couldn't afford to think about Alice; there was no point upsetting herself for no reason. Her daughter was happy and safe, for which she was thankful. Yet there was an ache in Nell's heart that couldn't be wished away. Passing Westminster Abbey, on an impulse she walked through the huge porch and down the nave to pay her respects at the tomb of the Unknown Soldier, brought back from France after the last war. How many more corpses were lying there now? She took a seat in an out-of-the-way pew near the back of the church, curled up with her head on a hassock and the helmet by her side, and slept.

She woke up a couple of hours later, yawned and stretched, then put on her helmet and returned to the Houses of Parliament, waving her pass with a casual air and strolling down to the vault. The door to the store cupboard was unlocked, which should have alerted her, but she pushed it open anyway. The light was on, and a girl with curly blonde hair was sitting on an upturned bucket, smoking.

'Well, hello,' she said, in an unexpectedly gravelly voice. 'Who are you?'

'The new firewatcher,' Nell replied, startled. 'I was just coming to check the cupboard.'

'How very keen of you. And in full regalia, I see. Even the helmet.' She looked at Nell with her head on one side like a bright, naughty bird. 'You don't have to wear it every minute of the day, you know.'

'Best to be prepared.' Nell put her hands in her pockets and stood there awkwardly.

The girl laughed. 'Dyb, dyb, dyb *et cetera*.' She was all rosy and gold, like a painted cherub on a chapel ceiling. 'Fancy a cig?' she went on. 'I was coming to check the cupboard too. We left it in a hell of a mess last night but some good fairy seems to have tidied everything away.'

'Thanks.' Nell took a cigarette, trying to act normally.

'My name's Henrietta Carmichael, by the way.' The cherub stood, extending her hand. 'Known generally as Hetta.'

'Eleanor Spelman. Do call me Nell.' She shook hands, and then remembered. 'Although, actually, Martha is my real name.'

'Is it, indeed?' Hetta extracted a lighter from her pocket, lit a cigarette of her own and held the flame towards Nell. She narrowed her eyes through a cloud of smoke. 'And where have you sprung from, Martha Nell?'

'I'm Arthur's wife. Arthur Spelman, that is. AS.' Nell nodded in the direction of the logbook. 'He's had to go away so I'm taking over his duties for a while.'

'Go away? That's rather sudden.'

'A family emergency, I'm afraid. But he didn't want to let anyone down.'

Hetta digested this information. 'And is that your haversack in the corner?' she asked. 'I was about to take it to Lost Property.'

'So it is.' Nell feigned surprise; she'd never been much good at acting. 'I knew I must have left it somewhere,' she added lamely.

Hetta gave her another appraising stare from round blue eyes that might have been childlike, were it not for their expression. She was tiny, a good head shorter than Nell, and although she was wearing the familiar uniform of tweed skirt, twinset and pearls, the cut and fabric of her clothes marked them out as singularly chic. Her small, shapely legs were clad in silk stockings, and she looked far too *soignée* to go scrambling about over roofs. If that's what firewatchers were supposed to do; Nell wasn't quite sure.

'Why don't I stand you a cup of tea?' Hetta said. 'To thank you for your sterling efforts in the tidying department.'

Nell sensed Hetta watching her closely as she collected her belongings and they made their way upstairs. She had to confess that she hadn't yet discovered the canteen, and indeed that Arthur hadn't shown her where anything was, not even the fire-watching post she was meant to be manning. 'But you've been vetted?' Hetta asked. 'You have a security pass?'

'Oh, yes,' Nell replied airily. 'All that's been sorted out.'

Several people greeted Hetta by name; she seemed particularly popular with the various policemen dotted about. 'Do you work here?' Nell asked, suddenly dreading she might have crossed paths with someone terribly important. Hetta gave her sardonic smile and said there was no need to look alarmed, she was merely a secretary.

The canteen was an airy room in an annexe beside Westminster Hall, laid out with the communal tables and self-service counter that the war had made familiar.

They queued for their tea and Hetta led the way to a secluded table. She heaped sugar into her cup, cut a Bath bun into quarters and said conversationally, 'So would you care to explain what you're really doing?'

'What do you mean?' Nell's heart lurched.

'I might be a lowly secretary but I'm not a fool. Why are you wandering around the Houses of Parliament without a clue where you're going or what you're supposed to be doing? I was in two minds whether to hand you over to the custodians straight away, but you intrigue me. And you did tidy the cupboard.'

Nell glanced around the room. 'Looking for an escape route?' Hetta asked. 'Or hoping for inspiration? You might as well tell me the truth.'

'All right then.' She took a deep breath, wondering where to begin. 'Do you know Arthur, my husband?'

'I've met him once or twice. He's a clockmaker, isn't he?'

Nell nodded. 'Well, he's been taken in for questioning by the police. I think he's stumbled across some kind of wrongdoing and decided to investigate on his own. Or maybe he's being framed. I found a Fascist badge in his jacket pocket but he wouldn't have anything to do with Mosley's lot. He's partly Jewish, you see.' Why did she always feel a desire to apologise when she said that?

'He seems an inoffensive chap,' Hetta said. 'Why would anyone want to frame him?'

'To get him out of the way, perhaps?' Nell leaned

forward. 'There's a man who's always resented Arthur and he was sniffing around the workshops this morning. He's not the only one, though. Someone else is involved, a member of the House of Lords. I've seen the two of them together and they're planning something, I'm sure of it.'

'And you think if you hang about here in your husband's siren suit, you're going to magically uncover the plot? Well, good luck with that.' Hetta took out her cigarettes.

'Have one of mine.' Nell reached in her satchel. She had become a confirmed smoker over the past few weeks; the habit helped calm her nerves, and she was sure Arthur wouldn't really mind, given the circumstances. 'What else can I do?' she went on, offering Hetta the pack. 'I've nothing else to go on, except—'

'Except what?' Hetta's eyes were bluer and sharper than ever as she helped herself to a cigarette.

'Arthur went to a meeting in West London, the day before he was arrested. I saw the address in his diary.'

'Would you mind telling me what that address was?'

'Park West, I don't remember the number.' Nell wasn't going to hand over everything on a plate. 'It's off the Edgware Road. I thought I might go there.'

'And do what?'

She shrugged. 'I don't know. Just have a look at the place, I suppose. See what kind of people live there.'

Hetta twirled a blonde curl thoughtfully around her finger. 'Be careful. If your husband has been framed, there's nothing to say you won't be, too. And if you start spreading rumours about a peer of the realm, you could end up in serious trouble.'

'I have to try. Arthur doesn't have anyone one else on his side.' Nell hesitated. 'Are you going to tell the authorities about me?'

'I'm not sure. May I see your pass?'

Nell pushed it across the table and Hetta took a look. She shook her head, raising her eyebrows. 'Martha and Arthur, the conveniently rhyming couple. Hardly sophisticated, is it? Still, full marks for ingenuity.' She passed it back. 'No, I'm going to keep you around for entertainment value. I could do with some company and I've a hunch you'll be good value. You'll have to do your bit, though. In the fire-watching department, I mean.'

'Oh, I will. Thanks.' Nell was dizzy with relief. 'That's jolly decent of you.'

'It is, isn't it?' Hetta smiled. 'I've rather surprised myself. Hope it's not a decision I'll come to regret.'

'The thing is, the Palace of Westminster – or the Houses of Parliament, or whatever you want to call the place – is a world unto itself, with smaller worlds inside it. Like a continent with different countries, or a galaxy whose planets don't communicate.' Hetta was warming to her theme. 'Or a country-house weekend, when the guests have each brought their own staff and there'll be trouble in the servants' hall.'

Nell laughed uncertainly. Hetta was taking her on a tour of the building, introducing this new volunteer to a variety of useful people. They had started off in the basement headquarters of the Westminster ARP, and from there she had met the ladies who ran the canteen, nurses in the First Aid post, several members of the Home Guard and, most important of all, many of the ex-servicemen who policed the whole building, known as custodians. 'Teddy bears, most of them, although some might look a little alarming.' Then they had walked along the colonnade, up a staircase and through an unobtrusive door onto what looked like a fire escape. 'Hold the handrail,' Hetta warned. 'It can get slippery up here.'

Nell followed her up the spiral metal steps and stepped out onto a flat roof. 'My goodness.' She gazed around, hands on hips. 'What a view!'

They'd emerged into another world: a landscape of iron and slate with gutters for paths, mountains made of tiles, and valleys that were courtyards far below. The same skilled Victorian workmanship was evident here, although few people would ever see it: carved stone ledges and pediments, domes and spires, some of them gilded, and small green crowns at the points where roofs and buildings intersected. Only a few birds wheeling through the darkening sky kept them company. Nell could see for miles in every direction – up the river to Waterloo Bridge, and across to the tall white towers of Battersea Power Station and the sprawl of St Thomas's Hospital on the opposite bank. A mist rolling off the water had settled in the streets like a soft grey blanket, pierced by the spires of churches and chimney pots crowning rooftops, and the silver barrage balloons swayed dreamily on their cables in the dusk. Soon there would be searchlights roaming the sky and anti-aircraft guns adding their thunder to the cacophony of sirens, aeroplane engines and bombs. For now, the fairy-tale city held its breath, waiting for whatever the night would bring.

'So this is our patch. Got your bearings?' Hetta asked. 'We're on the east side of the building, above the terrace. That's the roof of Westminster Hall,' she pointed in the opposite direction, 'and we're standing on top of the Commons Chamber, more or less. Big Ben and the clock tower are behind us, as you see, so you won't lose track of the time, and there,' she turned in a semicircle, 'is the tower over the central lobby, and the Victoria Tower beyond that. Covered in scaffolding at the moment, unfortunately, which doubles the fire risk.' She glanced at Nell. 'Think you can hold your nerve? It can get pretty hairy up here in a raid.'

'I've lived through a few of them,' Nell replied. 'But tell me what to do again.'

'If it's an incendiary, tackle it with your stirrup pump. Spray, remember? Only use the jet setting for fires; if you jet a bomb, you'll blow it to pieces. Or you can smother the thing with a sandbag if the pump's impossible. There's not much you can do with a high explosive except raise the alarm.'

'By the telephone downstairs?'

Hetta nodded. 'And blow your whistle too, to clear the building. The National Fire Service will take over.

Sometimes the Abbey firewatchers lend a hand – they're much better organised than we are. None of the MPs will go scrambling over roofs and the Home Guard aren't keen either. Your husband's not one of them, is he?'

'No. He doesn't like guns or marching about in a group.'

Hetta grinned. 'Very sensible. Now come down and I'll show you our sleeping quarters. Pretty basic, I'm afraid, so don't get your hopes up.'

Five or six truckle beds had been set up in a corridor on the floor below, with an army blanket folded on each thin mattress. 'This is where we girls bunk down,' Hetta said. 'A couple of nurses use the place too, but they'll be going once Parliament's in recess.'

'And if the alert doesn't sound, I can just sleep through?'

'That's right. Sounds appealing right now.' Hetta sat on one of the beds. 'I have the most thumping hangover.'

Nell sat on another. 'I can do a shift every night if that would be useful.'

'I'll say. Are you sure?' Hetta inspected her again. 'Where are you staying at the minute?'

'Various places. I was thinking of the shelter at Caxton Hall for tonight.'

'Flitting about, then, like me.' She lay back, folding her arms behind her head. 'You'd be better off here. One thing, though. If there's an axe propped outside the store cupboard, knock and come back in fifteen minutes.' She yawned. 'Hardly the most romantic place but it's hard to find any privacy these days. Think you can look after yourself for a while? I might get some shut-eye before it all kicks off. I'll be on duty in an hour or so. Join me if you like.'

Nell gathered her things and said goodbye but Hetta was already asleep, her angelic face pillowed in the crook of her arm. She went downstairs to change out of the siren suit and stow it with her helmet and rucksack back in the cupboard, feeling hopeful for the first time since she'd arrived in London. Once outside, she was sufficiently buoyed to set off for the Edgware Road, despite Hetta's warning. What was the harm in taking a look? With a bit of luck, she might be able to get there and back before the alert sounded.

She was about to descend the steps to the underground when she spotted Bill Talbot walking towards her. They were about to cross paths when he swerved abruptly to the right and yanked open the door to a pub. Without thinking, she followed him through. The blackout blinds had been drawn and the saloon bar was dimly lit by several red-shaded lamps, the air thick with cigarette smoke. It felt as though she were stepping onto a stage set. An elderly man with a dog at his feet stared into his glass while two Auxiliary Territorial Service girls murmured in low, confidential voices, their heads close together.

She walked past Bill Talbot and waited at the bar while he ordered a drink – she didn't catch what – leaning her bottom against the stool in a noncommittal way while working out her approach. She'd never been in a pub on her own and assumed people would think she was a tart, despite her sensible shoes. Yet the barmaid, a sallow-faced woman with dyed jet-black hair standing up like a guardsman's bearskin, greeted her pleasantly enough.

'I'll have a small sherry while I wait for my friend to arrive,' she said, cautiously edging one buttock onto the seat.

They were all out of sherry, the woman said, but Nell was welcome to a pink gin, or a gin and orange, or a gin on the rocks. She chose a pink gin because that sounded the most innocuous. Spotting a newspaper on the bar close to where Talbot was sitting, she asked him whether she might have a look. 'It's not yours, is it? I'm assuming someone's left it behind.'

'Feel free,' he grunted, scarcely bothering to look at her.

'Thank you so much.' She smiled pleasantly. He was utterly charmless, quite apart from the birthmark, yet she would persevere. What must it be like to present that face to the world, to know that a stranger's first reaction would be one of revulsion? Even in this subdued light, his eye stared out from what looked like a slab of raw meat, as though his skin had been flayed. And then she remembered all the times Arthur had come home smarting and anxious from a confrontation with Bill Talbot, and hardened her heart.

She leafed through the paper. Three babies had been lowered from a torpedoed liner in baskets, one of them marked, 'Baby – with care', and winched onto the rescue boat by crane. 'Would you believe it?' she exclaimed, showing the barmaid the headline and relaying snippets from the article beneath. The captain had gone down with his ship, which they agreed was heroic and just as it should be.

'More fool him.' Talbot gave a sour laugh.

A honeymoon couple had died, too, she read aloud, returning to their cabin to retrieve wedding presents, and a ship's steward, trying to find the Spitfire fund raised from staff wages and tips.

'Spitfire fund!' Bill Talbot snorted. 'I ask you.'

'Now then, Bill,' said the barmaid. 'Keep a civil tongue in your head.'

He muttered something inaudible, hunched over his tankard.

'Don't mind him,' the woman reassured Nell. 'I'm going through to the public bar but call if you need anything.'

Nell forced herself to smile chummily at Talbot. She told him that she'd given three good saucepans to the Spitfire fund and wished she hadn't now. 'They're probably rusting away in a scrapyard somewhere.'

'Course they bloody are,' he grunted. 'If my missus gave away three saucepans, I'd send her to fetch them back pretty sharpish.' He took out a packet of cigarettes and flipped open the lid, then crumpled it in disgust and tossed it on the floor.

'Have one of mine.' Nell slid her packet along the bar.

'All right, then,' he said warily, snatching at it as though she might change her mind. 'Don't mind if I do.'

Nell glanced over her shoulder; the two women were deep in conversation and the old man was still contemplating his beer. 'Feels like we've been taken for mugs, don't you think?' she said. 'Bet there are still plenty of saucepans in the kitchens at Buckingham Palace.'

Talbot struck a match and bent his head to the flame. His hair was flecked with dandruff along the parting and his clothes smelt of stale food. What was she doing?

'That's for sure.' He stared at her, inhaling deeply. 'Makes me sick, the Queen trying to pretend she's one of us. "Looking the East End in the face," my eye! She's not spending the night in an Anderson, is she?'

'What does she know what it's like, waiting three hours in a queue for a piece of scrag end?' Nell racked her brains for other examples of royal privilege. 'Or running out of coins for the gas meter?'

Talbot was still scrutinising her. 'Have we met before?' he asked.

'I don't think so.' She was flustered by the suddenness of the question. 'No, I would have remembered.' Of course she would; once seen, never forgotten.

He smiled. 'I know who you are. I've seen your photograph. You're Spelman's wife, aren't you? I've a good memory for faces.'

Nell thought about denying it, but in one swift

movement he had grabbed her handbag and spilled its contents on the bar.

'Well, well, well. Eleanor Spelman,' he said, examining her identity card. He gave an unpleasant laugh and said with a leer, 'So that's how it is, eh? When the cat's away, the mice will play.'

'I know who you are, too, Mr Talbot.' Nell managed to keep her voice steady. 'You've heard, then, about my husband? I've been trying to find out exactly what's happened but no luck so far.'

'Can't help you there.' Talbot turned away, raising the glass to his lips. Outside, the wail of a siren started. The old man's dog began to whine and the women drew apart, still talking as they reached for their caps.

'You're right, I was hoping to speak to you.' There wasn't much time. 'To offer my services. I'm not like Arthur, you see. I'd be discreet and not get into trouble.'

That caught his attention. He stared at her, waiting.

'I found this badge,' she said hastily, fumbling for the thing in her pocket and laying it on the bar. 'I wanted to come with Arthur to the meeting but he told me wives weren't allowed.' Talbot might think she was a fool but it was worth a shot.

'I don't know what you're talking about,' he said, glancing at the badge without any emotion. 'What meeting?'

'The one in Park West.' Nell gulped her gin, noticing the flicker of recognition in his eyes. 'It sounded like the sort of thing that would interest me.'

'Recipes and knitting patterns, you mean?' He drained his beer and pushed the glass away.

'A different way of thinking, if you catch my drift.' She was gabbling now, and tried to slow down. 'Fancy another? Let me buy you a chaser. A quick one, for the road. Set you up for the night ahead.' She waved at the barmaid whom she could see through an archway, putting on her coat. 'Whisky, please, if you have it. My husband thinks too much, that's his problem,' she went on as she turned back to Talbot, 'and it makes him indecisive. I'm more of a one for action.' Silently she apologised to Arthur for her disloyalty.

'Drink up,' the barmaid said. 'Best not to hang about.'

Nell paid for the whisky and slid it along the bar. 'Have you ever been to Park West?' she asked, glancing at Talbot with her head to one side in a manner she hoped was coquettish. 'Do you think I'd be welcome? If there are any more gatherings, I mean. Perhaps you could put in a good word for me.'

'Why would I want to do that? Because you gave me a fag and stood me a drink?' He downed the whisky in one, grimacing, and smacked his lips. 'I'm not that cheap.'

'Oh, suit yourself. I don't care.' She slung her handbag over her arm and pushed back the stool. 'I thought you'd be different, that's all. From what Arthur told me.'

Talbot chuckled. 'Well, you've got some spirit, I'll give you that.' He looked her up and down. 'What else do you have to offer?'

'A darn sight more than my husband,' Nell replied tartly; she knew Talbot would like that. Taking another leap in the dark, she added, 'Maybe I could help with Handle.'

His expression changed at once. He stood up, put his arm under her elbow and steered her roughly through the pub door and out into the night. The siren wailed louder than ever, too loud for her to think straight. She glanced up at the sky: no planes yet, but soon they would come.

His mouth close to her ear, Talbot said in a low, menacing tone, 'What exactly do you know about that?'

'Only the name.' His fingers were digging into her flesh and she was properly frightened now. 'No details.'

'Then keep your stupid mouth shut. Do you understand? Or someone will shut it for you.' He stood back, contemplating her as if making up his mind. Then he said abruptly, 'All right. Go to Park West and let's see what they make of you. They're meeting on Saturday at three. But don't repeat that word, not to anyone there or anywhere else.'

'I won't, I promise.' She forced a smile, her heart still beating a frantic tattoo. 'Will you be going, Mr Talbot? I should like to keep in touch.'

'Oh, we'll keep in touch,' he said, 'don't you worry about that. I'll see you here, midday on Sunday, and we can carry on the conversation.' He strode away, soon swallowed up by the night.

'Are you all right, Miss?' The black-haired barmaid

loomed towards her through the dark. 'Someone said you'd left together in a hurry and I was worried. He's a cold fish, that one.'

'Thanks. I'm fine, honestly.' Nell rubbed her arm, sore from the imprint of Talbot's grip. She had either made a terrible mistake or found her way to the heart of the matter – maybe both at once.

Chapter Sixteen

London, December 1940

It was a dark night with the merest sliver of moon only occasionally visible, yet still the bombers were coming – guided by radar, according to Hetta. The sirens carried on wailing, a pulsing wave of sound that washed across the city, gathering force as the alarm was taken up by one district after another. Every now and then, searchlight beams roamed the dense clouds. A gust of wind whipped over the rooftop, flapping the legs of Nell's siren suit and setting her swaying on her feet. There was no shelter, nothing even to grab for balance. The ground was too far below and the wide, dangerous sky too close above her head. Gradually, she became aware of a rumble through the soles of her feet. The building itself seemed to vibrate, a sound that deepened into a roar as vast black shapes came screaming out of the sky, heading directly for them.

Hetta threw back her head and yelled with wild exhilaration, 'Here they come!'

Nell dropped to her knees instinctively, clasping her hands over her helmet. Someone pulled her upright and the sudden burst of a flare revealed Hetta, laughing, her legs planted firmly apart and a sandbag over her shoulder like a miniature Father Christmas. The image flashed through the dark with startling clarity, as though projected onto a cinema screen. Hetta's lipstick had turned black in the surreal light and her skin was a porcelain mask; the St Christopher medal she wore round her neck glinted as though it were burning. 'You'll get used to it,' she shouted over the din.

More parachute flares were dropping around them, lighting up a turret here or a chimney stack there. The ack ack guns had begun firing and their shrapnel rained down; a chunk of metal clanged off the brim of Nell's helmet and she could feel its heat. The planes had roared past and now she heard a soft, steady swoosh as the hundreds of incendiaries they'd unloaded tumbled through the air. She strained to see where the bombs landed. Most seemed to be falling further away, detonating with a brilliant white light that fizzled into yellow flames as fire took hold in distant streets. Louder blasts and the crash of collapsing masonry suggested high explosives or parachute mines were dropping too.

'Over there!' She turned in the direction Hetta was pointing to find an incendiary had lodged on the ridge of a nearby roof. Hetta was already running towards it, having swapped the sandbag for an axe. Nell followed, in time to see her shin up a fixed ladder over the tiles and sit astride the ridge. Swinging her legs back and forth, she inched towards the white heart of the glare, then steadied herself for a moment before hooking the axe blade under the bomb's burning carcass and sending it flying through the air in a gleaming, fiery arc. The world plunged back into night; only seconds later, it seemed, Hetta was standing beside Nell, straightening her leather jacket.

'The boys on the ground should deal with it now.' She was hardly out of breath. 'Did you play lacrosse at school? It comes in rather handy.'

But now another bomber had come screaming overhead and more incendiaries were plummeting down. One landed a hundred yards or so away.

'That's mine!' Nell seized a stirrup pump and bucket from the heap of supplies by the parapet wall and ran towards it.

'Spray for bombs, remember?' Hetta said, chasing behind her.

Nell hastily changed the setting on the pump's nozzle and doused the writhing, spitting creature with water. It fizzled out in a sodden heap and Hetta gave her the thumbs up. Exhilarated, the blood pounding through her veins, Nell looked around for the next challenge. Tiny volcanoes of light flared up everywhere in the night; most were extinguished, only to emerge in other dark corners. A searchlight beam caught a spider crawling up the scaffolding of the Victoria Tower, and bells clanged in distant streets. At the far end of the roof on which they stood, an incendiary was burning behind the fretwork of a turret, scattering diamonds of orange light across the stone. They ran to deal with it, dodging shrapnel and debris, their feet crunching over the asphalt. Hetta had coiled a rope over her shoulder but it fell uselessly at their feet when she threw it: the tower's crenellations were too high. Above their heads, the bomb sizzled merrily.

'Think I can reach it on your shoulders,' Hetta shouted. 'Give me a leg up?'

She put her foot in the hammock of Nell's hands, climbed onto her back and then, grunting with exertion, somehow managed to balance upright as Nell leaned against the wall. The soles of her boots dug into Nell's shoulders but her weight was manageable. Nell held the bucket of water as Hetta sprayed with the pump until, at last, the fire had been extinguished and she was slithering to the ground. 'Got it. Thanks.'

They stood for a moment, taking stock. 'We could go into the circus when this is over,' Nell said.

Hetta was lithe and sure-footed as a cat; she must have been a wonderful dancer. She laughed. 'We make a good team, don't you think?'

And then the Westminster Chimes rang out, followed by Big Ben striking the hour across the rooftop – just for them, it seemed. The night had lasted a lifetime yet it was only nine o'clock. They were walking back towards the heap of sandbags and other supplies when a flickering glow in the gulley between two roofs to their right caught their eye. The ladder up which Hetta had climbed had itself caught fire, flames licking down from the top; they could see the roof spars underneath already smouldering.

'My turn,' Nell said, so Hetta held the bucket as she began to scramble up with the hose around her neck. A few feet up, her foot slipped on a smooth rung and she gasped, her heart in her mouth, but she was holding on tight; there was nothing to worry about, not really. Steadying herself, she took another step. Now she could feel the heat of the flames above and the breeze blew a gust of smoke in her face, making her eyes smart. What if another German plane flew out of the clouds? A fighter, equipped with a machine gun that could pick her off like the sitting duck she was, and send her cartwheeling through thin air like that incendiary, all the way down and down and down to the ground. She glanced over her right shoulder. A minuscule light shone in the courtyard below, with small dark figures swarming around it. The acrid taste of nausea burnt her throat; her hands were cold and damp with sweat. One more rung, one step at a time. But her legs were too heavy and too weak to move. She clung to the ladder, shaking and sick. Stuck.

'Nell?' Hetta's clear voice floated towards her. 'Look up, not down.'

Tentatively, she raised her head. The wind must have changed direction and the smoke had cleared. She took in a lungful of air, feeling the pounding in her chest ease a little. Flexing her fingers, she lifted one hand off the ladder and wiped it down her trouser leg before taking hold again. Her grip was strong.

'That's it,' Hetta called. 'Now find a star and fix your eyes on it. I'm coming to fetch you.'

Nell gazed into the sky. It was empty and quiet; the danger had passed. Clouds still hid the crescent moon but their cover was patchy and the longer she stared, the more stars she saw: three, then four, then dozens of pinpricks in the velvety sky, thousands of miles away in a galaxy that knew nothing of war. She chose the brightest one and focused on it until her breathing became regular and the buzzing in her head had cleared. And now, suddenly, the bells were chiming again for the quarter hour. She thought of Arthur, facing his own demons, and felt the warmth of his watch against her skin.

'All right?' Hetta's hand pressed against the small of her back, warm and firm.

'Yes, fine. Sorry.' Resting against the ladder, she unhooked the hose from around her neck, changed the setting on the nozzle to jet and doused the flames. Drops of cold water splashed on her upturned face as, slowly, she came back to herself.

'Don't worry. Happens to the best of us.' Hetta stamped out her cigarette. 'My fault, really, for letting you climb up there in those shoes. Another drink?' She offered the hip flask.

Nell accepted gratefully, took a sip of brandy and passed it back. 'I bet it's never happened to you.'

Hetta laughed, but didn't contradict her. 'We'll have to get you some decent boots.' She stretched out her legs to admire the thick rubber soles of her own. 'I'll talk to the controller when we sign off.' She had maintained her usual level of style in tailored trousers and a flying jacket with a sheepskin collar that must have been made for a child. They were sitting on a couple of upturned packing cases, passing the time before the All Clear sounded or another raid sent them rushing about like demented ants.

'Arthur never told me about fire watching,' Nell said. Then again, she had never asked. 'I suppose he didn't want to worry me.'

'How long have you been married?'

'Just over a year and a half.' Not long, was it? 'Our daughter's coming up for nine months.'

'You have a baby?' Hetta whistled. 'Then I definitely shouldn't have let you up the ladder. I'm expendable – you're not.'

'It doesn't feel like that. My mother's looking after Alice; she probably hasn't even noticed I've gone.' Nell sighed and changed the subject. 'How about you? Any boyfriends, I mean?'

'One or two. Nobody special.' Hetta took a bar of chocolate from her pocket, broke off a couple of squares and offered them to Nell. 'I had a fiancé but he was a fighter pilot and didn't last long, so now I'm fancy free. Living for the moment, you might say. Fewer complications.' She gave a wry laugh. 'Or at least that's the theory.'

Nell tried to imagine what she would be doing if she weren't a wife and mother. 'What do you think life will be like after the war?'

Hetta shrugged. 'Depends on whether we win or lose.'

Nell stared at her, shocked. She had never heard anyone voice the possibility of defeat; it was the sort of talk that could get you into serious trouble.

'It'll be different, that's for sure,' Hetta went on. 'Especially for us women. Now we've had a taste of freedom, we won't give it up in a hurry.'

And that idea was startling, too. Nell thought for a while. 'Do you actually want a career, though?'

'A career sounds frightfully serious.' Hetta stood and stretched. 'I want to live abroad, preferably somewhere scorching hot, sunbathe naked all day and swim in the sea, drink wine and eat delicious food with my fingers. I might do a little work to support myself but only of the strictly frivolous and entertaining kind. I'll be an artist's muse, perhaps, or run a louche hotel, or dance at the *Folies Bergère*. Then, when I'm old, I shall scandalise society by taking a succession of young lovers, male and female, and treating them all very badly. I shan't ever talk about the war and if anyone asks, I'll say I don't remember.'

Nell smiled. 'How wonderful. May we come and stay in your hotel?'

Hetta turned to her. 'Don't you see? This war is the start of something, not just an ending. For all the horror, at least we have that. You can negotiate new terms with your husband, tell him how you want to live. Especially since you're risking life and limb for his sake.' She sat again on the upturned packing case and yawned. 'I hope he's worth it.'

'He is,' Nell assured her. 'All I want is to live with him and our daughter. I don't care about the terms, as long as we're together.'

'How sweet.'

'Time for another cig?' Nell produced her pack. There wasn't much else to do and she wanted to share something with Hetta, who had already given her so much.

'How's your investigation going, by the way?' Hetta took one. 'Made any progress?'

'As a matter of fact, I have.' Nell suppressed an involuntary shiver of disquiet. 'I'm going to Park West on Saturday. To the meeting, remember, that I told you about?'

'Are you, indeed?' The flare of a match revealed Hetta's sharp glance. 'So you're going to pretend to be one of them. Think you can carry it off?'

'I'll give it my best shot. Like Arthur.' That must have been why he had the ghastly badge – either that, or Talbot had planted it in his pocket. 'I'll find out what they're up to and . . .' And then what? 'And make the police see he could have had nothing to do with it.'

'But what if you end up in trouble, too? Or discover he's involved in some Fascist plot after all?'

She shook her head. 'There has to be another explanation.'

'I suppose at least then you'd know,' Hetta said, as though Nell hadn't spoken.

At that moment, the continuous note of the All Clear rang out. 'Marvellous.' Hetta clamped the cigarette between her lips and started to gather together the various pieces of equipment. 'Let's get this lot downstairs,' she said out of the corner of her mouth, narrowing her eyes against the smoke. 'Don't mind holding the fort, do you? Now you know the ropes? There's a dry martini and a rather gorgeous navigator waiting for me at the Four Hundred.'

It took them a couple of trips to clear the roof, and another five minutes in the store cupboard for Hetta to change into a backless silk gown. She still wore her boots with the flying jacket on top, and carried her dancing shoes wrapped in a shawl. 'See you in the morning,' she said. 'Or maybe tomorrow night? Be careful! Don't do anything I wouldn't.'

Which didn't really limit Nell at all.

She lay fully dressed under a blanket on the truckle bed, waiting for the sirens to sound or the nurses to arrive. Sleep seemed a remote possibility. One thought consoled her: at least here she was safe from Bill Talbot.

Arthur had been transferred to Brixton Prison, Nell discovered, when she called at Scotland Yard the next morning. She would have to telephone there to find out about visiting times. Barring a miracle, it looked as though he wouldn't be out in time for Christmas. She couldn't bring herself to speak to her mother again so she sent a telegram instead, saying all was well and she hoped to be home early the next week, Tuesday at the latest. That was Christmas Eve, so she was cutting it fine. Rose would be worried but Alice wouldn't know the difference; one day was the same as another to her. Returning to the Palace of Westminster, Nell ate a hearty breakfast in the staff canteen before strolling out through Old Palace Yard. A few pieces of shrapnel lay here and there on the pavement, and an empty sandbag had been blown into the branches of a tree. Nell turned up her coat collar, wondering whether to sit in the Abbey for a while or walk to Regent Street and see whether her money would stretch to toys in Hamley's for all the evacuees. Malcolm would be reunited with his mother for Christmas so at least she didn't have to worry about him.

As she strolled along Whitehall, she became aware of someone following close behind. Glancing over her shoulder, she saw a nondescript man in an astrakhan overcoat and relaxed, because he wasn't Talbot. She wasn't unduly worried when the pace of his footsteps increased, and at the same time, a car that had been idling its way down the street drew up at the kerb alongside her and someone opened the rear door from inside. At that precise moment, the man in the astrakhan coat bumped into her. Instead of apologising, he took her by the elbow and bundled her into the back of the car, so swiftly and unexpectedly that she hadn't even time to cry out, let alone resist. Slamming the door behind her, he climbed into the front passenger seat and the car accelerated smoothly away past the Cenotaph.

'Help!' Nell screamed, beating on the window. 'I'm being kidnapped!'

'Don't be so melodramatic,' said the man wearily, as though she were a tiresome child. 'This car is soundproof and anyway, there's nobody about. And you're not being kidnapped.'

'Then what would you call it?'

'We want a word with you, that's all.' He hadn't even bothered to turn around.

'And who's "we"?' Nell demanded. He didn't reply so she tried her luck with the driver, a pale young woman with lank hair and a red nose. 'Where are you taking me?'

'Not far,' the girl said, taking a handkerchief out of her pocket with one hand and blowing her nose. The car swerved and the man in the overcoat tutted, putting a hand on the steering wheel to correct it. 'Just off St James's Street, actually,' she added, sniffing. 'Won't be long.'

Nell's heart was pounding. She had no idea what to do apart from shouting again, which would serve no purpose except to embarrass her, so she declared, 'This is outrageous!' and sat tall on the back seat with as much dignity as she could muster.

They drew up about ten minutes later outside an elegant four-storey house in red brick with a 'To Let' sign above the door. Nell was escorted from the car by the man who had pushed her into it, while the girl with the red nose drove off in search of a parking space. She wondered briefly about making a run for it but he was holding her arm tightly and actually, the part of her that wasn't frightened was intrigued. She wanted to see what would happen next.

Inside, the building had an atmosphere of frenetic activity. An urgent clatter of typewriter keys floated through open doors, footsteps thumped along corridors and a man with one arm, his empty sleeve pinned out of the way, ran past them down the stairs without breaking his stride. A telephone rang shrilly below. 'Will someone answer that bloody thing?' shouted a disembodied voice, but the demand was ignored, and on it trilled.

A uniformed Wren leaned over the banister above and called, 'Has anyone seen Standish?'

'Just left for Blenheim,' came a reply from the ground floor.

'Damn and blast,' she muttered, disappearing.

Nell's captor took her along a corridor on the third floor, knocked on one of the doors and waited, holding her in his cool gaze.

'Come in,' a woman called, whereupon he ushered Nell through.

'Mrs Spelman, ma'am,' he said and withdrew, leaving the door ajar.

Nell found herself in a small room, mainly taken up by a large desk covered in papers. A woman sat behind it with curly chestnut hair and a fresh complexion, wearing a heathery purple tweed suit. She looked as though she should have been striding over the moors with a spaniel at her heels, rather than being confined to an office overlooking the gun emplacements and barbed-wire barricades of Green Park.

'Have a seat, Mrs Spelman.' She waved at a chair on the other side of the desk. 'Thank you for coming.'

'I didn't have much choice,' Nell said, determined not to be cowed.

'I suppose not.' The woman stared at her thoughtfully for what seemed like an age, flipping a pencil between her fingers.

'Who are you?' Nell asked eventually. 'And how do you know my name?'

'I'm Jane Coker, and it's my job to know things,' the woman said, with a chilly smile. 'I work for the Ministry of Information. It's a pretty poor show if we don't know what's afoot. Would you like a cup of tea?'

'No, thank you,' Nell replied stiffly. 'I should like to know why I've been brought here in such a peremptory manner.' Nerves were making her pompous.

'All right, then.' Miss Coker – she wasn't wearing a wedding ring – dropped the pencil and said briskly, 'We think you should go home. There's nothing you can do to help your husband and, frankly, you're a distraction. There's a chance you could jeopardise an extremely delicate operation.'

A flash of fear shot through Nell's stomach. 'What on earth do you mean?'

Miss Coker gave an exasperated sigh. 'Don't act the innocent, it's a waste of everyone's time. Miss Carmichael has told us all about you.'

So Hetta had been taking a professional interest in her, rather than merely a friendly one. What a fool Nell had been! 'There's nothing I'd like more,' she said now, trying to recover some dignity. 'If Arthur were released from prison, I'd go home this minute. Couldn't you look into the case, Miss Coker?'

'I'm afraid it's a police matter. Beyond my jurisdiction.'

Nell leaned forward. 'My husband would never go to a Fascist meeting in the normal run of things. He's half Jewish, for heaven's sake! It's my belief he'd stumbled across some conspiracy and was trying to find out more. Either that, or he's been framed. Maybe these people wanted to get him out of the way because he'd found out what they were up to and wouldn't play along. Surely it's worth investigating?'

'But we are investigating, Mrs Spelman, and we'll get along better without your interference. We don't need anyone blundering in at Park West.' Her tone had become icy. 'This is a warning. If you don't co-operate, you could end up in prison, too. For quite some time.'

Nell's palms prickled with sweat. She had nothing to lose. 'I think Arthur was trying to find out about Handle.'

Miss Coker glanced at her sharply. 'I beg your pardon?'

'Handle,' Nell repeated, lowering her voice. 'That's what this is all about, isn't it?'

Miss Coker got up and closed the office door. Then she walked back, leant against the edge of her desk and folded her arms. 'Tell me everything you know about Operation Handle. And don't even think about playing games.'

So Nell explained the whole story, starting from that first meeting with Lord Winthrop the morning she'd been out shooting rabbits, and ending with what Bill Talbot had told her the evening before. 'He said I was to go to the meeting but not say anything about Handle. So they could see what they thought of me. Whoever "they" are.'

'And you're positive this man Winthrop used that word on the telephone? You couldn't have misheard?'

'Positive. "Handle's definitely going ahead," that's what he said.'

'Wait here.' Miss Coker disappeared, returning a few minutes later with a tall, grey-haired man whom she didn't introduce. 'Go through it all again, if you would,' she commanded Nell, 'just as you told me.'

They both listened intently as she spoke, their eyes fixed on her face. At the end of her account, the man said, 'Thank you, Mrs Spelman.' He nodded at Miss Coker. 'All right, then. If you think so,' and left the room.

'You should play along,' she told Nell. 'Go to the meeting, do exactly as Talbot said and let us know if he contacts you. One thing, though. What makes you think you'll have any more luck with these people than your husband?'

'Because I know how their minds work. I can say the things they want to hear as though I mean them.'

Nell had been subjected to her father's litany of resentment often enough: the sour refrain as he searched for someone to blame for his lack of success, and settled on the whole Jewish race as a scapegoat.

'I certainly hope so,' Miss Coker replied. 'For all our sakes.'

Chapter Seventeen

Oxfordshire, January 2022

Ellie hadn't wanted to find out any more about Eleanor Spelman. 'If you'd seen the things she was saying!' she'd told Dan. 'I mean, maybe anti-Semitism was widespread back then, but even so.'

Yet here they were, driving in a rental car towards Oxford. 'Seems crazy not to,' Dan had said, 'since we're here. Besides, it's my birthday so I get to choose. You can come along for the ride.' He slowed down, indicating as they took the off-ramp. 'Don't you want to see some more of England?'

He had a point. And it was relaxing to be driven through a changing landscape, the clogged city streets giving way to a three-lane freeway for a stretch, and then a cross-country route that Dan had planned. He'd brought some snacks for the journey – potato chips, peanut-butter cups and cans of soda – which surprised her, as he and Lisa had always been so strict about their diet. They sang along noisily to the radio while she ate with her feet up on the dash, feeling like a kid on spring break. It was a sunny winter's day and the future suddenly seemed full of promise, rather than all the wrong choices she was bound to make and spend years regretting. Dan would be going back to the States on Monday and she'd managed to control herself. She could carry on their easy, relaxed friendship and there would be no romantic entanglements to get in the way of her relationship with Beth, no embarrassment when Dan had to admit – as he inevitably would – that he thought of her as a sister and besides, there was no way he was ready to start dating again.

'Do you remember that time Beth and I came to visit you at Lehigh and I sneaked off to a party with your crazy roommate?' she asked him, out of the blue. 'And you went to every hall on campus trying to find us?'

'I do. And I also remember washing the floor and sheets and your clothes after you threw up on them. You were like Vesuvius; it just kept on coming.'

She laughed. 'Sorry.' He had seen her at her worst, that was for sure.

They'd been getting along fine, despite her initial reservations; it had been good to have someone to hang out with, especially now she'd given up her search into the Spelman family history. Dan had thrown himself into the task of finding interesting things to do. He'd queued up early for tickets to the theatre, found the best Chinese restaurant in Soho, got her up at dawn for a visit to the flower market, and discovered the oldest riverside pub in London, down by the docks, where smugglers and sailors used to drink. She would miss him when he went back to New York in a few days' time. She might even have considered travelling with him, but she'd promised to take Gillian to her next round of chemotherapy and stay at her house overnight. She'd felt awful the last time, and the side effects of the drug were cumulative so the next dose would be worse. After that, her daughter Lucy would be back from South Africa and she could take over.

'But you really ought to let Max know,' Ellie had said. 'How do you think he's going to feel when he finds out you've been keeping this secret?'

'Relieved, I should imagine,' Gillian had replied. Ellie hadn't dared ask why she wouldn't give him the chance to be kind, although she'd very much wanted to.

'You look very serious all of a sudden.' She turned away from the window to find Dan glancing at her. 'What's up?'

'Oh, nothing much.' She forced a smile. 'Just wondering what I'm going to tell Mom when she asks me about the trip. It's strange, I thought somehow I was meant to come to England, like my grandmother was calling me, but now I'm not so sure.'

'But you've made friends with your aunt, and Max and Nathan,' he said. 'So that's a plus. You don't have to say anything about Eleanor. It's not as though we know for certain what she was up to.'

'I guess not.' Ellie sighed. 'I'd like to be proud of her, that's all. Although why should it matter whether she was one of the good guys? Maybe I only wanted to feel better about myself, to know that I might not have amounted to much but my grandma was amazing.'

'That's deep. I'd say you've not turned out too badly, all things considered.' Dan was blushing, she noticed. He added, 'Well, at least you're through the vomiting drunk phase.'

Ellie laughed, reminded not to take herself too seriously. She felt warm and comfortable, and dangerously tempted to confide in him. That was an impulse she would have to control. They stopped for lunch in Oxford at a hotel with a huge log fire in the bar, ate steak-and-kidney pie and treacle tart, despite all the snacks in the car, and talked about inconsequential things: whether the Mets would beat the Yankees, which was the country they would most like to visit, what had happened to various people they'd known at high school.

After she'd finished a glass of red wine and they were drinking coffee, she said, 'If I tell you something, will you swear to keep it to yourself?' Because the knowledge was, after all, too much of a burden to carry alone.

'Go on.' Dan leaned back and folded his arms, his face flushed from the heat of the fire and all of his attention focused on her. A hundred butterflies beat their tiny wings in Ellie's stomach. Focus, she told herself.

'I've found out why my aunt thought I came here,' she began, 'and I'm not sure what to do about it.'

It had taken Gillian a while to come to the point. Ellie hadn't liked to press her; she'd looked so frail, lying back in the chair with her eyes closed while her body was flooded with drugs that would probably make her feel worse than the cancer. Eventually, she'd confessed that her mother, Mavis, had lied to Alice almost thirty years ago. Mavis had said that Arthur hadn't left her any money in his will, that his whole estate had gone to her and Gillian.

'She made sure Mom couldn't make it over in time for the funeral, and she told the solicitor she'd lost touch with her stepdaughter and no one knew where she was.'

'And your mom just accepted that?' Dan asked. 'Without making her own enquiries?'

'Ridiculous, isn't it? But you know what Alice is like – she's the least materialistic person in the world. And proud, too. Maybe she thought she didn't need or want her father's money. Apparently, Gillian knew what was happening but didn't do anything about it.' Ellie remembered what her aunt had said: 'I was angry with Alice. It might sound ridiculous but I hadn't forgiven her for leaving. She'd turned her back on me, too.'

'So what's happened to the money?'

'That's the thing. Apparently if a legacy isn't claimed, it's kept by the UK Treasury Department. It wasn't as though Mavis got Mom's share; she just didn't want her to have it.' Ellie drained her coffee cup. 'My aunt thought Mom had got wind of her inheritance somehow and sent me over to fetch it.'

'You mean, the funds are still available?'

'There's a chance, but we'd have to hurry. You have thirty years to make a claim, and it'll be thirty years at the end of this month since my grandfather died. That's why Gillian was rattled – she was sure we'd found out, that me turning up when I did wasn't a coincidence.'

'So how much money are we talking about?' Dan asked, steepling his fingers.

'Not millions, but a tidy sum. Forty thousand pounds initially, which was earning interest for some of the time. It would mean Mom could stay in her nursing home for a while longer.'

'Then what are you waiting for?'

'My mom already doesn't think much of Gillian. If she knows that Mavis lied to her and Gillian did nothing to put things right, she might not want anything to do with her English family. And what if the money doesn't come through?'

Even if the claim were successful, Gillian would have to face up to her complicity when she was already going through so much – although Ellie couldn't tell Dan about that.

'Look, you owe it to your mom to go after that legacy,' he said. 'Your grandfather's wishes ought to be respected, and Gillian should do what she can to help. Alice can decide whether or not she wants to keep the money if it comes through. But maybe don't tell her any of this until you know for sure that's going to happen.'

'Good idea.' Ellie waved at the waiter to bring their bill. 'Thanks, Dan. And happy birthday, by the way.'

'Now for the next excitement.' He pushed back his chair. 'Millbury, here we come.'

'Can't we explore the city instead? It looks so beautiful. We could visit one of the colleges, maybe, and then find a café for afternoon tea. Buttered crumpets? Scones with jam and cream?'

Ellie was familiar with these delights by now. She could see the two of them gazing at the medieval buildings, whose history Dan would probably know, soaking up the beauty and romance, then maybe taking a punt down the river and—

'Actually, you're right. Let's make a move.' She pushed back her chair. 'I guess we won't starve if we don't eat for a couple of hours.'

They left Oxford and drove along back roads into the country. The scenery was lovely even in the depths of winter, with leafless trees spiking fields of corrugated brown earth.

'This is too much,' Ellie murmured, as they passed through yet another storybook village. 'Can we stop? I want to see if it's real.'

Cottages of golden stone were set around a duck-pond, smoke rising from their chimneys into the still air. A design had been carved into one of the thatched roofs: rats chasing each other up the slope past an attic window set into the eaves. She had to take a picture, although the people who lived there were probably sick of tourists.

'OK,' she said, climbing back into the car, 'we can turn around now. I've had my fix.'

'It's only another few miles to Millbury.' Dan started the engine. 'You don't even have to knock on the door. We'll take a look at the house and then go home. What are you so afraid of?'

'Surprises,' Ellie said, yawning. 'I don't like them anymore.'

She fell asleep then, waking up with a start when he stopped the car. Orchard House wasn't at all picturesque: square and forbidding, it loomed at the end of a short gravel drive with dank rhododendron bushes on either side. It was built of red brick in the mock Tudor style, with a lot of insistent, heavy black beams. Dan got out of the car, stretching his back. Ellie didn't want to take a photograph; this house would mean nothing to Alice and it wasn't even quaint.

A woman they hadn't noticed approached Dan, wearing gardening gloves and holding a trowel. Ellie climbed out of the car to join him in explaining why they were there. She took her grandmother's identity card out of her purse, but the woman only glanced at it briefly.

'I can't help you, I'm afraid,' she said. 'We moved here just five years ago and the house has changed hands several times in the past twenty years or so. Sorry.'

'Of course. No problem,' Ellie said. Maybe now Dan would agree they could go back to London.

She had her hand on the car door when the woman called after her, 'There is someone you might want to talk to. Mrs Macdonald, in the middle of the village. She lived here when she was a girl and she's in her nineties now. Sharp as a tack, though, and quite the character. She might remember your grandmother. Millbury's a small place, after all.' She gave Dan instructions on where to find the apartment and wished them luck.

'All right, all right,' Ellie said, when they were back in the car and he'd turned to her, raising his eyebrows. 'We'll go there, for all the good it'll do.'

With any luck, this woman wouldn't have realised the sort of person her grandmother was, even if she had known her and could tell them anything at all, eighty years later. Anyway, it was getting dark; an elderly woman wasn't likely to open the door to two strangers calling out of the blue.

Mrs Macdonald lived on the ground floor of an apartment block overlooking the village green. There was a bench in the front garden, and geraniums in pots, still flowering despite the cold, and a tabby cat washing its fur. Ellie could imagine her mom being happy in a place like this. Dan rang the doorbell and they stood back.

'She's not answering,' Ellie said after a few seconds. 'C'mon, let's go.'

But Dan put his hand on her arm. 'I can hear

footsteps.' And now they could see a blurred shape approaching behind the frosted glass.

Mrs Macdonald was leaning on a walker, which must have been why it took her a while to open the door. She wore a pink velour tracksuit with the word JUICY picked out in diamanté across her chest, lipstick to match, and large turquoise-framed glasses. Another pair hung around her neck, along with a three-strand pearl necklace, and her white hair was scooped up with various tortoiseshell combs. This is how I want to look when I'm old, Ellie decided instantly.

'Who are you?' she said. 'If you're collecting for charity, you can bugger off. I donate by standing order.'

'We're so sorry to disturb you,' Ellie said, biting back a smile. 'This is a long shot, Mrs Macdonald, but is there any chance you might have known my grand-mother, Eleanor Spelman?'

'Never heard of her.' Mrs Macdonald began to close the door. For all of her reservations, Ellie felt a pang of disappointment. But then it slowly swung open again, and the old lady was staring at her. 'My God!' she said. 'You mean Nell, don't you?'

Ellie's heart leapt. 'That's right.'

'Good heavens.' Mrs Macdonald swayed, gripping the walker so tightly that her knuckles turned white. 'Well, I'll be damned. Do you mean to tell me you're Alice's daughter?'

'Yes, I am.' Ellie found there were tears in her eyes. She blinked furiously. 'Did you know her, too?'

'I'll say.' Mrs Macdonald shuffled a few steps closer,

gazing at Ellie as though she were drinking her up. Then she manoeuvred the walker in a semi-circle. 'You'd better come in,' she said over her shoulder. 'You're letting out all the heat, standing there with the door open. The place is a mess but you'll have to put up with that. I'd have tidied up if I'd known you were coming. Possibly.'

They followed her down the narrow hall and into a living room that overflowed with papers and books, covering every surface and stacked in heaps on the floor. 'I'm sorting out my library,' Mrs Macdonald said, sinking into a chair, 'but I keep getting distracted. Find a seat where you can. Would you like a cup of tea?'

'I'll make it,' Dan offered. 'Just point me in the right direction.'

Mrs Macdonald looked at him doubtfully. 'You can have a go, I suppose. But use the kettle, not the microwave. I've seen Americans making tea on the internet and it's not pretty. Follow your nose and it'll lead you to the kitchen.' She turned back to Ellie. 'Well, well, well. Who'd have thought it? Now, tell me all about yourself, and Alice too. Is she still alive? So many of us have gone and here I am, plodding on.' She laughed, lifting her glasses to dab her eyes with the tissue. 'What's your name, dear?'

When Ellie had introduced herself, she nodded. 'You're the image of your grandmother – I should have realised straight away. And named after her, too. How lovely.'

Ellie had to contain her impatience while she gave

Mrs Macdonald a brief history of her family and showed her pictures of Alice on her telephone. 'How did we all get so old,' she said, staring at the photograph. 'I'll always think of your mother as a five-year-old. That's when I last saw her.'

'Please, tell me everything,' Ellie begged, perched on the edge of the sofa. But then Dan arrived with the tea tray, and there was a lot of toing and froing with milk and sugar, and the clearing of side tables.

'Not bad,' Mrs Macdonald said, having taken her first sip. 'I was fearing the worst but this is perfectly acceptable.' She settled her cup back on the saucer. 'Now, where to start? At the beginning, I suppose. So, I first came to this village in 1940, when I was nine. We were evacuated from Coventry in the nick of time, my sisters and my brother and me, a few months before it was bombed. I know a lot of children suffered terribly, having to leave their families and live with strangers, but it was the making of us. She was a decent woman, you see.'

'My grandmother?' Ellie asked.

'No, I'm talking about her mother, Mrs Roberts. She took care of us all, in a way no one had done before. Our real mother was an alcoholic and pretty much a dead loss. We were dreading the thought of her fetching us back at the end of the war but, thank goodness, she simply disappeared. We never found out what became of her. Our father had left years before, so Rose Roberts fostered us and put our lives on the right track. My sister trained as a midwife and I ended up at grammar school and then university, would you believe. I became a history teacher, and it was all because of her and the wonderful teachers at our village school. And now I'm retired and widowed and living back here, where I started.'

'But what about Nell, Mrs Macdonald?' Ellie couldn't contain herself.

'Do call me Brenda, dear. We're virtually related, after all.' She wiped her eyes again. 'I met your grandmother only a few weeks before she was killed so I didn't know her long. Yet she made a great impression on me. I can picture her clearly, even now.'

Ellie found the photos of Nell on her phone. 'There she is, bless her.' Brenda sighed. 'I remember her being driven away that last time. She and the baby came to live in the village because they'd been bombed out, you see, but her husband stayed behind in London. And then for some reason, she went back to join him in the middle of the Blitz. Goodness knows why. I've no idea how she died, either. Children weren't told anything in those days. "Ask me no questions and I'll tell you no lies," that's what people used to say.'

'So what happened to my mother after that?' Ellie asked.

'Alice stayed with us at Orchard House for the rest of the war, and then her father came and fetched her back when it ended. It was terrible.' Brenda shook her head. 'Alice was all Rose had left by then, in the way of blood relations. First Nell was killed, and then Harry – he was Nell's brother – died a year later in a prisoner of war camp. He was shot, trying to escape. But Arthur was Alice's father, so Rose couldn't very well refuse. She poured her energies into us and I think that helped, but we all missed the baby terribly. Sparky little thing, she was. And still is, I imagine. I don't suppose she'll remember me now.'

'She's getting forgetful,' Ellie admitted.

'As am I. It's strange, though: I've no idea what happened yesterday but those childhood days are as clear as a bell. I remember Nell saying to me once that if anything happened to us children, she and Rose would never get over it. That was the first time I'd ever felt of any value. Up until then, I thought there was nobody in the world who cared whether we lived or died. It was a turning point for me, really.' Her hands shaking a little, she handed the phone back to Ellie.

'Did you know anything about her politics?' Ellie asked.

'Heavens, no. We didn't discuss that sort of thing, and this was the war, remember, when we had a government of national unity and were all pulling together. Everyone was too busy hating Hitler and rooting for Winnie to squabble the way they do now.'

Dan caught Ellie's eye. He'd been quiet, but now he said, 'So she wasn't a Fascist, as far as you know?'

Brenda stared at him. 'Why on earth would you suggest that? No, she most certainly wasn't. Now her father, Mr Roberts, he once sounded off about the Jews feathering their own nests but I remember Nell setting us children straight afterwards. You couldn't argue with him directly because he hated to lose face, but she made sure we knew what the Nazis were doing and how evil it was – especially as far as Jews were concerned.'

'Really?' Ellie felt a spark of hope. 'You're sure about that?'

'Positive. Oh, I thought she was marvellous. A Fascist, indeed!' Straightening her back, Brenda turned to Dan. 'Perhaps you could make yourself useful, young man, and clear away the tea things.'

'Of course.' He jumped to his feet and began loading the tray.

When they were alone, Ellie said, 'Just now, you mentioned Nell being driven away for the last time. Was anyone with her?'

Brenda leaned back in the chair and closed her eyes for a moment. 'I'm sorry, I'm rather tired. This has been quite a shock – a delightful one, of course, but all the same . . .'

'Yes, of course.' Ellie stood up, though she could hardly bear to go. She wanted to shake Brenda Macdonald until all the pictures she held locked away in her head came spilling out. Someone who had actually known her grandmother! And her mother, when she was a small child.

'Will you come back tomorrow morning?' Brenda asked. 'I need time to think everything through. And I have a few photographs you might like to see, although it'll take me a while to find them.'

‘I should love to, thank you.’ Ellie took Brenda’s hand in hers. The old lady’s skin was cold, although the central heating was going full blast. Please don’t die in the night, she wanted to beg her, but of course she only said, ‘Meeting you is more than I could have hoped for. And my mother will be so thrilled.’

The old lady looked up, her watery eyes swimming behind the thick lenses. ‘Don’t tell Alice anything yet. Wait until you hear what I have to say.’

Chapter Eighteen

Oxfordshire, January 2022

Ellie sat in front of the dressing-table mirror, wishing she'd brought some mascara with her. She'd slipped a lipstick into the pocket of her jeans but that would only go so far. If she'd known they'd end up having dinner and staying overnight, obviously she'd have brought three different outfits, a curling iron and a fully stocked make-up bag. As it was, she'd only just managed to buy a spare pair of knickers, a hairbrush and toothbrush before the stores closed. She stared grumpily at her reflection, then went to the mini bar in a corner of the room and found some gin to calm her jitters. She hadn't been able to sit still or settle for a minute since the car ride from Millbury.

'I can't believe it,' she'd said to Dan, once they were back in the car. 'To think we almost didn't come here, and I'd have missed the one woman alive in England who knew my grandmother! Thank you!'

She was so happy that she'd thrown her arms around him for a hug, and something had happened – she still wasn't quite sure what. When her cheek had touched his, it was as though an electric current had passed between them. Dan felt it, too, she could tell. He'd pulled away from her abruptly and started the engine. First he'd stalled, and then he'd gone into first gear instead of reverse, and they'd nearly hit the car in front.

'Damn stick shift,' he'd muttered.

She daren't look at him, so she'd gabbled about the chances of running into Brenda Macdonald, and how she couldn't wait to tell her mom about the visit, and what on earth could Brenda be going to say the next day, and so on.

Dan had cleared his throat. 'It's crazy to drive back to London. Why don't we see if they have rooms in that hotel where we had lunch?'

'Sure,' she'd replied brightly, her stomach doing a back flip.

'Rooms,' he'd said, not 'a room'. But still . . . What if he felt the same way she did? What if he didn't, though? She'd end up never being able to look him in the face again. Beth would either be mad that Ellie had risked their friendship or think she was pathetic and feel sorry for her, so she'd lose her best friend, too. The whole thing would be a catastrophe. To complicate matters further, when they'd arrived at the hotel and were checking in – Dan having telephoned in advance to book their rooms – the receptionist, a beautiful girl with olive skin and long black hair in a swishy ponytail, had flirted with him so outrageously that Ellie felt like slapping her.

'This way, Mr Scardino,' she'd said, glancing seductively at him over her shoulder and fluttering her extravagant eyelashes as she led the way along the corridor. She'd barely acknowledged Ellie's existence.

'Shall I test the bed for you, Mr Scardino? You'll find it very comfortable,' Ellie muttered, adding a splash of tonic. She kicked off her shoes and lay down. The bed was, in fact, very comfortable. What if there had been only one room left in the hotel? They'd have had to share; Dan would have insisted on taking the couch because he was a gentleman, but they'd have talked long into the night and then she'd have realised he couldn't sleep so she'd have pulled back the duvet and said, come on, this is ridiculous, and he'd have slipped in beside her, and everything would have been easy in the warm, forgiving dark.

'Get a grip,' she told herself, shuddering with embarrassment and lust. Had Dan always been so hot? He had an angular, bony face with deep-set eyes that could look brooding, but when he smiled, he could – as Alice also said – charm the birds out of the trees. Maybe England had cast some sort of spell over them both. Her heart was thudding and her hands felt clammy. If it were anyone else, she'd have been on the phone to Beth, but how could she tell her she was crushing on Dan? How could she tell anyone? Ugh, she was too old for this.

They had decided on a late dinner after such a big lunch. There was nothing else for it: Ellie finished her gin and went to meet Dan at the bar. She found him talking to the girl with the ponytail who was now behind it, serving drinks. Goodness, she was multi-talented. She'd put on gold hoop earrings for the evening and undone an extra button on her crisp white blouse, and her ponytail swung jauntily as she sashayed between the optics. Ellie imagined herself leaping over the counter with a machete clenched between her teeth and slicing it off.

'There you are,' Dan said. 'I was about to send out a search party.'

He seemed back to his old self but Ellie had become awkward. She wasn't hungry, had drunk too much gin and couldn't think what to say: a problem she'd never had with Dan before. 'I'm sorry,' she said eventually, when they were debating whether to have dessert, 'I know it's your birthday but would you mind if we called it a night? I'm running on fumes.'

Yet what with all the conflicting thoughts chasing each other around her head, it was some time before she fell asleep.

After a restless night, she woke early, way before the hotel restaurant opened for breakfast, and decided to explore Oxford by herself. Some fresh air might clear her head. She dressed quickly and crept out into the corridor – and there was Dan, emerging from his room.

'Great minds.' He smiled, and her heart leapt. 'Fancy a stroll?'

They went out into the dark, silent city, lit by street lamps and the slowly breaking dawn. A few stars were still bright in a sky that faded from black to moleskin as they walked, speaking in whispers. It was magical, as though they were stepping outside their everyday selves and into another world. Ellie became gradually calm. The sun would rise and the world would go on turning, despite her ridiculous preoccupations. A kerb-side café was opening so they bought coffees to go and strolled on until they came to a bridge, where they stopped to drink them. Morning had definitely broken; she could see as far as a distant bend in the river flowing beneath them, with boats moored on either side.

She looked at Dan, noticing every detail of his face: the scar that bisected his left eyebrow, the lick of hair that always curled the wrong way, his eyes that were either hazel or dark grey, depending on the light. They were grey now, and gazing into hers.

'Why did you come to England?' she asked.

'Because you invited me, remember?' But his eyes were kind.

'Fair enough.' There was no more to say. They would carry on dancing around each other and maybe in time, the awkwardness would fade.

Dan looked away, down into the water. 'And because

I thought it would be easier to tell you how I felt if we were somewhere different, miles from everybody else.' He took a sip of coffee. 'Hasn't quite worked out like that, though.'

A faint blush was spreading up his neck. 'So how *do* you feel?' she asked, slipping her arm through his.

Now he met her eye. 'I'm crazy about you, Ellie. I have been for years. Have you really never noticed? I thought the whole world must have known. Lisa certainly did.'

'Honestly, I had no idea.' She hesitated, searching for the right words.

'The timing never seemed right,' he went on. 'Whenever I split up with anyone, you always had some guy in tow.'

'Each one worse than the last.'

He laughed. 'Well, I wasn't going to say that, but yes. Didn't one of them pick up a girl at your birthday party and drive back to her place in your car?'

'Wilf.' Ellie winced. 'He was the worst.'

'And by then I was with Lisa. I think I only married her to get you out of my head. That didn't work either.'

'Oh, Dan.' She leaned against his shoulder.

'It's OK. You don't have to pity me.' He stroked her hair. 'I'll live with it. We can still be friends, can't we?'

'No.' She drew away from him. 'I don't want to be friends anymore.' His eyes had widened in alarm, so she put her arms around him. 'Dan, I've been such a fool. How could I have wasted so much time when you've been right in front of me all along?'

'What are you saying?'

Did she dare? 'I'm saying I want more than friendship. It's taken me long enough to realise it, but maybe I'm in love with you, too. Or at least I could be, given the chance.' She laughed. 'Shall we try to make a go of it, Mr Scardino? Better late than never.'

'I don't believe it,' he said. 'Are you sure? You're not just saying that because you feel sorry for me?'

'Why would I feel sorry for you? You're kind and funny and smart, and I should have jumped on you years ago.'

'I can't disagree with any of that,' he said, grinning. And then, oh God, he was leaning towards her.

'Stop!' she said, panicking. 'I haven't cleaned my teeth.'

'I couldn't care less.' He drew her close. 'Come on, I've waited twenty years for this.'

His lips were softer than she could have imagined. Closing her eyes, she gave herself up to the kiss, letting her fear and uncertainty dissolve in the sweetness of that moment. There could be no more misunderstanding; they were expressing their deepest feelings without the need for words. She had known Dan all her life, yet now it felt as though she were meeting him for the first time. He kissed her gently at first, then more fiercely as her body responded to his and their desire grew stronger. There was nobody else in the world except the two of them, and soon they had to take a taxi back to the hotel so as not to waste another minute that could be spent in bed.

All the way to Mrs Macdonald's house, they kept catching each other's eye and smiling for no reason. When Dan stopped the car, she had to kiss him again.

'Enough, we're late as it is,' he said, finally disentangling himself. 'You go in. I'll take a walk around the village and let you concentrate on family stuff.'

Perhaps it was for the best. Ellie walked a little unsteadily up the path and rang the bell.

Brenda opened the door at last, wearing a purple tartan shift and red tights. 'There you are,' she said. 'I was beginning to think you'd changed your mind.'

'I'm so sorry. I didn't sleep well and then—' Ellie spread her hands wide, shrugging.

'Neither did I,' Brenda replied. 'In fact, I've been up half the night. Come through, dear. We have plenty to talk about.'

As they went down the hall, Ellie spotted a tray in the kitchen, laid with teacups and a plate of biscuits.

'Thank you so much for having me,' she said, feeling guilty that Brenda had gone to so much trouble, and that she had managed to forget about Alice and Nell for half a day.

Brenda parked her walker by a table in the sitting room and pulled out a chair for Ellie. 'Now, sit down and pay attention. I don't know what's happened since yesterday but you look distracted and you'll need to concentrate.'

Ellie apologised again. Another English battle axe; she was getting used to them.

'This is the picture I thought you might like to see.' Brenda passed her a framed photograph. 'It's the only one I have of us all together: my brother and sisters and me, and your grandmother with us. We were at a Christmas party and someone took this photograph for the local paper.' She leaned over; Ellie caught a waft of peppermints. 'There's me sitting next to my older sister, Susan, and on my other side are the twins, Timothy and Janet. The lad in glasses beside them is poor Malcolm Parsons, who was evacuated with us. His mother took him back to London for the holiday and they were both killed a few days later.'

'How awful.' Ellie gazed at the little boy with the shy grin, destined never to grow old. 'And that's Nell, isn't it?' She'd spotted her grandmother in the back row, wearing the red hat and a dark coat. She wasn't smiling.

'That's right.' Brenda took a quick look and sat back, her eyes far away. 'It was the last time I saw her.' She gave a little shiver.

'So my mother wasn't there?' Ellie asked. 'I guess she was too young.'

'Maybe. I have other photographs of her, though.' Brenda reached for a battered black album on the table. 'There aren't many, but taking pictures was more of a palaver then. No one can eat a piece of toast nowadays without recording it for posterity.'

Ellie leafed through the pages. Alice was usually to be seen sitting on someone's lap or holding someone's hand, in the middle of the group. One photo showed her being towed along in a go-kart; in another, she was strapped into the most enormous pram, wearing a pixie hat, with Susan holding the handle.

'My older sister adored babies,' Brenda said. 'She's the one who became a midwife. We all loved Alice, though – she was our little mascot. It must have been so difficult for her, being suddenly taken away to live with her father. He brought her to visit once or twice but apparently she found it too unsettling, coming back and then having to leave again. Of course she did, poor little mite! The next thing we heard, he'd married someone else, and then Rose died a few years later, and so we lost touch.' She sighed. 'I thought the man was selfish, fetching his daughter back because he was lonely. He didn't stop to consider how she would feel, uprooted from the only people she knew. I'm glad she made a life for herself in America, and that she had a family of her own. Does she ever talk about her childhood?'

'Not often. All I knew was that her mother had died when she was a baby, and that she didn't get on with her stepmom. I wanted to come over here so I could fill in the gaps – for both of us. We don't even know how Nell died,' Ellie said. 'Sounds like you don't know either.'

'Not for certain, but I have a theory. You'll probably think I'm a mad old bat if I tell you.'

A shiver ran down Ellie's spine. 'Try me.'

'You make the tea, dear, and then I will. It's a long story and we'll need some refreshment.'

'I can see her clearly now, sitting in the front of that car next to the chauffeur. He was a cold fish. Cooke, his name was.' Brenda bent over the teacup, her glasses clouding with steam. She put down her cup and wiped the lenses slowly with a handkerchief.

'Go on.' Ellie smiled encouragingly, trying to hide her impatience.

'And Lord Winthrop was in the back. The Christmas party was at his house, you see. Millbury Manor, just up the road. It's been turned into luxury flats now – you wouldn't believe the prices. Nell had brought us there and then suddenly, she was off, leaving with him before the festivities were over. I tried to stop her but it was too late. Susan took us home that afternoon, and then it was Christmas a few days later, and then in the New Year, we were told she was dead.'

'But why did you try to stop her leaving?'

'Because I'd had my eye on Winthrop for a while and thought he was dodgy. Dodgy as a nine-bob note, we used to say. Timothy and I fancied ourselves as spies; there wasn't much going on in the village that we didn't know about. Lots of things about His Lordship made us suspicious. He kept a plane at Hatfield aerodrome, for a start, and there was a landing strip in a field next to the Manor, with comings and goings at all hours. We'd found a sort of shooting range in a wood behind the house, too, littered with cartridge cases and . . . other things. So we used this party as an excuse to have a look around the house. We said Malcolm needed the lavatory – he had problems in that department – and went exploring.' She took another sip of tea. 'The attic was full of guns, crates of them, and hand grenades, and boxes of God knows what else that there wasn't time to investigate. Lord Winthrop ran the Home Guard but they hardly had three rifles between them. This was his own private arsenal and if you ask me, he wouldn't have used it against the Germans. He was planning to throw them a welcome party.'

'Why didn't you tell the police what you'd seen?' Ellie asked.

'We probably should have done. But we were evacuees, remember, with a reputation for stirring up trouble. Lord and Lady Winthrop were the village bigwigs and we'd had no business poking around their house. Anyway, the police raided Millbury Manor the day after we'd heard Nell had died, and we saw all the weapons being carried out, so there was no need to come clean.'

'And what happened to Lord Winthrop?'

'Vanished into thin air, so far as anyone could tell. They took Lady Winthrop in for questioning but apparently she hadn't known what her husband was up to. Or at least, they couldn't pin anything on her.

Of course, there were all sorts of rumours flying around the village about the pair of them. Then, after the war, she sold the house to a stockbroker and moved abroad, and eventually everyone forgot about the Winthrops.'

'But you didn't.'

'No. I was convinced His Lordship had something to do with Nell's death. It seemed too much of a coincidence that she should have gone off with him to London, so soon before she was killed.'

'You're not saying he murdered her?'

'Who knows?' Brenda shrugged. 'He didn't look like the sort who'd be capable of murder but you can't judge from appearances. I did wonder whether she'd got wind of his activities, though, and had to be disposed of somehow.' She was quiet for a while, and then said, 'Why did your young man ask whether she was a Fascist? Such an odd question, it seemed to me afterwards.'

Brenda Macdonald was indeed sharp as a tack. 'Because I found a Fascist badge in her belongings, to start with,' Ellie replied. 'So I did some research at the Imperial War Museum in London, and saw Eleanor Spelman's name mentioned.'

Brenda leaned forward. 'Where?'

'In transcriptions from MI5 interviews. An undercover agent was running meetings, pumping suspected Fascists for information, and Nell was one of them. She was saying all kinds of anti-Semitic stuff.'

'Then she must have been working under cover,

too,' Brenda declared. 'Trust me, she'd never have said anything like that otherwise.' She fixed Ellie with a beady look. 'Those files must have been released fairly recently or I would have come across them.'

Ellie stared back at her. 'So you've been investigating as well? But why?'

'Because her death was such a mystery, and I was so angry about never being given a straight answer. I'd got the idea that her husband was a spy, I can't remember where from, and it seemed perfectly possible she might have been working with him, and that was why she'd gone rushing off to London. Her parents never talked about her after she'd died, or at least, not to us children, and I couldn't bear that. It was as though she'd never existed. Nell made a big impression on me. She spoke to me as though I was her equal, not a child, and she was so bright and talented. Here, I found her sketchbook in the loft. You should have it. Take it back for your mother.'

She passed a yellow-covered artist's pad across the table. Its pages were full of drawings of Alice as a baby: asleep with her thumb in her mouth, lying on her back with her chubby legs in the air, crawling up the stairs. The sketches were extraordinarily good, capturing her spirit in a few swift, assured strokes.

'You should take over where I left off,' Brenda said at last, when Ellie looked up from the pages. 'If you're serious about finding out what happened to your grandmother, that is. I'm positive a woman called Jane Coker holds the key to it all. I was making progress until the trail led to her and then I hit a brick wall. I haven't the energy to keep looking but somebody should, for Nell's sake. She deserves the truth to be known.' She patted Ellie's hand. 'Do your best, dear, and then I can die happy.'

Chapter Nineteen

London, December 1940

Nell forced herself to smile at the two women. 'Time for a cup of tea before you head home?'

'Sorry. Prior engagement.' Celia Dent checked her face in the mirror of her powder compact, then snapped it shut. 'So nice to meet you, Mrs Spelman. Hope to see you again in the new year.' She fastened the clasp of the fur stole around her throat, turned away from them and stalked off in the other direction down the Edgware Road.

'Don't mind if I do.' Miss Pardue's eyes gleamed, giving the lie to her words.

Celia Dent and Eunice Pardue had arrived at the address in Park West together, although they looked like unlikely friends. Mrs Dent was extremely slim and fashionably dressed in a cocktail frock and pillbox hat with a short veil. Her mouth beneath it was painted in bright red lipstick, and her fingernails were red to match. Miss Pardue, on the other hand, was stout and had a nervous tic which made her screw up her eyes and blink when she talked. She had a wet mouth, with tiny beads of spit collecting at the corners. The only other person at the gathering – apart from a Mr Kenneth Greene, who was in charge of proceedings – was a teenage youth called Martin something or other, who spent most of the time staring at his feet and blushed furiously whenever anyone spoke to him. He worked at a nearby munitions factory, while Miss Pardue was a secretary at Hatfield aerodrome. Mrs Dent 'lent a hand' at her local WVS, but her main claim to fame was her husband's internment at Brixton Prison along with Oswald Mosley, and the fact that she and her husband moved in the same social circles as Mosley and his wife.

'Diana's a great friend of mine, actually,' she told Nell in an offhand manner. 'It's a scandal, the way she's been treated. Locked up and her baby not even three months old.' Mrs Dent smoked incessantly from an ivory cigarette holder and had a hacking cough.

Nell had found the meeting an unsatisfactory affair. Martin was trying to find out where weapons were stored around the country but didn't seem to have got very far, while Miss Pardue could only make vague allusions to developments in design at the aerodrome. Mr Greene seemed amiable but slippery. They had all welcomed Nell, and her allegiance to the cause had apparently gone down well, yet she hadn't found out anything of value. There certainly weren't any plans for imminent action. The next meeting wasn't due to take place until after Christmas and she couldn't afford to wait that long. Still, maybe her 'fellow' Fascists could be persuaded to let something slip in a *tête-à-tête*. She knew she wouldn't have much luck making friends with Martin so the women it had to be, and now she was left with Eunice Pardue.

'There's a Kardomah,' Nell said, spying one in the other direction. 'My treat.'

When she and Miss Pardue were sitting at the most secluded table they could find in the café and had ordered their tea, she asked, 'I still can't find out exactly why my husband was arrested. Do you know anything about that?'

Miss Pardue leaned across the table, cupping her chin in one hand to shield her mouth. 'He was meant to have been putting up stickie-backs in telephone kiosks,' she whispered. 'I expect he got caught in the act. Not really cut out for that sort of thing, is he?'

Oh, Arthur! How he would have loathed such a grubby little escapade. Nell had seen the self-adhesive posters at bus stops and lampposts, proclaiming 'the Jew's war'. He must have been trying to prove himself. 'Fancy ending up in prison for something like that,' she said out loud.

Miss Pardue nodded vigorously. 'It's this Regulation 18B. The police can pick up anyone without a shred of evidence and lock them away for as long as they like. Honestly, it's a scandal.'

Her voice was rising. Nell put her finger to her lips and Miss Pardue glanced around. 'That's why we've got to do what we can to end this war as soon as possible,' she went on, her voice lowered to a malevolent hiss. 'We need a strong leader to throw out all the dirty Jews and Communists, and those councillors lining their own pockets. The Germans will make a better job of running the country than this shower. We'll soon have our empire back and get what's rightfully ours.'

Now, thank goodness, the waitress had arrived with their tea and crumpets. Miss Pardue inspected the tray greedily. 'Jam too! Shall I be mother?'

'Yes, please. I guessed Arthur was involved in some sort of plot,' Nell said, 'but he wouldn't tell me the details.'

'Men.' Miss Pardue sniffed. 'They want to keep all the glory for themselves.'

'I thought it was something big, though. Not just a few posters.' Nell sipped her tea reflectively. 'Have you heard any rumours?'

Miss Pardue was busy munching her crumpet and didn't reply. She swallowed and licked her greasy fingers, one by one, looking at Nell and blinking. 'I only want to play my part,' Nell added hastily, fearing she had gone too far.

'Me too. I've been trying to interest Mrs Dent in some sort of disruption but she's not keen. All talk, that one. And she's not as friendly with the Mosleys as she likes to make out. She went to a cocktail party at their house once, from what I gather.' Miss Pardue gave a cunning smile. 'Let's do something together, you and I.'

'Oh yes. Let's!' Nell played for time. 'What do you suggest?'

Eunice leaned forward, sheltering behind her hand again, and mouthed, 'There's a Jew tailor's shop near where I used to live on the Mile End Road. We could burn it down. All that cloth would make a lovely bonfire.'

'What a hoot!' Nell laughed, horrified. 'Except I think you'd need petrol and rags to start a fire and that would be difficult to explain if we were stopped on the way. Good idea, though.'

'All right, then. We'll throw a brick through the window.' Miss Pardue sat back, satisfied. 'And leave a few leaflets behind so they'll know it was us.'

'Marvellous.' Nell could wriggle out of it somehow; say she was ill, perhaps. 'When did you have in mind?'

'It'll have to be soon, before they shut for Christmas – not that they'll be celebrating, bloody heathens. Tomorrow evening would be a good time. We'll go after dark but early, so I can get home before the raids start. There won't be anyone around and Grossman will see the damage first thing on Monday. That'll start his week with a bang.' She giggled.

'Don't you think we ought to clear it with Mr Greene first, though?' Nell asked. 'It might be better to wait until the new year and see what he thinks.'

Miss Pardue pursed her lips. 'He'd probably try to

talk us out of it. I've got my doubts about our Kenneth.' She filled the teapot with hot water. 'Top up, Mrs Spelman?'

Nell pushed forward her cup. 'May I ask what you think of our friend Mr Talbot? Do you have your doubts about him, too?'

'Let's just say if I had to choose between the two of them in hopes of future glory, so to speak, I should throw in my lot with Bill. I'm sorry not to have seen him at Park West for a while.' Miss Pardue patted her hat complacently. 'Still, we speak from time to time.'

'Oh yes, I've been meaning to ask,' Nell said, as though she'd just remembered. 'Someone in my parents' village keeps a private plane at Hatfield. A Lord Winthrop? Have you by any chance come across him?'

'Can't say I have. There are so many people coming and going at the aerodrome, especially these days. You can imagine.'

'Of course. I thought he might have attended one of these gatherings, that's all. I've an inkling he's sympathetic to our cause.'

'I don't doubt it. Any fool can see which way the wind's blowing.' Miss Pardue blotted her mouth with a napkin. 'Well, thank you for the tea, Mrs Spelman. Most kind. I shall look forward to seeing you tomorrow evening. Shall we say six o'clock sharp at Mile End tube station?'

'I can't wait.' Nell did her best to smile again.

* * *

'It was sordid but somehow rather trivial,' Nell told Hetta. 'Not what I was expecting at all. I can't believe those people know anything about—' She stopped short, even though they were up on the roof with no one else in earshot. 'About you know what. And now I've got myself involved in this ridiculous scheme with the Pardue woman.'

'You don't have to go through with it,' Hetta said. 'You could go back to your baby and forget about the whole thing. Don't expect any support from the lot at St James's. Jane Coker might look like a curate's wife but she's ruthless. She'll drop you without a second thought if you end up in the soup.'

'I can't give up now. I have to stick up for Arthur and besides, if something big *is* being planned, surely it's my duty to help foil it?'

According to Hetta, several recent encrypted messages from sources at the very highest level had featured that word they dare not name. Hetta, Nell had discovered when she confronted her about her role in Miss Coker's organisation, was surprisingly well informed about a number of things.

'You should have been honest with me from the start,' Nell had reproached her, but Hetta had only laughed. And now they were working together. Hetta was to be her contact: Nell would tell her anything of interest, and she would pass it on to the team at St James's.

'Don't bother too much about reporting what happens at Park West,' she'd told Nell. 'That's already covered. This Talbot fellow sounds more interesting.'

And Lord Winthrop, too, Nell thought. She still felt certain he was involved. She'd remembered Brenda running after the car as it had left Millbury Manor. What had the girl been trying to say? She would have to telephone her mother again sooner or later, so perhaps she could talk to Brenda then.

'At least smashing a shopkeeper's window might convince Bill Talbot I'm serious,' she said.

Hetta stamped out her cigarette and got up from the packing-crate seat. 'Try not to get caught. Although they might let you share a cell with your husband, I suppose. Well, I'm off. Places to go, people to see, etcetera. I'll sound the alarm if you don't turn up tomorrow evening.' She picked up her lamp. 'Good luck.'

'Thanks.' Nell watched the small beam of light bob through the dark, feeling very much alone. She had been nervous, standing outside the flat in Park West, but the thought of Bill Talbot terrified her. The danger from bombs was more straightforward. Yet all the same, she was relieved to find the sirens didn't sound once that night. She was able to have a leisurely supper in the staff canteen with the nurses, who were a jolly, uncomplicated trio, and sleep through with only the odd distant thump to disturb her.

She found Talbot hunched over an empty glass at the bar of 'their' pub the next morning. 'Time for another?' she asked, shamed by the tremor in her voice. A quick drink and then she could go.

He gave her a sour smile. 'Well, look what the cat dragged in.' And she had to laugh, as though it were funny.

When the drinks had arrived, she lit a cigarette, hoping he hadn't noticed her hand shaking, and waited for him to speak. 'So,' he said eventually. 'Did you have a good time yesterday?'

'It was all right, I suppose.' She blew out a cool plume of smoke. 'A little tame, though. I was hoping for some more direct action.'

'Well, aren't you the one.' He didn't like women, she could tell. He'd probably had his share of rejections and was determined to take his humiliation out on all of them. Or perhaps he just hated everyone.

She gulped the fiery gin. 'Miss Pardue seems a decent sort, though. She was enquiring after you. Said you hadn't dropped in for a while.'

'I've had other fish to fry.' Talbot swallowed a mouthful of beer and wiped his mouth with the back of his hand.

'Oh?' Nell raised a flirty eyebrow, which he ignored. There was so much she wanted to ask: whether he had taken over Arthur's work, for a start, because surely somebody had to be maintaining the clocks if her husband wasn't. Yet Talbot would become suspicious if she were too inquisitive. She wondered whether he had mentioned her name to Lord Winthrop. The two of them were working together, she was certain, but the connection seemed impossible to prove when she daren't risk showing her hand.

When the silence was becoming awkward, she said, 'As a matter of fact, Miss Pardue and I are planning a little jaunt together this evening.'

Talbot stared at her without speaking. 'Yes,' she went on, as though he'd just declared that was the most riveting thing he'd ever heard, 'we're going to surprise a certain Jewish tailor with a brick through his shop window.' She smiled, copying Miss Pardue's glee.

Talbot lit a cigarette of his own. 'Think that's going to make much difference?'

'Well, it's a start!' The man was infuriating. Why had he arranged to meet her if he wasn't interested in what she had to say? She was so irritated that for a moment, she forgot to be frightened. 'I'd have thought you'd be pleased.'

'Better not get yourself arrested, like someone we know.'

Nell was encouraged by the 'we'.

'I won't,' she said. 'I told you I'd be more careful. But you should understand I'm serious, Mr Talbot. About helping the cause, I mean.'

'Maybe you are.' He pushed back his cap and gave her a long, appraising look. What was he thinking? She was proud that she managed to meet his eyes without flinching. At last he said, 'All right. If you're so keen, there might be something you could do. I'll have to talk to a few people and get back to you.'

'Well, don't take too long about it.' Nell drained her glass. 'You'll find I'm in demand.' Oh God, why had she said that?

'Spare me the details,' he muttered. 'I'll see you here, then, tomorrow evening at six.'

The barmaid smiled at Nell as she left the pub; she was turning into a regular. What would Arthur have said?

Miss Pardue was waiting for Nell outside the tube station in a camelhair coat with a paisley headscarf, her handbag over her arm. Nell was respectably dressed, too; they had to look like a couple of friends, out for an evening stroll. Although Nell couldn't see much of the area in the blackout, she could tell by the way the wind howled around them that it had been badly knocked about.

'Got your brick?' Miss Pardue asked her, but she said she would pick one up along the way. She was spoilt for choice; they were constantly stumbling over rubble and her torch beam revealed craters in the pavement.

Miss Pardue had brought leaflets and delegated the brick-throwing to Nell because of her sciatica. 'I can't raise my arm above the shoulder,' she'd said, 'otherwise I'd have loved to join in.'

Nell thought of Arthur's father, Henry, so anxious never to do or say anything that might cause offence. She imagined him in 1915, hurrying to sweep up the glass from his smashed shop windows before anyone could witness his shame. Miss Pardue walked ahead, occasionally darting into a telephone kiosk or bus shelter; a flutter of white paper in the dark and she'd return, breathing fast. 'It's easy,' she whispered, giggling. 'I can't imagine how your husband managed to get himself picked up.'

There weren't many people around. A pub door opened, letting out a gust of smoky air and conversation, and a man walked by, the tip of his cigarette glowing. Trams clattered up and down the Mile End Road and the odd bus roared past, its shrouded headlights reduced to narrow slits.

When they had been walking for fifteen minutes or so, Miss Pardue pulled her into a nearby doorway. 'It's just there, on the corner,' she whispered, blinking furiously as she shone her torch up the road. A fleck of spittle landed on Nell's cheek, making her recoil. 'Take a look at the lie of the land. I'll keep a lookout here. If anyone comes, I'll cough.'

Nell went ahead on her own. So far, she had done nothing wrong. She waited for a tram to pass by, shining her torch at the window of Grossman and Sons. 'Tailors and alteration experts since 1920', proclaimed a sign on the door. 'Let Grossman's dress you and cut your tailoring bills by half'. The glass was criss-crossed with brown tape; behind it, she could make out a tailor's dummy, dressed in a half-finished dinner jacket tacked together with long white stitches, a tape measure draped around its neck. A giant reel of thread had been fashioned from a wooden cable drum wound with tinsel, against which was propped a pair of silver-painted cardboard scissors. There were pine cones scattered on the floor, and fake snow that she guessed was Lux soap flakes.

Lowering the torch, she strolled around the corner into a side road lined with dilapidated terraced houses, their doors opening onto the street. She tripped over an empty bottle ready for collection by the milkman the next morning, sending it rolling into the gutter. Soon, she found the inevitable broken-down wall, and kicked over the rubble until a suitable missile emerged from the pile. Tucking it inside her siren suit, she walked back to Miss Pardue.

'This should do,' she said, drawing back her lapel to reveal the brick.

Miss Pardue thrust a folded paper into her hand. 'Don't forget to leave the leaflet behind.' Then she added in an entirely different voice, 'Goodness, Gladys, I've a terrible stitch. Do let me catch my breath.'

'All right, ladies?' An approaching warden flashed his torch briefly into their faces.

'Fine, thank you,' Nell replied, putting her arm behind her back. 'Just making our way home.'

'Well, don't hang about.' He nodded and strolled past them towards the tube station. Nell let out her breath, wondering whether he'd noticed her rooting through the debris, but he didn't glance back.

'That was a close one.' Miss Pardue let out a giggle, blinking furiously.

Anyone might loom out of the dark at the wrong moment and catch Nell with a brick in one hand and *A Last Appeal to Reason* by Adolf Hitler, in the other. She saw herself up before the magistrate for vandalism – but of course, she would have been charged with a more serious crime. Maybe Hetta's suggestion she might end up sharing a cell with Arthur wasn't so laughable after all.

'After I've done the deed, we must split up,' she said. 'Pretend we don't know each other, it'll be safer.'

Miss Pardue nodded, not quite as full of bravado now. Nell headed into the dark, a sense of resolution overcoming the sick dread in her stomach. A safe distance away, she dropped the brick in the gutter and stuffed the leaflet in her bag. When she had reached Grossman's, she turned down the side street, picked up a milk bottle from the nearest doorstep and paused for a moment, watching and listening for trams or wardens or Miss Pardue's warning cough. Then she hurled the bottle with all her strength at the wall beside the shop, where it shattered with a satisfying crash.

''Ere! What's going on?' Somewhere above her head, a window had been pulled up and a voice was shouting into the darkness.

Nell was already hurrying down the road. She broke into a run with her torch trained on the white linc at the edge of the pavement, heedless of the uneven ground, hissing only to Miss Pardue that she had been spotted, and somebody might be after her. She ran away from what she had so nearly done, not stopping until she had reached the station and joined the stream of people heading underground, some with bedding rolled under their arms. Their tired faces, at once so commonplace and heroic, looked at her with indifference as she struggled to catch her breath. Spotting a couple of policemen standing by the ticket barrier, she dropped her eyes, her heart racing. Yet she was able to walk past them and down to the platform unchallenged, still carrying her secret burden of guilt.

'I'd say our little scheme was a success, wouldn't you?' Miss Pardue screwed up her eyes, blinking wildly. 'There must have been glass everywhere, judging from the noise. Shame we couldn't go back to inspect the damage.'

Bill Talbot glanced at them both with what seemed to Nell like contempt. 'So now you're partners in crime. Who'd have thought it?'

Miss Pardue laughed uncertainly. 'Sabotage is actually rather fun.' She had made up her sallow cheeks with rouge, which added to her general air of hysteria.

Nell hadn't been expecting to see her again so soon, but when she arrived at the pub, there was Eunice Pardue, sporting a pink tam-o'-shanter with matching scarf and drinking a glass of stout opposite Bill Talbot. At first, Nell had been relieved to have an ally in dealing with the man. That feeling had soon turned to frustration, however, because what could she say of any importance in front of Miss Pardue? She had no idea why Talbot had invited her; he seemed to take no more pleasure in her company than he did in Nell's. Miss Pardue seemed desperate for his approval, suggesting other windows that might be smashed and other places where leaflets could be dropped. She was outlining a plan to daub graffiti on the door of a synagogue in Shoreditch (Nell guessed that task would be delegated to her) when Talbot interrupted.

'That's all amateur stuff. How'd you like to be involved in something really important? Think you'd be up to it?'

'What, us?' Miss Pardue asked.

'We'd be honoured,' Nell said quickly. 'Wouldn't we, Miss Pardue? Anything for the cause.'

'It's a high-profile job,' Talbot said. 'Your names would be noticed by our friends in high places. Might even be a medal in it for you both.'

Miss Pardue blushed and blinked, struck dumb. Nell's palms prickled with excitement and dread. She lit a cigarette, inhaling deeply to control her nerves, and asked Talbot to tell them more.

'Not here,' he replied. 'And not now. The less you know, the less you'll be tempted to blab.' His expression made her quail.

'Oh, we wouldn't breathe a word to anyone,' Miss Pardue assured him.

'But can you at least say when we'll be needed?' Nell asked. 'I'll be going away shortly, you see.'

'New Year's,' he said. 'So you won't have to wait too long. Think you'll be free?'

After they'd assured him they were – Miss Pardue had a tentative engagement, apparently, but nothing that couldn't be rearranged – he said they were to meet in the pub at midday on New Year's Eve itself, when he would tell them precisely what they'd have to do.

‘And is this—?’ Nell stopped, uncertain how to continue. ‘The plan, I mean, is it—?’

‘Yes, it’s the big one.’ Talbot smiled, revealing a row of surprisingly small yellow teeth. ‘You’ve got what you wanted.’

Chapter Twenty

London, December 1940

'Really, darling? I don't understand,' Rose said. 'Why do you have to stay in London over Christmas? It seems very odd to me. Why can't Arthur manage this business by himself?'

'I'm so sorry,' Nell replied. 'I'd love nothing more than to come home, you know that, but I simply have to stay in London for another week. Arthur's been – called away. I can't explain over the telephone, I'll tell you when I see you. How's Alice?' She could hardly bear to ask.

'Oh, she's all right. Susan's been a great help, I must say. But she's missing her mother. Still, I suppose your husband needs you more than we do.' Rose sounded so disappointed that Nell could hardly bear it.

'I'll see you in the new year, Ma, I promise,' she said. 'Thanks for being such a brick.'

There was a click as Rose replaced the receiver, followed by the dialling tone buzzing in Nell's ear. She wrenched open the door of the telephone kiosk and stepped out into the grey gloom of a winter day. Christmas in Oxfordshire would have been impossible, even if she could have travelled by magic carpet instead of a fully-booked train; she couldn't have borne to leave Alice again and Rose wouldn't have let her go back to London a second time without the most tremendous fuss. There was no alternative but to stay put until the new year. She would do whatever was asked of her – she couldn't begin to imagine what that might be – and go back to Millbury after the job was done. Arthur was right: there would be other Christmases.

The Palace of Westminster had an abandoned air. Parliament had gone into recess the week before and by now most of the maintenance, cleaning and catering staff had left. Hetta was deserting Nell, too. She was off to spend Christmas with friends in Scotland. The combination of danger and shared confidences over brandy and cigarettes on the roof had brought the two of them closer than Nell would have believed possible in such a short time. Hetta was unshockable; one could say absolutely anything and she wouldn't flinch. Nell trusted her completely. After all, there seemed little point hiding anything from her when she knew so much of the story already. She was an ally at a time when Nell was in desperate need of one, and her courage made the dangerous, rackety life they were leading seem almost ordinary. Or manageable, at least.

They were having a farewell lunch together before Hetta left for the station. The canteen had been decorated with paperchains made out of newspaper and Dolly behind the counter wore a hat trimmed with tinsel, though her expression was as dour as usual. She slopped a portion of marbled pink corned-beef hash onto Nell's plate and added a spoonful of tinned peas swimming in water. There was to be a grand Christmas lunch for the remaining staff the next day; clearly the kitchen staff were conserving their energy.

'Grim, isn't it?' Hetta surveyed her meal. 'Like someone's insides, scraped off the pavement after a particularly nasty accident.' She pushed her plate aside after a few mouthfuls and lit a cigarette. 'So, you're clear about everything?'

Nell nodded. Hetta had given her a Whitehall telephone number to ring in case of emergencies. She had to tell whoever answered that she had left her suitcase at Paddington Station, and wait for the reply: 'The lockers there are so convenient.' Then she would know it was safe to speak, and that her message would reach Miss Coker. The dialogue sounded like something out of a film, although no doubt she'd feel differently if she actually had a reason to say the phrase.

'Anyway, I'll be back by the weekend. And it does look as though Jerry's giving us a few days off. I'm sure you'll be fine.' Hetta gave Nell a shrewd look. 'What's on your mind?'

No one else was in earshot. 'I just wish we knew who was behind the whole thing,' Nell said. 'I'm sure Talbot couldn't have planned it, he hasn't the authority. And why involve Eunice Pardue? She's the proverbial leaky bucket.'

'Let the Ministry lot worry about that,' Hetta replied. 'You don't want to muddy the waters. Just stick to your part and let them get on with theirs.'

She was probably right, yet Nell's thoughts kept circling back to Lord Winthrop. His interest in Arthur had led her husband to the flat in Park West, she was certain, and ultimately to his arrest. And then there had been the question of Winthrop's meeting with Bill Talbot, and above all, what he had said on the telephone at Millbury Manor. She hoped Miss Coker had taken her suspicions seriously. But what if she had misheard? And what if those other events had been merely a series of coincidences?

'Made any plans for tomorrow?' Hetta asked, bringing her back to the present with a jolt.

'Lunch here, which is bound to be a veritable feast.' They laughed. 'And then, later, the usual shift upstairs, I suppose. You never know, Jerry might surprise us.'

'Not going to see your husband?'

Nell shook her head. 'Visits have to be booked days ahead.' She knew Arthur would have hated her to see him in jail; it would be the final humiliation. 'I'll drop off a card and present,' she added. A small token, it would have to be, since her money had to last another week. Hetta had given her some knickers made out of parachute silk, but there was still the question of food and cigarettes. She had to marshal her resources.

After Hetta had gone, Nell resisted the temptation to fall into limbo. She walked to Victoria Station, finding a draper's along the way, which was about to close, where she managed to buy Arthur a pair of socks entirely with clothing coupons. 'Your husband will be glad of these,' the shop assistant had said, wrapping them in brown paper, and Nell had resisted the urge to reply, 'Yes, he's probably cold in prison,' just to see the expression on her face. It seemed wasteful to spend money on a card so, sitting on the underground train to Brixton, she wrote a cheery message on the back of a flattened cigarette packet and tucked it inside the parcel. The prison looked as forbidding as one might have expected. She shivered, looking up at the grim façade and imagining Arthur behind it. What kind of state could he be in? Not long, my darling, she promised. I'll get you out of there.

After she had dropped off his modest present, she took the train to Green Park and wandered about for a while, past the Ritz and the ruined church, with pigeons nesting in its burnt rafters. The pavements were crowded with last-minute shoppers, although the few shops that were still open had meagre window displays; even the dressers at Fortnum & Mason had restricted themselves to hampers filled with pretend presents – cardboard boxes beneath the gay paper, Nell guessed – and pyramids of papier mâché fruit. To distract herself, she walked on to Leicester Square and bought a ticket to see *Gone with the Wind*. It was an extravagance but at least she could sit in the dark, safe and warm, until it was time for her vigil on the roof. It occurred to her, later, looking out over the sleeping city, that fire watching was the only responsibility she had for the next few days. Apart from that, she could please herself entirely, and she might as well, because there was no knowing when the chance would come again. So she got up early on Christmas morning and walked for miles along the river, up to Tower Bridge and beyond, as far as the docks, where roofless warehouses lay open to the sky and the skeletons of wharves cooled their blackened bones in the water. She had to witness the devastation, awful though it was. When Alice was older, she would bring her here and describe what she saw now, so that her daughter would know what the country had endured, and do her utmost to make sure it never happened again.

'So how was it? Predictably gruesome?' Hetta was back from Scotland, bearing slices of cake wrapped in greaseproof paper, a cooked pheasant and fresh supplies of brandy and cigarettes. They were sitting on one of the truckle beds, having a debrief.

'Actually, the lunch was surprisingly good,' Nell said. 'Only mutton but it was jolly tender, with onion sauce and as many potatoes and carrots as one could want. And plenty of booze, too. Sherry to start and someone produced a bottle of whisky later, which certainly helped with the sing-song. And then we listened to the King.'

'So did we. He didn't make too bad a job of it, did he? Though I can't imagine why they had to make him say "ready to resist". It seemed almost cruel.' They laughed. Poor King George, with his stammer and his speech impediment: the whole country must have been willing him through the Christmas address. 'So who was there?' Hetta went on. 'Just you, the custodians and the Home Guard?'

'Some WVS ladies came along, too. As a matter of fact, it was one of them who provided the whisky.' Nell picked off a crumb of yellow paste and chewed thoughtfully. 'Does this marzipan taste rather odd or is it just me?'

'Sorry, I should have warned you. It's a heady concoction of flour, marge and almond essence.' Hetta passed over the hip flask. 'Have a swig to cleanse your palate and tell me what else you've been up to.'

'Not much. I walked about a lot, and I've seen *Gone with the Wind* three times and *The Thief of Baghdad* twice. Nothing to touch your celebrations.'

Hetta's friends were very grand, from what Nell could make out. There had been twenty around the table for Christmas lunch, a hunt on Boxing Day and a shoot the day after that. There was going to be a ball for Hogmanay, too, featuring Scottish reels and men in kilts. 'Don't worry, I couldn't possibly leave you in the lurch,' Hetta had said. 'New Year's Eve is your moment of glory, isn't it?'

Nell was already sick with nerves; waiting with nothing much to do only made the ordeal worse. Still, only a couple more days and then it would be over – one way or another. At that moment, the siren's pulsing note started. 'Here we go.' Hetta scrambled to her feet. 'The holidays are over.'

They'd already assembled a collection of sandbags, pumps and buckets to hand on the roof. Hetta was first up the metal staircase. 'Looks like we're going to be busy,' she called down. The roaming searchlight beams picked up scores of enemy bombers streaming across the sky, their engines chugging steadily beneath the thunder of ack ack guns, and now they heard the gentle swoosh of falling incendiaries. Soon hundreds of those spitting magnesium flowers were blossoming in the dark, some extinguished only to pop up again close by, others fizzing steadily until their white hearts were swallowed up by tongues of yellow flame. It was a windy night and everywhere Nell looked, blazing rivers were flowing into one great sea of fire.

Nell stared around in disbelief. Surely there had never been bombing on such a scale – although miraculously, so far not a single incendiary had landed on their part of the roof. They were standing on an island in the middle of an inferno that was roaring as loudly as any bomber.

'What shall we do?' she shouted, but Hetta only shrugged.

On the planes thundered, and now the scream of high explosives close by added to the din. Hetta grabbed

Nell's arm and dragged her to the shelter of a nearby turret, where they hunkered down behind a pile of sandbags as the world around them was torn apart.

Some time later, an incendiary landed not far away – still only the one – and Nell was able to dispatch it with her stirrup pump. Taking advantage of a lull in the wave of bombing she ran, crouching, to the low parapet wall at the edge of the roof and looked out.

'My God.' Hetta had arrived and stood at her shoulder, mesmerised.

The darkness was gone. A false dawn had broken, leaving the city bathed in a surreal rosy glow. A pall of pink smoke drifted across the livid crimson sky, brilliant diamonds of light flashing within it as anti-aircraft shells exploded harmlessly around the enemy planes. Fewer now, though still coming. The barrage balloons had flushed the colour of candy floss and the Thames had turned into a shining golden ribbon, with a tug boat ablaze on it like a flaming torch. The whole of London was on fire. It was the most terrible, beautiful thing Nell had ever seen.

Lorries and fire engines hurtled through the streets, their bells clanging; already, turntable ladders were swinging into position and jets of water arcing against the blaze. Nell scanned the horizon. The smoke seemed to be thickest upriver, towards the City and around St Paul's. For a moment, the dense cloud swirled apart to reveal the pale, serene dome of the cathedral, still intact so far – but for how long? And all they could do was watch. They saw extraordinary things: bombs curling through the sky like shooting stars; a vast building with flames spilling from every window falling gently forward as if in slow motion; a fireman three storeys high swept from his ladder by the cable of a drifting barrage balloon. Shrapnel clanged on the roof as the ack ack guns continued to fire, people shouted and screamed in the streets below, and every fifteen minutes the Westminster Chimes rang out regardless.

'There'll probably be a second wave.' Hetta lit two cigarettes and passed one to Nell, her hand shaking. 'We must stay alert.'

Yet, extraordinarily, an hour or so later, they heard the piercing wail of the All Clear. They climbed off the roof, dazed, and went down into the street with sandbags over their shoulders. The ground was awash with water, hissing shrapnel and chunks of masonry, the air full of ash and cinders. Sparks showered down on them like golden rain; Nell had to duck as a spar of burning wood narrowly missed her. Firemen were everywhere, dragging unwieldy hoses that writhed like snakes, shouting instructions, their reddened eyes staring from faces black with soot.

'We might as well piss on it for all the good we're doing,' said one, throwing the nozzle down in disgust.

'Can we help?' Nell asked, but he brushed past her without a reply.

They dealt with a couple of small fires in the gutter and walked on, not knowing where they were heading or what they hoped to find. A woman wearing a dressing gown and a saucepan on her head instead of a helmet ran down the road, which might have been funny had she not been weeping. Rounding a corner, they came across a small knot of people in front of a partly demolished house. The front wall had been sheered away, revealing a kitchen on the ground floor with a table set for breakfast – two bowls and spoons, two side plates, two cups and saucers – and a flight of stairs leading to nowhere. The first floor was a mass of beams piled higgledy-piggledy on top of each other, plasterboard, bricks and roof tiles. An unbearable sound was coming from somewhere within the chaos, midway between a howl and a scream.

Catching sight of them, a man turned away from the group and called, 'Sonny? Over here!' And then, 'Oh, sorry, Miss. My mistake.'

A woman and her twin babies were trapped at the back of the house, he said when Hetta and Nell were in earshot. Someone had tried to reach them several times – a ladder stood propped against the wall – but the gap between the beams was too small for a man to crawl through. They were having to wait for the heavy rescue boys with a crane, and who knew how long that was going to take.

'Would you be prepared to have a go?' the warden asked Hetta. 'Think you're about the right size. If you could at least get close enough to tell us exactly where they are, it would be a help.'

'I'll do my best.' She was already taking off her jacket.

'Is the building stable, though?' Nell said.

'As far as we can tell.' A woman in uniform and a peaked cap had joined them, and now Nell noticed the St John Ambulance waiting nearby with its doors open. 'I'd go myself, but . . .' She gestured at her ample hips.

'Don't worry. Of course I'll do it.' Hetta took a brief swig from the hip flask and passed it to Nell, along with the cigarettes that were in her trouser pockets. 'Keep these for me?'

'Just a minute,' the woman said. 'I'll give you something for that poor soul, if you can get near her.' She hurried over to the ambulance, returning moments later with a folded cloth that smelt sickly sweet. 'Put this over her mouth and nose. Try not to breathe it in yourself.'

Hetta nodded. Seconds later, she was shinning up the ladder.

'Stand back, just in case.' The warden shooed them a safe distance away. There were five people altogether in their group: the ambulance driver and her nurse, an off-duty fireman from the next street who'd come to help, Nell and himself. The fireman followed Hetta, taking up position at the foot of the ladder. Cinders swirled towards them on a gust of wind and a column of smoke rose from the back of the house; water gushed from a broken pipe on the first floor to the kitchen table below and the china fell off it, piece by piece, to smash on the tiled floor. Nell could hear it, she realised, because the woman who'd been screaming had stopped. She let out her breath with a shudder.

Hetta emerged backwards from the wreckage a few minutes later, on her stomach. They saw her boots feeling for a foothold on the ladder before the rest of her body appeared and she was climbing down. Once on the ground, she bent double and vomited. Nell started forward but the warden reached out a restraining arm. 'Leave her be.'

At last she walked unsteadily towards them. 'The woman's dead, I'm afraid,' she said. 'Pretty sure I can reach one of the babies but I can't see the other. Don't know if either of them are alive.' Her face was a greenish white. The nurse gave her water from a vacuum flask and she took a mouthful of brandy after that.

'Should I come too?' Nell asked, but Hetta shook her head, saying there was no point; it was a tight squeeze, even for her. The warden decided that the fireman should follow her up the ladder and she would pass the babies out to him. Or not, as the case might be.

Nell could hardly bear to watch. She turned and walked a short distance away, worried she might be sick herself, and drank some brandy too. When she looked again, Hetta had disappeared from view. A few minutes later, the fireman called to her and a reply came from somewhere inside the wreck, but the wind snatched their voices away. Nell paced back and forth, her mind blank. A cheer from the nurse made her whirl around, to see the fireman climbing back down the ladder. After he'd reached the ground, he paused for a moment to reach inside his tunic, and soon the reedy, indignant wail of a baby drifted towards them.

'Now there's a thing!' cried the ambulance driver. The warden laughed, taking out a packet of cigarettes, and the nurse squeezed Nell's arm. 'See?'

Nell's breasts throbbed in response to the cry and she felt the milk rise in them, seeping through her brassiere. The visceral reaction took her by surprise. She'd thought her milk had all gone but the flow only increased when she saw the little mite, not more than three months old, wrapped in a filthy sheet and bawling now, its eyes screwed up and red in the face. The nurse had taken the baby from the fireman's arms and wrapped it in a blanket. Nell followed her to the ambulance, already unbuttoning her siren suit.

'May I?' she asked, reaching out for the baby.

After a brief, astonished pause, the nurse said, 'Well, I can't see why not,' and handed him over. She clearly thought it was a very odd request, though, and watched Nell dubiously as she sat on the ambulance step and settled the baby on her lap. His cries became more frantic as he smelt her milk and his open mouth searched desperately for the nipple. Gently she guided his small, hard head to her breast. He latched on with grim determination and began to suck, kneading her flesh with his tiny fingers, intent on the business of survival. Occasionally, he paused to give an outraged hiccup, milk dribbling down his dirty chin. It couldn't have been much of a feed but the familiar action and warmth of her skin must have been a comfort. Nell stroked his matted hair, glad to be of use at last, and the baby stared back at her with ancient, inscrutable eyes.

And then a number of things happened all at once, in a split second. The air was sucked out of Nell's lungs, leaving her breathless and panicky. She saw the remaining walls of the house bulge outwards, and thc ladder fall away, and the fireman who had been about to climb it blown backwards as the most tremendous explosion set the ambulance rocking. Nell hugged the baby, bent over him, her ears ringing with the sound as missiles clanged against its metal side. When at last the noise had died away, she looked up to find the ground littered with stones and splintered wood. All that remained of the building was a mountain of rubble. She might have been looking at the wreck of her old home in Hathaway Road – except this time, there were people buried under the debris, and one of them was Hetta.

Chapter Twenty-One

London, December 1940

It was most probably a delayed-action fuse on the bomb, that's what they said, or maybe some movement in the house had triggered the explosion: a settling of beams, or the collapse of an internal wall. Nell stayed at the site all night; she couldn't leave Hetta alone in that desolate place. Somebody gave her a blanket and a WVS refreshment van arrived as the true dawn broke. She sat on a sandbag with her back against the wall, drinking hot, sweet tea. The heavy rescue boys had turned up by then and three or four men and a dog were picking over the rubble. There was no need for a crane, because the building had been so thoroughly blown apart. The men grunted with exertion, calling to each other in terse voices. Occasionally the dog scrabbled with renewed vigour and they would cluster around it, calling for silence, and listen with their heads bent low to the rock. Nell had offered to help but they wouldn't let her, and she was glad, because she dreaded what she might find.

She had drifted into a fitful sleep when a cheer woke her and she leapt to her feet, dazed. A miracle had occurred, although not the one she'd been hoping for: something small and soft and human was being lifted from the pit and passed from one pair of arms to another. The second twin had been dug out.

'Who'd have believed it?' said one of the WVS ladies. 'As if anything could have come out of there alive!' Somebody shushed her, most likely for Nell's sake.

The baby had been sleeping in a drawer, it emerged, and a door had been blown across it that formed a perfect shelter, with enough air to breathe. The little bundle was cuddled and exclaimed over, and a second ambulance was called to take him to hospital, as the first had long gone by then. Nell wondered whether the twins would ever be reunited; everything seemed such a muddle that she doubted it. The baby was quiet and she couldn't bear to look at him. The only way to get through this ordeal, she felt, was to keep her mind as quiet and blank as possible. She watched the men work, huddled in her blanket; occasionally she stood up to stretch her legs and smoke a cigarette.

The pale sun was rising in a peachy sky streaked with crimson when a warden approached her. 'Do you recognise this?'

A chain swung, glinting, from his hands: Hetta's St Christopher medal. When Nell confirmed that it belonged to her friend, he patted her awkwardly on the back and said there was little point in her staying any longer. 'There's no hope, I'm afraid,' he added, in case she had somehow missed the point. 'Go home now and get some sleep.'

He'd taken her gently by the shoulders and guided her away. She had walked in a dream, not knowing where to go. The people she passed wore the same blank, baffled expression as they picked their way over the ground. One elderly couple had no shoes. She saw a woman being helped into an ambulance, burned skin hanging down from her elbows in shreds. Fires were still burning; columns of smoke rose up everywhere she looked, fire engines tore through the streets and the gutters ran with dirty water. The air was full of ashes so she tied a handkerchief over her nose, which helped a little. There were cinders in her hair and her hands were filthy, her fingernails rimmed in black. She stood for a moment, looking about. There was something important she had to do, but she couldn't think what. Finding herself in St James's Park, the idea came to her that, of course, she must go to the house off St James's Street and tell Miss Coker that Hetta was dead.

Hetta was dead. She repeated the words in her head, not wanting to believe them. Hetta, so full of life, so brave and seemingly indestructible; how could she possibly have gone? Nell had jumped out of her old life and landed in another, and it had been Hetta who'd been there to guide her, Hetta who had scooped her up and become her friend. She sank onto a bench with her head in her hands, clutching her hair so hard that it hurt. The pain would help her focus.

'Pull yourself together, old girl,' she heard Hetta say, as clearly as though she had been sitting beside her. 'Sitting here won't get the job done.'

A mouthful of brandy was left in the hip flask. She pulled off her handkerchief mask, drank it and stood up. One foot in front of the other, one step at a time; that's how it was done. She fastened Hetta's St Christopher medal around her neck, next to the watch Arthur had given her, fearing that she might lose it. The two chains soon became tangled, which she found comforting; it made her feel as though she and Hetta were still together. As she walked, she overheard snatches of conversation from the people emerging from shelters or standing at bus stops. The fire had spread rapidly between empty buildings. Being a Sunday, there had been no workers to sound the alarm, and no firewatchers either; the fire service had been overwhelmed and the tide in the river too low to pump more water. St Paul's had been saved, a policeman said, but only by a miracle, and all the books had been burned in the publishers' warehouses in Paternoster Row. Nell felt as though she were living through a nightmare, the sort one feels relieved to have woken up from. There could be no wakening and no relief now, though, only a grim process of counting the cost.

She didn't know the name of the street off St James's but after a certain amount of wandering about, managed to find the house with the 'To Let' sign outside. It was still early. She was shown to a cloakroom where she managed to clean herself up a little, and then to a small windowless room where she paced up and down as she waited, bracing herself. She could hear the familiar sounds of chaos in the corridor outside, the same atmosphere of frenetic activity.

At last she was taken to see Miss Coker, who sat in state behind her vast desk. 'You shouldn't have come here,' she said, by way of a greeting. 'Don't do it again.'

Her expression hardly changed when Nell passed on the news of Hetta's death, although she swivelled her chair around to look out of the window and didn't speak for what seemed a long time. Eventually she said, 'You're due to meet this man at midday tomorrow?' When Nell nodded, she picked up the telephone receiver and barked into it, 'Ask Miss Hart to come to my office. At once, please.'

Miss Hart was the girl with the streaming cold who'd driven Nell here the last time; she didn't look much better now. They nodded at each other while she dabbed her nose with a handkerchief. Miss Coker informed her she was to wait for Nell the next day, under the statue of the lion on the south side of Westminster Bridge. They would walk beside the river until they were sure of being unobserved, and then Nell could relay whatever information she'd gleaned.

'I was given a Whitehall telephone number, too,' Nell said. 'Is that still valid?' The line about leaving her suitcase at Paddington Station had suddenly come back to her.

'Only for emergencies,' Miss Coker replied. 'We trust it won't be necessary.' She stood. 'Well, if that's everything, I won't keep you. Good luck for tomorrow.'

'Could I rest here for a while?' Nell asked, no longer giving a damn about social niceties. 'I've been up all night and I don't have anywhere else to go.'

Miss Coker didn't seem at all put out. 'Of course. Take Mrs Spelman upstairs, Felicity, and make her a cup of tea.'

'Upstairs' turned out to mean another cubby hole, just big enough for a camp bed. Nell was swilling in tea; if she drank any more, she'd dissolve. She thanked Miss Hart but declined her offer, kicked off her boots, crawled under the blanket fully dressed and fell instantly asleep.

She slept all day, waking only when Miss Hart reappeared to tell her the office was closing and show her the back door through which she could leave unobtrusively. That night she kept vigil at her spot on the roof, remembering each time she had been there with Hetta, every conversation they'd had in the still, small hours. All was quiet; perhaps the Germans had run out of bombs. The next day, she woke with the dawn and on a whim, walked over to the clock tower and used Arthur's keys to unlock the door. She climbed the endless spiral steps to the belfry and then up to the Ayrton light. Then, at last, she wept. St Paul's stood alone in a wasteland. The maze of narrow streets that once surrounded it had been reduced to rubble, from which plumes of smoke still rose into the cold morning air. So many irreplaceable, ancient buildings, destroyed in a single night. It was unbearable.

'It's chronic catarrh,' Miss Hart said, as they strolled together beside the Thames after Nell's meeting with Talbot. 'Can't seem to shake it off but I'm not contagious.'

'Poor you,' Nell replied, as though she cared. 'How grim. I've had one eye infection after another. I expect we shall all end up with scurvy.'

They had walked downriver as far as Lambeth Bridge, then turned and headed back again. 'This'll do.' Miss Hart stood looking about, then plumped herself down on a bench. 'All right, fire away.'

Nell sat beside her. 'The target is Church House.' She spoke quietly but clearly. 'We're to plant a bomb at the front door this evening, at nine o'clock. I have to keep a lookout at Dean's Yard from an hour before. Miss Pardue will be waiting by the archway at the entrance to the Yard, with the bomb in a brown holdall. If the coast's clear, I'll give her the nod and she'll leave it at the door. It'll be primed to explode fifteen minutes later.'

Miss Hart nodded. 'Got it. Church House, nine this evening.'

'But Miss Pardue's small fry,' Nell said urgently. 'You have to bring in the people who've organised this, they're the real villains.'

'Just play your part and don't worry about anything else.' Miss Hart trumpeted into a sodden handkerchief. 'It's all under control.'

'And in return, Miss Coker's going to look into my husband's case. Will you remind her?' Nell laid her hand on Miss Hart's arm. 'She gave me her word.'

'And I'm sure she'll keep it.' She got to her feet. 'Well, I'd better be off. Best if we separate now, don't you think? Good luck.'

Nell wandered over to the low wall overlooking the river and smoked a cigarette, looking into the swirling grey water. The meeting with Bill Talbot had been strangely unsatisfactory. Miss Pardue hadn't turned up; apparently, she'd already been given her instructions in a private briefing. Nell doubted Eunice had the guts to go through with her role, but when she expressed those doubts to Talbot, he only gave that oddly child-like smile and said she should give the woman more credit. He seemed excited, jubilant even, rubbing his hands as he talked about the 'proper drubbing' London had taken a couple of nights before. She and Miss Pardue were going to deliver the final bobby dazzler, he said; the cherry on the cake, so to speak. Nell had said she couldn't wait and felt honoured to have been chosen. In fact, she felt nothing at all, not even fear. She had been scoured clean of emotion.

She spent the afternoon in the cinema, watching *Gone with the Wind* for the fourth time, followed by the Movietone News. The Italians had been routed in Egypt, declared a cheery announcer, over footage of embarrassed-looking prisoners being marched through the desert. They might as well have been actors, too. After that, an extract was played from

President Roosevelt's latest fireside chat, during which he promised Britain that although his fellow Americans wouldn't join in the fighting, they would act as the 'arsenal of democracy' and send over planes, ships and weapons – which Nell supposed had to be better than nothing. She just hoped they would hurry up about it. She ate an early supper at the Corner House in Piccadilly, then went back to the Palace of Westminster to change into the siren suit and marshal her belongings. She slung the haversack containing her purse and papers on her back, while the Beretta went into one deep trouser pocket and its ammunition into the other, along with her torch, her pass and Arthur's keys, just in case.

The waiting was nearly over. She would play her part as agreed and the next day she would pay a final visit to Miss Coker, no matter what she'd said, and extract some sort of commitment from her to help Arthur. And then, at last, she could go home to Alice. She had rung Orchard House that morning but her father had answered, and said in an offhand voice that Rose was too busy with the children to come to the telephone. Nell would have some apologising to do. She set off for Church House, about fifteen minutes' walk away; better to be early than late. A snatch of piano music floated through an open pub doorway and three girls passed her in a cloud of scent, their arms linked. She had forgotten it was New Year's Eve, and wondered whether she could be bothered to stay up until midnight. Arthur would want her to hear Big Ben ringing in the new year, but she felt little enthusiasm at the prospect of 1941.

Shining her torch through the arch leading to Dean's Yard, the grassy quadrangle outside Church House, she found the place deserted. Yet the night was pitch black and she could only see a few feet ahead. There might have been a hundred people lying in wait under cover of darkness, and indeed, she hoped there were, ready to pounce on Miss Pardue and deal with the bomb she was carrying. Or would they be waiting inside the building? A dim blue lamp illuminated the entrance to Church House; the three doors were locked and there was no sign of a caretaker.

Nell walked on, wondering why she felt so uneasy. Bill Talbot was not to be trusted, she knew that. Why had he chosen Miss Pardue to plant the bomb, while Nell herself had the secondary role of keeping watch? Did he suspect her? What if the bomb were primed to explode as soon as Eunice Pardue set it down, rather than half an hour later? And yet there wouldn't be much point in killing Eunice, annoying though she was. Actually, what was the point in bombing Church House at all? The place was empty and nobody was meant to know Parliament had been meeting there, so the public wouldn't appreciate its significance. And for another thing, why was the plot called Operation Handle? The handles of the holdall, perhaps? It seemed a tenuous link. Nell stopped for a moment to listen as the familiar sound of the Westminster Chimes rang out, followed by Big Ben striking eight. An hour to go.

That was when she realised. She stood for a moment, transfixed with horror. How could she have been so stupid? Bill Talbot had lured her here to get her out of the way. Church House was merely a distraction. She ran back through the arch and out into the street, her mind racing. There wasn't much time; she would have to make every minute count. Think! Where was the nearest telephone box? There was one on Great George Street, near the corner of Parliament Square. She arrived out of breath, her heart thudding, to find it occupied. She yanked open the door. A red-faced man stinking of whisky was bellowing into the receiver, 'You know I love you, Beryl.' He broke off. 'What on earth—?'

'Forgive me. This is a matter of national importance,' Nell said, fighting for breath. 'I must use that telephone.'

'You'll wait your turn, young lady.' He made as if to push the door closed, but Nell kept her foot in the way and produced the Beretta, thumbing back the safety catch. With a bit of luck, he wouldn't notice the gun was unloaded.

'I mean it,' she said. 'Don't make me shoot you.'

'Good God.' He hung up and stumbled past her without another word, weaving into the night.

Her hands trembling, Nell shook out some coins from her purse and dialled the Whitehall number. It was answered by a man on the third ring. 'I've an urgent message for Miss Coker,' Nell began, and then,

'Oh, sorry.' What was the damn phrase? 'I've left my suitcase at Paddington Station.'

'The lockers there are so convenient,' came the laconic reply, and she could go ahead.

'You must tell Miss Coker immediately that Church House is a red herring.' Her voice shook. 'Have you got that? Call off the men at Church House. The intended target is Big Ben. I repeat: the intended target is Big Ben.'

Chapter Twenty-Two

London, December 1940

The tune of the Westminster Chimes, Arthur had told Nell more than once, was based on a passage from Handel's *Messiah*. Once Nell realised Operation Handle was in fact Operation Handel, everything fell into place. Attacking Big Ben at the very moment that people all over the country – all over the world, even – were gathered to hear him ring out would be a far worse blow to morale than an explosion in some deserted building. There probably wasn't even a bomb in the holdall, which was no doubt why Miss Pardue had been deputed to carry it. Eunice would do as she was told and not look inside the bag. Talbot must have realised Nell was working with the Ministry and knew she would pass on everything he told her. If attention was focused on Church House at the precise moment an attack was taking place elsewhere, he would have free rein. Nell couldn't bear to think of an explosion rather than Big Ben announcing the nine o'clock news, and the new year being greeted by silence. But would Miss Coker get her message in time and if she did, would she act on it?

She stood for a moment outside the telephone box, dithering. She could sense people moving around her in the blackout, hear their footsteps and muffled laughter. War or no war, this was still a night for celebration, and she was the only one with any idea of the danger they were in. Panicking, she ran down the steps to the underground station and through the secret entrance to the Palace of Westminster, flashing her pass at the guard, who knew her by now. There was no point asking anyone for help; it would take too long to explain, and who would believe such an extraordinary story? She could hardly believe it herself.

As she hurried through the colonnade, the smaller bells sounded the quarter hour. If her theory was right, there were forty-five minutes to go. Shc tried to think calmly. What was the plan? Talbot must have planted a bomb inside the belfry; it would be impossible for an aeroplane to target the clock tower accurately in the dark. That was why Lord Winthrop had wanted to be shown around the belfry, and why Arthur had to be got out of the way so he wouldn't stumble across the bomb and raise the alarm. And Ralph Watkinson, too. There had to be a clockmaker on standby in the tower on New Year's Eve, but it could only be Talbot and not either of them. She stopped for a moment to load the Beretta, her fingers trembling so violently that it took several minutes, making sure the safety catch was on before she replaced it in her pocket.

At the foot of the clock tower, she waited for a second by the heavy wooden door, listening, then slowly, gingerly, tried the handle. It was unlocked and swung open more quickly than she'd anticipated, with an alarming creak. She grabbed to reach it, and stood on the threshold with her heart pounding loudly enough to drown anything else. Faint noises came from above, but shining her torch up the stairwell would be an immediate giveaway. The idea came to her that she must learn from Hetta, and become lithe and stealthy as a cat. Putting her foot on the first stone step, she began to climb, her ears attuned to the slightest sound and her heart pounding. There was no time to waste, yet she had to keep quiet. Nearing the belfry at last, she heard the sound of voices and people descending the staircase towards her; a couple of people, she thought, and most probably men, their tread heavy and deliberate. Uncertain whether to carry on or turn back, she gambled on hurrying ahead, taking the stairs two at a time as quietly as she could, grasping the banister with one hand and her gun in the other. The clock-makers' room was unlocked, thank God, so she slipped inside, her breath tearing at her chest. Keeping the door open a crack, she listened as the footsteps grew louder.

'It all seems to be running smoothly,' someone said,

and she recognised Lord Winthrop's voice. 'Like clockwork, if you'll pardon the pun.'

The other man laughed.

'The pilot's on his way,' Winthrop went on, 'so the rest is up to you and Cooke. He's outside with the searchlight but that's only a backup. We're relying on you, Talbot. Don't let us down.'

'Never fear, sir,' he replied. 'I'll be in position, ready and waiting.'

The sound of footsteps grew fainter as they descended. She leaned against the wall. It had come as no surprise to hear Lord Winthrop's voice. The man was a snake; she'd known that all along. 'The pilot,' he had said. So the tower was to be bombed from the air after all! Cooke was outside with the searchlight, yet Talbot had the starring role. He was going to be 'in position', but where? She remembered the expression he'd used: 'the final bobby dazzler', that's what he'd said about the operation. And then she remembered Arthur telling her Lord Winthrop had been particularly interested in the Ayrton light above the belfry. She sank to her haunches, horrified. They were going to illuminate the tower from inside and out.

Think, she told herself, trying to remember everything Arthur had told her about the Ayrton light. Before the war, it had been lit whenever Parliament was sitting after dark. There was a control switch by the Speaker's chair in the Commons chamber, and she was sure Arthur had mentioned another, in the engineers' workshop. Talbot would switch on the light from there when the time came; he wouldn't risk venturing into the House of Commons. Putting the gun back in her pocket, she opened the door and stepped outside.

Immediately she was seized from behind, her arms pinioned, and thrust back into the room. A light shone in her face, and behind it was Bill Talbot.

'Thought I heard something.' He twisted her arm behind her back, making her cry out, and spun her around. 'You're meant to be at Church House. How's Miss Pardue going to manage on her own?'

'You won't get away with this,' she muttered between clenched teeth, struggling in his grip. He was surprisingly strong. 'The police know about your plan and they're on their way.'

He held her easily with one arm, cupping a hand to his ear. 'Funny, I don't hear them. Well, apologies, but I can't stay here chatting. Goodbye, Mrs Spelman. For the last time.'

He shoved her across the floor, so violently that she stumbled and fell. She heard the door slam shut behind her and bolts on the other side being slid across, top and bottom. Struggling to her feet, she threw herself against it, hammering with her fists, shouting at the top of her voice although there was nobody to hear. Talbot's footsteps receded below and she was left entirely alone. Far above her head came a tremendous clatter and rumble, as though huge rocks were falling down the stairwell. The smaller bells were ringing out. She had half an hour left to live.

* * *

She had screamed, losing control for a moment, and then driven her fingernails so fiercely into her palms that they drew blood. If she panicked, she had no chance. Shining the torch around, she took stock. Escaping via the door was impossible: the bolts that had been fitted on the outside for extra security were impregnable. The windows were too small to squeeze through and anyway, she was over a hundred feet above the ground.

'Help me, Arthur,' she begged, trying frantically to remember everything he had shown her that evening – a lifetime ago, it seemed now – in this very room. And then, looking up, she found her one chance of escape: the inspection hatch directly opposite, set into the curved wall of the weight shaft. 'Danger, void behind this door,' read a notice on the front.

Her hands shaking, at last she found the key that would fit and managed to unlock it. The shaft stretched down into a dark, bottomless abyss. She knew there were sandbags at its base, although she couldn't see them, but they wouldn't be enough to save her if she fell. A safety bar had been placed across the entrance to warn the unwary; holding on to it, she looked up and down the shaft in search of the weights. Two of them were out of her reach below, but the middle one (Arthur would know which gear train it controlled) hung above her head, descending by halting degrees every couple of seconds. The weights hung beneath a circular wheel, suspended by steel wires that ran around this pulley and back up to a barrel on the clock mechanism. The wires had to be strong, of course. Strong enough to support her weight? Well, she was about to find out. The bile rose in her throat as she wiped her clammy palms down her thighs. Her hands would slip and the wires would cut them to pieces. She ran back to the workbench, scattering tools and clock parts until she found a couple of chamois leather polishing cloths that she wrapped around each hand.

Rushing back to the door, she saw the weight hanging directly opposite in the shaft. It was now or never. Screwing up every ounce of courage she possessed, she ducked under the safety bar and leapt into the void. She was aiming for the wire cable, slender as a cotton thread. She missed it, of course, but was able to grab the rim of the pulley with one hand. Her legs thrashed in mid-air and the cylindrical weight beneath the pulley bucketed from side to side, yet she managed to grip the pulley with her other hand and achieve some sort of equilibrium, wrapping her legs around the weight and clinging on for dear life. She daren't look down so she lifted her head to gaze up at the clock mechanism. Dear God, if Arthur could see her now! If she weren't so terrified, she might have laughed. But this was no time for humour: the cables that supported her were too insubstantial and she was dangling hundreds of feet above the ground, the weight still lurching haphazardly. Already her legs were cramping and her hands burned where they gripped the sharp pulley rim. The weight was descending agonisingly slowly; she couldn't hold on much longer.

She didn't need to. Daring to glance down for the first time, she spotted another opening in the weight shaft, a few feet below. It was covered by a wire grille that looked flimsy enough, framed at the top and bottom by another two projecting safety bars. If she could use her body to swing the weight a little nearer, she might be able to reach the top bar. It wasn't easy, but at last she gained some momentum. Not enough, though: her fingers only brushed the bar as the weight descended. Soon she would miss her chance. Gripping the cables above the pulley, she hauled herself up so that she was standing on top of the weight, holding on at each side. Bending her knees, she crouched down, reaching for the top bar with one hand. The chamois leather fell away, fluttering down into the empty dark, but her grip was firm enough without it. She waited a couple of seconds, steadying herself, then grabbed hold of the bar with her other hand and swung her legs off the weight to kick at the grille. It stood firm. For a moment she hung from the top bar, dangling, until she managed by dint of frantic scrabbling to find purchase with one foot on the bottom bar, and then the other.

The grille was secured by a padlock on the other side. Very slowly, steadying herself against the wall, Nell reached into her pocket with one hand, drew out the Beretta and released the safety catch with her thumb. She lined up the shot, then turned her face away and squeezed the trigger. The noise was deafening, ricocheting around the shaft. When she looked again, the padlock had disintegrated into a mess of twisted metal. She pushed open the grille and climbed through, dropping down into what turned out to be a storeroom. And there she crouched for a moment, taking great shuddering breaths. But there was no time to lose. Arthur's watch on the chain around her neck showed her it was almost a quarter to nine. She had to find Bill Talbot in the engineers' workshop and stop him switching on the Ayrton light. Leaping down the stairs, she ran out of the clock tower and along the colonnade as the quarter bells rang out. Somebody called after her, but she didn't slow down, keeping one hand on the gun in her pocket. Had anyone tried to stop her, she would have used it.

The door to the engineers' workshop was locked. What if Talbot were somewhere else? She took out Arthur's keys and sifted through them to find the right one, her breath coming hard and fast. If anyone were inside, they might hear her, but there was no helping that. She unlocked the door, clicked the safety catch off the Beretta and stepped through. Talbot was standing in front of the control centre. He stared at her in disbelief.

She had to make sure. 'You're about to switch on the Ayrton light, aren't you?' she asked breathlessly, holding the gun by her side.

'That's right.' Talbot leaned forward and flicked a switch on the bank of controls. 'I just have, see? And now I'm going to deal with you, because you're starting to get on my nerves.'

As he walked towards her, she saw the glint of a

knife blade in his hand. Before she had time to think, she had raised the gun and shot him squarely in the chest. He dropped like a stone, face forward onto the tiled floor. She stood for a moment, looking at his body and the blood already seeping underneath it, feeling nothing. Then she stepped over him and ran to the control panel, searching the rows of switches and lamps. One tiny red bulb was blinking steadily, and the switch beneath it was labelled with the initials AL. Another flick from her and the Ayrton light had been extinguished – simple as that.

She made the gun safe and put it back in her pocket. The job wasn't over yet, though: she had to find Cooke with the searchlight. He was the backup, Lord Winthrop had said. Where exactly could he be? Not on Westminster Bridge, nor Speaker's Green; those places were too public and confined. The only possible place one could park a searchlight was Parliament Square. She checked her watch. It was ten to nine. Time was running out; the pilot must be close.

One of the custodians called out as she raced towards the exit and made as if to follow her. Ignoring him, she showed the guard her pass, gabbling something about an emergency, and then broke free, hurtling out into the night. Now, at least, no one could see her, and no one seemed to be following her, either. She looked about, one hand on her heaving chest, then dashed across the road, hardly bothering to pause for traffic. A taxi swerved, its horn blaring, but her eyes were fixed on a finger of light that swung drunkenly across the sky. She flashed her torch towards it. A gap had been cut in the barbed wire enclosing Parliament Square, and a lorry had been parked on the grass in the middle, towing a searchlight mounted on a mobile chassis. By the time Nell had reached it, the beam had come to rest on the clock face, towering hundreds of feet into the sky behind her. Cooke was standing on the bed of the lorry, his hands on a control wheel at the base of the light.

'Get back!' he shouted when he saw her. 'You're too late.'

'I have a gun,' she called. 'Turn off the searchlight or I'll shoot.'

But he only turned, leapt down from the other side of the lorry and disappeared into the night.

Nell climbed onto the vehicle and wrenched at the searchlight's controls with all the strength she had left. The wheel wouldn't budge an inch, no matter how hard she hauled, sobbing with fear and frustration, and she could see no way of extinguishing the beam. There was only one other option. Shoving the gun back in her pocket, she ran to the lorry's cab, opened the door and climbed in. The keys were still in the ignition. Her foot on the clutch, her heart hammering, she attempted to start the engine – which promptly stalled. She'd forgotten to double de-clutch. Frantically, she tried to remember her ambulance-driving days. At last she managed to get the motor running, wrenched off the handbrake and set the lorry lurching over the grass, the searchlight swaying behind. She had to take it away, that was all she knew, and there wasn't a second to lose. Pulling out into the road, she found herself driving against the direction of traffic but ploughed on regardless, holding her breath, her palms damp with sweat. A bus mounted the pavement to avoid her, and someone screamed. Now she fell in behind a taxi rounding the corner of the square and realised with a surge of relief that she must be nearing St James's Park. She'd turned the headlights full on and kept her fist on the lorry's horn as she bucketed down Birdcage Walk, waiting until she could cut across to the park on her right, praying other drivers would keep out of her way. She had passed Storey's Gate at the corner and the lodge beside it, so now only a line of trees separated the park from the road. Spotting a gap between them, she veered out, ignoring the scream of metal and skidding tyres, and jolted through the undergrowth. Branches cracked and splintered against the windscreen, but when she glanced in the mirror, she saw the searchlight was still attached.

And then with an almighty crash, the lorry came to an abrupt halt – so abrupt that she was thrown forward. A stab of pain made her gasp, and she realised it was because her watch had been caught between her chest and the steering wheel. Pulling it free, she saw firstly that the face had cracked across, and secondly, that the time was dead on nine o'clock. And now Big Ben was ringing out the hour. She had to get out; there wasn't a second to waste. Yet the door handle rattled uselessly when she attempted to open it.

Throwing herself against the door, she only succeeded in bruising her shoulder. It wouldn't budge. When she wound down the window, she was confronted by a massive tree trunk and a shower of twigs falling around her feet. Sliding along the seat, she tried the passenger door, too, with the same result. She had managed to wedge the lorry fast between trees. Perhaps she could shoot her way out: make a hole in the windscreen, smash it somehow and climb through. When she felt for the Beretta, however, her pocket was empty. The gun must have fallen out when she climbed onto the lorry.

All she could do was wait. Wait to be rescued, or wait to die.

'Look up!' Hetta's voice rang in her ear. 'Find a star. I'm coming to fetch you.'

Nell gazed up at the sky. She had done what she'd set out to do; done her bit, and it had been enough. Everyone she had ever loved was beside her and she wasn't afraid. She felt Alice's soft cheek against hers, Arthur's arm around her shoulder, her mother's tentative embrace. All shall be well, and all manner of things shall be well, she thought, at peace now. And then the night became darker still as the stars were blotted out by the aeroplane diving towards her, its engine screaming, and the string of bombs that tumbled from its hold, falling straight and true towards the searchlight's glare.

After that: nothing.

Chapter Twenty-Three

Westchester County/New York, January 2022

Ellie arrived back in New York on the early-morning flight. She had told Dan not to worry about meeting her – it seemed too soon to make that kind of assumption – yet there he was, unshaven and yawning, waiting for her at the barrier. She'd worried on the plane that he might have had second thoughts during the week they'd been apart, that England might have cast some kind of temporary spell over them both that would dissipate once they were back home, but as soon as she'd caught sight of him, she'd known the magic was still there. Dan had wanted to know everything Ellie had found out about her grandmother – she'd told him over the phone that she'd finally unravelled the mystery in the few days they'd been apart – but he would have to wait. Alice should be the first to hear. So after a quick shower and some strong coffee, Ellie had headed out to the nursing home with a bag full of precious memories from England. Brenda Macdonald had said she had no children to pass the snaps on to, so Ellie might as well have them since they wouldn't mean much to anyone else. And of course, she must take Nell's sketchbook; that belonged to Alice by rights.

'I know these children,' Alice said now, gazing at the photographs. 'I used to think I'd made them up: my imaginary friends. But look, they're real.' She turned to Ellie with a radiant smile. 'I'm one of the gang, aren't I?'

'Completely. Brenda said you were their mascot.'

'Which one is Brenda again?' Alice asked. Ellie pointed her out. 'And she really remembers my mother? She's got all of her marbles, then. But you said she uses a walking frame?' Ellie nodded. 'I don't need mine anymore,' her mother went on, with great satisfaction. 'I shall even be managing without a stick before long.'

'Mom, it's not a competition. You'd like Brenda, she's a kindred spirit. I have her phone number and she says you're to call whenever you feel like it.'

'Maybe.' Alice frowned. 'Now tell me again about this trouble my mother got mixed up in. I'm not sure I've got it straight.'

'There was a plot to bomb Big Ben during the Second World War,' Ellie began. 'Your father stumbled across it but the police didn't believe him, so he tried to investigate by himself. And then—' She hesitated.

'And then Nell took over where he'd left off and saved the day.' Going into detail was confusing, and confusion frightened Alice.

'She saved the clock tower, single-handed,' her mother repeated. 'That's what you said, wasn't it?'

'Absolutely. She was a heroine, as brave as she was beautiful.'

'As brave as she was beautiful.' Alice sighed, reaching for the sketchbook. 'And these wonderful drawings! My mother must have loved me very much, don't you think?'

'Of course,' Ellie replied. 'Everyone did. The evacuees, and your grandparents, too. Anyone can see that in the pictures.'

'But then my father took me away.' Alice found the photograph of herself as a teenager with Arthur. 'Because he loved me, too. I suppose he was terrified of losing me, although I didn't realise it then. He suffocated me, always wanting to know what I was doing and who I was doing it with. It drove me mad. Poor man, he must have been so lonely. Even after he married Mavis.' She closed the sketchbook. 'Now, tell me what you made of Gillian.'

'We had a rocky start,' Ellie replied, 'but she grew on me. Sounds like she didn't have the happiest of childhoods, either. I think it was hard for her when you left home.'

Alice raised her eyebrows. 'Whatever gave you that idea?'

'Because she told me so. She said she felt abandoned.'

'Maybe she did.' Alice folded her hands together. 'That never occurred to me. Of course, I was in love for the first time and too excited about making a new life in America to think about anyone else. My father married Mavis when I was around Gillian's age then – actually, I was a couple of years older.' She sighed. 'I should have understood how she would feel. Too late now, I suppose.'

Ellie took her mother's hand. 'Aunt Gillian has breast cancer, Mom. She's going through a tough time.'

'All right, then,' Alice said reluctantly. 'I suppose we'll have to do that thing that everyone's up to these days: skipping or swooshing, or whatever it's called. You know, on the computer.'

'You mean Skype? Or Zoom?' Ellie laughed in disbelief. 'Sure, that would be great. I can bring in my laptop and we'll fix up a call.'

'It would be interesting to see what she looks like.'

'She looks like a bird with a broken wing,' Ellie replied, without thinking.

'And does she know my mother was a wartime heroine?' Alice asked, perking up. 'Have you told her the whole story?'

Ellie had. They'd had a long chat over a farewell dinner in Gillian's house on Ellie's last night, together with Max and Nathan, and looked through the photograph album again. Gillian had mainly wanted to talk about her father, though.

'Not being able to protect his wife must have tormented him,' she'd said. 'I can understand why he didn't want to mention her name. Yet she was always with us, this perfect ghost in the background that my mother could never live up to, no matter how hard she tried. I'm not making excuses for her but life wasn't easy for my mum, either.'

Ellie had decided not to tell Alice about the money from Arthur's will that might or might not be coming to her in due course. With Gillian's help, she'd submitted a claim to the Treasury before she'd left the UK, making the deadline by the skin of her teeth, so they would just have to wait and see.

In a few weeks' time, Gillian would be having an operation to remove her tumour. Still, at least now she had told her children what was happening, so Ellie had gone home with a clear conscience. She had become fond of her aunt in a restrained, undemonstrative way that seemed appropriately English.

She and her mother looked out of the window for a while, and then Alice said, 'You know the picnic in my dream, the one my mother brought? With the cheese triangles and sandwiches with the crust cut off? Well, it was Mavis who made that picnic, I remember it now, for my twelfth birthday. Gillian wasn't born then. I'd invited a couple of friends from school and we climbed up the hill and flew a kite. Mavis had baked a cake, too.' Her eyes were far away. 'I suppose she did her best, given what she was.'

'A butcher's daughter,' Ellie teased.

'I might have got that wrong,' Alice admitted. 'We certainly never had much meat in the house. Do you know, meat rationing didn't end until I was fourteen?'

'You might have mentioned it once or twice.' Ellie gathered her coat. 'Mom, I have to go or I'll be late for supper. But I'll bring in my laptop tomorrow and we can speak to Gillian.'

She and Dan were eating at the Italian place on the corner where she'd been a regular for years, only now it felt like her first visit, because they were there together.

'My sister's been asking me a load of questions about the trip,' Dan told her as they were waiting for their spaghetti, 'but I didn't say anything about us. I thought I'd leave that delicate task to you. If you're still OK with me being around, that is.'

She squeezed his hand, smiling. 'I think so. On balance.'

He poured her a glass of red wine. 'So, now you can tell me everything you learned about your grandmother after I went home? The whole story. Come on, shoot.'

After Dan had left, Ellie had visited the National Archives in Kew to find out what she could about the woman Brenda Macdonald had mentioned: Jane Coker. And there, among a sheaf of dusty files, she had struck gold. Miss Coker (she'd never married), had been a brilliant and high-ranking civil servant, working for MI5 both during and after the war. During her retirement, she had written an account of several sensitive operations with which she'd been involved, to be released after her death. The information had been kept secret for thirty years, much to Brenda Macdonald's frustration, and only recently declassified.

Operation Handel, Ellie read, had been one of the most audacious conspiracies of the Second World War, intended to strike a blow at the very heart of the nation. Winston Churchill had been well awarc of the vulnerability of the Houses of Parliament, lying between three railway stations and so easily found by flying up the Thames. The Palace of Westminster had suffered bomb damage already in 1940 but that had been incidental, rather than targeted. Precision bombing wasn't thought possible at that stage of the war, yet a new aeroplane was in development at Hatfield aerodrome that was capable of far greater accuracy: the Mosquito. It was lighter, faster and far more deadly than the lumbering Hurricanes and Spitfires. Although its existence wasn't widely known, a certain Lord Lionel Winthrop had come to hear of it. He was a Fascist sympathiser who'd travelled widely in Germany after the First World War, met Adolf Hitler on several occasions and admired him greatly. Violently anti-Semitic, Winthrop was convinced Great Britain would become a stronger nation if Hitler were in charge. Following the death of his only son in a tragic incident of friendly fire, early in the war, His Lordship's distrust of the British government had turned to hatred. Under cover of running the local Home Guard regiment, he was in touch with other Fifth Columnists, preparing to smooth the way for an inevitable German invasion. They were all deeply frustrated by the Luftwaffe's inability to win the Battle of Britain, so Winthrop had come up with the plan to destroy Big Ben on New Year's Eve. It would delight the Führer and dismay the sheep-like British, gathering around their wirelesses to hear those famous chimes announce the news.

Winthrop had assembled a cell of various disgruntled activists, one of whom was a test pilot at Hatfield. Both men had been present at trials of the Mosquito prototype in late December 1940, and taken account of security measures around the hangar in which it was stored. The pilot was popular around the aerodrome – 'a blokey sort of chap' – and on New Year's Eve he had plied the security guards with whisky and bribed them to let him take out the prototype that night for a spin. The Mosquito was probably the only plane in Britain able to fly low enough, in the hands of a skilful pilot, to negotiate the barrage-balloon cables along the Thames and drop a bomb on a specific target with any degree of accuracy. Arrangements had been made for the clock tower to be illuminated as the plane approached by switching on the Ayrton light above the belfry or, failing that, shining a searchlight beam on the clock face.

The plan had so nearly succeeded, Miss Coker wrote. The police and security services had been fed false information and were assembled elsewhere. Only one woman had realised what was about to happen and tried to alert the Ministry. Her name was Eleanor

Spelman, and she had been killed by a bomb in St James's Park on New Year's Eve at five minutes past nine in the evening. A watch recovered from the site of the explosion was presumed to have given the time of her death.

'It appears,' Miss Coker had written, 'that Mrs Spelman had towed the searchlight away from Parliament Square to a place of safety, despite the risk to herself. It is a matter of lasting regret to me that her warning telephone message was not taken sufficiently seriously to be acted upon.'

'Something of an understatement,' Dan said, topping up Ellie's glass. 'Do you know how it all came out?'

'They arrested Lord Winthrop's chauffeur the next day and he told them everything.' Tears came to her eyes; these days, her emotions always seemed to be spilling over. 'I can't bear it for Nell, yet I'm so proud. Everyone ought to know what she did.'

'So what happened to this Winthrop guy?'

'He was shot by a British agent in France, a few days later. Presumably he'd been trying to make his way overland to Germany, or maybe he wanted to join the German high command in Paris. The test pilot didn't make it that far: he drowned in the English Channel when his boat was torpedoed. They'd already found the Mosquito, abandoned at an RAF station in Kent. It was painted bright yellow, you see, and would have been far too conspicuous in daylight.' She took a sip of wine. 'Of course, the theft was hushed up. It was a terrible breach of national security.'

'And what about your grandfather?' Dan asked. 'Did you find out how long he was kept in jail?'

'Apparently he was released without charge shortly after Nell was killed. Who knows whether Miss Coker had anything to do with it? He was declared a low risk, with no previous convictions or links to the Fascist party. Maybe they wouldn't have detained him much longer, anyway.'

Their spaghetti had arrived, fragrant with garlic and chilli. Ellie concentrated on eating; love had made her incredibly hungry, as well as emotionally unstable. 'I'm just so glad,' she said eventually, wiping her mouth, 'that I've been able to tell my mom the story while she can still make sense of it.'

'Do you really think she's declining that quickly?' Dan asked.

'I talked to the staff at the nursing home today. They think Mom's been covering up her memory loss, but it's significant and getting worse. She can't live on her own anymore.' She put down her fork, suddenly losing her appetite. 'She knows what's happening, I'm sure of it. She was glad I went to England, she said, because now the Spelmans can look out for me when she's gone.'

'And you have me, too,' Dan said, reaching for her hand. 'I'm not going anywhere. It's like you said, we've wasted enough time. I want to spend the rest of my life with you, and maybe' – he hesitated – 'maybe try for kids, if that's what you want, too. Lisa never did, and I was fine with that, but it would be an adventure, wouldn't it? Having a family of our own.'

'I'm thirty-eight, though,' she replied. 'We might not be lucky. Remember how hard things were for Beth?'

'Then I guess we'd better start trying right away,' he said, with a grin. 'Eat up and I'll ask for the check.'

Epilogue

London, July 2024

After the ceremony, they all pile back to Gillian's house in a couple of cabs: Max and Nathan, Gillian, Lucy and her husband Richard, Ellie and Dan and little Ali, who's fallen asleep on her father's shoulder. Everyone agrees she's been amazingly well-behaved; it's almost as though she could tell something important was happening. Now they're sitting around the kitchen table, having a cup of tea and a debrief.

'Of course, we knew about Dan and Ellie before she did,' Max is telling Lucy. 'It was written all over his face, poor man. Those puppy-dog eyes, that look of hopeless devotion . . . Though goodness knows why he had to wait until she'd left the States to tell her.'

They all laugh, and then Ellie yawns. 'Sorry. It's been a long day. Dan, maybe we should get going.' Because Gillian looks exhausted, too. She's put on some weight, which suits her, and her hair is silvery grey now, which suits her as well, but there are dark circles under her eyes and she could probably do with a rest. She's had another round of chemotherapy recently, and it's taken a toll.

'Let the poor man finish his tea,' Lucy says with a proprietorial air. Ellie tries to suppress a flash of irritation – Lucy's bossiness is annoying – and Max catches her eye and smiles.

She and Dan ought to be leaving fairly soon. They're driving to Millbury tomorrow to visit Brenda MacDonald, who's still going strong at ninety-four. She's aiming for a hundred, she's told Ellie, hanging on for her message of congratulation from Buckingham Palace. Ellie wants to show Brenda her daughter: Alice Eleanor Elizabeth Scardino. Quite a mouthful for a nine-month old, so just Ali for now. She settles the baby on her lap and buries her face in the nape of her neck, then blows on Ali's curls to make her laugh.

'She really is the jolliest little thing there ever was,' Gillian says. 'So sad that Alice never got to know her.'

'Mother! You've said that at least three times already,' Max exclaims. 'Change the record, please.'

'I'm sorry.' Gillian's not offended; Max can still get away with murder.

'But I think Mom does know her on some level,' Ellie says. 'In fact, I think she's with us right now.'

It's coming up for a year since Alice died. It was a peaceful passing, and somehow not what anyone had been expecting. She had softened, seeming to conquer the fear of losing her mind and enjoy the limited life she led. To Ellie's huge relief, Arthur's legacy had come through, so her mother could stay at the Willows without any financial worries. She spent her last months in a happier place, sleeping more each day and talking less. Occasionally she would recount some story from her childhood, but the memories didn't distress her. Even when she was no longer talking at all, Ellie felt her mother always knew who she was. She would pull up a chair beside Alice's bed, take her hand and place it on her stomach so that her mother could feel the baby kicking.

'See?' she would tell her. 'This is my child, Mom. I'm going to be fine, I promise. You don't have to worry.'

And Alice would smile with a tender, secret expression that might have shown she understood, or might have meant nothing at all.

They had all been hoping her mother could hang on to see the baby born, but a week before Ellie's due date, Alice had gone to sleep one night and not woken up in the morning. She had simply drifted away. Ellie was glad her mother had been spared any suffering. She had gone into labour the same day – probably because of the shock, they said – and baby Ali had been born that afternoon. Only after the birth had Ellie been able to tell Dan how much she'd been longing for a girl. She hadn't dare pray for anything other than a healthy baby, yet a daughter seemed a direct link to Alice, and to Nell. Ali had been baptised in the gown Ellie had found in Alice's apartment, and today she was wearing one of the hand-smocked dresses, in honour of the occasion.

'I've been thinking about Alice all day,' Gillian says. 'She would have been so proud of her mother. A plaque in the belfry, no less!'

That morning, there had been a small ceremony conducted by the Keeper of the Clock to unveil the memorial. 'To honour the courage of Eleanor Spelman,' read the plaque, 'who gave her life during the Second World War to save this monument for the people of London and all around the world who cherish it. Her valour will never be forgotten.'

'It would never have happened without your help,' Dan says. 'Thank you for everything.'

'A pleasure.' Gillian smiles, and Ellie smiles too. All of her English family like Dan, she can tell; they have great taste. When he catches her eye, her heart gives a fluttery leap. She's still besotted, still in the honeymoon phase although they're not married yet. They've just never gotten around to it. One day soon, though.

'Before everyone goes, Nathan and I have some news,' Max says. 'Not to steal the limelight or anything, but we're getting hitched. After fifteen years together, we thought it was time.'

Now everyone's laughing and talking at once, and Gillian produces a bottle of champagne from the fridge, which Lucy opens. She twists the cork, not the bottle, Ellie notices, though she knows better than to point out the mistake.

She looks around the table at these faces who have become so dear to her, despite their imperfections (and heaven knows, she has plenty of those herself). Like Gillian, she's also been thinking about her mother all day. She often talks to Alice in her head and Alice invariably answers back. They're linked to each other, inextricably and forever. Nell is bound up with them too, and Rose before her; a web of connections stretching back generations, its strands made up of love and desire, birth and death, failure, success, jealousy, forgiveness, and a hundred other emotions besides. Meanwhile, Arthur's grandfather clock ticks in the hall, counting out the seconds that make up a life.

Acknowledgements

I'm grateful to the following people for their encouragement and expertise: my agent, Sallyanne Sweeney at MMB Creative; the fantastically professional and creative team at Avon Books, including Phoebe Morgan, who first broached the idea for this book, and editor Molly Walker-Sharp; copy editor Laura McCallen, and proofreader Linda Joyce; Caroline Young and the HarperCollins design team who produced such a stunning cover; Catherine Moss and Lindsay Schusman from the Parliamentary Estate; my American family, Mary-Kate Serratelli and Gillian Weiner, who advised on all things transatlantic; Michael Stallibrass and Philip Walters, for their help with knotty plot points; Andrew Walters, formerly of the RAF, for his knowledge of aircraft during the Second World War. Any remaining errors are all my own work.

Last but not least, I should like to thank my

husband, to whom this book is dedicated, and my sons, whose help comes in the vital form of making me laugh and reminding me not to take myself too seriously.

If you loved *The Clockmaker's Wife*, we think you'll love Mandy Robotham.

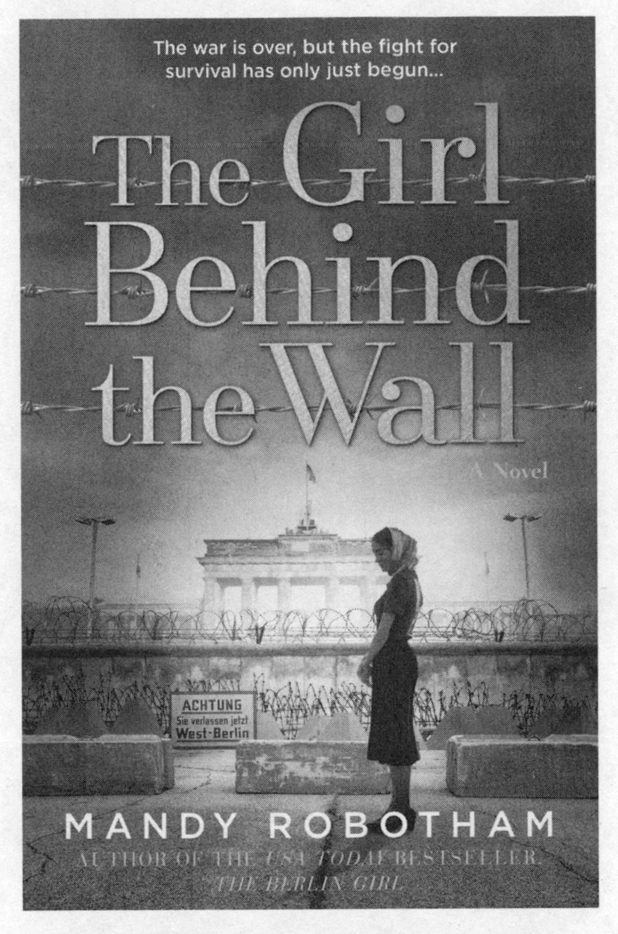

A city divided. Two sisters torn apart.
One impossible choice . . .

The highly awaited new novel from the author of internationally bestselling WWII fiction.

Or why not try *The Girl from the Island*?

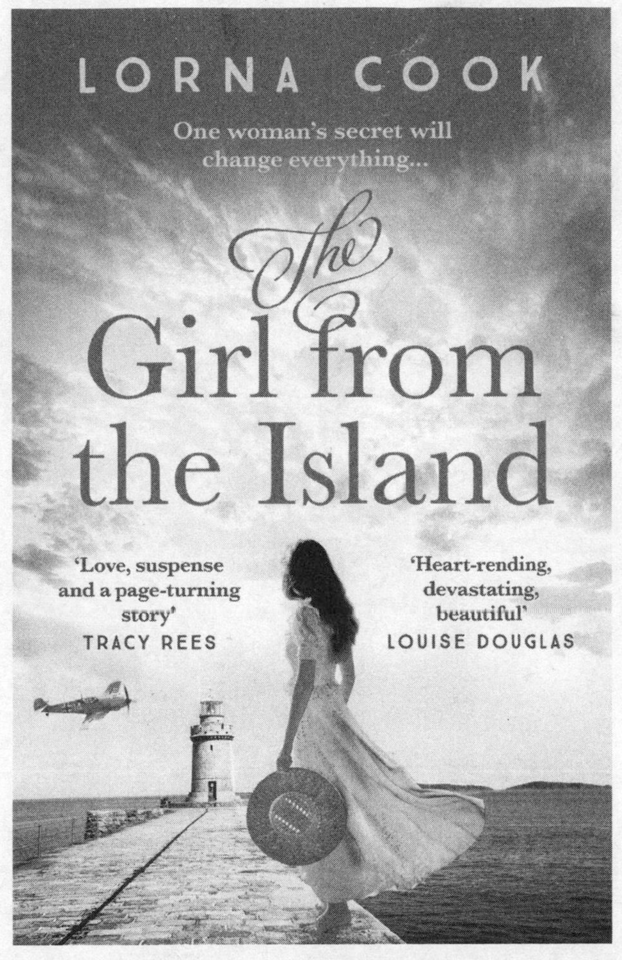

A world at war. One woman will risk everything. Another will uncover her story.

A timeless story of love and bravery, perfect for fans of Kate Morton and Rachel Hore.